KS

D0098654

THE
ADVOCATE'S
DEVIL

Other Books by Alan M. Dershowitz

THE BEST DEFENSE

REVERSAL OF FORTUNE: Inside the von Bülow Case

TAKING LIBERTIES: A Decade of Hard Cases, Bad Laws, and Bum Raps

CHUTZPAH

CONTRARY TO POPULAR OPINION

THE ABUSE EXCUSE: And Other Cop-outs, SOB Stories, and Evasions of Responsibility

THE
ADVOCATE'S
DEVIL

———

Alan M. Dershowitz

WARNER BOOKS

A Time Warner Company

Publisher's Note: This is a work of fiction. Names, characters, places, and incidents either are the product of the author's imagination or are used fictitiously, and any resemblance to actual persons, living or dead, events, or locales is entirely coincidental.

Copyright © 1994 by Alan M. Dershowitz
All rights reserved.

Warner Books, Inc., 1271 Avenue of the Americas, New York, NY 10020

  A Time Warner Company

Printed in the United States of America

First Printing: November 1994

10 9 8 7 6 5 4 3 2

ISBN: 0-446-51759-3

LC: 94-61318

My first novel is lovingly dedicated
to my firstborn, Elon,
who has inspired me,
encouraged me,
and improved everything
I have written.

ACKNOWLEDGMENTS

I would never have had the chutzpah to write a novel without the encouragement and help of so many family members, friends, and professional associates. Early drafts were read and critiqued—I mean really critiqued—by family members, especially Carolyn, Elon, Jamin, Tully, Marilyn, Adam, Rana, Claire, Hedgy, Dutch, Mortie, Marvin, and Julie. Later drafts were read and improved upon by Mitch Kapour, Alex McDonald, Justin, Ken and Jerry Sweeder, Jim Hamilton, Michael Schneider, Sue Levkof, Alan Stone, and Jerrold Rapaport. Much appreciation for editorial assistance by Sandy Gelles-Cole, Larry Kirshbaum, Sona Vogel, and my agent, Helen Rees, and for secretarial and proofreading assistance from Maura Kelley, who burned the midnight oil, Gayle Muello, Eileen Weisslinger, and Ruth Stefanides.

Finally, a debt of gratitude to the several generations of Harvard Law School students with whom I have debated these ethical issues. I hope this book contributes to the continuation of that debate.

Prologue

"Terrific. Another weekend trashed."

Jennifer Dowling was recalling the pain of the past year as she noticed the tall, attractive man walking in her direction from Avenue of the Americas. A cold March rain drenched West Fifty-fifth Street, forming pools wherever there were faults in the sidewalk. Every weekend since New Year's had been a weather disaster, making it unbearable for Jennifer to travel to her weekend hideaway in the Catskills. Not that she had been much in the mood for solitude during her recent legal ordeal. Now that it was finally over, she craved the healing isolation of her simple country bungalow. Yet the prospect of driving up alone along dark, icy roads late on a winter Friday night was not something she found comforting, so she had decided to remain in the city again. Nor had her mood been brightened any by the notice she had received that this was the weekend the water heater in her co-op was scheduled for maintenance—no hot water for twenty-four hours. "Make that trashed and grungy," she complained to herself.

The man walking toward her crossed into her path, halting her progress. She veered to the right to pass him, but he seemed to have the same idea, so they ended up in a balletlike to and fro

1

until they both stopped. The man was so tall that Jennifer, who was five feet six, came up only to his chest.

"Care to dance in the rain?" His smile, punctuated by blue eyes looking down at her, was magnetic.

"This isn't a movie; I'm drenched."

"Dry off with a cup of coffee, then?"

"Are you crazy? This is New York. You're obviously dangerous—"

"Or deranged," he finished for her, and they both smiled.

The man gently took her elbow and steered her to the lobby of the skyscraper looming beside them. Oh, why not, Jennifer rationalized. It was broad daylight. What's the worst that could happen? Jennifer allowed the man to lead her out of the rain.

The bistro inside was crowded and noisy, but her tall companion shouldered his way to a small window table, miraculously empty. "Do you know this place?" he asked her as he gracefully shed his black leather coat.

"I've never been here, though I work in the neighborhood."

"Let me guess, public relations?"

Jennifer started to say yes but corrected herself. "Used to be, now it's advertising. How did you know?"

"It's a gift. I'm intuitive, intelligent, and observant."

"And modest—a Virgo, perhaps?"

He put one huge hand over the table, and she shook it, "I'm Joe Campbell." He waited to see her reaction; there was none. Only her own strong handshake in response.

"I'm Jennifer Dowling," she said as the waiter appeared.

"Cappuccino all right?"

"With skim milk."

"Make that two," Joe Campbell said, not taking his eyes from her face.

Thank you, God, Jennifer said to herself. And to think she had written off this weekend.

BOSTON—WEDNESDAY, MARCH 15

The evening had started with drinks in the "Quiet Lounge" of the Charles, the hotel in Cambridge where Jennifer was staying. "It was fortuitous, you're having to be in Boston." He raised his mineral water in a toast and allowed his eyes to play over the sleek, sophisticated woman seated opposite him. "As in fortunate."

"A word lover, I see. Let me guess, Oxford University, Rhodes scholar. Degree in classic literature."

"Totally wrong. Northeastern University, chemical engineering, 1984."

Actually Jennifer already knew that. They had planned this date over their cup of coffee five days ago, and she had managed to collect a lot of information about him in the meantime. He was the real item, no question about it. Everything he'd told her about himself checked out—including the fact that he was the starting point guard for the New York Knicks. What he hadn't told her was how famous he was. And not being a pro basketball fan, she didn't know that the Knicks had acquired the star point guard from Golden State after losing the final game of the 1994 playoffs. He had been dubbed "the White Knight" by the fickle New York fans, who were counting on him as their last hope for an NBA championship during the Patrick Ewing era.

A group of young men dressed in business suits wandered into the bar, and Jennifer could feel Joe recede. "Any minute those guys are going to come over here and bug us," he said quietly. "You ready for dinner?"

Jennifer nodded, getting up from her seat. He led them away from the group, and as they passed from the dimly lit lounge to the lobby, he bent his head and adjusted his hat lower. He was really quite shy, for all his bravado, Jennifer thought to herself.

A nice-looking man in jeans and a sport jacket politely ac-

costed them at the hotel door just as they were leaving. "Get the Celtics good tomorrow night, please, Joe. I'm from New York, and the Celt fans torment me." Campbell smiled without looking up.

The driver of the white Lexus limo had the door open before they got there, and Joe politely guided her onto the rear seat. "Nice car. Is it white because of your nickname?" She smiled coyly. To Jennifer the idea of a "White Knight" in her life made a good deal of sense.

"Maybe, I guess, now that you mention it."

"Why do they call you that?"

"Well, there's the official and the unofficial explanation. For one thing, I was the only white starter when I played for Northeastern. And now, of course, the Knicks fans hope I can get them a championship."

"Is that official or not?" Her voice was teasing. Joe looked slightly edgy for a moment.

"Official. The unofficial reason is because I was always the cleanest ballplayer on the team."

"What does that mean, you didn't tell dirty jokes?"

"I didn't have a garbage mouth—you know, dis' my opponent and stuff like that. It also means I didn't use my elbows—unless absolutely necessary."

"And what about now? Do you roughhouse now?"

He almost was going to answer her until he realized she was teasing again. Jennifer was smart. He liked that. "Depends on the circumstances. Seriously, it's impossible to stay clean in the pros. Too many muscular bodies banging around in too little space."

The thought of Joe Campbell's muscular torso under his suede jacket flashed pleasantly, almost electrically, through her mind.

There was always that undefined moment when Jennifer knew it was time to take a relationship to the physical. When she was younger she wouldn't let herself acknowledge it, though her body told her often in unmistakable ways. Now that she had turned the corner into her thirties, her mind often took over from her body. It had been a rough year for Jennifer, what with the legal mess she had just gotten through. There had not been much time for fun: not much inclination to be sexual. In the last few weeks the cloud of pain had begun to lift, and she could feel herself reawakening. Her body was telling her she was responding to Joe Campbell.

The large limo ambled through the streets of Cambridge. "I hope Italian is okay," he said, and before she could reply he turned away to look out the window.

The restaurant, Stellina's, a northern Italian gourmet eatery in Watertown, was a bit off the beaten track. At dinner Joe proved to be something of a control freak, ordering for both of them without asking, even insisting she change her mind over the choice of salad. At first this was offputting, but as the meal went on, she began to see him as refreshingly different from the usual wimps she tended to attract. And, in fact, Campbell turned out to be right about the delicious tricolore salad with sun-dried tomatoes.

Back in the limo on their way to Cambridge, he made sure she was relaxed, offering her a cognac from the limo's bar. There was a comfortable silence between them. Jennifer had to admit the truth to herself: she was already a little bit crazy about him.

And this was not lost on Campbell. In fact, nothing was lost on Joe. He was one of the most instinctual ballplayers in the NBA, with a reputation for having the smartest hands in the league. He could sense from the look in an opponent's eyes which way he was going to pass, or whether he would drive toward the hoop. Joe's hands were always there a split second before—deflecting, poking, flicking. Offense might be a function of raw athletic talent, but defense was intuitive. You had to sense what your opponent was thinking, planning, and doing in order to beat him to the move.

Joe Campbell was the master of instinct. Whenever Coach

Riley showed the video of opposing teams' games, he would freeze-frame the action at crucial points and ask the players to guess what came next. Campbell was rarely wrong in his predictions. He understood the flow of the game better than any player in the league.

And Joe understood women the way he understood opposing point guards. He could tell from a glimmer, a smile, or a gesture whether his date needed coaxing—whether her "no" really meant "maybe" or her "maybe" really meant "yes"—or whether she wanted to be taken without foreplay or game playing. Had there been video replays of dates, Joe would have been just as adept at predicting the flow of the action. And he saw in Jennifer's body language that she was heating up. For now his style of aloof gentlemanliness, punctured with playfulness, was working quite well.

"For a tough guy, you're very sweet, you know," she whispered.

"Don't tell that to the Rockets."

The limo driver chuckled . . . Jennifer was put off by the intrusion and quickly recoiled, as Joe raised the glass partition.

"You must be reading my mind."

Soon the driver stopped in front of the Charles Hotel, and just as Jennifer was thinking of a way to ask Joe upstairs without appearing eager, he turned to her. "Listen, I can leave you here if you want or escort you up to your room. I mean, you know, we can kick off our shoes, maybe have a drink from the minibar. I'm safe, I promise." He flashed his famous small-town-boy smile.

Jennifer nodded, and on some signal from Campbell, the driver jumped out and opened her door in one graceful motion. The hotel doorman took over from there, as though escorting them into the hotel were a kind of relay. There was no way anyone in Boston could possibly have known that Jennifer Dowling and Joe Campbell would wind up at the Charles Hotel in Cambridge that evening, yet five or six women appeared to be waiting for him as they stepped into the lobby. They called after him by name and tried to touch him. To Jennifer it was surprising—and a bit revolting.

"How did they know where to find you?" she asked, keeping close by his side, though not touching him.

"They don't have to know. The groupies go to all the hotels when a game is in town, waiting for whoever might show. As soon as someone is spotted, the word spreads."

As they stepped through the crowd, a tall, raven-haired woman approached them.

"Hey, Joe, remember me?" she said, her voice low and insinuating. The woman's breasts were spilling over the tank top of her red body suit. Jennifer was repulsed, but Campbell smiled and acknowledged the woman as she handed him a videocassette.

"An 'audition' tape. I get them all the time," he confided. "Some of the guys think they're funny, but I find them pathetic."

Jennifer assessed the group of women as having a median age of twenty-five. They were beauties, dressed to kill with bodies to die for. She could not imagine what would possess any one of these handsome young women to humiliate herself this way. But who was she to judge? she asked herself as she made her way through the hotel lobby with Joe Campbell. Maybe she was just one of them in a way. Certainly her friends and colleagues in New York would wonder what she was doing, inviting a man she hardly knew, and a jock at that, up to her hotel room.

Campbell kept his eyes down, and Jennifer felt sorry for him. He was a very gentle man, cultured, charming, and maybe even a bit vulnerable. He really seemed nice—the kind of man she could like, both as a friend and as a lover. She thought suddenly of her boss last year, who had not been gentle, cultured, or kind. Jennifer was glad that Joe had chosen to be with her—that she wasn't one of those women down there.

Now all she had to do was sweep him into her fantasy.

Once in her hotel room, Campbell absentmindedly picked up the copy of Boston magazine that had been placed in each room, quickly flipping through the pages while looking down to the street. Somewhere below, a siren wailed. There was lots of activity on the river side of the hotel. "Wonder what's happening down there," he said without turning his head toward her.

Jennifer joined him at the window, pretending to share in his absorption with the scene below. "Looks like some sort of fire."

"Uh-huh," Campbell responded, looking out into the night.

"You seem to have lost your concentration," Jennifer joked. "If you were dribbling that way, I'd be able to steal the ball from you in a minute." She playfully flicked the magazine Campbell was holding out of his hands and onto the floor.

Campbell quickly reached for the magazine. "I never lose my concentration in a ball game, but off the court I'm entitled to daydream." He turned toward her, and her perfect American face became a blur, blending into the black-haired girl they'd seen downstairs, whose name, he seemed to remember, was Charlotte or maybe Cherise. They all became the same after a while. This woman offered the chance of something different. Maybe she wouldn't disappoint him like the last one. The crack about his concentration had thrown him off. How could she tell so much about him so easily?

"I'm sorry," Jennifer said. "I obviously pressed a button I shouldn't have gone near."

"No, no, it's okay, sometimes I do lose my concentration in situations like this."

Jennifer didn't know what to make of Joe's comment, so she left it alone.

Joe kicked off his loafers. Jennifer noticed that they had thick heels, so as to give him an extra inch or two of height. How odd, she thought, since he was at least six feet three in his stocking feet. He then took off his jacket and hung it meticulously on the back of a chair. He was wearing short sleeves, something her lawyer and banker friends never wore under jack-

ets, exposing muscular upper arms. God, he was beautiful. Then she saw a bandage around his right wrist.

"What happened?"

"I ran into Patrick during practice."

"Tell me a little about basketball. You know, some inside stuff that I could only get from actually having a date with a bona fide superstar." Jennifer was kidding, actually mocking what she imagined a groupie might say. Joe uncharacteristically missed the irony. A look of disgust crossed his face.

"Did I say something wrong?"

"No, no, it's not that. Look, I didn't come here to talk about basketball. I'm sure there are subjects you would rather not discuss." There was an edge in Campbell's voice, and Jennifer's paranoia kicked in—what did he know about her?

"I was just messing around." She smiled. "The last thing I want to hear about is basketball, any more than you would want to hear about advertising."

"Hey, I'd love to hear about advertising. I'm fascinated by how you can sell some of that junk that they're marketing these days. I'm also fascinated with how women like you make it to the top in a man's world. You must be something special."

She felt the mood tottering in the wrong direction. "Let's make a deal. No basketball, no advertising, no bullshit." Then she paused, and the next words came out of her mouth as if someone else were saying them. "I like you, I'm attracted to you, I'd love to spend the night with you, and I hope you feel the same way." After she uttered these words, she couldn't be-lieve that she had been so bold.

He said nothing in response, just moved gently closer and put his arms around her so as to leave absolutely no doubt about his reply.

Jennifer luxuriated in his embrace. She felt electrified by the feel of his hard body through his soft cashmere pants. She found herself pushing him closer, hoping to feel his erection. Yet when she felt nothing, she was not surprised. This was a guy who could get it on with a different girl every night, not some adolescent kid having sex for the first time. She would have to use some imagination tonight.

Gently she brushed her hand down his chest toward his belt. Joe moved away from her embrace, asking whether she would like some champagne. That was the last thing Jennifer wanted, but she said yes, thinking perhaps this was a part of his ritual. She went to the minibar and took out the only champagne she could find—a half bottle of cheap "brut" from California. She handed the bottle and corkscrew to Joe, then went to the bathroom and undressed, leaving on only her black silk shirt. After inserting her diaphragm and some spermicidal jelly, she returned to the living room with the shirt unbuttoned to her waist, exposing her well-toned breasts.

Jennifer had worked long and hard on her body, lifting weights and doing Nautilus every other day with a personal trainer who called himself a "body sculptor." Since the legal mess that had started at the office last year, she had thrown herself into hardening her body. "If I keep my body hard," she kept saying to herself, "maybe I can keep my soul from hardening." Now it was time to show off her new body. Joe would be the first man she'd slept with in a long time.

Jennifer had kept on her black pumps, and she forced herself to walk slowly and gracefully toward where he sat on the couch. She relaxed herself against his body in a gesture that was not so much sexual as kittenish. "Are you comfortable here?" she whispered. "Would you like to go into the bedroom?" Not waiting for his reply, she took him by the hand and urged him into the adjoining room.

Now, lying beside her, Joe found himself holding back. Her eyes flicked open, and he saw so much there: wanting, hurt, need, uncertainty, maybe even a touch of fear. When she closed her eyes again, he ran his strong fingers across her forehead gently. This relaxed her, and he let his touch radiate from there, arranging her hair on the pillow piece by piece, taking his time, holding back. His reticence inflamed her even more; her chest rose faster, and a small anticipatory sigh escaped her lips. She pulled him closer to her and kissed him, tempting him first just by offering little kisses, little nips. She hesitated, waiting for some sign of interest, but no part of Joe stirred. Still, his hand found its way idly beneath the silk shirt, and her soft breasts welcomed his large palms.

Jennifer began to tremble, moving her hand down his body, but he stopped her. He could sense the warm, moist heat emanating from her. They kissed deeply, and soon Jennifer arched her body upward to engulf his touch. His fingers danced in and out as she slowly directed his face toward her belly. She moved in harmony with his caresses, spinning toward that place where she would shortly be out of control.

Slowly, almost languidly, Joe came up for air. Jennifer took that as a cue to move her face down his body. As she did so, he kissed her neck and whispered in her ear. At first Jennifer paid no attention to the words themselves, only the sensual feel of his breath on her earlobe. She thought she was hearing sweet nothings, and it was the feeling that mattered. Joe's manner was sweet and soft.

Joe repeated the words, more insistently this time, his strong fingers squeezing her cheeks, as if to make certain that she understood him clearly. This time Jennifer heard Joe's tortured voice. In an instant her mood changed. She gasped and started to speak as he grew hard and rolled on top of her. . . .

PART I

Innocent until Proven Guilty

Chapter One

"God, another groupie filing rape charges against an athlete to get money," Abe Ringel couldn't help musing to himself as he sat reading the sports pages in the small breakfast nook nestled at the back of his Cambridge home. This must be the third or fourth this year alone, the lawyer thought, shaking his head in disbelief. Warm morning sun filtered through a dozen places in the house open to the sun—skylights, floor-to-ceiling windows, even apertures cut into the doors.

The house had been built by a disciple of Frank Lloyd Wright. Abe's wife, Hannah, had fallen in love with the minimalist effusion of bricks, the dark unexpected spaces, the curved windows that bounded the corners. The Ringel home was one of the few contemporary houses in a neighborhood of Early American classics. Abe had insisted on solar collectors, which illuminated the artwork covering every conceivable space—even the seductive hiding place at the bottom of the steps that beckoned one to sit and contemplate the early Magritte watercolor that had been Hannah's favorite. For Abe, the challenge was not finding art—it was finding wall space.

All the light bouncing off the windows seemed to confuse the Canadian geese that passed over Cambridge each winter and

15

early spring. Last month one of the big black birds had become entranced by its own reflection ("Just like some of my clients," Abe had quipped) and dive-bombed hara-kiri style into the living room window, knocking itself unconscious. Emma, Abe's seventeen-year-old daughter, had been distraught about the traumatized bird and had insisted they call the Humane Society to put the poor thing out of its misery.

But then the most amazing thing had happened: the flock had shrieked and called out for their fallen mate to wake up. While father and daughter were standing around feeling helpless and arguing over what to do, the fallen bird had risen and flown up to join its flock.

"There's a lesson in this." Abe had turned to Emma, warming up to his subject.

"I'm sure there is, Dad, and I'm even surer that you're going to share it with me." Emma often teased her father about his morality lessons, which to her marked him as an old-fashioned man still stuck in the 1960s. Yet Abe had the distinct feeling that this was the part of him she also found most appealing. These modern young women were so hard to understand!

The sound of Birkenstocks clumping on the stairs alerted Abe to his daughter's impending entrance for her usual breakfast of carrot juice and figs. "What kind of pants are those?" Abe asked as he inspected her outfit of blue jeans and a work shirt. As always, Emma had distracted him from any more gentle preoccupation. "I can practically see your tush through that cutout."

"You can tell it's cut out, Daddy? It's supposed to look worn out."

"I don't care if it looks cut or worn, Emma," Abe declared with the tone a father uses only when confronted by his teenage daughter's burgeoning womanhood. "The point is your tush is showing, and you're sending an unintentional sexual message."

As soon as he uttered those words, Abe knew he was in for trouble. But it was too late. Emma was ahead of him, as usual.

Someday he'd like to figure out why it was that his doctorate in jurisprudence from Harvard, his nearly twenty years as an attorney, his reputation as a raconteur, and his speaking tours around the globe—how it was that all this experience had not prepared him ever to win an argument with Emma.

"Who said it's unintended, Daddy?" Emma's smile was so like Hannah's, with the funny way her heart-shaped mouth turned slightly down at the corners, flirting unconsciously with him. This child, who had become his sole responsibility at such a fragile time in both their lives, had the power instantly to transport him back to another time when her mother was alive, when all three of them shared this house and their lives together.

"I'm a woman," Emma continued, pointing unsubtly to her breasts. "And I have a constitutional right to send whatever messages I want to whoever I please."

"That's whomever." Abe heard the supercilious tone in his voice and sensed that he was quickly losing his authority.

"Hey, Dad, it's cool, they're just messages. I'm still, you know—"

"Spare me the details." Abe held up his hand.

But Emma was not to be silenced now that she had her father where she wanted him. "I don't pet below the waist even if I do send messages with my a—" She looked at him with those gorgeous deep brown eyes and completed her thought: "Tush. . . ." With that, Emma gave an exaggerated wiggle of Exhibit A.

It was all too much for Abe. Hannah's death in an automobile accident had left him to deal with Emma's puberty, which had been bad enough. Now Emma's emerging sexuality seemed to be raging out of control. Not out of Emma's control—out of Abe's control. As a result, he found himself trying to figure out how Hannah would have handled these situations. Abe realized, of course, that he would soon be spared the daily burden of overseeing Emma's transition from girl to woman, since this was her last year at home before she left for college. Maybe that was why he treasured and dreaded these final months of being Emma's live-in chaperon. By this time next year he wouldn't even know what Emma was wearing and to whom she was transmitting what messages.

Emma quickly sensed that it was time to change the subject. Her father was squirming in the way he always did when they had one of these talks. And that was too bad, because if she couldn't talk to her father about this stuff, then she'd never get a man's point of view—the boys in her class really didn't count, since they were, well, boys. Thank God at least there was Rendi, her father's girlfriend or whatever, to talk to, though Rendi seemed to have lots of hangups about sex discussions. What was wrong with these people, anyway? It seemed like the more experience people had with sex, the more nervous they got about discussing sexuality. She'd have to think about this concept for a while.

Not that Abe was prudish about discussing sex in general—as long as it didn't involve his own family. Just last week he had helped Emma resolve a dilemma that her friend Janie Warren had imposed on her. Janie had become pregnant and had asked Emma to help her get an abortion without her parents finding out. Emma felt strongly that Janie should tell her parents, but Janie said she was afraid. Emma sought her father's advice. After listening, Abe asked one question: "Does Janie know that you're telling me?"

"Yes, she does. I asked her permission to seek your advice, and she said, 'Sure.' "

"Then I know what I have to do," Abe said. "Janie understands that I *have* to tell Charlie and Mary now that I know. She *wants* me to tell them."

Emma was worried. "But what if you're wrong, Daddy?"

Abe responded by quoting Shakespeare, his frequent source for resolving tough ethical conundrums: "To do a great right," Abe said, "you sometimes have to risk doing a little wrong."

Emma did not object as Abe walked to the phone and called

his old friend Charles Warren to tell him about his daughter's problem and fear.

Janie was enormously relieved when her parents told her that they knew of her situation and that she could count on their support and love. It was vintage Abe—perceptive, direct, proactive, and right. Emma was proud of how her father had cut through everything so quickly and helped her friend.

Indeed, this uncanny ability to see through complexity and cut to the chase was one of Abe's great strengths as a lawyer. His working rule was that every complex problem had a simple and obvious solution. And so far it had proved to be a good rule for Abe. He never obsessed over issues. He reasoned, he decided, he acted, and he didn't look back. And if he sometimes wondered whether he was guilty of oversimplification, he quickly reassured himself: not a great vice for a busy trial lawyer.

Both Abe and Emma were news junkies who channel-surfed their way through the network morning news shows while dressing and leafed through the newspapers while in the bathroom. Emma was just about to begin the morning Ringel ritual of discussing the headlines when Abe preempted her.

"Did you hear about Joe Campbell being arrested?"

"Yeah, it's all over the news. It's about time they did something to athletes who think they're God's gift to women." Wait a minute, Emma thought to herself. Here she was, sitting across the table from a bona fide expert on a topic that Jon, her main love interest these days, was bound to want to talk about, and she was wasting time making a political point on a man who wouldn't even understand it! Wake up, girl!

She placed a respectful look on her face. "Do you think Campbell's arrest will get him suspended?" Jon would just die if Campbell weren't able to participate in the playoffs.

"No, I don't think so. Even the NBA has to live with the presumption of innocence, and in this case it seems more than a mere presumption." He was comfortable now, warming up to a more impersonal subject. "I imagine the league will assume it's just another frustrated groupie crying rape because the ballplayer didn't ask her out again, or another gold digger looking for a pot of cash at the end of a rainbow."

"That's not fair, Dad. It's just another example of your Jurassic attitudes toward women. Have you ever stopped to consider the possibility that Campbell might actually have raped this woman?"

Abe realized he wasn't going to get out of this conversation without another lecture. "All right, maybe," he said, "but I find it hard to believe. I mean, the woman had been out on a date with him, not once, twice. You read about that, right? And why would Joe Campbell have to force a woman to have sex with him? He's got groupies following him around wherever he goes. You can't very well rape a groupie."

"Daddy, that's ridiculous. Anyone can be raped, even a prostitute. And it doesn't matter if she knew him—if they had two dates or ten. We're not talking about sex, Dad, we're talking about violence—you should know that."

"Well, maybe," Abe said grudgingly, yet without really believing it. "Campbell gets all the violence he needs driving to the hoop. Have you watched him recently, since Oakley sprained his ankle? He's banging more bodies on the boards than the power forwards."

"You just don't get it, Daddy." For a moment Emma's expression turned thoughtful, serious, as though she were in touch with a feeling he could never totally appreciate or understand. Maybe it was true what Rendi said, that all women were born with the precognitive experience of being raped—"gender memory," she called it. Whatever the case, Abe wasn't about to ignore his daughter's opinion, even though he didn't believe for a minute that Campbell had raped the woman.

"I get it all right. Remember, I belonged to a fraternity once. I knew some guys who could be real assholes when left alone with a woman—but rapists? Clods, maybe, cavemen, even, but I don't see how an average guy could change over the course of an evening from a good date to a violent predator."

Abe was a 1960s liberal who believed in free speech, equality for minorities, environmentalism, abortion rights—the whole agenda. This new feminism, on the other hand, had him confused and a bit hostile. On sexual issues, *he*—along with all men—was the target, the bad guy. He really *didn't* get it, and he wasn't sure he wanted to. He had always treated women as equals, hiring several as associates even before it was voguish. And then there was Rendi, who was any man's equal. But when it came to issues such as date rape, Abe had real difficulty understanding what all the fuss was about. What did they want from him?

As usual, Emma read his mind. "Why do guys have such a hard time believing date rape can happen, anyway? It's not like we're saying you're all rapists or anything. Yet it happens, guys get crazy. You can't change facts just by saying it's the victim's fault."

Hannah, where are you? Abe thought. What do I say now? Out loud he asked: "Is this what they teach you in school?"

"No, of course not. You know our headmaster, Mr. Cravers. Talk about antiques! He'd never let us discuss this stuff. No way. We study it in our feminist group."

"I thought your feminist group was about politics—you know, women candidates and all that."

"It is about politics. We discuss the politics of rape, the politics of sex, of marriage. It's great."

I can't deal with this, Abe thought to himself, removing his glasses and massaging his temples, which he had noticed just that morning were showing small streaks of gray. Suddenly he was looking his age, unlike his father, who had remained youthful looking until his death at seventy-five a year ago. Harry Ringel had died at work while cutting the hair of a friend whom he had barbered for more than fifty years.

A tear formed in Abe's eye as he thought about his father. Harry Ringel had been a real barber, Abe recalled with tender pride—not a hairdresser. He cut and shaved, never coifed or layered. He was proud of having been the first white barber in the Boston area to cut the hair of Negroes, as he insisted on calling them till his dying day. "I've got plenty of Jewish customers with curly hair. I know how to cut curly hair. I'm in the hair business, not the skin business." He drew the line, however, at women. "I'm a man's barber," he would insist. Harry was not only a man's barber, he was a man's man. He loved his customers. He loved his three sons. And he respected his wife, Sylvia, in whose presence he rarely uttered a word.

Sylvia, who had moved to Florida following Harry's death, had written "the book" on Jewish mothers. Less than five feet tall and under a hundred pounds, she was a benevolent despot. She insisted on being addressed as "Mrs. Ringel" by anyone other than her immediate family and a few close friends. When Abe had briefly dated a southern woman, it had created a minor confrontation when the woman had once used the term *you-all* to Sylvia's face. Sylvia was an absolute master of the put-down, capable of humiliating the strongest man or woman with a well-chosen word or phrase. She was also capable of seeing the dark cloud in any silver lining. When her sons and grandchildren had gotten together and bought her a beautiful diamond watch for her seventy-fifth birthday, her response had been, "Oy, now I have to decide which one of you I should leave it to in my will." Abe loved his mother, but his personality was closer to his father's.

Emma quickly brought Abe back to the moment. "Tonight in our group, the topic is 'Taking Control of Your Own Sexuality.' "

"Enough, my darling daughter. Can we please not talk about your sexual comings and goings anymore? You really have to try to understand. I was brought up in a different world. We never talked about those kinds of things. I'm not good at it. If you have to talk to someone, could you talk to Rendi?"

"Dad, that's the whole point. I don't want to talk to Rendi.

I mean, I love Rendi and I'm glad you two are, you know, well, whatever it is you two are, but I need a parent to talk to." Emma paused. "You don't know how it feels to grow up without Mom."

Oh, yes, I do, little one, Abe said to himself. He had hardly been a grown-up himself when Hannah had died. At least that's what he thought looking back on it now. These were not emotions he could share with Emma. Or anyone. Abe had worked hard to keep himself one step removed from the rest of the world. It was part of the advocate's territory. And perhaps more to the point, it served to remove him from the never-ending pain over losing Hannah. Seeing his daughter's face, her eyes like Hannah's, suddenly glinting with the tears that came so quickly in adolescence, he realized that he couldn't use his distancing tactic with her.

Abe glanced at the old-fashioned watch his father had given him as a Bar Mitzvah gift. "You have only so much time on this earth," his father had said. "Always make the most of it. Don't waste a precious minute. You'll never get it back."

Abe had lived by those words. He was one of those people who was always doing something productive. He squeezed a tennis ball to strengthen his hands as he read a good novel, listened to classical music while enjoying his art. Abe was something of an overachiever, a man who tried hard to do the right thing, even though he sometimes had difficulty figuring out what the right thing was these days. He yearned for the black-and-white simplicity of his youth and even his young adulthood. During the late 1960s and early 1970s he really thought he was at peace with himself about the moral issues of the day. Then along came the feminists, the radicals, the black separatists, the gay activists. Part of him resented these young upstarts for complicating his life, for making new and sometimes incomprehensible demands on his moral bank account. Even his own daughter confused him. "Isn't it time for you to be off to school?"

"Yeah, I guess. . . ." Emma was small-boned, and when her thoughts grew cloudy, her whole face seemed to close down.

These were the times Abe would have lain down and died for her, if only she would smile. "Come on, kid, what's bugging you?"

Without a word, Emma came over and hugged her father. Not knowing if Jon still liked her was what was eating her—not knowing why he hadn't telephoned last night and feeling too proud to call any of her friends to talk about it, not wanting the hurt to show. That was bothering her. And her difficulty with calculus was really bothering her. And her painful period. Everything was bothering her, and she didn't know how to get started. If she did get started, would her father even listen? That's the way it always was. He'd give her attention for a minute and then he'd be off, to the office, to the phone, to his briefs, to wherever he went when he wasn't being her father.

Over the years Emma had learned the secret passageways to Abe's soul. Either she had to provoke him, as she was doing this morning, or she had to engage his lawyer's mind, as she had done several months earlier while Abe was totally focused on a murder trial.

The case involved a businessman named Hamilton who had taken out a life insurance policy on his partner ten days before the partner was gunned down by a professional hit man. The DA was finding it easy to persuade the jury that the timing could not possibly be coincidental, and Abe had been racking his mind for an answer. Emma, finding that she simply couldn't get his attention, had decided to try to help him figure out a common-sense rebuttal to the DA's circumstantial case.

And she had.

"Daddy," she said, popping into his home office late one night, "the answer is Chekhov."

"Why Chekhov?" Abe asked, his head still buried in the books.

"Because Chekhov once told an aspiring dramatist that if you hang a gun on the wall in the first act, you had better use it by the third act. We read it in lit class."

"So what does that have to do with the Hamilton case, my bright young daughter?"

"Everything, Daddy. Don't you see?"

"No, I don't see; show me," Abe said, finally lifting his head to look at her.

"Your jurors see Chekhov's theory on TV and in the movies every day. Don't you get it, Daddy? On TV, when they show a businessman or a wife buying life insurance on someone, every viewer knows there's going to be a murder, and they know who the murderer will be. It's a setup."

"You've got a point. Sure, on TV, when a character coughs or has a chest pain, you know he's dying. There's no such thing as a cold or indigestion. Everything has to be relevant to the drama."

"But in real life, Daddy, the world is full of irrelevant actions and coincidences. People take out insurance policies all the time, and then the person lives till Willard Scott can put him on the *Today* show."

"You've really got something there, Emma. I think I may use it."

And Abe had used it. He'd convinced the jury not to look at the Hamilton case as if it were a made-for-TV movie, but rather as a slice of real life, full of irrelevant actions and coincidences. He'd asked the jurors how many of them had taken out life insurance on a loved one and what their neighbors would have thought if that loved one had died shortly thereafter.

After he'd won, several jurors had told him that his TV argument had turned them around.

Abe had taken Emma to Olives, her favorite restaurant, and charged the meal to the appreciative Hamilton. Over dinner Emma had informed Abe that coming up with the Chekhov idea had convinced her to become a criminal lawyer. Abe had smiled proudly but said nothing, afraid that if he were too encouraging, it might provoke her rebellious streak. Every time he told the story of the Hamilton case, he credited Emma with the victory.

25

Sometimes Emma couldn't use her precocious intelligence to get her father's attention. Sometimes she just wanted to be his little girl. Like now. This was the part he really loved—being the protective father. It took him back to a simpler time, when his role was much easier, to remove a splinter, to tell a story. Now it was so much harder, watching her make her own mistakes and knowing that he could not protect her very much.

Emma pulled herself from her father's arms. Abe knew that for all his daughter's apparent emotionality, she was most definitely his daughter. So he allowed her to move the conversation back into the comfort zone.

"So, Daddy, tell me how you would defend Campbell if you were asked to take the case."

"I should be so lucky. This case is lose proof."

"So you've already decided the victim is guilty."

"Wait a minute, Emma dear. Who *is* the victim? All we know so far is that there is an accuser and an accused, and the accused is presumed innocent. That means the accuser is not presumed to be a victim—at least not yet."

"Yeah, yeah, I know *that*. Do you think after all these years of being your daughter I don't know *that*? What I want to know is: Would you do the sleaze thing and try to put the victim on trial? You know, go into her sexual history, what she was wearing, stuff like that?"

"Sure I would. If the court would let me. Because when I defend someone, I can only think about one thing: winning."

"Even when the defendant is guilty of rape?"

"Look, Emma, not everyone accused of rape is guilty. Did I ever tell you about the ninety-nine-pound MIT nerd who was accused of raping the one-hundred-forty-five-pound woman rugby player?"

Emma interrupted: "Only about a hundred times. I even brought it up in my women's group when we were discussing William Kennedy Smith. To defend you. Everyone gave me such a hard time about your stand on that Oprah show where you came down on the side of Smith and Tyson that I had to do something to protect our family reputation. After all, you're my father, even if you are a dinosaur."

"And did the girls buy the notion that the defendant just might be innocent?"

"Women, Dad, women! All right? My group believes that rape is the most heinous crime, even more heinous than murder, because it continues to hurt the victim for the rest of her life and because a rape victim who complains gets raped again on the witness stand."

"I'm sure there are some in your group who believe that rape is so heinous an offense that even *innocence* shouldn't be recognized as a defense," Abe remarked, hoping to lighten the conversation. Emma gave another groan.

"Do *you* believe me when I tell you that the MIT kid was innocent?"

"I guess so. It depends what you mean by innocent. He certainly took advantage of her by threatening to stop studying with her the night before the final exam unless she slept with him."

"That's not rape," Abe insisted.

"Not in a legal sense," Emma agreed. "But a lot of feminists would regard it as moral rape to blackmail a woman by threatening to cut off an important relationship unless you 'agree' to do it."

"Well, I'll leave the moral distinctions to you and your friends. You leave the legal distinctions to me and to the law," Abe said, aware that his haughty tone sounded somewhat hollow in his daughter's court.

"As for Campbell," he continued, "it sounds like an easy case to defend. Most athletes, particularly popular white athletes, tend to be acquitted of those kinds of charges. I don't remember anything about Campbell's background to suggest that he's been in this kind of trouble before."

"Unlike Mike Tyson." Emma was familiar with her father's perspective on the boxer's case.

"That was a real tough one for Tyson's lawyers, because Tyson came into the case with a reputation. And then his own trial lawyer portrayed him as an out-of-control animal. I would have handled it entirely differently, emphasizing his positive qualities. I remember reading that one of the jurors said after the conviction that it seemed as if his own trial lawyer thought he was probably guilty."

"Well, he probably was."

"I don't believe it. From what I've read, Tyson was known as a pretty direct guy. The woman knew what he wanted from her before she went to his hotel room at two A.M."

"See, Daddy, now you're talking just like Tyson's lawyer. He was a direct guy, and everyone knew he was only interested in sex. Not a great jury argument, Daddy."

"You're not a jury, my dear, bright daughter. I was making that argument to *you*."

"Well, it didn't work. And it wouldn't work if you made that argument about Joe Campbell, either."

"Look, Emma, you can't generalize about athletes. They're all different. Campbell has to be judged on his own merits and demerits."

"Daddy, why do you always side with the men in these cases? You do have a daughter, you know. I would think that might make it easier to see the woman's point of view."

"It does. And I don't side with the *men*. I side with the *defendants*."

"Who just always happen to be men. Next you'll be telling me that O. J. Simpson is innocent."

"He is innocent, unless and until he were to be found guilty and the conviction affirmed on appeal. He's presumed innocent."

"Unfortunately his victims aren't *presumed* dead. They're really dead."

"The question remains, who killed them. And in the Campbell case, the question is who is telling the truth."

"All I know about Campbell is he's soo cute. Some of my friends at school think he's the sexiest player in the NBA. If you do get to represent him, can I get to meet him? Maybe even get into the Knicks locker room next time they play the Celts?"

"You're not going into *any* locker room, little girl, unless you become a sportswriter, and then I'll bring a lawsuit to make the guys cover up before I get you in."

Emma got up from the table, placed her dish in the sink, and gave her father a kiss good-bye.

"What time are you going to be home from school?"

"Late, after our feminist group meeting. It's about how all women are part lesbian and how to bring that part of you out of the closet." Emma smiled to let him know she was teasing. She made a quick check of her hair and a glance at her body, using the full-length mirror kept expressly for this purpose in the foyer. Then she was out the door, leaving the smoky scent of her patchouli oil behind her.

As Abe packed his briefcase for the short walk to his office, his mind turned from Emma to Charlie Odell—the last and most painful in a series of recent losses that had begun to tarnish his golden touch. All tough ones, but the media didn't understand. How could they know that his "loss" in the Johnny Brill case was really a victory? Sure, Brill had been wrongly convicted of insurance fraud for torching his own bankrupt bar. What the media didn't know was that the bar was actually turning a profit that Brill was hiding by keeping two sets of books. Abe could easily have proved that Brill was making so much money that he had no motive to burn down his cash cow for insurance, but then he'd have exposed Brill's long history of tax fraud, which carried a much longer sentence. What a mess that had turned out to be, along with several other of Abe's recent cases.

At least Abe still had a chance to undo the mess in the Charlie Odell case. Today would be devoted to planning the next battle in the legal war to save Charlie O.'s life.

Chapter Two

Abe walked briskly to his office atop a three-floor walk-up on Mt. Auburn Street. The building had once been an old-fashioned boardinghouse. Now it was an old-fashioned office building, housing a psychiatrist, a nutritionist, a private investigator, and a mysterious outfit called Resources Limited.

As he opened the front door, Abe heard a breathless voice calling from the stairs on the landing below: "Abie baby." Without even turning, he knew it was his old friend from Dorchester, Alex O'Donnell, who was obviously on his way up to Abe's office. Since hearing about Campbell's arrest, Abe had hoped Alex might get in touch. For a moment he had even thought about calling him. In the end he'd decided not to because he didn't want to become the kind of lawyer who solicits business.

O'Donnell had grown up down the block from Abe in what was then, and still remained, Boston's largest working-class community. The Dorchester of Abe's childhood was an economically poor but culturally rich amalgam of "first generation" Irish, Italian, and Jewish offspring of parents who had left Europe in the proverbial quest of "a better life for their children." As Abe's life showed, the long journey from the working class to Harvard *could* occur in a single generation—it just required, as his father had always counseled him, "an equal measure of brains and breaks." Abe, fortunately, had gotten plenty of both.

In the neighborhood where Abe and Alex grew up, the confluence of immigrant families, in the same tightly packed neighborhoods—often in triple-decker houses with three identical apartments—led to bonds of trust and tolerance that, sadly, were all too rare in the larger society. In childhood the parental mistrusts of the "stranger" or the "other" were diluted for Abe, Alex, and their friends because daily they were each other's best evidence that "the mick," "the wop," or "the kike" could be your confidant, your ally, your most trusted friend. The commonality of a working-class childhood forged their bond: in adulthood Abe had come to understand what a gift that special upbringing had bestowed upon him.

These childhood memories had been transformed into friendships Abe measured in decades. The one shared with Alex O'Donnell ranked among the longest. They had played punchball, stickball, basketball, and Scrabble together. Alex had been a great athlete as a kid, a short playmaker and shooting guard who had gotten a scholarship to play basketball at Boston College. But he'd hurt his knee during freshman year and become the team manager. After college he'd become an agent, specializing in basketball players. Though they had drifted apart over the years, O'Donnell always sent Abe a Jewish New Year's card— the only one he usually got—as well as news clips about his famous clients.

"I've got a gift for you, Abie baby," Alex said as he hugged Abe. "It will more than pay you back for fixing me up with 'Chesty' Chessowics back in junior year at Boston Latin. I came to deliver it in person because I wanted to see the look on your face."

"What could possibly be a sufficient payback for your first copped feel?" Abe asked, hoping he knew the answer.

"Joe Campbell," Alex said, beaming.

"I talked him into meeting with you," Alex continued as the two men walked back down the stairs and toward O'Donnell's dove gray Jaguar. "He's gotta be at practice this afternoon, and he's spending the morning looking for a good local lawyer. I had breakfast with him and told him about you. He wants to meet with you right now."

"Great. Thanks, Alex. What does Campbell know about me?"

"Only the good things. I didn't tell him about your most recent cases. I went back to the glory days. This one's gonna break your streak."

"Those were tough—"

"I know, Abie baby," Alex cut in. "You don't have to make excuses to me. We go back too far."

While Abe and Alex drove down Storrow Drive, Alex began to tell him about Campbell. "The man's a walking flytrap for broads. We should be so lucky. No way he raped this woman. She wanted him. We can prove it. Let Joe tell you what happened. He's smart as hell, this guy. Brainiest ballplayer I ever represented. And we can get hard evidence to back up everything Joe is going to tell you."

"What do you mean, 'we can *get* hard evidence'?"

"I mean there are hospital reports, physical evidence, and other stuff that will knock your socks off. This is going to be the easiest case you ever couldn't lose. And you'll be the hero of the sports world. We just gotta win this one real quick. Reebok is holding off on a megabuck endorsement deal until this mess is out of the way. So no typical lawyer delaying tactics to pad the bill."

They arrived at the Four Seasons, where O'Donnell came to a stop right in front of the hotel. Alex seemed to throw the Jag into park and hurl his compact body out of the illegally parked sports car all in one energetic motion. At the lobby house phones, he called the hotel operator and asked for Mitch White.

"Who the hell is Mitch White?" Abe asked.

"Oh, that's the name he registers under—White—'White Knight.' That way only his friends know how to reach him."

"Joe," Alex practically yelled into the phone. Abe wondered just how Campbell kept his identity secret with the exuberant O'Donnell as his agent. "I've got Ringel down here with me in the lobby. Okay to come up?" Alex nodded to Abe, and they headed to the elevator bank.

Alex knocked on room 535, a corner suite, and Joe Campbell opened the door. Alex hugged him, and he reciprocated with obvious reluctance and a shrug directed at Abe as if to ask "Does he make you go through this, too?"

Abe immediately liked Joe. Of course, he had seen him play many times and felt that he knew him in the one-sided way that spectators and audiences always thought they knew popular stars.

"Mr. Ringel, come in. I've heard only good things about you." Abe hoped that was literally true.

"Come, sit down." Campbell led them to the sitting room of his elaborate suite. "I'm sorry to have dragged you down here. I'm interviewing several lawyers this morning, and it was easier this way."

"No problem. I like to make house calls."

While they bantered, Abe and Joe were casually sizing each other up. It was always like that at a first meeting between lawyer and client. The lawyer looked for telltale signs of innocence or guilt, quickly assessed what kind of impression the client was likely to make on the judge or jury, and tried to sense whether the client was going to be straight with his lawyer. For his part, the client inspected the merchandise he was considering buying—the sincerity of the lawyer, his energy level, his appearance, and, most important, his commitment to the case.

Abe assumed Joe liked what he saw, because the athlete began to move the conversation from banter to substance. Yet he started his story in an oddly elliptic manner, perhaps because he was uncertain or embarrassed, Abe reflected.

"Well . . . we met in New York last—"

"Please, don't tell me what happened," Abe said, cutting him off. "Let me ask you specific questions."

"Why? I've got nothing to hide."

"It's much better this way," Abe said. "I want to frame the questions so that you don't tell me more than I need to know."

It was the way Abe always structured his initial interviews. Don't let the client tell you his story before he understands the implications of what he is saying. The Supreme Court had recently ruled that if a lawyer knows his client is lying, he is not permitted to put him on the witness stand, since that would constitute suborning perjury. The ruling had grown out of a murder case in which the client pleaded self-defense. When he first told his defense attorney the story, he said he had not seen any gun in the hand of the man he stabbed. Then, after talking to some jailhouse lawyers, he changed his story and claimed that he *had* seen the metallic object he had previously denied seeing. The upshot of the case was that the Supreme Court ruled it improper under those circumstances to allow the client to swear that he had seen a metallic object. Thus if a client told one story at the outset and then changed it, this created big problems both for the lawyer and client. Most criminal defense lawyers had become much more cautious about letting their clients ramble on without some structure.

Abe was not as controlling as some lawyers. Anthony Albino—the lawyer Joe was scheduled to interview next—was infamous for his technique. At a recent bar association dinner roasting Albino, there was a skit about a fictitious defense lawyer named "Tony Alibi." "Alibi" was shown interviewing a woman charged with murdering her husband. "He beat you, right? He threatened the kids, right? Oh, you don't have kids. Well, how about nephews? nieces? a dog? the goldfish." Abe didn't create defenses the way Albino did, but neither did he want to hear his client's untutored version of the facts during the first interview. It was a dicey little game, and every lawyer was playing it by somewhat different rules.

Abe remembered his first interview with a client following the Supreme Court's new ruling. He'd started by telling his client that if he were guilty, he couldn't take the stand. The client had responded matter-of-factly, "Just tell me what I have to tell you if I want to take the stand, and I'll tell it to you." What a relief it was to have a client like Joe Campbell.

Campbell, to his credit, had stopped talking and was waiting politely for Abe to lead the conversation, which signaled to Abe that he would not be one of those pain-in-the-ass clients who fought with you about everything. Nor did Joe seem like a liar. Abe relaxed a little on his chair.

"First a few preliminaries. Everything you tell me is confidential. Alex has to leave the room. Although he's your agent and friend, he isn't your lawyer, and what you tell him isn't privileged."

"Wait a minute," Alex protested. "I won't tell anyone. I want to stay."

"Sorry, but the rule says that if you stay, we can all be subpoenaed to testify about our conversation. You've got to go. Just wait outside."

"What about your fee? Don't you want me to be here for that part of the discussion."

"There's really nothing to discuss. My fee is three hundred an hour for my time, and a hundred and seventy-five an hour for my associate's time, plus expenses. In Joe's case, I don't need a retainer. He's good for it. I read in the paper how much you got for him in his recent contract negotiations."

"And that's without endorsements," Alex added as he shrugged into his coat. "Joe, I'll call you before the game. Abe, you can get home without me since I'm dismissed."

"Go, Alex," Abe said as he made a shooing gesture with his hand. Alex left, and Abe turned to Joe.

"Let's start at the end and work backward. When were you arrested?"

"Last night about 10 P.M., when I got back to my hotel. The police were waiting in the lobby. They were very polite.

Said I would have to come with them to the Berkeley Street station."

"What did they tell you?"

"That I was under arrest for raping Jennifer Dowling."

"Did they book you?"

"Yes, and then they let me go. Said I should get a lawyer and be in court today for the arraignment."

"Did you tell them anything?"

"Yes, I did."

"What exactly did you say?"

"I told them it was a date, consensual sex, that she had inserted a spermicide."

"Why did you tell them all that? Didn't they give you a *Miranda* warning?"

"Sure, but they made it sound like it was a warning for guilty people. I had nothing to hide, so why not tell them? I thought maybe they would drop the charges once they learned that Jennifer had gone into the bathroom and put in her stuff. They took notes and said they would look into what I said."

"Are you leaving anything out?"

"Yeah, I told them how we met in New York, where we went to dinner here in Boston. I gave them the American Express receipt for the Watertown restaurant, and the name of the limo company and the driver."

"Did you talk to anyone else other than the police?"

"Yes. Mike Black of the *Boston Globe* was at the booking. Someone had tipped him. I told him what I had told the cops, since I figured he would be printing a story about my arrest, and I wanted my version in the story."

"Is there anything else I should know? Maybe some info you held back from the police or Black?"

"Yes, there is, Mr. Ringel. I was too embarrassed to tell them about it."

"What is it, Joe? And please call me Abe."

"It's in the bathroom, let me get it."

Joe came out of the bathroom holding a crumpled handkerchief in a plastic Baggie. "I wiped off my penis with this after we finished, and I'm sure it contains some of her jelly. Can you use that?"

"Sure, let me take it and send it over to the lab."

As Joe handed him the bag, Abe asked, "Does this mean you've decided on me as your lawyer?"

"I guess so. You seem very able, and Alex says you're a 'mensch,' which he translated to me as 'a good egg.' "

"I'll win this case, Joe—if it ever becomes a case. The DA may well decide to drop it after they follow up on the leads you gave them."

"That would be great."

"Joe, I have just one more question."

"Shoot."

"How do you explain why Jennifer Dowling filed this rape charge? If you're telling me the truth, then it seems clear she will have a difficult time winning. Is she trying to shake you down for money?"

"No, I don't think so. I think she *feels* raped. I acted like a real shit after we made love. I just picked up and left. I didn't kiss her or thank her. She was a lousy lay, and I guess I let her know it. I shouldn't have done that, and I guess now I'm paying the price."

"And it's a darned heavy price," Abe added.

"I hope you never experience it, Mr. Ringel. You can't imagine how it feels to be accused of something so terrible. My mother is so upset. She knows that this is not the boy she raised. And it's my own fault. I should have realized how vulnerable I am to this sort of accusation, and I should have been more sensitive to her needs."

As Joe spoke, Abe was listening not only to the words, but also to the music and the rhythm. Almost all clients spoke the words of innocence at the initial meeting with their lawyer, but Joe spoke them with sincerity that was not at all typical of Abe's

37

clients. The look on Joe's face reminded Abe of Oliver North's. It exuded all-American integrity. What a great witness he will make, thought Abe. He quickly put the idea out of his mind as reality set in. This case would never get to trial. The really good ones rarely did. The prosecutor wouldn't want to lose a high-visibility case like this one. She'd drop it before she got too much egg on her face. Maybe Jennifer Dowling would change her mind when she found out what she'd have to go through. They often did back out, Abe knew. It would be a good win for him, not a great win. Nobody ever credited the defense lawyer when the case got dropped.

"I'll get to work today—interviewing witnesses, calling the lab, talking to the cops. A young lawyer—your age—will be down to see you in half an hour. His name is John Justin Aldrich, but he goes by Justin. Give him all the specifics: names, addresses, times. Everything you know about Jennifer Dowling. We'll follow up on everything, and he'll represent you at the arraignment, which is nothing more than a formality. And no more talking to anybody. Not the police, not the press, not your teammates, not your coaches, not even Alex. From now on, everything goes through me and Justin. No one else. Here's my private home phone number. Call me anytime, day or night. If my daughter answers, leave a message. I'll get right back."

"Abe, I don't know if this is proper. . . . Would you and your daughter, or whoever, want a couple of tickets to tonight's game? I can't promise I'll be in top form after this. Then again, that's good for you. You're a Celts fan, right?"

"Right, from now on I'm a Campbell fan first. Sure, we'll take the tickets. My daughter, Emma, and her entire class seems to have a crush on you. Maybe I can use it as an excuse to talk her out of going to her feminist group." Abe winked as the two men shook hands. He had to restrain himself from emitting a cheer as he flew along the corridor to the elevator.

Chapter Three

Back once again in his office, Abe had time to process the meeting with Campbell. He sat on the antique carved oak chair that his mentor, Haskel Levine, had given him when he'd first opened his practice. Abe wondered what the old man would make of the case. He dialed Haskel, but the phone was busy. Haskel had good days and bad, mostly bad lately.

Once, Haskel Levine had been Boston's most brilliant doctor of law, with an emphasis on "doctor." In his practice, Levine's approach had been more healing than adversarial. Haskel understood that law was a symphony, a blending of many different instruments and personalities that shaped a system. He did everything possible to avoid conflict, relying on reason, investigation, and compromise to achieve resolution. He became "counsel to the situation," in the spirit of his hero Louis Brandeis. But if all else failed, Haskel Levine, in his prime, was also an awesome advocate in the style of Brandeis. As his student, Abe had subsumed Haskel's approach, adding to it his own driving need to win.

Now Haskel's incredible brain was being diminished by Alzheimer's. It was horrible to watch. And to make matters worse, Haskel had become deeply depressed, to the point where he was being heavily medicated. Abe spoke to his mentor every day and visited him frequently. He found that whether Haskel was in a lucid phase or not, Abe needed to talk to the old man. Whatever Abe was struggling with would be filtered through Haskel's ear. It was strange behavior, especially for Abe. Yet it never failed that after he'd talked things over with Haskel, the answers would come to him—not from Haskel, but through Haskel's very presence. It was as if being near Haskel helped Abe to absorb Haskel's wisdom. When Abe soliloquized in Haskel's presence, he spoke a deeper, more honest, and more introspective truth than ever emerged in the presence of others—or even when he was alone. Haskel was Abe's superego, his conscience, his Jiminy Cricket.

Not that Haskel would give him answers. Even when he had been in his prime, Haskel didn't give advice in the traditional way. He had been the indisputable master of the "Socratic method"—or, as he preferred to call it, "the Talmudic method." He asked questions, digging deeper and deeper with each layer. "We are archaeologists of ideas," he once said. "There is always a deeper level, with more interesting artifacts. We must continue to dig until we are satisfied with what we have found. Then we must dig more, because we should never be satisfied."

Abe had not yet quite internalized all of Haskel's values. He still needed the reinforcement of Haskel's physical presence to bring out the best in him. He was aware that he was insuring for himself that by the time Haskel's mind was entirely gone, he would have internalized him completely. Sometimes he wondered if this process of consuming his mentor was morally okay or not, if in fact he was being selfish by eating up the old man in this fashion.

"You're the only person I can talk to about certain things," Abe would say, "because you're the only lawyer I know who never had any difficulty being an advocate as well as a human being." That was true. Abe needed Haskel to bring out the part of him he was most proud of, and most afraid of. His vulnerable side, his human side. This was a serious potential character flaw in a tough advocate!

40

When the phone was still busy at Haskel's, Abe buzzed Justin Aldrich on the intercom.

"Could you come into my office?"

Justin sat erect on the worn leather chair opposite Abe at the ancient partner's desk, the desk from Abe's original street-front office. John Justin Aldrich was in his early thirties, with straight blond hair, aristocratic in talk and dress. He was everything Abe wasn't, which is why he had been hired.

"You know we got Campbell?"

"I knew before you got back from the meeting."

"How's that?"

"I caught Gayle making out the file."

"Always efficient, isn't she? You're to go over there, debrief him, and walk him through the arraignment."

"Well done, Abe."

"Now, catch me up on Charlie O., please."

"We've got a complication."

"What else is new?"

Charlie Odell was a black man in his early twenties who had been convicted of gunning down Monty Williams, a controversial black politician, as Williams was leaving a McDonald's in Newark following a campaign stop for reelection to the city council. Odell, who had a severe overbite that made him appear always to be smiling, was easy to recognize and had been identified by two eyewitnesses, one white and one black. While Odell had proclaimed his innocence from the moment of his arrest, a jury had convicted him and the judge had imposed the death penalty.

Abe, who believed in his gut that Odell was innocent of this crime, had taken over the case on appeal on a pro bono basis and had lost in the state and federal courts. The judge had set an execution date—two months hence. Now the case had taken several new twists.

First, Charlie Odell had developed prison psychosis. He had literally gone crazy on death row and had to be given massive

41

doses of Thorazine, Librium, Valium, and other antipsychotic drugs just to keep him from banging his head against the brick walls and killing himself. How ironic, Abe thought. The state wants to kill Charlie. Now Charlie wants to kill himself. So the state has to stop him from killing himself so that they can kill him. The Supreme Court had ruled that a condemned man must be cured of his insanity before he can be executed, so that he could understand the nature of the punishment.

Now apparently fate had thrown them another curveball.

"So what's the latest?"

"I went to law school with a woman named Nancy Rosen," Justin said. "She was one of Haskel Levine's students during his last couple of teaching years. Her parents were wealthy New York real estate people. Predictably, she rebelled, became a radical, and went to work for Bill Kunstler. She didn't get along with him, so she opened a storefront law office in Newark."

"Another baby boomer who rejected the silver spoon in her mouth?"

"Don't stereotype us, Abe. I drove a cab to get through law school. The spoon was silver all right, but it had tarnished a long time ago, and we didn't have enough money to polish it. Poor *Mayflower* trash, my mother calls us. Poor but proud."

"So what about Ms. Rosen?"

"Well, you're not going to believe this. She called me to say that she knows who killed Monty Williams but she can't tell us because it was told to her by a client and falls under the rule of confidentiality."

"My God, Justin, can't you plead with her? We're talking about life and death."

"I begged her to reconsider. Her exact words were 'My client's life is also on the line. I have to protect my client even if he's guilty as sin.' "

Nancy Rosen was right under the rules of legal profession, of course. But she was wrong, Abe thought, a hundred percent wrong, according to the rules of decency and morality.

"Please, Justin, get her to think about it."

"I can only try, Abe. Meanwhile, I better get over to Campbell's hotel. I'll check in later."

Abe nodded absently, absorbed in the situation Justin had just presented to him. How much influence could Justin have over a former classmate? He tried to put himself in the young woman's position.

Abe needed Haskel's wisdom—or at least his presence—to help him make some tough decisions about the Charlie O. case. It was almost twelve weeks to injection day, and in the world of legal remedies, twelve weeks was a blink of the eye. The fact that Haskel's phone was still busy was a good sign. Perhaps it meant that the old man was having a good day.

Briefcase in hand, Abe left the office, flinging himself into the cool March air. He walked briskly, covering the half mile to Haskel's house in seven minutes. Abe always had been somewhat frightened by Haskel's home. It was almost exactly the opposite of his own—closed off, stuffy, the windows covered by heavy drapes. After Jerome, the home companion, let him in, it was clear that illness was hanging in the air, advancing toward its ultimate destination.

When Jerome took Abe into Haskel's study, the older man was quite alert, poring over the *Boston Globe* with his glasses pushed up on his forehead in the old way he had that made Abe's heart hurt. How often had he seen his mentor with just those same glasses pushed back up on the great dome of his head.

Haskel motioned for Abe to move closer to his desk chair. There were so many books and periodicals in Haskel's office that he arranged them in stacks like giant toadstools on the floor. Abe usually ended up seated on the ancient mahogany desk, his back against the room's lone window, facing Haskel. Above Haskel's large head were a series of old oil paintings of bearded European rabbis. "My inspirations," Haskel would call them. Now Abe leaned toward the elderly man, who whispered, "Abraham, can I confide in you?"

Haskel always insisted on calling Abe by his full biblical name, though Abe clearly preferred the shortened, more American version. To Haskel, Abe would always be Abraham, since the mentor thought it appropriate to his protégé's confrontational legal style. "The patriarch Abraham was, after all, the first defense attorney in recorded history," Haskel had long ago told Abe. "He argued with God in defense of the condemned cities of Sodom and Gomorrah."

"Yeah, but he lost," Abe had replied.

"It's not a disgrace to lose an argument with God," Haskel had replied. "You've lost to some lesser opponents."

As Abe recalled that story, he placed his hand on the old man's shoulder and nodded. "You can always confide in me, Haskel."

Haskel whispered in his ear, "I don't always take all the medicine they give me. Sometimes, when I feel like being myself, I hide the pills under my lips and flush them down the toilet later." Haskel then put a gnarled finger to his mouth, removed the pill Jerome had given him earlier, and crushed it with surprising strength into powder. "This makes me feel a little more in control of my life. Is there anything so terrible about that? Who, after all, am I cheating?"

"You're cheating yourself, you're cheating me, Haskel," Abe pleaded. "They're miracle drugs. They really do make a difference. You're entitled not to suffer."

Haskel shook his head vehemently. "It's my decision, not yours or anyone else's. I'll think about what you said, but it is very important for me to make the decision. Do you understand?"

Abe nodded—how could he not agree?

"So, tell. It's about Charlie O.?"

"How do you know?"

"Because you came to see me in the middle of a workday. You do that only if it is something important. And I know that the most important case you have now is that young man on death row."

Abe was astonished at the things Levine remembered, compared with the things he let go. It seemed as though his diseased memory still had a very refined selectivity about it. Haskel could forget that he was eating cereal in the middle of breakfast. Yet he could instantly remember the most painful case of his protégé's career.

Haskel and Abe had previously discussed Charlie's prison psychosis. Now Abe filled him in on Nancy's phone call to Justin.

"Your Mr. Charlie faces the same struggle I do. People want to keep him alive, so he can die when *they* are ready."

Haskel's eyes were changing focus, and Abe knew any minute he would be lost. He had learned that if he sat quietly for a few minutes, his mentor would sometimes snap back. As he watched Haskel, he noticed a stain on the old man's pants. Haskel was struggling against the dementia trying to overpower him—a battle he could sometimes win by recounting stories from his youth in Vilna, where as a twelve-year-old yeshiva student he had mastered the Jewish sacred texts, as well as calculus, geometry, and algebra.

"Have I told you about the trip my father and I took to Berlin before the war?" Levine's father was a melamed, a simple Hebrew-school teacher.

"Many times."

"About the swimming lesson?" Haskel asked, then continued without giving Abe a chance to reply. "My father wanted so much for me to attend the University of Berlin. We traveled there. As it happened, Hitler was giving a speech that day."

Haskel had told Abe a number of times about this trip, painting a spooky picture of himself and his father in their side locks and dark clothing as they were taunted and spat upon by Nazi hoodlums. They had stayed long enough to hear Hitler speak, then he and his father had taken the next train back to Lithuania.

"On the ride home, my father asked me this question: 'According to Jewish law, what are the three things a father must teach his son by the time he becomes a Bar Mitzvah?' Well, I was frightened by the hoodlums, but not so much that I could not answer this question, since it had been ingrained in me. 'First Torah; then a trade'—and the third, which had always fascinated me—'to swim.' "

" 'And which is the most important?' my father asked me. The correct answer, I thought, was Torah, of course, because it includes everything. So then my father asked, 'But what is the most important mitzvah in the Torah?' The answer, I knew, was 'Pickuach nefish'—the obligation to save life.

"Then my father smiled at me and asked: 'Which of the three obligations comes closest to the saving of life?' Without answering, I smiled back at my father, signaling to him that I understood what he was telling me. By then my father had already taught me Torah. He had directed me toward a profession. But that day in Berlin he taught me how to swim. I remember his words exactly. He said, 'Never swim against the current; always look for dangers beneath the surface; and always anticipate a change in the weather.' This was my father's way of gently telling me I would not be going to Berlin—that the climate, the weather, was wrong there. And so he sent me here. And you know the rest of my story." As indeed Abe did.

Haskel's father had sent him first to study in Boston at a Jewish high school and then on to Harvard and Harvard Law School. After one year at the law school, Haskel volunteered for the United States Army, served as a translator near the front, and made heroic efforts to locate his family. After the war he found out that they had all perished at Treblinka. Haskel returned to Harvard, completed his degree, served as a law clerk to Justice Felix Frankfurter, and began his brilliant career at the bar. In his spare time he taught trial practice at Harvard, wrote three books about jurisprudence, learned half a dozen more languages—each one of which he spoke with hardly a trace of an accent—and cultivated flowers, a hobby that Abe believed kept Haskel more firmly grounded than most of his colleagues. In his late thirties he married Estelle, the widow of one of his colleagues and a woman several years his senior. They had no children.

Abe had been one of Haskel's first students in trial practice, and a close relationship had developed between them.

Haskel's method of teaching confused many of the students, who were looking for answers, especially in a course as practical as trial strategy. But Haskel didn't give answers, only more questions. "I don't answer questions," he would gently advise his students. "I question answers.

"My job," he said, "is to deepen the level of your confusion. Your job is to find answers that work for you. Only you can do that. I can help by questioning your answers."

Abe had a natural affinity both toward Haskel's method of teaching and toward Haskel as a person. Both were old-fashioned men, though very different in their attitudes toward spirituality and religion. While Haskel had initially abandoned his faith in God after learning of his family's fate, he had gradually returned to it. Now, facing death, Haskel was more spiritual than ever. Abe was a skeptic. "How can you still believe," he had once asked Haskel, "after what God allowed to happen to your family?"

"My dear friend Abraham," a much younger and more impish Haskel had replied, "I must respond to your probing question with a question of my own: After surviving an event as cataclysmic as the Holocaust, how can one not believe?"

"Believe in what? A God who punishes the virtuous and rewards the evil? That's what happened during and after the Holocaust. Innocent Jews died, and guilty Germans lived a good life."

"Let me tell you a story about the Holocaust that my friend

Elie Wiesel once told me," Haskel had responded. "It took place during the darkest days at Auschwitz, when all was hopeless. A great Hasidic rabbi summoned God to a *din Torah*—a lawsuit. The rabbi accused God of abandoning his people in their time of greatest need. Witnesses were summoned, evidence was taken, and the jury voted. Elie told me that God was unanimously convicted by the jury—and then everyone prayed."

"But then after they prayed, they were gassed," Abe had replied in a tone of anger. "Wouldn't they have been better off trying to resist than relying on a God who doesn't keep his promises?"

"Is it so much better to rely on human beings who fail to keep their promises to God?"

It was typical Haskel—always answering hard questions with harder questions and with stories—filled with rabbis, talmudic scholars, and, of course, lawyers. Haskel's stories reflected the dual worlds that his mind and soul would always inhabit: the rational world of secular law and the mystical world of religion.

Abe had never been religiously observant, but he identified strongly with Jewish ethics and the historical experience of Jewish persecution. He was also a respectful skeptic—about everything. He had once bought a T-shirt for Haskel that read "Question authority—but raise your hand first." It perfectly captured the attitude of respectful skepticism by which both Abe and Haskel lived their lives. Haskel treasured the T-shirt, though he never wore it. "I am not the T-shirt type," he'd explained apologetically.

Though Abe was skeptical about nearly everything, he believed in rules. Even during the freewheeling sixties and seventies, he had never smoked pot, engaged in civil disobedience, or flouted the law. He was, he acknowledged with a mixture of pride and embarrassment, something of a square. Never do anything in private you wouldn't be proud to defend in public, he would tell Emma. Abe had broken that rule once, and it still haunted him.

Now he tried to draw Haskel back to the present. It wasn't clear how much Haskel understood as Abe recounted Nancy Rosen's call. When Abe explained that Nancy knew who the real killer was, Haskel responded by reminiscing about Nancy, to whom he had taught trial strategy at Harvard Law School.

"She was a dedicated soul," he recalled, "always calling into question the conventional wisdom." Haskel asked one of his traditional questions, but this time Abe's mind was wandering and he did not immediately grasp its relevance: "Can a lawyer who defends civil disobedience by others refuse to engage in it herself?"

Haskel wanted to keep talking, ostensibly about the Odell case, but really about his own situation. Or maybe it was about the Odell case. "Is a man himself," Haskel asked, "when he takes medicine that makes him so different? Is Charlie alive on those drugs? Or is he already dead?"

Abe pleaded with him to take his medicine, then noticed that Haskel had drifted away. Gently he kissed his mentor on the head and thanked him for his advice.

Haskel suddenly awoke. "What advice? Why thanks? For asking a few questions and complaining about my medicine? It's you I must thank, for listening and for trusting me, even now."

Abe walked down Brattle Street, passing the pre-Revolutionary wooden homes and the nineteenth-century brick mansions. He began to wonder what would happen when Haskel died. Would he become one of those blubbering fools who visit their parents' graves and "talk" to them? Abe understood that strange phenomenon a bit better now that he would sit with Haskel and "talk" to his nearly unconscious body.

While Abe contemplated life without Haskel's physical presence, an idea popped into his head about how to win the battle for time in the Odell case. Had Haskel knowingly put it there? It was impossible to tell, since by this time their two minds were as one.

It didn't really matter whose idea it was. It was a doozy.

Abe glanced at his watch: 5:45. He stopped on the sidewalk and pulled his cellular phone from his briefcase.

"Justin? It's me. Can you hear me all right? . . . Good, listen. Haskel just gave me a way to buy some time for Charlie. It's chancy, but . . ."

Chapter Four

It was hot that night at the old Boston Garden. Maybe it was one of Red Auerbach's fabled tricks for putting his opponent at a disadvantage—like not repairing parts of the famed parquet floor so that only the home team would know where the dead spots were. Abe had managed to reach Emma at school and talk her into leaving her feminist group a bit early in order to meet him in front of the "will call" window, where two loge tickets were waiting in Abe's name.

Abe loved these opportunities to be alone with Emma at a sports event. He found it easier to talk to her when they were both looking at something else rather than at each other. And sports—especially basketball—were a shared passion. Abe enjoyed the periodic father-daughter, one-on-one games in their backyard court, most of which Emma won.

The evening news had carried the story that Abe was representing Campbell, and several fans congratulated Abe on his new client. When the opposing players were introduced, the fans gave the usual friendly boos to Ewing and Oakley, but when Campbell's name was called, there was a smattering of cheers. One fan yelled out, "She asked for it," and another screamed, "Now that you're through with her, I want her!"

Emma turned to her father in disgust. "These guys have

51

already tried and convicted the woman. It's revolting, but typical. Now do you understand why so few rape victims complain?"

"C'mon," Abe replied, "lighten up. These are sports fans. What do you expect? They've obviously had a few brews."

Joe was right about his game not being up to par. His performance during most of the first half was well below his usual aggressive style of play. He seemed lethargic, uninvolved. But near the end of the second quarter, he hit two quick jump shots, one of them from three-point land. He seemed to smile at Abe as the official put his arms in the air to signify the three. The half ended with the Knicks ahead by four points.

During the half-time break, Abe phoned the office and reached Justin. "I'm glad you called. I found something unbelievable."

"What?"

"I plugged the name *Jennifer Dowling* into Nexus to see if she was ever involved in another case. And bingo! Last year she accused her boss of sexually harassing her. And that's not all. The case was dismissed—as unfounded. I don't know why yet, because the papers seem to be sealed. The bottom line is she lost."

"That is great," Abe shouted into the pay phone. "Find out whatever we can about the case. If she falsely accused someone else of sexual misconduct, her credibility will be shot."

"Can we get a false accusation of sexual misconduct into evidence under the rape shield laws?"

"Probably. It's not about her sexual history. It's about her history of lying."

"Great. Should you tell Campbell?"

"Sure, after the game. I'll go into the locker room, while my lovely daughter waits outside. Why don't you meet us at the Harvest for a late dinner and we can discuss the good news."

"Right, I'll see you there—what—ten-thirty?"

"Sounds good."

They hung up and Abe rejoined Emma, who was munching

popcorn and was by now lost in the game. "You missed a great shot by your new client, Dad."

The game ended with a blowout by the Knicks, 124–103. Campbell finished with fourteen points and three steals.

The Knicks' media relations man, Todd Curtis, was standing guard in front of the visitors dressing room, checking the press credentials of those reporters he didn't recognize. When Abe identified himself as Campbell's lawyer, Curtis immediately waved him in, cautioning him that "nothing is off the record in a locker room swarming with press people."

Emma waited outside with a pouting look on her face. She was used to being sent away when her father discussed confidential information, and usually she didn't mind. This time she had really wanted to accompany her father. What a story that would have made for tomorrow's lunchroom.

Abe had never been in a professional sports locker room before. It was a strange sight. Naked men were talking unselfconsciously to women reporters as the reporters tried hard to avoid looking at their private parts. Some of the ballplayers were stark naked, some wore towels, others were in underwear or fully dressed. An air of teasing macho sexuality pervaded the scene. Emma wasn't coming near this place, ever, Abe thought.

The sights and sounds of victory were all around. There was a lot of loud laughter, friendly cursing, sports lingo, and back slapping. Abe made his way through the mélange of tall bodies, finally spotting Campbell, fully dressed and surrounded by TV and print journalists. A woman from WBZ asked him about the rape charge, and he replied, "I'm here to talk about the game. I have no comment on anything else. Lawyer's instructions." A male reporter from *Newsday* asked him whether he thought his game was affected by the rape accusation, and Joe acknowledged candidly that during the beginning of the first half, his concentration had been off. "They don't teach you how to deal with this sort of thing in training camp." He quickly added that once he had made those two jump shots near the end of the second quarter, his concentration had returned.

Then he spotted Abe and, without missing a beat, politely introduced him to the press. "Ladies and gentlemen, this is my lawyer, Abraham Ringel. From now on, he will be speaking for me in all matters regarding the case."

The TV cameras turned immediately to Abe as a barrage of questions were directed at him simultaneously.

"Did he do it?"

"What's your defense gonna be?"

"Has the NBA front office been in touch?"

"How much are you charging him?"

Abe waited for the shouts to subside, then in a firm voice said: "I have a brief statement at this time. Joe Campbell asserts his complete innocence and is looking forward to proving that at trial. Mr. Campbell is cooperating totally with the police and has already turned over to them several leads and items of exculpatory evidence. Beyond that I have no further comment at this time. I'm sure you understand why."

The questions continued, but Abe ignored them as he whispered in Joe's ear. "Something important has come up. Something very good. We have to talk to you about it. Can you meet us at the Harvest restaurant in Harvard Square in about half an hour?"

Joe said he would have to check with one of the coaches to see if it was okay to miss the team flight back to New York. After a brief conversation with a short, graying man, he returned and said, "Okay."

Abe made his way through the crowd and rejoined Emma, standing among the several Knicks fans and groupies hoping to catch a glimpse of their heroes.

"Did you get to see him?" Emma inquired.

"Yes, he's meeting us at the Harvest."

"What did he look like naked?" Emma asked with a teasing smile.

"I didn't see him naked, and neither will you. Most of them were dressed. The others had towels around them," Abe fibbed. "Let's get off that subject. Justin and I have to meet with Campbell, and you have to go home."

"Can't I meet him? I'd love to just say hello. Jon would die if he knew I met him."

"You know you can't come to a lawyer-client meeting, Emma. You know the rules of confidentiality."

"How about if I stay just to meet him, and then I'll go home like a good little girl." She flashed him her most irresistible smile.

"All right, but just for five minutes. We have a lot to discuss, and Campbell didn't miss his team flight to talk to *you*, my dear daughter. So after a polite introduction, off you go into a cab and home to bed."

"Deal. Thanks, Dad."

The Harvest was a trendy restaurant, housed in a building designed by noted architect Ben Thompson and patronized mostly by academics. Although famous for its nouvelle cuisine as well as its discretion and privacy, it could sometimes be a bit too politically correct. A few days earlier a woman had stormed out of the restaurant as soon as she'd recognized Abe at the next table, muttering loudly about how she didn't want to sit next to a sexist who always defended rapists on TV.

Abe had called ahead for his favorite corner table and had alerted the maître d' that a tall man would soon be joining them. Now he also looked around to make sure the woman who had walked out was not there tonight. The last thing he needed was a scene in front of his new client. When Joe Campbell arrived, he was shown immediately to Abe's table. Almost no one stared at him as he made his way through the dining room. Among the academic crowd, Campbell went almost unrecognized.

"Joe, you know Justin. This is my daughter, Emma. She wanted to meet you. Her boyfriend is a big Knicks fan. She'll be able to dine out on this meeting for a long time."

"It's nice to meet you, Emma. You're very pretty."

Emma blushed, unprepared—for once—to respond to the unexpected flattery. "It's nice to meet you, too, Mr. Campbell. Good game, especially the second half. But can I ask you a question?"

"Sure, go ahead."

"Why did Riley have you guarding Douglas? Don't you usually match up with Dee Brown?"

"I asked him the same question. I guess he anticipated that my concentration might be off, and he couldn't take a chance on Brown walking all over me. Douglas isn't that much of a scoring threat."

Abe tapped on his watch. "Time's up, my dear. It's home for you now. You can get a cab in front of the out-of-town newsstand. Bye, we've got to get down to business."

Emma frowned, picked up her book bag, kissed Abe on the cheek, waved to Justin across the table, and extended a hand to Campbell. Joe shook her hand. "Fine grip you've got there. Not used to that in a female." Emma giggled, uncharacteristically, and walked off.

Abe leaned in toward Campbell and began to talk in a tone that made it clear the chitchat part of the meeting was over.

"Justin has discovered a very important fact. We're not quite sure of its implications—or even whether it will be admissible at a trial—but it is potential dynamite."

"What is it?" Campbell asked.

"It seems that you're not the first man this Jennifer Dowling has accused of sexual misconduct. Last year she accused her boss at a public relations firm of sexually harassing her."

"Well, maybe he did," Campbell replied.

"It doesn't look that way. We don't know for sure, but it appears that her complaint was dismissed as unfounded. That means she had no case."

"Do you know the specifics?"

"Not yet. The records appear to have been sealed."

"Can this help you get the case against me dropped?"

"Can't hurt. Could help. Don't know yet."

"I'm not surprised," Joe said. "She mentioned something about a legal mess she had just gotten finished with, and she seemed to have a lot of animosity toward men. I think I have a better sense now of why she did this."

Abe wasn't so sure. "I still can't figure it. She had to know we would find out about this prior accusation. Her case seems weaker and weaker. Why did she cry rape if she knew she had no case?"

"She probably didn't think much about it," Joe speculated. "She must have called 911 as soon as I left the room, since the police were waiting for me by the time I got back to my hotel. Maybe she's thinking about it now, and she'll reconsider."

"Could be," Abe said, feeling mixed emotions about that prospect. "But we've got to act as if she's going full steam ahead. We can't leave anything to chance."

"Is there anything else I can do?" Campbell asked.

"Not for now, other than trying to think of anything else she might have said that could be relevant."

The waitress interrupted the conversation by telling them that the kitchen was about to close. Campbell asked for a lemonade and some berries. Abe ordered decaf cappuccino and a chocolate torte. Justin wanted a glass of white wine and some pâté.

As they were waiting for their snack, Joe said, "There is something I remember."

"What is it?" Abe asked.

"It's a little embarrassing for me to talk about."

"Think of us as your doctors. You've got to tell us anything that could help you."

"I'm not sure this helps, but all right, here goes."

Campbell took a deep breath, as if he were preparing to shoot a crucial free throw. "When we were in bed going hot and heavy, I went down on her, and she seemed to enjoy it a lot. She sure was moaning. I then asked her if she would . . . you know, do the same for me. They usually do. But she didn't want to. She said something about having a bad experience with oral sex."

"Stop, please," Abe insisted, putting his hand gently on Joe's arm. "This is just the kind of thing I was warning you about this morning when we first met. We could be getting into some dangerous territory here. Let me talk for a minute, before you go on."

"Fine, but I think I know what you're worried about, and it's not a problem."

"Maybe so, but let me guide you."

Abe thought for a minute how to put what he wanted to say. "Okay, let me tell you something about the law of rape that you probably already know."

Campbell looked at Abe intently as the lawyer continued. "If a woman consents to foreplay or even intercourse, she can still say no at any time, and she can refuse any *kind* of sex, even after agreeing to any other kind of sex."

"I do know that," Campbell interjected. "I remember the Marcus Webb case." Joe was referring to a former Celtic who was accused of forcing a woman to have anal sex after she agreed to have ordinary sex. "Don't worry, that's not what happened here."

Abe insisted on maintaining some control over the conversation, even though his original concerns had abated. "So she told you that she did not want to perform fellatio on you, and you did not insist that she do so, is that right?"

"Yes, that's right. She—"

"Wait, please let me continue. You didn't force her to perform fellatio. Is that right?"

"That's exactly right."

"Whatever she did, she did of her own free will. Right?"

"Right."

"Okay," Abe said with a sigh of relief. "Now we can get back to talking like normal people."

Justin asked Campbell if Jennifer had explained what her bad experience was.

"All she told me was that it didn't have anything to do with any kind of disease or anything like that. It was something emotional. She made it clear it was none of my business, and that we should go ahead and have intercourse."

"And you did," Abe continued.

"Yes, we did, but it was lousy sex from then on. I don't know, it kind of threw me off my game, and she seemed nervous, too, but she didn't want to stop. It was almost as if we both wanted to get it over with. I certainly did. And I was out of there like a bat out of hell."

"Did she ask you to stay?"

"No, but I think she wanted to talk about it. I sure as hell didn't."

"Did she accuse you of anything before you left?"

"No, except with her eyes. Her eyes accused me of insensitivity, and my eyes admitted guilt."

"I think that's enough for now," Abe said, again looking at his watch. "We have a busy day tomorrow. Not on your case. On a death row case we have in New Jersey. On our way back, we'll drop by to see you in New York. We can go over the next steps in the case. In the meantime, think of anything else that could be helpful. Investigative leads, witnesses, anything. When's your next game?"

"Saturday night. Cleveland. Tough team. Great city."

With that Campbell seemed to turn off his concern about the case. When the waiter brought the food the three men rehashed the game. What a kick to be reviewing an NBA game with one of the players, Abe thought. He couldn't wait to fill Emma in on Campbell's analysis of the third quarter. That pleasant task would have to await his return from his morning visit to New Jersey's death row.

Chapter Five

The sight of a prison housing death row always sent shivers down Abe's spine. The idea of a state deliberately taking a human life was incomprehensible to him, especially in light of his skepticism about the accuracy of the criminal justice system. Now he knew for sure that at least one innocent man was scheduled to be strapped onto a gurney and injected with an infernal chemical concoction designed specifically to snuff out life. The prison in this instance was an imposing gray building surrounded by bright silver barbed wire. When the morning sun reflected off the glistening metal, it created the appearance of a heavenly halo, masking what Abe knew was a hellish reality inside the walls.

Death row, Abe thought as he contemplated his visit with Charlie O., was more alive than Haskel's house. At least there was hope that some of the young men would survive. New Jersey had a fairly liberal supreme court, and although state law authorized capital punishment for murderers, the courts had deprived the executioner of his designated victims several times in recent years. In fact, no one had actually been executed in New Jersey for several decades.

Charlie's case was different. He had killed a black man. Since the opponents of capital punishment had long argued that

60

no one in America was ever executed for killing blacks, Charlie made a good case for the state. Almost everyone who believed in capital punishment wanted Charlie Odell to die. It would make an important statement.

Even Charlie wanted to die—or he had before he started taking his medicine. Now he wanted to live. He wanted Abe to keep him alive until he could prove his innocence.

Charlie had never once deviated from his original story, a case of mistaken identity. He was doing a drug deal downtown in Newark at the time of the Williams murder. He was blocks away. Of course, the guy he was selling drugs to—his alibi witness—would never come forward. Charlie wanted Abe to look for another skinny black kid with an overbite like his.

And Abe had done just that. He had hired a black private investigator from Newark to comb the city. No luck. Newark was a place where people came to hide for a while—to blend into the neighborhood—and then leave. There were lots of transients, especially in the world of crime. If there were another skinny black kid with an overbite who'd actually killed Williams, the PI finally reported to Abe, he was probably gone by now.

After they parked, the two attorneys locked their valuables in the car they had rented at the Philadelphia airport. This was mandatory for visitors to death row. No one was allowed to carry anything into the prison. Guards even searched the bottom of Justin's right shoe when the hand-held metal detector buzzed. Justin had stepped on a thumbtack, which had embedded itself in his heel. The guards removed it before letting Justin through security. Then Abe and Justin had their hands stamped and were led into a room that locked from both sides. From there they were led to a visiting area that adjoined death row. A special lawyer's room was reserved for them so they could meet their client in private. The room was divided by a Plexiglas panel separating the lawyers from the condemned inmate. The panel had airholes through which they could talk. All touching was prohibited.

Charlie was already seated as Abe and Justin took their places. Charlie placed his hand against the glass partition, and Abe placed his on the other side so that their fingers met across the glass. It was the death row handshake. Justin did the same. The young black man then placed his face in his hands and spoke in a monotone. "Please don't let them kill me. I'm scared. Please help me. I didn't do it."

The ill-fitting orange prison uniform flapped against his body as the man rocked back and forth—the only physical evidence of his anxiety. Abe had been working with the prisoner long enough to recognize that beneath this young man's relatively calm exterior were buried the emotions of a lifetime in poverty—the pain of neglect, despair, and hopelessness.

"We know you didn't do it." Abe stood and placed a hand reassuringly near Charlie's head across the partition. It was the best he could do to comfort the young man in a setting where actual touching was impossible. Abe could see the initials of Charlie's "old lady" sculpted into his Brillo-like hair. Abe spoke through the holes in the glass partition. "I've got some promising news. Justin has somebody who knows who did do it."

"Who?'

"She won't tell me yet," Justin interjected. "I'm working on her. It may take some time, but I'm confident that I will eventually find out."

"That's just what I got none of—time. It's less than six weeks now." Charlie was rocking faster.

"Look, Charlie, I do have an idea."

"What?"

"It's a gamble, but we've got no choice."

The rocking stopped. "What?"

Abe leaned over and whispered through the holes in the glass into Charlie's ear. "Charlie, you're gonna have to stop taking your medicine for a while."

Charlie looked bewildered. "If I stop, I'll go crazy again. Do you want me to go crazy?"

"Yes, I do," Abe said somberly. "Try to follow me."

Charlie listened as Abe tried to explain the idea he had gotten from Haskel's refusal to take his medicine.

"They can't execute you under New Jersey law if you're crazy—if you're legally insane. And without your medicine, you *are* legally insane, psychotic. You don't have to help them kill you. You don't have to help them keep you sane so that they can execute you. Just stop taking the medicine."

"They'll force me to take it."

"They may try, but we'll take them to court. Under New Jersey law, they can't force you to take medicine unless you are dangerous to others or yourself."

"When I don't take the medicine I try to kill myself. I bang my head against the wall."

"They can protect you by putting you in a padded cell. It's worth a shot. It will certainly buy me time."

Justin remained silent. He was doubtful, both about the likelihood of succeeding and about the ethical implications of a lawyer advising his client to stop taking his medicine. In the airplane on the way to the prison, Abe had told Justin about a Texas case in which a death row inmate had stopped taking antipsychotic medicine and a judge had postponed his scheduled execution. "If it worked in Texas, it could certainly work in New Jersey."

"That may be true," Justin replied. "But what about the ethics of advising a client to stop taking his medicine? He might kill himself."

"There are different rules on death row. This is about saving life, *not* covering our asses. We've got to take some risks here."

Charlie was even more frightened now. "You don't know what it feels like to be crazy. When I stop taking the medicine, I'm really out of control. I don't know what I'm doing. I just want to die. I don't want to feel like that."

"It must be terrible," Abe agreed. "Sadly, we've got no choice. You've got to stop taking the pills if you want to stay alive."

Charlie looked at Abe tearfully. "I think I understand. If I don't want *them* to kill me," he said, pointing to the guard who was standing outside, "then I have to want to kill *myself.*"

Charlie understood. So did Abe and Justin—to the extent anyone could understand this theater of the absurd. It was a bizarre twist in the macabre dance of death row justice.

Soon enough the interview was over. Before the guards took Charlie away, he gave Abe a thumbs-up sign. "You're my man. Do right by me, Mr. Ringel."

"I'll try, Charlie. I sure to God will try," Abe said as he looked back at the man he had just condemned to a potentially suicidal insanity.

Chapter Six

Back in the parking lot of the prison, Abe retrieved his portable cellular phone and called the office.

"Am I glad you called, Abe," Gayle said, her voice crackling through the static. "Rendi is desperate to reach you *before* you see Joe."

"Where is she?" Abe asked. Rendi, in addition to being Abe's on-again-off-again lover, was also a top-notch investigator who was working with them on the Campbell case.

"She's waiting for you in front of Campbell's apartment building. Figured she couldn't miss you that way."

"What does she have?"

"She doesn't want me to talk about it on the cellular phone."

"I thought we bought one of those secure ones—the kind that scramble."

"We did. But still . . ."

"That good?"

"Or bad!"

"Which one?"

"I don't know. She'll explain."

"What's up?" Justin asked as Abe pocketed his Motorola flip-top.

"We're meeting Rendi in New York City."

Justin could barely squelch a groan. "She couldn't tell you what it was over the phone?" He hated when Abe included Rendi—a nonlawyer—in their legal strategy, believing that it reflected Abe's lack of faith in him. However, that wasn't true in this instance. Abe knew that his always hyper investigator had a feel for the hot buttons in any case. Whatever made her rush to New York was guaranteed to be important. Rendi didn't usually overreact.

"You know how I feel about Rendi's instincts, Justin. We've been over this before."

Justin closed his car window and sighed. "I know, I know, she's an intuitive genius."

"It's true. Look, I don't use her for legal maneuvers. That's what I count on you for. But when it comes to understanding people, Rendi is the best. The fact is Rendi can walk into a roomful of partying strangers and in seconds figure out who's having an affair with whom, who hates whom, who's sucking up to whom, and who's stabbing whom in the back. That's intuition. You can't learn that in law school."

"Listen, Abe, if we need mental CAT scans, I suggest we call Mass. General."

Abe pinched Justin's cheek playfully. "Come on, boychick, smile. We've got the hottest case in the country right now, and we can't lose it. So what have we got to worry about?"

"She just gets to me—"

"That's Rendi's stock in trade. That's what we hire her for."

Rendi was waiting for them, her jeans and pullover blending perfectly with the merchandise showcased in the window of the Gap store that occupied the ground floor of Campbell's apartment building. As Abe looked at Rendi from inside the car, he reflected on the woman who had come to mean so much to all of his different lives.

He had first met Rendi ten years ago, and at the time he

wouldn't have been able to guess if she were twenty-eight or forty. Dark-skinned, with a European face, she was a strange and mysterious woman of indeterminate ethnicity, culture, and age. "I have no native language," she was fond of saying, "because I have no home." In fact, he knew Rendi spoke eleven languages, each with a slight accent. It wasn't until much later that Abe would discover she had been born in Algeria, moved to Israel as a child, worked for the Mossad, where she'd acquired her skills as an investigator, and was closer to thirty-five than twenty-eight.

For all his fascination, however, their relationship was a troubled one. Though Hannah had been dead for nine years, Abe still felt a strong sense of guilt about his wife's death. He and Rendi had engaged in a one-night foray a week or so before Hannah had been killed in the crash. It had tortured Abe, who frequently indulged in the self-lacerating belief that Hannah might have been distracted by her suspicions when she'd driven the car into the tree. The indiscretion had made both Abe and Rendi feel so terrible that it had been several years before they could begin to explore their own feelings for each other. Even now their relationship was rocky, and Abe had not yet been able to commit himself to her.

"Abe, look, a spot. Grab it."

The reality of parking in Manhattan brought Abe back to the present as he backed the rental car into the metered space between two trucks right in front of Campbell's building on Broadway between Eighty-sixth and Eighty-seventh Streets.

"Let's walk down to Zabar's and grab a bagel," Abe suggested, grabbing Rendi's arm.

"Forget eating, Abe, you don't have time."

It was so like Rendi to rush headlong into a conversation that Abe had to suppress his smile. Every part of her lovely frame was infused with nervous energy. In fact, it was impossible to relax around her. And the last thing Rendi ever wanted anyone to do around her was relax.

Naturally Justin had to react. "What's the matter, Rendi, the Campbell case isn't making us crazy enough for you?"

Rendi ignored Justin and motioned the two men around the corner to Eighty-seventh Street.

"This won't take long. I did not want to do this over the telephone. And I thought if you were going to see Campbell, you might want to give him a sense of how urgent this matter is. So I brought you the original instead of faxing you a copy." She opened her attaché case and pulled out a piece of paper that Abe recognized as a printout of the police report.

"Listen to this. When I got this it read just like your basic report: 'The complaining witness acknowledges that she initially consented to perpetrator's advances, including cunnilingus, blah, blah.' Now listen: 'Perpetrator then'—here's the part that got me—'made reference to a sexual harassment complaint she had filed against a former boss, which involved oral sex.' Then the report goes on, 'Witness insisted that perp stop and leave. Perp ignored her expressed lack of consent and proceeded to force intercourse.'

"Here's another little goody: 'Small microabrasion on vagina consistent with forced intercourse according to examining Dr. Mary Stiller.' "

"Yeah, but that could be related to a few things," Justin commented.

"Something's not right here. You guys told me that Campbell had seemed surprised to learn about Jennifer Dowling's sexual harassment complaint when you told him after the game. Now it looks like he knew about it earlier."

"There could be a few explanations," Abe said. "My clients frequently hold information back for a while until they trust me. It's been my experience that criminal defendants—even innocent ones—often lie about details of the case that may be embarrassing to them or that they believe may hurt their defense. Then when they see the hard evidence, they begin to get with the program."

"Still, how would he know about it?" Justin asked. "Did she tell him?"

"And if she did tell him, why didn't he tell us? And why did he cover up that he knew about it since that fact would help him?" Rendi handed the report to Abe as she spoke.

"Maybe she's not telling the truth," Abe said.

"Abe, take the stars out of your eyes, at least for a minute," Rendi cautioned. "Something's not right. I have a funny feeling about this report."

"Funny feelings don't usually make a good underpinning for a defense—or a prosecution." Abe heard how caustic he sounded, but he couldn't help it. Rendi was always good at popping holes in his balloons—too good. "Listen, I really appreciate your dashing down here like this. As usual, you're right on the spot. Now, if we're going to make that meeting before Campbell leaves for Cleveland, Justin and I have to go. Where's your car?"

"In a lot. You are paying my expenses."

"I'll walk you. Justin, wait for me here."

They walked in step together, though Abe had to push it to keep up with Rendi's brisk pace. Rendi seemed to grow slimmer and taller as Abe thickened a bit around the middle. It was her discipline about working out, he was sure. "Listen, you know I'm not going to let this slide, Rendi. I just don't want to be confrontational. Campbell is a good client for us."

They walked in silence. Rendi did not try to force the Campbell issue. She was quiet, which was unusual for her. In fact, she seemed distracted. "What's on your mind?" Abe asked.

"Nothing, really. You know . . . the Campbell case."

"There's *never* nothing on your mind, Rendi. Now tell me the real reason you drove this report from Cambridge to New York."

"I wanted to show it to you in person—and, I missed you."

Abe was surprised. This was unlike Rendi, whom he considered to be without a vulnerable bone or soft streak in her limber body. Rendi was all muscle and heat and courage.

"I haven't seen you since you took on the Campbell case," she went on.

"Correct me if I'm wrong, but it's been two days."

"Two days can be a long time or a short time, depending."

"You sound like Haskel."

"I consider that a great compliment."

"It is." He ruffled her hair. "I'll see you tonight."

"Ciao."

When Abe returned to Justin, the younger man did not hide his annoyance at having been abandoned on the streets of New York. Abe tried to mollify him: placing an arm around his shoulder, he asked Justin's advice as to how to confront Campbell with the apparent inconsistency. "I don't want Campbell to think we're calling him a liar. This is one client we don't want to lose. I've got to get him to trust us with the truth. An innocent defendant can really get hung out to dry if he starts prevaricating."

"For a start, don't use the word *prevaricate* with Joe. He strikes me as the kind of guy who would prefer to be called a liar than a prevaricator."

"Well, I don't think he's either. He's probably just scared."

Joe greeted them at the door of his spacious penthouse apartment, which—to Abe's surprise—was full of books, magazines, fine lithographs on the wall, and classical CDs. Joe led them through the living room to a den that was dominated by a large computer, with a laser printer, a modem/fax, and all sorts of programs and instruction books. It looked like the apartment of a young assistant professor in Cambridge.

Campbell saw Abe's look as he took in the room. "Surprised?" he asked, smiling. "Did you expect to see girlie pictures and sports magazines?"

Abe was visibly embarrassed. "Well, I certainly didn't expect to see an intellectual's pad. You're a more complex man than you seem."

"You can't tell a man by his books and art, although I do read a lot, and I love to do research on my computer. You can find out anything, you know," Joe said, handing Abe a printout of about forty law cases. "This is your won-and-lost record over the last ten years. Pretty impressive, especially if you discount the past few months."

"It's getting harder to win these days," Abe said, then added casually, "Joe . . . before I forget, I'd like you to take a look at this." He handed Campbell the entire police report, so as not to alert him to his specific concern.

Joe read the report carefully, making some notes as he read. When he finished he said calmly: "There are some falsehoods in this report, though a good deal of it appears to be accurate. I guess that rape is in the eye of the beholder. I didn't force myself on her, that's clear to me. She did consent to cunnilingus. In fact, she invited it. I didn't force her to do anything against her will."

Abe waited for Joe to mention the earlier harassment complaint. When he didn't, he put the question directly. "What about the harassment complaint? You didn't indicate last night that you knew about it."

"I did know about it, I just didn't use it in the way the report says I did. She told me about her previous problems with men, and I tried to be sympathetic. That's when she got a little weird, but she never said no. To the contrary, she seemed to want to get it over with, like I did. If that's rape, then I've raped and been raped by several women over the years."

"No, that's not rape—at least not according to the law. My daughter's feminism group may have a different idea, but legally that's just mutually lousy sex, which I bet you now wish you hadn't gone through with."

"You're darn right. I can get all the lousy sex I want, every night of the week. Why would I endanger my freedom—my entire career—to get more of something I have unlimited amounts of?"

"Not a very good defense, Joe," Abe said, smiling. "Most

of my guilty clients risk the things they have limited quantities of—namely, their freedom and reputation—to get a little bit more of what they have unlimited amounts of, generally money." He was thinking of the dozens of wealthy clients he had represented who had risked, and sometimes experienced, imprisonment for a couple of extra bucks. As Emma had put it when she'd heard about one rich client's indictment: "Why did she have to cheat people? Did she need yet another Porsche?" Somehow, Abe mused, people with everything seemed to have a psychological compulsion for even more. It was a bizarre reality.

"To tell you the truth," Joe continued, "I went through with it as much for her as for me. She took some emotional risks, being as forward as she was. She actually propositioned me, though I would surely have asked her if she hadn't. And she had been through some tough times with that previous business. If I had said no, I really would have hurt her. Or at least that's what I thought at the time."

"All right, that sounds plausible—at least to me. Now back to the sexual harassment suit. When and how did you first learn about it?"

"Do I have to tell you, Abe? It's embarrassing."

"Yes, you've got to tell me, Joe. I'm your lawyer. I've got to know everything."

"I'd really rather not get into that, if you don't mind. I don't think it has anything to do with the case, and it makes me uncomfortable to talk about it."

"Joe, you've got to tell me. It may turn out to be important to the case, especially if the prosecutor digs it up. I don't want to be blindsided."

"If I tell you," Joe replied, "will it be entirely confidential? Do I have your promise that you will never disclose it to anyone?"

"Look, Joe, there are clear rules of confidentiality and clear exceptions in the Code of Professional Responsibility. I live both by the rules and by the exceptions."

"If I tell you what you want to know, will that be within the rule or the exception?"

"If it's about anything in the *past,* it's within the rule, and I can never tell anyone. If you tell me that you're planning a *future* crime, then it's within the exception and I can disclose it."

"I'm not planning any future crimes, Abe. I didn't commit any past crimes, either. Everything you want to know relates to the past. But I still don't know whether I should tell you. It's not that I don't trust you personally. But I'm a, you know, a celebrity, and stuff gets out. Your secretary, your daughter—anyone could gossip."

"You can trust me. And everyone on my staff. We're all professionals. We live and die by our oath of confidentiality. As far as my daughter or anyone else not on my staff is concerned, I don't tell her anything confidential. That's why she had to leave our meeting at the Harvest. You have my word about all this. I *have to* know. I can't defend you successfully without it. I can't afford the risk of being sandbagged by the prosecutor."

"Okay, if you promise me you'll never tell anyone what I tell you, I guess I have no choice."

"No one except my law associates and investigators, and only on a professional need-to-know basis."

"Okay, Abe, I'm putting myself in your hands. It's not pretty. If it ever got out, it would ruin my life. It would make me look like a sicko."

"What is it?" Abe asked, wondering if he might have been better off in the dark.

"Whenever I meet, or hear about, a woman I'm interested in, I check her out on my personal computer."

"That's your big secret?" Justin asked incredulously. "Lots of people check out their dates. I bet she scoped you out, too."

"Well, I guess I'm old-fashioned about this sort of thing. I've got to be especially careful considering my position."

"It's totally understandable," Abe said. "How do you do it?"

"As you can see, I've got a modem, and all this fancy software, even a password-cracking program. It's probably illegal to use it. I got it off a computer network."

"What does it do?"

"Every secret file has a password that you need in order to get into the database. You'd be amazed how obvious most passwords are. A large jeans company used 'zipper' as its password. An advertising agency I know uses 'subliminal.' A lot of people use their birthdays, sports teams, children's names. This program can figure out almost any password that appears in a standard dictionary."

"But what if it isn't a Scrabble word?"

"No problem. If it's a big company, I learn whatever I can from the open files and then call a secretary, pretending I'm in the accounting department. You'd be amazed how gullible some people are and how easy it is to get them to give up the password."

"How did this help you find out about Dowling's lawsuit?"

"Piece of cake," Joe said proudly. "First, I checked her out in the open databases—CompuLaw, Nexis—and found out that she had filed a lawsuit, that it had been dismissed, and that the reasons for the dismissal had been sealed. So I figured that the company she used to work for must have a closed file on the lawsuit. It took me a few hours to break their password. A little more subtle than most, but not that difficult. It was 'spin.' I got into the database and there it was. No problem."

"I can't believe it's so easy to break into."

"Watch your own files, Abe. I bet you don't even know the password to your secret files."

"You're right, I don't. You can be damn sure that I'm going to change them tomorrow."

"Randomize them, Abe, randomize them. Just a series of random numbers with no rhyme or reason. That's impossible to break—and change them every month. And tell your secretary not to give them to anyone."

"Thanks for the excellent advice, Joe."

"Just remember your promise. Nobody learns about my little secret. Right?"

"Right. Your secret is safe with me. I don't understand why you care so much. It's not that bad a secret—wanting to learn more about a woman you're about to go out with."

"It makes me seem so damn calculating, so devious. It's also probably illegal. By the way," Joe added almost as an afterthought. "I've got the Dowling printouts in a file. You want them?"

"Darn right I do. And anything else you've got."

Campbell opened a drawer in his desk, pulled out a neatly labeled file, and handed Abe several pages. The first was a case denying the motion to dismiss the complaint, the second a case stating that the complaint had later been dismissed by the judge, and the third a memorandum from the secret file of the defendant's company, setting out the reasons for the dismissal in cryptic legalese. There was enough to show that Jennifer Dowling had lied in a sworn deposition and had destroyed her credibility. It was a great investigative lead.

Abe took the first two printouts, then he gave the third back to Joe after reading it carefully. "I don't want this one in my file," he explained. "It's probably stolen property."

"Why the hell didn't you tell us about this yesterday?" Justin asked with a distinct edge to his voice.

"I told you that I was a little embarrassed to admit that I check out my dates by computer before I see them again. It's not very gentlemanly. Remember, we were in the Harvest. Anyone could have been listening. Also, I wasn't sure I could trust you. I needed to hear you promise me that everything would be kept confidential. I value my reputation as a gentleman."

"This is not about being a gentleman," Abe interjected. "This is about defending a false rape charge. You just can't hold anything back. And you did worse than that just holding this back. You actively led us to believe that you were hearing about the harassment charge for the first time last night."

"You're right. I'm really sorry. It won't happen again."

"It *can't* happen again. This kind of thing can really come back to bite us in the ass at a trial. Do we have an understanding?"

"We certainly do. I never make the same mistake twice, just ask Coach Riley. You can count on it."

Chapter Seven

When Abe got back to Cambridge that night, Emma, Jon, and Rendi were watching the evening news. Jon was working on a class project with Emma. Rendi—who was making dinner—had invited Jon to join them for a Sabbath meal.

Abe liked Jon. He was a child of academia. His mother was a law professor at Harvard, and his father was an aeronautical engineer at the Lincoln Lab, connected with MIT. Jon was born in New York, hence his loyalty to the Knicks. His family had moved to Cambridge after he finished the first year of high school.

Jon was polite and considerate to Emma, and he always called Abe "Mr. Ringel."

"Hi, Mr. Ringel. Great case. I'm sure you'll win. Even Emma got converted last night, and if you can win over Emma, you can persuade anyone."

"Dad didn't win me over," she corrected him. "His antediluvian arguments couldn't convince anyone who knows anything about rape. Joe Campbell won me over. He was really nice. Put him on the stand, Dad, he'll win his own case."

"What a show of confidence in your own father, my dear. The client will win without any help from his lawyer. Don't let Campbell hear that—especially before he pays my very considerable bill."

"Oh, you know what I mean, Daddy. I've heard you say it a million times. An innocent client is more important than a good lawyer. You're a great lawyer, Dad, but in this case you have a rare innocent client. It should be a piece of cake."

"It's never a piece of cake," Rendi said. "Something always makes the cake crumble."

The Ringel family and guests always seemed to gravitate to the kitchen, and tonight was no exception. And because they were hooked on news, a miniature TV was permanently placed on the counter. Suddenly Campbell's picture flashed across the small screen. The voice was the familiar one of Cheryl Puccio, the sex prosecutor from Middlesex County. She was being interviewed by Bob Maverick, the sports reporter. Puccio was holding forth:

"Rape by athletes is becoming an epidemic. It's got to be stopped. We're going to make an example of Joe Campbell. He was invited to Boston to play basketball, not to attack women. Now he's being invited back to Boston to stand trial, and I predict that he'll be spending a lot more time in Massachusetts, living at the taxpayers' expense in a prison."

Maverick asked Puccio whether she had a strong case, then reminded her that several other allegations against athletes had been dropped.

"This one is much stronger than the Coleman and Webber cases," she replied. "We've got a good witness. She's a successful businesswoman, not some fly-by-night groupie, and we have physical corroboration, which I can't go into at this time. Nor am I at liberty to disclose the victim's name, since she does not want it in the press. You can certainly understand why. I am confident that there will be a conviction and a long prison sentence."

The sex prosecutor spoke some more, referring to other athlete sex scandals.

Abe was furious. The media and the other lawyers were always complaining when he "tried his cases in the press."

Didn't they understand? He had no choice. He had to defend against this kind of preemptive strike in the "court" of public opinion. Unchallenged, an interview of this type could really hurt Campbell. The public often didn't adequately analyze the news—they tended to believe whichever talking head was talking at the time.

"You've got to respond to her," Rendi insisted. "You can't let that kind of stuff remain unrebutted."

"Please don't put the victim on trial, Daddy."

"*She's* not the victim," Abe countered. "She's the accuser, and I think she's a false accuser."

"It sure doesn't sound that way, when her name is kept secret and Campbell's name is all over the news," Rendi said.

"You know, that really always bugs me," Abe said, "the way they keep the names of rape accusers secret."

"Rape *victims*, Daddy, *victims.*"

"We don't know that until after the trial, Emma. As of now, Jennifer Dowling is an accuser, not a victim."

"Daddy, if her name were to be published, she would become a victim."

"Why? The names of all other accusers are made public."

"Rape is different. It's so personal, so private."

"Not when she publicly accuses someone."

"And anyway, Daddy, not all accusers' names are made public. Remember when Rudy Warren, Janie's younger brother, got mugged in Harvard Square last year? They didn't release *his* name."

"That's because he was a juvenile. Do you think adult women should be treated like juveniles?"

"When they've been raped? Maybe. Yes."

"Not very egalitarian, Emma."

"But practical, Daddy. If they start publishing the names of rape victims—"

"Accusers, Emma, accusers."

"Okay, accusers—a lot of rape victims won't become accusers. Already many rape victims don't report the rape. If they knew that their names would be all over the papers, even fewer would."

"That's the price we may have to pay for the presumption of innocence."

"You know, Abe," Rendi joined in, "it would certainly make my job as an investigator easier if Jennifer Dowling's name were out there. People who know her might call with leads."

"That's it!" Abe said assertively. "That convinces me. I'm going to disclose her name at the press conference."

"No, Daddy, don't do that. Everybody will get on your case."

"I can't help that. Rendi has convinced me that I owe it to Campbell. We can't afford to blow any opportunity to get information on Dowling."

"You mean dirt, Daddy, don't you?"

"If there's dirt out there, and its relevant, yes, I mean dirt. As a defense attorney, that's my job. I'm in the dirt business."

"Daddy, you hate when the press digs up dirt on people. You're being inconsistent."

"No, I'm not," Abe said with a hint of defensiveness. "I'm not a journalist. I'm a lawyer representing a client. I have no choice but to do everything I can to help my client."

"Everything?" Emma asked skeptically.

"As long as it's legal and ethical. Remember the puppet case? You even helped me make 'Pepe' out of papier-mâché."

"What puppet case?" Jon asked. "Emma never told me about a puppet case."

Abe and Emma both smiled as Abe recounted one of his favorite cases, which had become part of his repertoire of war stories. There was a bizarre judge named Crosby in southern Texas who sat on the bench with a hand puppet. Whenever he had a tough decision to make, he would take out his puppet and ask him how he should rule. Abe had been briefed by a Texas lawyer about this character and his puppet, named "Pedro," and asked how a buffoon like that could be reelected. The Texas lawyer replied, "Well, I guess the folks around here like the way Pedro rules."

The case involved a well-known entertainer in a drug bust, and Abe's only chance was to get the search declared unconstitutional. At the conclusion of the hearing, Judge Crosby pulled out his puppet and asked him, "How should I rule?" Before Pedro could answer, however, Abe stood up and asked whether "local counsel" could briefly address Pedro. The judge happily agreed, and Abe pulled out his own hand puppet, named "Pepe," who made an eloquent argument to Pedro.

Judge Crosby had such a good laugh that he—or rather Pedro—ruled in favor of Abe's—or rather Pepe's—client.

As they left the courtroom, the Texas lawyer couldn't get over Abe's audacity. "No one around here ever thought of doing that."

"It's nothing special," Abe replied. "Every trial lawyer knows that when you have a woman judge, it's often better to have a woman argue. Same for a black or Hispanic judge. I just took it to its logical conclusion."

Jon and Emma laughed when Abe finished his story, then Emma grew serious again. "Daddy, that case was different. It involved drugs. This one involves rape."

"Alleged rape, my dear, alleged. And by disclosing the accuser's name, it may help us prove that the allegation is false. Sorry, Emma, I've got to do it."

Abe began calling his media contacts, telling each one of them that he wanted to respond to the interview. "Tomorrow morning, eleven o'clock, my office. I'm answering Puccio. It will be a good story." Within fifteen minutes he had an impromptu press meeting set up. Abe was accessible to the media—most of the time. He had spent years building these relationships because that was how the legal system worked—for better or for worse, press coverage was part of the game, and spin was the first rule.

Abe had another rule—this one about dinner at home. No

matter how important the case on which he was working, there was no discussion of it during dinner. During breakfast, fine. During lunch, okay. But never during dinner. There were no exceptions, not even for the Campbell case. Emma hated "the rule," much as she hated other arbitrary restrictions.

"It's a rule for children, not for grownups," she had complained.

"You're right," Abe had responded. "But it's *me* who's the child, not you. I *need* an arbitrary restriction, or else I would never get off my cases."

Dinner tonight was a Mideastern couscous, one of Rendi's specialties. It was delicious, and Emma, Abe, and Jon all complimented the chef. "I don't understand you, Rendi," Emma said as she picked through the couscous to avoid eating any meat. "You're the most modern, liberated, independent, and uncompromising woman I know, and yet you cook for my father as if you were his slave. How come?"

"Because I choose to," Rendi answered without a trace of ambivalence. "I love to cook for your dad and for you. It brings out the domestic side of me that I rarely get to feel in my work."

"But why don't you make Dad help—at least do the dishes?"

"Because he doesn't enjoy that, and it would make it seem like a trade-off. I don't *need* your father to do the dishes in order to prove that he regards me as an equal. He shows that in every way. Our relationship, whatever else it may not be, is certainly equal."

"Wow!" Jon exclaimed. "What a beautiful statement."

"Don't get too excited," Emma said, resting an arm on his shoulder. "That was Rendi talking, not me. If you ever want *me* to make *you* dinner, it's shopping, dishes, and dessert from you."

Over baklava and Turkish coffee, the foursome talked about Jon's decision to pick Stanford over Harvard and Emma's choice to attend Barnard rather than Brown. Abe was happy they would be in different places. Although he would be pleased to have a son-in-law like Jon *eventually*, he really wanted Emma to date other guys. Abe wasn't thrilled with Barnard's location on the Upper West Side of Manhattan, but he knew it was exactly the right kind of school for his very political daughter.

Abe would miss these dinners. He would miss Emma's physical presence in the house. When Emma left for college, his real period of mourning for Hannah would begin.

By ten-thirty the next morning, Abe's whole office suite was packed with reporters, TV cameras, and microphones. It was not the first time. In fact, the office neighbors had complained that the sight of cameras in the building was upsetting their clients. Well, there was nothing Abe could do, except try to explain that it was hard to practice law these days without an occasional media blitz.

At exactly eleven A.M., Abe began. "This case endangers the civil liberties of all Americans. If a rape charge can be brought on the basis of this evidence—or really lack of evidence—then nobody is safe from false charges. If you read the arrest report—which I am making available now—carefully, you will see several important facts. First, the alleged victim acknowledges that she originally consented to sex. Second, it does not take much reading between the lines to see that this is not the first time this woman has falsely accused someone of sexual misconduct. I urge you to look into this carefully and have the courage to report as fully on the relevant background of an accuser as you report on the background of a celebrity accused."

Abe paused and looked directly at Mike Black—who had published a column that morning, saying that if Abe Ringel really believed in his client's innocence, why didn't he put his own credibility on the line, rather than hiding behind Campbell's boilerplate assertion of innocence? "I will stake my professional reputation on the prediction that Joe Campbell will be acquitted, if this case even goes to trial. No responsible prosecutor should be willing to go forward with this kind of case."

As soon as he finished his statement, questions began.

"Mr. Ringel, I noticed that in the police report you gave out, you didn't white out the name of the victim. Was that inadvertent?"

"No, I gave you the entire report with no omissions. Jennifer Dowling is not presumed to be a victim. She's an accuser, and we intend to prove that she's a false accuser."

"Do you want us to publish her name?"

"That's your decision. I certainly hope you will. And I urge anyone out there with information about Jennifer Dowling to call my office. That is why we decided to release her name. We are hoping that people who know her will come forward with factual information that might be relevant to the case."

More questions followed.

"Why are you attacking an alleged rape victim?"

"Isn't putting the victim on trial a discredited tactic?"

"Can we interview Campbell?"

Abe responded to the last question first. "Why don't you try to interview Ms. Dowling? She is the accuser. My client has a presumption of innocence. An accuser is always on trial under the American system. And rape should be no exception."

Abe took a few more questions, gave a few more answers, and ended the press conference.

Justin quickly ushered Abe into a conference room. "You really put yourself out on a limb—staking your professional reputation. That's on videotape. Forever! If Campbell loses, the TV stations will play that clip all day and all night. Why did you do it?"

"Because this guy is not only innocent. He's gonna be found innocent. Not like Charlie O. He has everything going for him—and for us. Let's make the most of it. I know what I'm doing. Give me a break, huh?"

"You're the boss. And it's your reputation on the line. I could always say I never heard of you," Justin joked.

"What do you hear from Charlie Odell? Has he stopped taking his pills?"

"I spoke to him an hour ago. He's stopped. The psychopharmacologist I consulted said it could take a few days before they can see any difference."

"Does the prison know he's stopped?"

"I don't know for sure, but when they do find out, they're certainly going to try to force him to take the medicine."

"What a world we live in," Abe mused. "A lawyer has to literally drive his client crazy in order to save his life. No wonder they tell so many nasty lawyer jokes."

On Monday night Abe was invited by Larry King to debate Gloria McDermot, the feminist attorney who specialized in representing rape victims. King hardly got a word in as McDermot and Ringel argued whether the usual rules of evidence—including the presumption of innocence—should apply in rape cases.

Gloria began, "Abe, you know that rape is the most underreported serious crime in America. And the major reason rape victims don't prosecute their rapists is lawyers like you, who drag them through the mud, disclosing their names, cross-examining them as if they were the criminals."

"You're right, Gloria. Rape is underreported, and that's a serious problem which we all recognize. However, there's an equally serious problem that you insist on ignoring."

"What's that?"

"Rape is also the most falsely reported crime, especially acquaintance rape. There are more fabricated date rape accusations than any other serious crime, and that's precisely why we need lawyers who challenge every alleged victim's story."

"See, you're doing it right now, Abe. You're accusing rape victims of lying."

"Not all, not even most, certainly some. That's why we need rigorous rules of evidence, especially in rape cases."

The debate continued for half an hour, with most of the

callers supporting McDermot. Nonetheless, Abe felt that he got his point across.

The morning after the Larry King show, Rendi burst into Abe's office. "I got all you need on the Dowling harassment case."

Abe stopped his dictation to Gayle in midsentence. "I'm sorry to have interrupted the beginning of your sentence with the middle of mine," he quipped.

Ignoring the put-down, Rendi launched into her findings. "I got the details of why Dowling's case was dismissed."

"Give."

"Ms. Dowling sued her boss, Nick Armstrong, after he promised her a promotion if she had oral sex with him."

"Where the heck did you come up with that? The records are sealed."

"An anonymous call—from a guy who used to work with Dowling. He heard your press conference. NBC disclosed her name. The others didn't."

"What did he tell you?"

"Lots of rumors and gossip, most of which we can't use. But the stuff about Nick Armstrong I was able to confirm with a good source."

"Who?"

"Armstrong's lawyer. I've done some work for him. He likes you. Hopes you might refer him some cases."

"So what else did he tell you?"

"She came through and he didn't."

"I wonder what made her stoop so low?"

"I got the answer to that from a former colleague of Jennifer's. It seems the company had lost its major client, Drexel Burnham, when they went into bankruptcy. The PR business, as you well know, is definitely not great right now. Jennifer was desperate and needed Armstrong's influence to keep her job."

"So she gave him a blow job?"

"It gets worse."

Justin joined them after finishing up a phone call. "Did I miss anything good?'

"So far the false harassment case is confirmed. Okay, Rendi, go on," Abe urged her.

To Rendi, who knew him so well, Abe's contained excitement was apparent. "Okay. Not only did Armstrong 'renege,' if that is an appropriate term, he did something even worse. I'm telling you, this guy is a real slime bucket. This Armstrong character recommended her to another vice president of the company as, and I quote, 'giving the best head in New York.' Jennifer, mortified, sued both men."

"Who told you this?" Justin had missed the early part of the conversation.

"Her colleague, who still works at the company. This is the same colleague who finally broke down under pressure from the company and disclosed that Jennifer had told her everything."

"Which is how the company got the case dismissed—yes?" Abe was ahead of everybody, as usual.

"Right you are. Jennifer lied in her deposition, claiming that she had turned down both men, when, in fact, of course, she hadn't refused Mr. Armstrong. It destroyed her credibility. All she got out of this nightmare was a deal—a crummy one, if you ask me—that her deposition would be sealed and the reason for her dismissal kept secret if she agreed to have the charges dropped as unfounded."

"Case, as they say, dismissed," Justin said.

"I feel sorry for her," Rendi said.

"Well, I understand that. It just happens to be a bonanza for our client. Can you get me a witness who knows the circumstances and will testify—maybe this colleague?"

"No, she won't testify, but I'll try to find someone who will."

And there was more. The limo driver had confirmed that there was necking in the car and that Jennifer had willingly invited Campbell back to her room.

Even the one bit of physical corroboration—a small abrasion on her vagina, which an expert said was "consistent with rape"—turned out to be, at best, ambiguous. The leading authority on vaginal abrasions, Dr. Joshua Weisburger of the Massachusetts General Hospital, had confirmed that although Jennifer's abrasion was indeed consistent with rape, it was also consistent with consensual sex, especially if the man's penis was unusually large and the woman had not borne children.

In Abe's view there was nothing left to the prosecution's case except the word of an alleged victim who had falsely accused her previous boss of sexual harassment—or, at least, the formal record so showed. If this were any other crime or any other defendant, Abe thought, the prosecution would fold. Yet Puccio wasn't folding. She wasn't even offering a deal—not that Abe would accept a deal at this point. This case had high-visibility trial written all over it.

Things looked good. Abe's losing streak was about to end. Though he was confident he had thought of every realistic possibility, he decided to have Justin and Rendi review every piece of evidence again, more out of habit than necessity. Nothing could go wrong.

Chapter Eight

"They're forcing the pills into his stomach!" Justin announced, coming into Abe's office. "The judge has scheduled a hearing for Odell an hour from now. Our local guy is handling it. "He's on his way to court. The shit has really hit the fan. The prosecutor is blaming it all on you. Says you're grandstanding at your client's expense."

"Are we ready to appeal if the judge approves the force-feeding?"

"Poised for action."

"Abe, it's CNN on the phone for you," Gayle said. "About the force-feeding. It's all over the wires."

"Hi, Abe Ringel here. What can I do for you?"

The reporter wanted to know if it was true that Abe had advised his client to stop taking drugs.

"I never discuss what advice I give my client," Abe said. Then he posed a rhetorical question to the reporter. "What advice would you give a friend who would be killed unless he stopped taking his sanity pills?"

Justin listened to Abe's side of the interview.

"No, I'm not confirming that I gave him the advice, but I'm not denying it, either. I'm letting you draw your own inference.

89

. . . Of course I understand the risks. Do you understand the risks of doing nothing? . . . No, I don't want to be interviewed live on television." An interview would not help his client, Abe knew. The public would never agree with what he was doing.

More calls: ABC, NBC, CBS, PBS, *The New York Times*, the *Post*. It was a hot story, and it could get hotter, regardless of which way the judge ruled.

"Abe, the judge has ruled." Gayle appeared in the doorway. "Stein is on the phone."

"Hey, Max, up or down?" Abe asked his old law school classmate Max Stein, who was handling the case for him locally.

"In the middle," Max replied. "Judge Cox granted the temporary restraining order. No force for now. He wants you and Odell in court next Monday. The restraining order stays in effect only till then. It's anyone's guess what he'll do. But he had some not-so-nice words to say about you."

"What's his gripe?"

"You should have done it more directly, by bringing a lawsuit to stop the medicine instead of advising him to throw the pills down the drain."

"Now he's telling me how to practice law. He knows damn well we have a better shot if the state has to force him."

"That's what he doesn't like."

"All right, we'll be ready for Monday. We have a great expert on psychopharmacology."

"See if you can find a great expert on legal ethics. You may need one."

Abe and Justin planned to spend the next couple of days preparing for the Odell hearing and the Campbell trial. Abe loved this part of the practice. No clients around, no billing problems, no judges. Just legal strategy. It was like a surgeon planning a complicated operation or a general planning a major battle. In this kind of chess game, Abe was at his very best in anticipating his opponents' tactics and countering them.

Everything was falling into place for both cases, when suddenly, out of the blue, Justin noticed something curious he might have seen a dozen times but never focused on before. While thumbing through the file folder containing the computer printouts that Joe Campbell had given Abe, he caught sight of the last page of Abe's won-and-lost record, on the very bottom of which were printed the numbers *08:43*. Justin then looked at Campbell's printout of the Jennifer Dowling case to see what the comparable numbers were.

There were no numbers at the bottom of that page.

Justin's first instinct was to ignore this apparently insignificant detail and turn to more promising leads, since the most likely explanation for this minor difference in formatting was probably of no relevance to the Campbell case. But he remembered what Abe had told him on his first day at work: "Always look for clues in places that aren't obvious." Abe had illustrated his lesson by relating how he had won a civil case several years earlier by noticing something at the top of a faxed page that had been turned over to him as part of the "discovery" process. The *contents* of that fax, Abe told Justin, were not particularly significant, but the digits at the top were the telephone number from which the fax had originally been sent to the defendant. *That* number proved to be extraordinarily significant, since it pointed to a source that no one previously had suspected of complicity in the conspiracy to destroy the plaintiff's business.

Justin thought about this story as he peered at the bottom of both printouts. Was there something significant here? Or would it turn out to be a dead end, as most leads did? Sure, Abe loved to tell the fax story, but he never told the hundreds of other stories where the lead took him down a dark alley to nowhere. No harm checking it out, though, even if it meant wasted steps, Justin thought as he dialed the number of the database company.

The recorded message for the database's customer support

system was frustratingly long, offering menus within menus, but finally Justin received an actual human being on the line.

"Thank you for calling CompuLaw Customer Support Systems, this is John Tierney, how can I help you?"

"I have a question about some numbers at the bottom of a printout from your reference system."

"I'll see if I can help you, sir."

"What does '08:43' mean?"

"That means the subscriber was interfacing with the database for eight minutes and forty-three seconds."

"Well, I have another printout without that notation. This one made a few days earlier. What could that mean?"

"I'm not sure. But it may have something to do with the change of format we instituted recently."

"What do you mean?"

"If you're certain that it's the entire printout you have in front of you, then it may mean that the printout without the numbers was generated before we changed the format to include the time logged. We had gotten a lot of complaints from law firms that they need the time for their billing records. So we changed it."

Justin's interest was piqued by this information. "And when was it that you changed the format?"

"I'll check the exact date for you, sir."

The technician came back on the line after a brief time-out. "That would be March first of this year."

"Thanks."

"Will there be anything else we can help you with today?"

"No, that'll do it."

"Have a good one."

After he hung up Justin sat back, put his feet on his desk, and meditated on the information. Just then Abe wandered into the computer room.

"Anything new?"

"Yes, in fact, there is." Justin placed his feet back on the floor and handed Abe the printout with the numbers circled. "See this?"

"Yes."

Next Justin handed him the sexual harassment print. "See this—no numbers."

"Yes, so?"

Abe didn't know anything about computer retrieval systems. He didn't use them, and he didn't believe in them. He hated them. "I like to write on long yellow pads. That's the way I think." Still, he did insist that the office have a complete and up-to-date system and that everyone else, especially his young associates, master them. "So that I don't have to," was his constant refrain. Justin loved to tell his computer age buddies about the first time Abe got a fax over the wireless portable that Gayle had ordered. "There's paper coming out of this infernal machine!" Abe had marveled. "And there aren't even any wires."

"The fax paper doesn't travel through wires," Justin had explained, "even when there are wires. It's all electronic."

"I know that," Abe had said defensively. "But at least when there are wires, I can see that it's connected to something."

Today's episode proved it worthwhile for Abe's office to be high tech—without Abe ever having to touch a machine.

"I don't even understand what it is I don't understand." Puzzled, Abe looked down at Justin. "Why is it significant that one printout has time figures at the end and the other doesn't?"

"*That's* not what's significant, Abe. What's significant is that the formatting was changed on March first."

"So?"

"So, Joe told us that he first met Jennifer in New York on March 10. But if her printouts were generated *before* March 1—as the technician seems to be saying—then Joe would have *had* to meet her at least ten days before he told us he met her."

"But why would he lie about *that?*"

"I don't know, Abe. But what I do know is that he may

have had some justification for his first lie, but two lies are harder to explain away. I'm beginning to get worried about this guy."

"Is it possible," Abe asked, "that you could be wrong about this formatting stuff?"

"It is possible," Justin acknowledged. "But only if the printout without the numbers was somehow incomplete."

"Okay, hang on a minute," Abe said, shuffling through the unfamiliar computer printouts. "Show me what I'm supposed to be looking for."

Justin stood and pointed to the time notation on the bottom of Abe's won-and-lost record and then to the end of the Dowling cases, where there was no comparable notation. Abe looked closely at the blank space following the end of the last Dowling case. His eyes fixed on what appeared to be some ink marks at the very bottom of the page. This is what he saw:

"What the heck are these?" he asked Justin.

"I don't know. They look like the very tops of some numbers or letters, but there are too many to be a time notation."

"Where do you suppose these things came from?" Abe insisted, looking at the indecipherable marks.

"Maybe from the next case," Justin surmised.

"But if there *is* a next case," Abe said, beaming, "doesn't that mean there was more material generated by Campbell's request?"

"Could be," Justin admitted.

"And if that's true," Abe continued, "then it follows that *this* is not the end of the search request, and that there may well be a time notation at the end of the entire search. And if that's true, then this search could have been requested *after* March 10, as Campbell said it was."

"Maybe," Justin acknowledged sheepishly.

"Maybe you jumped the gun, Justin. Maybe Joe didn't lie to us a second time. Please let's not presume our client guilty of lying again without proof. We've got nothing to go on."

"Nothing except that he lied once already, and we now know that he may not have given us the whole printout. Why would he hold something back if he is as innocent as he claims?"

"I don't know. Innocent people lie all the time, especially to their lawyers. Still, I am curious about what these notations mean. Maybe you can figure that out if you decipher those little marks at the bottom of the page."

"I'll try, but it won't be easy," Justin said, retrieving the pages from Abe and heading back around the computer room desk.

As Justin stared at the obscure marks over and over again, they began to make some sense to him. They could be the very tops of a group of words or letters that covered an entire line of print. But they were too fragmentary for him to reconstruct into the letters that would form the underlying words.

Suddenly Justin got a brainstorm. He photocopied a page from the printout and cut out enough words to form an entire alphabet on one very long line. Then he covered his "decoder" line with an index card so that only the very tops of the letters were visible. He could now compare what he was able to see in his "decoder" alphabet with the top parts of the letters that appeared at the bottom of the Dowling printout.

Instantly he was able to recognize most of the capital letters, which appeared to be "T," "P," "S," "N," "Y," "M," and "P," as well as the tops of several high noncapital letters, such as "i," "k," and "t." Now his job was to fill in the blanks to form a coherent series of words. It was like playing the old game of hangman or the new *Wheel of Fortune*. He spent about fifteen minutes puzzling over the possibilities, comparing the tops of letters, then came up with the following:

"Th_ P___l_ _ ___ St_t _ N_ Y___ _ M__k P_t___."

After several attempts at filling in these blanks, he deduced a logical combination of words and names: "The People of the State of New York v. Mark Peters."

It wasn't the only possibility, but it seemed to fit, both literally and contextually. It appeared to be the title of a New York criminal case. Justin plugged the case name into his CompuLaw search program and waited anxiously to see whether the computer would come up with a case by that name.

After several minutes words began to appear on Justin's flickering screen. Sure enough, there was such a case. It involved a criminal prosecution back in 1987 against a man charged with playing three-card monte—a variation of the shell game—in downtown Brooklyn.

Now Justin was really baffled. What did Mark Peters have to do with Jennifer Dowling—or Joe Campbell? Why would a three-card-monte case be included in a search that produced Jennifer Dowling's sexual harassment cases?

Justin brought his little decoder kit and the Peters case into Abe's office. "I think I decoded the marks, Abe, but it looks like another dead end." He showed Abe how he had filled in the blanks.

Abe was enormously impressed with Justin's resourcefulness. "How in hell did you figure that out?"

"Comes from watching Vanna White on *Wheel of Fortune* instead of studying during law school."

Then he showed Abe the Peters case. Abe read it over and over again, searching for some possible relevance to the Campbell case. There was no relevance. It really was a dead end.

Abe looked again at Justin's anagram. "Is it possible that your 'Mark' is really a 'Mary'?"

"Unlikely," Justin said with an air of newly found expertise. "The top of the 'k' shows, but a 'y' wouldn't."

"How about 'Merle'? An 'l' would look like a 'k,' wouldn't it?"

"Could be, but then there would be a spacing problem."

"How about Merl?"

"No harm trying them all," Justin said, heading back to the computer room.

A few minutes later he returned. "No cases under 'Merle,' 'Merl,' or even 'Mary.' I think it's Mark."

"But the Mark Peters case has nothing to do with Jennifer Dowling or Joe Campbell. I guess that means it's back to the salt mines for you. Now you've got me really intrigued by this print-out stuff. Let's try to get to the bottom of it."

"I'll try my best, but I'm not optimistic."

"I'm out of here for a few minutes," Abe said, yawning. "I need some fresh air. Be back in half an hour. Do you need anything from the square?"

"Yeah, a good book on anagrams."

Abe walked the three blocks to Harvard Square to pick up a newspaper and think. As he approached the kiosk, he realized he was hungry and glanced at the window of the corner sandwich shop. It had a sign advertising the daily special, a "Po' Boy" sandwich. Abe had no idea what that was, but it didn't sound appetizing. Inexplicably he found his eyes transfixed on the words *Po' Boy*.

Suddenly it hit him. Of course! How could he—how could Justin—have missed it! As he stared at the sign, he realized that the capital letters *P* and *B* were indistinguishable from the top. Their friend Mark could have the unlikely last name of Beters or Belers or even Belare. They had missed this obvious possibility because "Peters"—which fit the blanks—was such a common name.

Abe raced the three blocks back to the office and found Justin fiddling with the computer. "It could be a 'B,' Justin, not a 'P,' " Abe said, pointing to Mark's last name on the printout.

"Damn, you're right." Justin shrugged. "I was sure I had the capital letters down pat. I was playing only with the small letters. But what kind of name is Beters with one 't'?"

"A strange one, to be sure, but it's worth a try," Abe insisted, showing some pride at his discovery of the similarity between the tops of capital "B" and "P."

Justin punched in the case name, first using "Beters" instead of "Peters." Bingo! After several seconds a recent case appeared under the heading "The People of the State of New York v. Mark Beters." Maybe this case would bear some relationship to the Jennifer Dowling case.

But again, a careful reading of the case showed absolutely no connection. The Beters case involved a rape prosecution in which an Albany gas station owner named Mark Beters had been convicted of one count of rape and sentenced to eight years in prison. The conviction had been affirmed in a one paragraph order. It looked quite routine and ordinary.

Suddenly another case name appeared on the screen: "People ex rel Beters vs. McGrath, Superintendent." It, too, involved Mark Beters. It was a state habeas corpus proceeding ordering Beters to be released on the ground that his accuser, a woman named Prudence Crane, had recanted her accusation after becoming a born-again Christian and seeking counsel from a minister.

"This is all very interesting," Abe said, "but what does it have to do with Jennifer Dowling? Why would Beters's case come up in a search for information about Jennifer Dowling?"

"I don't know, but I'm going to check out this guy Beters until I find out what the connection is."

Chapter Nine

Haskel had deteriorated significantly. His hands were shaking. His lips were trembling. There were tears in his eyes. He looked sadder than Abe had seen him since his wife had died three years ago. It was obvious he was not taking his medicine. It broke Abe's heart to see his old friend suffer so much. And it hurt him doubly to know that Charlie Odell was also experiencing his own particular devils because of Abe's advice.

After a few minutes of imploring Haskel to take his medicine, Abe described the computer dilemma to the old man. Haskel thought for a few minutes and then began to ask his usual questions.

"If this Dowling woman has nothing to do with this Beters man, then what do their stories have in common? Why would one person be interested in reading about these two people at the same time?"

"That's a good question," Abe said, his mind racing to find an answer. Suddenly it came to him.

"Thanks, Haskel, you did it again." Abe left for his office, hoping to find someone there who could work the computer.

But the office was empty. He called Justin: no answer. Abe walked into the computer room and saw that the Macintosh was on, and that the search program Justin had been using was still up on the screen. He started to fiddle with the keys, trying to figure out how to search for a topic. As he was standing around scratching his head in frustration, Justin walked in.

Seeing Abe with his fingers on the computer keyboard, Justin began to yell. "Don't touch anything! Don't you know you could erase the memory? What are you trying to do?"

"Haskel asked me why anyone would want to read about both the Dowling and Beters cases at the same time. He's on the right track. Now, can you translate that sensible question into computerese?"

"Sure," Justin replied eagerly. "Which word or words are both narrow and broad enough to generate both of these cases in the same search?"

"That sounds easy enough," Abe mused. "We need to find categories that cover several different cases with common features."

"You've got it, Abe. If you lose the Campbell trial, you can always become a programmer."

"Let's see," Abe began. "Rape is too narrow, because Jennifer Dowling's case doesn't involve rape. It involves consensual sex given for a promotion."

"Sexual harassment."

"Yeah, but that's too narrow to include the Beters case."

"How about 'sexual misconduct'?"

"Much too broad. There are probably thousands of cases under that heading. We have to narrow it."

"What about 'false sexual allegations,' or 'false accusations'?"

"Or 'recantations,' " Abe added. "Something like that?"

"Sounds promising." Justin began to press buttons on his computer. After a few minutes of trial and error, he settled on "sexual misconduct—unfounded—current year—New York."

Seven listings! Over to the printer. Again some fiddling. Then the printout, and there they were. The two cases dealing with Jennifer Dowling; then a case about a woman who falsely accused a man of raping her at gunpoint in Central Park; a date rape case in which a teenager admitted making up the charge after her father learned that she had lost her virginity; a case in which a woman claimed that her estranged husband had raped her and then recanted after they reconciled; one case about a recantation of a recantation of rape.

And then the Beters case! But the Beters case did not immediately follow the Dowling stories in this printout, and Abe asked Justin why it didn't track as it had in Campbell's original printout. Justin explained that the sequence of the printout could change over time as new items were added to the categories. It was certainly possible that when Campbell ordered the printout, the Beters case had followed immediately after the Dowling stories. Or maybe, Justin conceded, he hadn't gotten the search request precisely right. But one thing was crystal clear: Campbell had not gotten the Dowling cases by searching under "Jennifer Dowling." Maybe he had started with her name. But that was not how he'd gotten her cases and Beters's cases on the same printout. He had almost certainly gotten them by searching under a more general category involving recent stories about unfounded charges of sexual misconduct.

"I don't know what this all means," Justin said with an air of triumph. "One thing is clear: Campbell lied to us again."

"Hold your prosecutorial horses, young man," Abe said. "I understand how proud you are of your little computer discovery, and it's only natural that you want it to mean something. But you're way out of line here. It raises some questions, maybe. But it doesn't prove anything."

"Look, Abe," Justin responded with an edge in his voice. "We have to presume our client innocent. I'm not arguing with that. But it doesn't mean we have to close our eyes to the truth."

"Justin, I'm as interested in the truth as you are. And I'm not sure I appreciate your sanctimonious tone. Sure, go ahead. Get to the bottom of this. Just don't start with an attitude toward Joe. He probably has an explanation for all of this. We haven't even given him a chance."

"So let's give him a chance. Let's confront him with what I found."

"Too early. If we confront him, it will make him sound like our adversary, not our client. He will lose whatever trust he still has, and he'll never level with us."

"How about a trip to Zimmerman?" Justin asked, referring to Gustav Zimmerman, Boston's leading polygrapher.

"Wouldn't work with Campbell," Abe snapped back.

"I don't mean the *machine*," Justin explained, "I mean the *ruse*."

"I know what you mean, and that won't work either."

By the "ruse," Justin was referring to a technique that Abe sometimes used on clients who he suspected weren't leveling with him but whom he wasn't yet ready to confront directly. First he would suggest that they submit to a lie detector test that could convince the prosecutor to drop the charges. Then, on the way downtown to the polygrapher, he would explain how no one could trick Zimmerman—he was foolproof. Typically the client would admit he was lying before they even got to Zimmerman's office. Justin wasn't even sure there *was* a Zimmerman.

"Joe knows that passing a lie detector test wouldn't persuade Cheryl Puccio to drop such a high-profile case," Abe was saying. "He'd figure out the ruse and find some reason for not taking the test. Remember, this guy is really smart. Second highest SATs in the NBA—after David Robinson. Unless and until we come up with hard facts—not your ambiguous computer inferences—we continue to treat Joe Campbell as our innocent client. Got that?"

"Yes, sir," Justin said, giving Abe a mock salute.

"Now, while I'm down in Trenton for the Charlie O. hearing, I want you to find out everything you can about this computer stuff. The presumption of innocence is just a presumption. Something we start with. It can be overcome by hard facts. Until it is, I believe in Campbell's innocence. Got it?"

Before taking the job with Abe, Justin Aldrich had worked

for a number of lawyers, some famous, some notorious. He'd never before had one who was always so emotionally committed to his clients, and as a result he'd come personally to think a great deal of his boss. In this case, however, he was worried that Abe's commendable commitment might create a blind spot.

"You know, Abe," he said, "I appreciate your candor toward me and that you don't pull your punches."

"Stick around, kiddo, you might learn something they didn't teach you in those downtown firms!"

Chapter Ten

Abe and his pharmacological expert, Dr. Ralph Hoxie, arrived at the old brownstone courthouse in Newark at 8:30 A.M. for the scheduled hearing for Charlie O.

Judge Cox convened the hearing at 9:00 A.M. Charlie was brought in wearing shackles and cuffs. The bailiff sat Charlie next to Abe. Dr. Hoxie had briefed Abe about Charlie's muscle spasms—they were related to the withdrawal from the antipsychotic medicines. Worse than that was the empty stare, the deadened look, in Charlie's eyes and the relentless rocking that caused the shackles to clank against the table. Abe knew that no young man who grew up in the projects would want the world to see him as this pathetic haunted creature.

The judge got right to it. "Mr. Ringel, I want to know one thing, and I want to know it now. Did you advise your mentally ill client not to take his drugs?"

Abe saw an opening in the judge's question. "If this court is prepared to find that my client, Mr. Odell, was mentally ill at the time he *began* not taking his medicine, then we can end this matter right now."

"Stop playing games with me, Counselor, and answer my question."

104

"I am most certainly not playing games, Your Honor. The issue is whether Mr. Odell was mentally competent at the time he was still taking the medicine. If he was not, then he can begin taking his medicine and still not be executed. If he was competent, then it doesn't matter what advice anyone gave him. It would be his decision. Therefore, Your Honor, I'm entitled to a ruling on his competence before I answer your question."

"How should I know whether he was competent *then?*" the judge replied angrily. "I never saw him then. He was *presumed* competent, since he was scheduled to be executed, and now I'm advised by the prison psychiatrist that he is not competent. He certainly doesn't look competent. Now answer my question."

With that, the attention of the courtroom shifted to the black man by Abe's side. Abe had to stop himself from throwing a protective arm around Charlie's shoulder. It would not serve his purpose now to offer Charlie any comfort that might appease him, yet Abe yearned with every nurturing and protective cell in his body to smash the TV cameras that zoomed in on his client's twitching face.

"Yes, I advised him to stop taking his medicine, and I am now once again formally instructing the prison authorities to stop giving him any drugs that could affect his mind, his brain, or his emotions."

"Is that what *he* wants, Counselor? Maybe I should appoint a guardian to act in *his* best interest, rather than in *your* best interest."

"I *am* acting in his best interest, and any reasonable guardian would agree that his best interest is to stay alive, even if that requires him to be crazy for a period of time."

The prosecutor called the prison psychiatrist, Dr. John Blanchard, a dour man in his fifties who wore his gray hair in a 1950s-type crew cut. Dr. Blanchard testified that Charles Odell had a full-blown psychotic episode after his final appeal had been denied, that he did not comprehend what was happening to him, and that, in his professional opinion, Odell was then incompetent to be executed under the relevant legal standards. The psychiatrist described the drug regime he had prescribed for Odell and how it had restored his competency to be executed. Then he described what had happened to Odell since he'd stopped taking the pills.

The judge asked, "In your professional opinion, is Mr. Odell competent to be executed today, as he sits here?"

"No. He has no understanding of the punishment he faces. He's totally psychotic and suicidal. We have him on a twenty-four-hour suicide watch."

"One more question. In your professional opinion, would he be restored to competency if I ordered him to receive his medication by force?"

"Yes, Your Honor."

Abe then cross-examined Dr. Blanchard.

"Doctor, before you began to practice medicine, did you take the Hippocratic oath?"

"Yes."

"Do you recall what its first principle is?"

"Yes."

"Tell the court, please."

"First, do no harm."

"Do you abide by that oath?"

"I try to."

"Were you aware when you prescribed the drugs that if they worked, Odell would be executed?"

"That he *might* be executed. You never know for sure in these cases."

"But by prescribing the drugs, you were increasing Odell's chances of being executed?"

"Yes, but—"

"Before we get to the 'but,' I want to be sure of the 'yes.' You *would* be increasing his chances of being executed."

"Yes—but not his chances of actually dying," the doctor added quickly.

"Why, Doctor, because in your view he was suicidal without the drugs?"

"Exactly."

"Through your procedures, can you reduce that risk?"

"We can certainly try."

"There's nothing you can do to reduce the risk that Odell will be executed if he's returned to competency, is there?"

"No, Counselor, that's your job and the court's. Not mine."

"Is it your job to help the state execute Charles Odell?"

"No," Dr. Blanchard said, his voice moving up in volume. "It's my job to help restore him to competency."

"You *know* that if you help restore him to competency, the state will try to execute him, right?"

"Right, but—"

"So *you* would be doing Odell harm by restoring him to competency, right?"

"No, wrong!" the doctor said emphatically, pointing a finger at Abe's face. "I would be doing him *good* by eliminating his psychosis. The *state* would be executing him."

"Not without your help, right?"

'Right, but that's not my responsibility. I don't write the laws."

"You just follow orders, right?" Abe asked contemptuously, not even waiting for an answer. The prosecutor's expectant objection was sustained, and the doctor left the witness stand seething with anger.

The judge was visibly frustrated. "Mr. Ringel, do you want your client to commit suicide or don't you?"

Abe responded, "No, we don't *want* him to commit suicide. But we also don't want him to take the antisuicide medicine, because it's really not *anti*-suicide medicine. It's *pro*-execution medicine. If he takes it, he will die. What we want is for you to stop him from killing himself without making him take the medicine."

Now the judge was furious. "I know what you want. You

want him to be sui*cidal*, just not to actually *commit* suicide. You want him to remain incompetent but alive."

"That's right, Your Honor. That's my job—to keep him alive."

"That's not my job," the judge barked. "My job is to make sure that lawyers like you don't play the system for a fool and manipulate the law so as to make it look ridiculous. Does the state have any more witnesses?"

"Not at this time, Your Honor."

"Call your first witness, Mr. Ringel," said the judge. For some reason he reminded Abe at that moment of his Boston Latin trigonometry teacher, who taught every equation by rote.

"The defense calls Dr. Ralph Hoxie."

Dr. Ralph Hoxie was a small, somewhat effeminate man with a nervous twitch, but his face, covered with red hair and a red beard, projected warmth and compassion. He looked as though he worked in a laboratory all day, which he did.

After Dr. Hoxie cataloged his very extensive professional background, Abe asked him to tell how the drugs prescribed by the prison psychiatrist had worked. There followed a detailed two-hour account of the pharmacological operation of various antipsychotic drugs and their side effects. Most of the spectators had left the courtroom as Dr. Hoxie's testimony began to wind down. Courtroom TV switched to a rape case in California.

The judge then asked the prosecutor how long it had been since Odell had last been given the drugs. "Since before your temporary restraining order, Your Honor. I guess about four or five days."

The judge asked the bailiff to bring Charlie to the bench. A predictable hush fell over the court as the bailiff complied. Shackles dragging along the linoleum floor, the prisoner wavered back and forth before the bench. The judge addressed him:

"Mr. Odell, do you know who I am?"

Abe jumped up. "Your Honor, please address my client *only*

through me. Mr. Odell pleads his Fifth Amendment privilege not to answer any questions."

"Sit down, Mr. Ringel. I want to find out for myself whether Mr. Odell wants to continue taking his medicine."

"I'm sorry, Your Honor. Mr. Odell cannot and will not answer any questions."

The judge then turned to Dr. Hoxie, who had laid out several of the antipsychotic drugs on the desk in front of him as part of his testimony.

"Dr. Hoxie, will you please hold up a Thorazine capsule so that Mr. Odell can see it?"

"Objection, objection!" Abe screamed. "This is absolutely improper."

"Sit down and be quiet, Mr. Ringel. This is my courtroom, and I decide what's proper. You have your objection and your appeal. Now, Dr. Hoxie, hold up the capsule."

Dr. Hoxie followed the judge's order, nervously holding the large yellow pill in front of him between his thumb and forefinger.

"Now, Mr. Odell, you can have this pill if you want it," the judge said slowly and loudly as he pointed to the capsule between Dr. Hoxie's fingers.

"Objection!" Abe shouted. Then, turning to Odell, he said, "Charlie, go back to your seat. Bailiff, take Mr. Odell back to his seat."

"Do no such thing, Mr. Bailiff. Keep Mr. Odell right here at the bench," the judge ordered.

Charlie, who was standing about two feet from Dr. Hoxie, looked intently at the doctor. Then he looked at the pill in the doctor's outstretched hand. Then he looked at the judge. Then he looked back at the pill. Abe was seething. The courtroom was absolutely silent except for quiet murmuring among the camera crew, who were urging Court TV to switch back to this proceeding.

Suddenly Charlie Odell thrust his entire body—shackles

109

and all—at the terrified Dr. Hoxie, biting the doctor's hand as he tried to grasp the pill between his lips.

Pandemonium broke out in the courtroom. The bailiff tried to separate Charlie from Dr. Hoxie. Abe jumped up to try to stop Charlie from swallowing the pill. The pill fell on the floor, and Abe grabbed it.

The judge said, "Mr. Ringel, give that pill to your client. He obviously wants it."

"I will not," Abe said defiantly. "My client is incompetent. He can't decide whether he wants to take the pills." With that Abe threw the pill on the floor and stamped on it, crushing it into powder.

"I hereby order the prison authorities to require Mr. Odell to take his medicine," the judge bellowed, banging his gavel. "My ruling is that taking his medicine is in Mr. Odell's best interest and that he wants to take the pill. You probably won't even have to use force," the judge said, turning to the prison psychiatrist. "If you do, you're authorized to use reasonable force."

"I hereby request that Your Honor's order be stayed for twenty-four hours so as to allow me to appeal."

"No more game playing, Mr. Ringel. Mr. Odell begins taking his pills right now. Court is adjourned. Remove the prisoner. Have a nice day."

"A nice day!" Abe repeated cynically as he left the courtroom, thinking of the Texas case in which a judge had signed a condemned man's execution warrant with a signature that included a happy face. Over the din of yapping reporters and gawkers he could hear only one sound—the clanking of Charlie's shackles as the bailiff led an innocent man back to his private hell and closer to his appointment with the executioner.

Abe left Judge Cox's courtroom feeling miserable. The Odell hearing had been a disaster. Odell's only hope was to appeal Judge Cox's order. Judge Cox's behavior might well offend the appellate judges, Abe hoped.

110

While in the judge's courtroom, Abe hadn't thought about the Campbell problem. When he got outside, his focus shifted back to the basketball player; he took out his cellular phone and tried to reach Justin. The cells were all busy, so Abe had to keep redialing.

The pattern in the screen saver danced before Justin's eyes as he puzzled over the printout before him. His concentration was shattered by the ringing telephone.

"Bad news," Abe said, and filled Justin in on Charlie's situation.

"You'll get Cox reversed, Abe. The court of appeals will never tolerate Cox's shenanigans. That was bullshit, offering a crazy man his drugs."

"I sure hope so."

"Listen, Abe, back to Campbell for a minute. There's something weird going on."

"Something new?'

"Yeah. Remember that when we punched up the search for 'false allegations,' the Beters case didn't come right after the Dowling stuff?"

"Yeah, you couldn't explain that."

"Well, now I think I can. It turns out that all of the cases that now come between Dowling and Beters were inputted into the database between February 20 and March 10. That means Campbell probably did the search sometime before February 20—not after March 10, as he told us."

"Justin, are you back on the timing thing? I thought you agreed that was a dead end."

"It sure looked that way after you noticed the markings at the bottom, but now I'm not so sure. I still think that Joe may have first met Jennifer sometime before the March 10 day he gave us."

"Why would he lie about *that?*"

Abe waited for Justin's answer in vain as the phone went

dead. After a quick battery replacement, Justin was back on the phone.

"Yeah, anyway, Abe, I have no idea why Campbell would lie about anything—if he's as innocent as you insist he is. What are you going to do about this new information?"

"Nothing," Abe shot back. "At least not yet. We don't have enough to confront him. It's all just suspicion so far. We need more."

"We've got plenty. This computer information—"

"I have to tell you, Justin," Abe cut in, "I don't have much faith in your little computer games. I admire your persistence and creativity, but I have more faith in my human instincts than in your technology. I would need something a lot more convincing, something conclusive, before I would be ready to believe Campbell's guilty of lying to us—or of rape. I've got Rendi working the human angle. Let's see if she comes up with anything. Remember how weak Jennifer Dowling's story is. We've got an innocent client, and nothing you've come up with makes me think differently. Keep digging. It's only a presumption."

Chapter Eleven

It just didn't feel right. The idea of investigating a client's sexual habits without telling him made Rendi squirm. And when Rendi squirmed, her whole body literally pulsated. She was the kind of woman who put her entire being into every gesture, every emotion, every reaction. Justin had once described Rendi as "emotion in motion."

Rendi was the most captivating women Abe knew—dark, wiry, quick moving, fast talking, and even faster thinking. Though they had been intimate friends and associates for nearly a decade, there was still much about her that was shrouded in mystery. She loved to say, "I came from everywhere and nowhere. I don't know where I will be next month." She had lived in Cambridge longer than she'd ever lived in one place before. She loved to relate the joke about the Romanian Gypsy who told her friend that she was moving to America. Her friend said, "But that's so far," to which the Gypsy responded, "From where?" Rendi was a spiritual Gypsy, a nomad. She had no "where" from which to be far.

Abe hoped he would learn more about her in time, though she seemed to agonize over revealing anything personal about herself. As a teenager she had been an actress, traveling with the

113

road company of an international troupe that specialized in doing Ibsen in several languages. Indeed, it was during that stint, which had lasted about two years, that she had been recruited to do her first undercover job for the Mossad: nothing particularly dangerous; mostly taking pictures of specified locations in Turkey, Greece, Czechoslovakia, Egypt, and once in Lebanon—before the current chaos. Twice she was caught and her film confiscated, but she played the innocent tourist to perfection.

Everything about Rendi was unpredictable, especially her opinions. She was a strident feminist—by her own lights and by her own actions. She wouldn't—couldn't—accept second-class status, in employment or anything else. For her, rape was the ultimate degradation, but she also believed that women had to take responsibility for their own actions, which was why the Campbell case was such an enigma for her. Her own feelings about Jennifer Dowling's role in the crime were upsetting to her.

Several months ago she and Emma had engaged in a shouting match over dinner about the "dressed for sex" defense.

"Of course no man has the right to rape a woman who is wearing a see-through dress with no underwear," Rendi agreed with Emma. "But," she continued, emphasizing her point with her whole body, "only an idiot woman would wear such clothing in front of a man with whom she did not want to have sex. Clothing, my dear, sends a powerful message. Wear it with extreme care."

Emma went ballistic. "A woman has the right to wear anything she pleases, in front of anyone she pleases, without inviting some animal to read that as an invitation to rape."

"You are right, of course, my dear. When you live in a world full of animals, you must never make the mistake of assuming they will not act like animals. A zookeeper never keeps the cage unlocked, even though he has a right not to be eaten by the lion."

Rendi was Abe's crack investigator. Because she was chameleonlike, she could get inside any closed group. He had used her to infiltrate the Newark Black Muslims in a futile effort to find out if they were responsible for the Monty Williams murder. In another instance she had passed as Italian and sat around a North End coffee shop for days, listening to conversations that had helped Abe discredit a government witness in a money-laundering case.

In addition to her role as Abe's trusted investigator, Rendi also served as resident cynic and realist. She had seen it all and trusted no one. She had strong personal values, such as fierce loyalty and honesty, but she was nihilistic about rules. To her, the golden rule was "He who has the gold, rules." Her version of the rule of reciprocity was "Do it unto others before they do it unto you." She was a complex person, this woman Rendi.

Besides being Abe's episodic lover, Rendi was Emma's best adult friend. Watching Rendi with her father, Emma often wondered why the two of them, who seemed to get on so well, couldn't "just get married, and stop this on-again, off-again romance." Abe wished he could tell Emma about their "problem," but that was one secret he could never share with her.

Now Abe was asking Rendi to pretend she was part of a most bizarre culture. "You want me to become a basketball groupie?" Rendi asked incredulously. "What in hell is that?"

Abe tried his best to explain, and Rendi agreed to come over to his house that evening to be prepped and dressed for her new role. Rendi arrived with her box full of props. Abe handed her a pair of falsies, which she examined and then tossed in the air. "I like my breasts just the way they are," she insisted.

"It's not *you* we're sending to the sports bar, Rendi. It's a *groupie* we're sending, and you have to *look* like a groupie if you're going to get inside that circle."

"Why can't I go with her, Daddy?" Emma asked, knowing the answer. "It wouldn't really be *me*. I would just be pretending like Rendi. And *I* would *love* to have big breasts—at least for one night." Emma reached for the discarded falsies on the floor and held them up to her chest.

"I knew I shouldn't even have told you about what Rendi is going to be doing," Abe said. "I certainly shouldn't have let you help her with her costume."

"Does that mean I can't go?"

"Yes, that means you can't go. Rendi is a trained investigator. She knows how to handle this kind of undercover role. It takes a lot of experience. You're not old enough to go to a bar of any kind, and certainly not a sports pickup bar like Champion's. I don't want you becoming a jock groupie."

"No chance of that, Daddy."

As Abe and Emma were arguing with—really more like teasing—each other, Rendi donned her costume: black leather minisheath, red belt, black spiked heels, fishnet stockings, and a shoulder-length blond fall.

"To die for," Rendi said, stroking the blond hair.

"To *dye* for," mocked Emma, spelling out the word.

The black-and-red heart-shaped tattoo that Emma had bought in the head shop adjoining her school was too much, even for Abe, especially when he found out where Rendi was thinking of placing it.

Emma let loose with a wolf whistle that would have made a construction worker proud. Rendi laughed out loud, remembering her little lecture to Emma about not dressing for sex unless you meant it. Now, here she was, dressing up as veritable man-bait. Rendi explained, "It's a costume, all right? It's just a costume. I'll be careful. I'm going to meet *women*, not *men*."

Abe laughed nervously as he once again offered Rendi the falsies. "Alex O'Donnell tells me you've got to wear these things to be a credible groupie. Athletes tend to evaluate women by their breast size. His exact words were 'broads with bazooms.'"

"Do guys still talk that way?" Rendi asked.

"Apparently in locker rooms they still do—at least according to Alex, who sounds like he knows," Abe replied.

"That's sick," Emma said.

"Don't attack the messenger, Emma," Abe responded defensively. "I'm just repeating what my expert on jocks tells me."

"No wonder they call them jocks. They ought to call them—"

"A little respect, my dear," Abe cut in quickly. "One of them is paying for your college education."

"I'm not talking about Joe Campbell, Daddy. He seems different from the stereotype Alex was describing."

"Maybe, but all stereotypes are wrong," Abe said.

Rendi saw her opening. "Well, if that's true, why are you making me wear these damn falsies?"

"Precisely because you have to look like a stereotype."

So Rendi stuffed some tissues into her bra and became a miniskirted broad with big bazooms. On one level she didn't really care. It wasn't her; it was just another one of her assignments, though not a particularly appealing one. Rendi hated basketball and could never understand Abe's and Emma's fascination with it. Once Abe had persuaded her to accompany him to an important playoff game, and she'd mortified him by reading a poetry book during the overtime. It was the last invitation she'd gotten to a basketball game, which was just fine with her.

Now Abe had invited her to enter the tawdry world of sexual hero worship—or was it whoreship, she thought—that followed professional athletes wherever they performed.

Her job was to find out everything she could about Joe Campbell's sexual proclivities—and, in the process, to learn about the life of groupies. Abe had told Campbell and Alex that he was sending his investigator into the groupie scene to get background on groupies for the trial. He'd told Emma the same thing. He could not tell them the real purpose of the undercover operation, nor what had stimulated his need to investigate what Justin suspected about Campbell's sex life.

Chapter Twelve

"How did you know I'd be here?" Nancy Rosen asked as she looked up at Justin from the weight-lifting bench in the old broken-down gym located in downtown Newark. Muscle Discipline attracted few women, especially white women, into its spidery depths. Justin stood out like a sore thumb in his gray lawyer's suit.

"Your reputation as a jock precedes you," Justin replied. "I can't get to talk to you any other way. Why the heck haven't you been returning my calls? We need an answer. Who killed Monty Williams?"

"I haven't called back because I can't tell you. It's your turn to put your sorry, out-of-shape butt on the line. Get out there and follow up some leads."

"You should only know how much investigative work we've done," Justin said, covering his mouth to avoid being overheard by the muscular black man on the next bench. "Even some of *your* clients, such as those Black Muslims in Newark who threatened Williams. So far we've come up dry."

"You're looking in the wrong place. The Muslims are clean on this one. That much I can tell you. No more."

"That's good," Justin acknowledged. "At least we won't go

down that blind alley again. Now all I've got to figure out is who the rest of your clients are. Any more clues for today, Superwoman?"

Nancy continued to curl the barbell. "Only that it won't be easy. I'm sorry, Justin. I just can't tell you more. The Code of Professional Responsibility makes no exception even for an innocent man on death row. I've got to play by the rules. I actually found a case just like this one, down in Georgia—eighty years ago."

"Just like this one?" Justin asked incredulously.

"Yeah. It involved a man named Leo Frank."

"I've heard of that case. A Jewish businessman who was convicted of murdering a young girl who worked for him."

"That's the one. Well, it turns out that one of Frank's other employees confessed to his own lawyer that *he,* not Frank, actually did it."

"Did the lawyer blow the whistle on his client?"

"No, he didn't. In fact, after the case was over, the lawyer wrote an article about his dilemma. That's how I found out about it."

"What did he say?"

"That he would be disbarred if he disclosed what his client told him in confidence. I can't break the rules, Justin."

Justin quickly jumped on Nancy's words. "That wasn't the position you took in the Jimmy Hawkins case."

Hawkins, a black preacher in Newark who had practiced civil disobedience, had been arrested for staging sit-ins at city council meetings. The prosecutor had argued that rules and statutes had to be obeyed regardless of the moral consequences. Nancy had made an impassioned and successful argument in defense of those who "break the rules to create a moral world, rather than those who play by the rules to preserve an immoral system." Nancy had proudly sent her press clippings to Justin after the case was over.

"How do you want to be remembered?" Justin asked, peering down into Nancy's eyes. "As a woman who played by the rules and allowed an innocent black man to be executed? Or as a woman who broke a rule and saved an innocent life?"

Nancy rose from the bench on which she had been reclining and stood face-to-face with Justin. "That's just not fair, and you know it. When I argued that Jimmy Hawkins should not be punished for breaking the rules, *I* was playing by the rules. That's a permissible closing argument in New Jersey. Now you're asking *me* to break the rules—to put my bar certificate at risk. Would you do that, Justin? Would you?"

Without pausing for an instant, Justin responded, "You're darned right I would—if an innocent human life were at stake." He knew he was not being entirely candid with Nancy. He knew he would do anything now to get Charlie off death row—to win the case. He didn't even care whether he was being fair to Nancy.

For now, Justin had made his point. It was a good exit line. It would leave Nancy thinking—and perhaps feeling enough guilt to loosen her tongue.

Chapter Thirteen

Rendi had been in the Westin Hotel many times for dinners, on assignment, even once for a romantic interlude with an old friend from her childhood. But she had never been in the Champion Bar, a watering hole for professional athletes, fans, and groupies. If she wanted to become part of the groupie scene, this was the place to begin.

The large room was filled with the mixed scent of smoke and perfume. Champion's was a brassy sort of place, adorned with shiny metal, glass, and oak. Several television sets were tuned to different sports events and programs. The sound was always low, producing a rhythmic mumble of sports jargon. Nobody appeared to be watching the lighted tubes; they were there more for ambiance. A dozen women or so, ranging in age from about twenty to thirty-five, were sitting at tables and at the bar. And half a dozen men, all beefy, were standing around the bar.

Rendi sat down at the bar next to a short, voluptuous woman, who introduced herself as Patsy. She appeared to be in her middle twenties. A cigarette hung from her lips as her eyes stared vacantly at the smoke.

"I just moved to Boston from Los Angeles," Rendi said, hoping her inflection would make her sound like a Southern

California girl. "I used to follow the Lakers in a big way. Have you ever been to the Forum Club?" She had prepped herself by reading a series of clips about groupies published by the *L.A. Times* following Magic Johnson's retirement.

"I wish!" Patsy replied in a perky voice. "I've only been in Boston, New York, and Philadelphia. I hear the scene is great out in L.A."

"It's a mixed bag," Rendi offered. "Lots of guys, what with the Lakers, the Clippers, and the college kids. Lots of competition, too, especially among the young girls who come to L.A. from the farm belt. The guys are always looking for new young blood."

"Washed up at twenty-seven." Patsy sighed. "And the athletes think *they* have it tough."

"How's the scene here?"

"It's okay. Some of the Celts are goody-two-shoes. They always seem to have a Mormon or two on the bench to keep them holy. Still, there are some real fun guys. Mostly I go for the out-of-town players. It's a lot looser with the visiting team. No wives or girlfriends to worry about."

"Did you hear about 'Riley's rule,' when he was coaching the Lakers?" Rendi asked.

"No, what is it? Some kind of curfew thing?"

"Pretty much the opposite."

"What do you mean?"

"Some of the Lakers' wives were accompanying the husbands on road trips, and it was getting the other players uptight. You know, wives stick together and that sort of thing. The action guys were nervous that the traveling wives would report what *they* were doing on the road back to their wives."

"Yeah, so?"

"So it was beginning to affect their play on the road—their nervousness and all."

"So what did Riley do?"

"He went and banned all wives from road trips, and the Lakers started winning again on the road."

"How did the wives react?"

"Some of them had a cow."

"So?"

"So Riley tells them, 'Look, wives don't score points, players do, and players have to be loose.'"

"Goes to show that sex on the road is good for morale."

"As long as it's not with your wife," Rendi added. Patsy joined in the laughter as they both ordered another drink.

"There's a guy in New York I'm really hot for," she confided, leaning over while trying to avoid the smoke from Patsy's cigarette.

"Yeah, who?"

"Campbell, the big white guy."

"You and half the borough of Manhattan. He's the best-looking spook in the NBA."

Rendi hadn't come across the word *spook* in her research, but it didn't take much imagination for her to figure out that its ghostly reference was to Campbell's white skin in a league where most of the players were black.

"A girl can fantasize, can't she?" Rendi responded.

"Ain't much for fantasizing, when you can't touch and feel." Patsy giggled. "It may be a whole lot safer."

"That Magic stuff has certainly put a damper on the fun," Rendi said.

"Not so much here in Boston. It's never been as wild here as everyone said it used to be in L.A. and Chicago."

"Oh, for the good old days, when all you had to worry about was getting knocked up or a dose of the clap."

"You got nothing to worry about with your heartthrob, baby. He's very selective, very discreet, none of this Wilt Chamberlain 'I've screwed everyone in California' stuff with Campbell."

"What else do you know about him?" Rendi asked, her voice in near perfect California modulation.

"Not much. I know he's shy. He reads a lot. Carries a portable computer with him sometimes."

"Anything else?"

"Yeah, one thing that should help *you*. He doesn't go for the very young ones so much—the teenyboppers. He likes mature, serious women. At least that's the rep."

"Is he kinky?" Rendi asked, not showing even a hint of embarrassment.

"I don't know. I've never been with him. I do know one girl who says she has been with him."

"What do you mean, 'says'?"

"Oh, you know. There's a whole lot of bullshit around. Some girls get off by just bragging. Didn't you get some of them types in L.A.?"

"I don't know—yeah, sure, maybe . . ."

"Are you sure you know this scene?"

For a moment Rendi feared her cover might be blown. "You know—I'm a little older than you. What are you—twenty-five, twenty-six?"

"I'm twenty-seven, like I said."

"Well, I'm older," Rendi declared. "We older girls weren't as brave as you kids. Things were less blatant earlier on. You know, rock star girls got all the attention for a long time—the competition wasn't so fierce."

"Yeah. It's so competitive nowadays that some of the girls even make stuff up." Patsy pointed in the direction of an older woman with flaming red hair, sitting alone in the rear of the bar. "Do you see Cynthia, over there? Don't look, just peek."

"Yeah."

"She's one of the bullshitters. Hardly ever gets it on with anyone anymore. Anyone important, I mean. Yet she brags about everyone—even some guys who never do it. Nobody believes her."

"Who's the lucky girl you know who made it with Campbell?"

"*Says* she made it with Campbell," Patsy cautioned. "It's a woman named Chrissy. Doesn't hang here. Doesn't really hang anywhere. I haven't seen her around for a while."

"I'd love to talk to her. Just for the thrill of hearing what it's like to be with Campbell."

"She *says* she's been with Campbell. Remember that you can't believe everything you hear in this scene."

"Do you have any idea where I could find her?"

"Nah, I never much liked her. We hardly ever talked. Once or twice. Now Bev over there"—Patsy pointed to a tall woman deep in conversation with a former-jock-now-corporate type—"she knew Chrissy real well. Maybe she can help you."

Rendi kept her eye on Bev while continuing to talk with Patsy. When Bev got up to go to the ladies' room, Rendi quickly followed.

As Rendi expected, the ladies' room was a face and body repair shop with indirect lighting that flattered the faces of the five women who were helping themselves to the ointments and toilet waters lined up in designer label perfume bottles. Rendi positioned herself next to Bev at the mirror. The other woman was dressed completely in red and was touching up her scarlet lipstick.

"Hey, Bev, haven't seen Chrissy around much lately. I've got a message for her, and I haven't run into her."

"Haven't you heard?" Bev replied without even glancing up. "Chrissy got married. To some jerk in the meat-packing business. Big bucks, big muscles, big jerk."

"What's his name?"

"I don't know. Stan something. Maybe Kowalski or Karinski, something Polish. I do remember his company is called Merit Meats. I remember that because she once had him send me a package of free steaks, before they got married. Haven't heard from her since she moved to the burbs."

"Which suburbs?"

"I don't know, south shore somewhere. He has a boat. Maybe Cohasset or Marshfield or somewhere."

"Thanks, Bev."

"Hey, you're not gonna call her with some message from some guy from the scene? That could cause complications. I don't think her Stan knows how deep she was into the scene before she regained her virginity for him."

"Nah, don't worry. It's a message from an old girlfriend of hers."

"Yeah. Who?"

"It's private, Bev, sorry. You understand."

"What do I give a shit. Just don't tell her you got the info from me."

Rendi made a zipper motion across her mouth and walked out of the bathroom and the bar. She needed some air. She wanted to go home. Her work for the night was done. Now all she had to do was find a woman named Chrissy, married to a Polish guy named Stan, who owned a meat company called Merit and lived on the south shore with his boat.

Piece of cake, Rendi said to herself as she drove toward Cambridge.

Chapter Fourteen

"What have you got for us, Rendi?"

Abe had arranged a joint debriefing with Rendi and Justin in his Cambridge office. Rendi disliked Justin, as much as he was put off by her. She regarded the tall, good-looking young lawyer as a spoiled brat who did not deserve the enviable opportunity of apprenticing for Abe. "Why him?" she had demanded when Abe told her he had selected Justin from the thirty-five Yale, Harvard, and Columbia applicants.

"Because he's so different from me. He's really a prosecutor at heart. He's better at seeing the other side of the issue. I need a different perspective. The rest of us—me, you, Gayle—we're all so much alike."

"How can you work with a wire strung as tight as Rendi?" Justin had once asked Abe. She scared him. He had never quite met anyone like her. He was fascinated and a bit repelled by her, but he was also in awe of her energy and impatience.

Justin loved to tell "Rendi stories" around the office. "You know the ketchup commercial—the one about how slow it drips out of the bottle? I swear, Rendi told me it drives her crazy to watch it drip so slowly. Why would anyone want a slow-pouring ketchup? For her the quicker the better. I can just imagine her in bed." One day Justin came out of the bathroom laughing hysterically. "Rendi went into the adjoining ladies' bathroom the same time I went into the men's room. As soon as she got in, I hear her flush. So when we came out, I asked her, and she told me she flushes as soon as she starts to go, so that the flush will finish when she finishes, and she won't have to waste an extra second. The woman is nuts. A terrific investigator, but a weird person."

Now the investigator was reporting on the follow-up to her bizarre evening. "I've got a lot of gossip, but nothing hard," Rendi said, spreading out her notes. "I found this woman named Chrissy Kachinski. She used to date Campbell—at least she says she did. Seems to be telling the truth. Nothing unusual. Slutty type. A couple of one-night stands with Campbell here in Boston. One weekend on Martha's Vineyard. Nothing kinky. She says he seemed bored by the sex. They left early. He was upset."

"Anything more?"

"Not from Chrissy. She told me about another woman he went out with named Darlene Walters. A Boston financial type. Worked as a bond analyst with First Boston. Chrissy got a call from her after she saw her out with Campbell one night at the Ritz. Warned Chrissy about Campbell's violent side. Chrissy thought Darlene was just jealous, because she never saw that side of Campbell, but she kept Darlene's name and number just in case."

"So, did you follow up with Darlene?"

"I tried, only she didn't want to talk to me."

"Dead end?"

"Abe, you know there are no dead ends with Rendi Renaad."

"So what did you find out?"

"I spoke to several of Darlene's friends. Mostly they wouldn't talk. One woman named Margie told me something quite interesting that Darlene had confided in her."

"What?"

"It seems that Campbell couldn't get it up with her. Darlene really liked Campbell, but he didn't just leave early, like he did with Chrissy."

"What did he do?"

"I'm not sure. Margie didn't know the details. Or else she wasn't prepared to get down and dirty with me. All she would tell me was that it was very unpleasant for Darlene. She had some black-and-blue marks on her legs, and she cried when she talked about it."

"Anything else?"

"Nothing specific. It certainly didn't make your client look good."

"Pretty vague. Maybe Darlene likes a little bit of rough stuff and it got out of hand. Not pretty, but I can handle it if the state finds out.

"Justin, how about you?" Abe continued. "What have you got from the computer stuff you've been working on?"

"My stuff is also a bit vague and circumstantial. I'm afraid that an ugly little picture is beginning to emerge."

"Paint it for us," Abe said.

"Okay. As I've already told you, I suspect, though I can't prove, that Campbell may have punched up the Dowling sexual harassment cases sometime before he claims he ever met her. Whenever he punched it up, we know—and this we know for sure—that he didn't just search for her name. He searched for *all* names and cases under a broader category involving false sexual allegations."

"So, my friend, what's the explanation?"

"I can think of several, none of them good."

"How bad?" Abe asked with a worried look.

"Bad is the best I've got," Justin replied. "From there it gets worse."

"That good, huh?" Rendi interjected.

"That good."

Abe quoted Shakespeare: " 'The worse is not, so long as we

can say, "*This* is the worst." ' " Then he shook his head. "You guys are perennial pessimists."

"Okay." Justin took up the challenge. "Possibility one, Campbell lied about when he first met Dowling. He actually met her before March tenth, made the Boston date, and *then* punched up the story, like he told us."

"Could be," Abe said. "But why would Campbell lie about *that* date? Dowling would probably be able to prove—by her friends, office mates—when she first met him. And what the hell difference would it make if he *had* met her earlier? That one's not so bad. Okay, what's next in your list of possible disasters?"

"I guess we're up to possibility two—'worse.' Well, worse is if Campbell is telling the truth about when he first met Dowling."

"Why?"

"Because then—if I'm right about when he punched up her case—then it would seem that he may have punched up her case before he *really* met her."

"What do you mean, 'really met' her?"

"Well, it's possible that he had seen her before—at a party or something. Maybe she didn't even remember him, yet he remembered her. Maybe a friend told him about her, and they hadn't actually met—yet. He punched up her story in order to check her out, and then he met her *again*, and they made a date."

"Okay. That sounds plausible. And it's also not that terrible from a jury's point of view."

"Remember, Abe, he didn't punch up information only about her. His search was for a broader category."

"What's your explanation, then, Justin?"

"It seems pretty obvious. Campbell probably cross-checks that category periodically, to make sure that none of the women he wants to date are the kind who go around falsely accusing people. Remember what he told you about how much he values his reputation as a gentleman."

Rendi nodded. "That does sound logical—"

"My God," Abe broke in, "have things gotten so bad out there that guys have to check their dates out in advance to head off false accusations of rape?"

Rendi ignored Abe's question as she continued to explore the thought she had begun. "Logical—but not certain," she said slowly.

"What do you mean?" Justin asked.

"There is another possible explanation."

"Better than mine?"

"No," Rendi replied somberly, "much worse."

"Okay, we're up to possibility three—worser," Abe said, and winced.

Rendi got up and started pacing. "What if *this* is what happened. It's completely speculative, I admit. And it probably didn't happen this way. What if—just what if—before Campbell ever even heard of Dowling, he placed a computer search for recent New York cases in which women had filed false complaints of sexual misconduct. And then he *deliberately* picked these women to go out with?"

"What, are you crazy?" Justin asked her. "Why would a man intentionally go out with women who he *knew* had falsely charged men with sexually abusing them? Those women are poison ivy to most men. They won't go near them. No one *wants* to be charged with sexual harassment or rape, especially a jock."

"That's right," Rendi said. "For *most* men these women are poison—because *most* men aren't rapists." Then, after pausing as if to reconsider whether to take her point farther, Rendi slowly continued. "What if a guy deliberately set out to rape a woman, and wanted to get away with it? Who might he pick as the least likely type of woman to be believed?" She quickly answered her own question. "A woman who *once before* had filed a *false* complaint and who had been exposed as a liar. A woman like Jennifer Dowling."

"Rendi, that's the most paranoid thing I've ever heard,"

Abe said angrily. "You sound like that radical feminist Gloria McDermot. I really expect more from you—"

"I'm not so sure that Rendi's off base," Justin interrupted. "It's certainly possible—though I also admit it's rank speculation—that Campbell made a calculated decision to date Jennifer because he planned in advance to rape her, and he knew she wouldn't be believed if she cried rape."

"My God, Justin, now you're joining Rendi's paranoia. That dog just won't hunt. It doesn't make any sense. Think about what you're suggesting."

"Could be true, Abe. Just could be. Maybe Campbell understood the story of the little boy who falsely cried 'Wolf!' and he applied it to a grown-up woman who had falsely cried harassment."

"Let's don't jump to any ridiculous conclusions," Abe cautioned. "You're both reading an awful lot into a couple of computer printouts and an incomplete field investigation. It's highly circumstantial at best, and Campbell may have a good explanation for the whole thing. We're letting our fantasies run away with us."

"You're probably right," Justin agreed. "Remember that Campbell and Dowling met by chance near her office building. That doesn't fit in with your theory, Rendi, does it?"

"Not all chance meetings are really chance," Rendi shot back. "I arrange 'chance' meetings with my investigative subjects all the time. It's not all that hard to do."

"Stop this now," Abe insisted. "We're Campbell's *defense* team. Let's stop thinking like prosecutors, and start thinking like defense lawyers. I'm going to defend this man—and win."

Chapter Fifteen

At law school Justin had been active in the Federalist Society, a conservative group that prided itself on being politically incorrect on issues of race, sex, and politics. He took courses mostly from the right wing professors, steering clear of teachers like Haskel Levine and others who had been Abe's favorites a generation earlier. Justin had written a term paper on how feminism was dangerous to liberty. Though he was always polite to women personally, his political views, especially about rape, sometimes provoked his women friends into displays of rage.

"Big deal," he had once infuriated Rendi by saying. "Rape is not like a broken bone or even a cracked tooth. It doesn't cause any real damage. There's nothing to heal, except some bruised feelings." Rendi had almost given him a cracked tooth following that display of male insensitivity. Instead she'd given him a lecture about how it felt to be violated to one's core. Justin had pretended to listen, but it had just sounded like feminist rhetoric to him even when coming with the passion that accompanied all of Rendi's lectures.

The Campbell case was subtly changing Justin. As his suspicions about Joe Campbell mounted, his compassion for Jennifer Dowling increased. What if Campbell had really exploited her vulnerable past? It was only a theory. What if it were true? He felt a growing kinship with Jennifer Dowling, since, like her, he had originally been taken in by the smooth-talking basketball star. Sure Abe was right: Justin had to act like a defense lawyer. That didn't mean he couldn't think and feel like a human being.

Justin and Abe sat over lunch at the Bombay Restaurant across the street from the Kennedy School near Harvard Square, the usual venue for their weekly strategy session. "You can't defend Campbell as though there weren't something fishy—as though you didn't know more than what he told you."

"I can't just act on your suspicions, either," Abe replied, taking a bite of his tandoori chicken. "He's our client, and I have a legal and ethical responsibility toward him."

"He lied to you, and more than once."

"All my clients lie to me, and more than once."

"This guy is bad."

"Most of my clients are bad. I think it was Mark Twain who once said, 'If there were no bad people, there would be no good lawyers.' "

"Abe, my gut tells me Campbell is guilty."

"That's your opinion, and you have the right to hold it and to express it to me—in private. I don't necessarily share your opinion."

"That's because you have DLBS."

"What the hell is DLBS?"

"Defense lawyer's blind spot. That's what we called it when I interned at the DA's office."

"Listen, every good defense attorney develops a nose for guilt over time. We're not easily fooled by our clients."

"Oh, yeah? What about the Patrick case?"

In the case Justin was referring to, Abe had been appointed to represent an indigent black man named Orlando Patrick, who was accused of killing a cabdriver during a holdup. Orlando's brother, Marcel, testified that he was the real killer. The jury believed him and acquitted Orlando. Marcel was then charged with murder, and Orlando testified that *he* had killed the cab-driver. The second jury acquitted Marcel. There was a terrible public outcry, especially when it became clear that neither brother could be retried for the murder because of double jeopardy.

"That case was unusual," Abe said defensively. "Those Patrick brothers were the best damn liars I ever met. To this day I still don't know which of them was telling the truth."

"How about neither of them." Justin sighed. "Abe, you represent so many obviously guilty defendants that you become desperate to believe that you're representing the occasional innocent—so you can justify what we're doing for a living."

"Who taught you that nonsense, Justin?"

"You did. I can see it in your desperation to believe Campbell is innocent. How many times have you heard defense lawyers mouth the platitude about how it's better for ten guilty men to go free than for even one innocent defendant to be wrongly convicted?"

"Oh, about once a day. And it's not a platitude. I assumed that you believed in it."

"I do believe in it. There's no greater exhilaration for a defense lawyer than representing an innocent defendant."

"Except when you lose. It's even worse losing for someone you know is innocent."

"Even when you lose, you know you're doing God's work if your client is innocent. I envy Mike Tyson's lawyers, despite the fact they lost. They knew he was innocent. In fact, in many respects, the Campbell case is the exact opposite—the mirror image—of Tyson."

"How so?" Abe asked.

"Lots of people thought Tyson was guilty because of his media reputation, his rough edges, and his direct way. Yet we both think he was really innocent. With Campbell, everybody seems to think he's innocent because of his charm and polish. And because he's white. I think he's guilty as hell."

"I'm glad everyone thinks Joe is innocent," Abe said. "That can't hurt in front of the jury. In this game, there's only one bottom line—winning—whether the client is black or white, innocent or guilty."

"Still, it feels a lot better expending all that energy when the guy is innocent.

"It sure does, and that's the attitude I'm approaching the Campbell case with."

"Tell me, Abe, how does it feel when you get a guilty guy off?"

"It's a terrible feeling, especially when it's a horrible crime like murder or rape. It's even worse when you lose a case for an innocent client, because it's your job to win.

"Even for the guilty?"

"Yes, even for the guilty. It's not part of your job to enjoy it—that's why I never go to victory parties for guilty clients."

"God, it must feel just terrible to see a murderer or rapist go free because you outsmarted the prosecution."

"You'll experience it some time yourself, Justin."

"I can't wait," Justin said cynically.

"You're right about one thing—that for the principle of 'better ten guilty go free' to have any meaning to a defense attorney, we have to actually meet that one innocent defendant every so often. I still believe Campbell is that one innocent."

"Sure you do, Abe, because if you can't find the one innocent, you have to make him up."

"Not so. Any good lawyer worth his salt does a better job if he truly believes his client is innocent."

"I understand that. That's precisely my point. You *really* do believe that your client is innocent, if there is *any* plausible basis for that belief. Then when evidence of guilt begins to emerge, you develop that blind spot. You just don't see it, even if it's right in front of your eyes. I'm amazed that with your experience you still don't see through Campbell's charm."

"Campbell's charm has nothing to do with it, Justin. He

may have charmed Emma. I'm looking at the evidence. *Your* evidence. It just doesn't persuade me. It does shake me a little bit, and I appreciate that. Without hard proof what would you have me do?"

"You should drop him like you did Kraus," Justin offered.

For an instant, Abe's mind flashed on an image of the goose-stepping Henry Kraus, a neo-Nazi "Uberführer" who had been arrested at Downtown Crossing in Boston for demanding that blacks be sent back to Africa, and that Jews be sent back to Russia. Abe had agreed to represent Kraus on the First Amendment issue. Kraus then went on TV and announced that he had picked Abraham Ringel to represent him only because he wanted "a sharp Jewish lawyer," Abe immediately left the case, announcing that he would never allow a Nazi to select him for anything because he was a Jew. His decision had caused quite a stir, especially when Kraus sued him for breach of contract.

Abe had won the case after an undercover agent working for the Anti-Defamation League testified that Kraus had deliberately orchestrated the entire episode in order to show that Jewish lawyers couldn't be trusted.

"You dropped that Nazi son of a bitch before you even knew it was a setup," Justin reminded him.

"Yeah, but when I dropped Kraus, nobody thought I was doing it because I believed he was guilty. I went out of my way publicly to defend his right to make racist and anti-Semitic speeches. I just didn't want to be his lawyer. This case is different. If I dump Campbell without any explanation, everyone will believe that I learned something that led me to conclude Campbell is guilty. I couldn't do that even if it were true—which it isn't."

"Please don't tell me you're stuck with Campbell," Justin said plaintively. "I really don't want to hear that."

"I am stuck with Campbell," Abe concluded. "Even if I agreed with you that he was guilty—which I don't. Better ten guilty men go free—"

"I *know* the rule," Justin interrupted. "Somehow it feels so different when we're the ones who are freeing the guilty rapist."

"First of all, we're not. And second of all, we have no other option," Abe said.

"Yes, we do. You've gotta confront Campbell with what we've learned—all the computer stuff—his reputation. The whole schmear. Campbell has the right to know what we know about him. Some clients just don't want to be represented by lawyers who are aware of the skeletons in their closets."

"What do you think I should tell him, Justin?"

"Everything we've got, the whole messy ball of wax. And tell him how we found it."

"You really do want him to fire us."

"It's his decision, and he's entitled to know exactly what we think of him, and precisely what we are, and are not, prepared to do for him."

Abe thought about this for a moment. "I think you're right about that. We should give him a chance to explain what you and Rendi have conjured up. And I'm not going to sugar-coat anything."

"Sounds like you've got to confront him before the trial," Justin said.

"It sure does."

"Want me to hold your hand?" Justin asked.

"Not on this one. This time, it's going to be one on one, with no referee."

Chapter Sixteen

In preparation for Abe's meeting with Campbell, Justin went back to the computer room and Rendi headed back out to the field. Abe needed documentation—hard evidence—to support everything he was going to throw at Campbell, even if it took some time to gather it. Abe knew that Campbell's intuitive ability to psych out his opponent would serve him well in this confrontation. Abe prided himself, as well, on being an intuitive lawyer. His advantage lay, as it always did, in superior preparation. Abe did not want to ask any question to which he did not have the answer—and the proof to back it up.

Justin's computer research had uncovered that Campbell had been married as a senior in college to a smart and beautiful classmate named Annie Higgins. Captain of the Northeastern University ski team and a standout slalom competitor, she was herself a star athlete. The marriage had lasted five years, though they had separated after two.

Rendi got right on the lead and managed to locate Annie Higgins, who was working as a buyer for Filene's. Higgins made it clear she didn't want to talk about Campbell. "That part of my life is behind me." When Rendi persisted, she agreed to meet for a quick dinner—with no promises. They met at Biba's, a trendy restaurant overlooking the Boston Common, which had some quiet corner tables.

"My husband was a good man," Annie Higgins said as soon as she was seated.

Rendi observed the other woman. She was clean-cut, pretty in a peaches-and-cream way. She looked a little like Jennifer Dowling: early thirties, tastefully dressed.

"How long have you been divorced?"

"Couple of years. Joe was generous. He even put me through school."

"Sounds like he felt responsible for your breakup."

Annie looked out the picture window in the direction of the duck pond made famous by the children's book *Make Way for Ducklings*. Tears began to well up in her eyes. "It's not really his fault," she said defensively. "He was fine before all those groupies got to him. He used to love to take me on the swan boats while we dated."

Rendi had the feeling that if she scratched just beneath the surface, Higgins would talk—maybe even wanted to—now that they'd met. This woman wanted her story told. "What do you mean, it's not his fault?"

"The sex between us was great in college, before we got married—even afterward for a few months. Then when he got into the NBA, he started to fool around a little on the road."

"That must have hurt you."

"In the beginning. And then you kind of get used to it. The wives all talk about it. It goes with the turf. In those days, no one worried about diseases. I could deal with the occasional one-night road stand. We all could."

"Then what was the problem?"

"The problem was that after a while, it got worse."

"More groupies?"

"No, that wasn't the problem. Sure, there were more groupies. I'm sure that contributed to the problem. Sex became boring to Joe. It was no challenge when he was home with me, it was still good—at least in the beginning. I could still, you know, satisfy him."

"So what changed that?"

"I don't know. Maybe it was the groupies. Maybe it was something else. All I know is that after a while, when he got home, he couldn't, you know, perform. He would be limp. I tried to be understanding, to help him. We even went to a marriage counselor for a couple of sessions, but he was embarrassed talking about it."

"About what?"

"About his impotency."

"Was he impotent with everybody, with the groupies, too?"

"That's what he told me. And that's what he told the therapist. Now I know it wasn't true."

"How do you know?"

"I once found a letter from some slut in Phoenix—and I mean this girl was the worst kind of trash—which described their lovemaking. It had the ring of truth. It sounded like the Joe Campbell I loved in college. Why he would want to make it with that kind of woman is beyond me."

"So what did you do?"

"I should have left him right there and then. The handwriting was on the wall. I stayed a few more months, and they were the worst."

"In what way?"

"This is really embarrassing, Miss Renaad. Can we talk in absolute confidence?"

"Yes, we can. This is just between us girls. We're trying to help Joe Campbell and other women."

"All right, let me tell you what happened. God, I've never told anybody about this."

"Good, keep talking. You'll feel better."

"Joe really tried to make it good between us. Some guys might just have given up on the sex or just kept going out with the sluts. To his credit, Joe put a lot of effort into solving his, you know, his problem."

"Why do you think he went through the effort, since he was able to satisfy himself with the groupies?"

"You have to understand Joe," Annie said. "He hates to think of himself as a low-class jock who only makes it with dumb sluts. He came out of a low-class background, and he prides himself on having overcome that. He wants very badly to be able to love intelligent, accomplished women. Only he can't. At least not without some weird stuff."

"What kind of weird stuff?"

"He tried to make it more exciting for himself."

"In what way?"

"This is really difficult to talk about," Annie said, her voice choked with emotion.

"Please keep trying. It's important." Rendi placed an arm around Annie's shoulder.

"All right. Let me just say it. He started to play games with me. He made me pretend that I didn't want to have sex with him. I would say no, at first in a kind of joking way, but that didn't work. So he made me say it and act like I really meant it. That turned him on, and we had good sex."

"So did that solve the problem?"

"For a while it did. Then it stopped working. He couldn't arouse himself if he knew that I really wanted to have sex with him. So he started to have sex with me when I *really* didn't want to."

"What do you mean?"

"Well, I didn't like having sex during my period. He knew that, and he made me do it, while I was menstruating. Then he would wake me up in the middle of the night, especially after a long day, and force himself on me."

"You mean he raped you?"

"No, it wasn't rape. We were married."

"A marriage license is not a license to rape," Rendi insisted, becoming a bit strident.

"I know. I know," Annie said defensively. "But I sort of went along with it. I wanted him to become aroused, even if I didn't enjoy the sex. It was a kind of bargain with the devil. It wasn't rape. At least not in my book."

"But is that why you left him?"

"No. I left him because it got even worse. During our last few weeks together, he could only get aroused when he really hurt me. He would tie me up—force me—I had bruises. The last time he held me down so hard I almost lost consciousness. So he slapped me and then he . . ." Annie couldn't go on. She was sobbing uncontrollably.

"That *was* rape," Rendi said quietly as she reached out to touch the other woman's hand.

"It really wasn't his fault," Annie insisted. "Those groupies—the lifestyle—screwed him up. That wasn't the real Joe."

"That may be the real Joe now," Rendi said as she signaled the waiter for the check.

Chapter Seventeen

While Abe was preparing for his confrontation with Campbell, Justin had to tend to some unfinished business with Nancy Rosen in Newark.

This time they met in her office. Out of the blue Nancy had called Justin, inviting him down for a chat.

Nancy's "office" was actually a storefront on Springfield Avenue, tucked between a rib joint and a Jehovah's Witnesses "temple."

"My law store used to be Cohen's haberdashery," Nancy said proudly, pointing to a framed photo on her wall of the old store with a Jewish man standing in front.

"Things change," Nancy mused. "The Jews used to be the haberdashers, the workers, even the petty thieves." Pointing to a small newsstand across the street, she told Justin that the Silverstein gang used to run numbers from that stand in the 1950s. "Now the African Americans own the stores, along with some Koreans. We have to remember our roots."

Justin was not particularly interested in Nancy's nostalgia trip. He had traveled to Newark for one specific purpose. "Why did you call me, after refusing to return my calls?"

"Because I realized that you were right," Nancy said. "I

144

can't just play by the rules and let Odell die. I've got to do something. After all, how can a lawyer who defends civil disobedience refuse to engage in it herself?"

"That sounds like something Haskel Levine would say."

"It is. I called him. Luckily, he was having a good day."

"You're kidding! *You* called Haskel?"

"Why? You think Abe's his only former student who values his advice?"

"Thank God, Nancy. You're doing the right thing. What made you call Haskel?"

"A number of things. First, I did further checking on that Leo Frank case—the one that I told you about last time we met. I discovered that the sanctimonious old lawyer who wouldn't break the rules actually bent them a bit in an effort to save Frank's life."

"What did he do?" Justin asked.

"It's not completely clear, but he apparently did *something*. In his autobiography, which I managed to dig up, he implies that he *somehow* let the governor know that Frank was innocent." After pulling out an old volume, Nancy read a cryptic sentence: "Without ever having revealed to Governor Slayton the facts which were revealed to me in confidence, I have reason to believe that, in some way, these facts got to him."

"Coy old son of a bitch," Justin said. "He sounds like he's part of my WASP roots. So what did the governor do?"

"He commuted Frank's death sentence to life, but he couldn't explain why he was doing it, and there was an outraged reaction from the people."

"So what happened?"

"A group of upstanding citizens marched on the prison, grabbed Frank, and lynched him."

"Wow, what a story. And that's what made you change your mind?"

"I can't let him die," Nancy said. "I read in the advance sheets that your emergency appeal was denied."

"Yeah, the appellate court chastised Judge Cox for his antics, but agreed with his bottom line."

"And Charlie's taking his pills?"

"Yes, he is, and they're beginning to work."

"So he will soon be competent to be executed?"

"Yes, he will. And what are you going to do to stop it?" Justin asked. "Can you tell me who killed Williams?"

"No, I can't tell *you*. I'm going to try to make a deal with the prosecutor."

"What kind of deal?"

"I'll offer him the name of the killer in exchange for total immunity for my client. I won't give him my client's name until he agrees to the immunity."

"Do you think Duncan will go for that? He's a real hard-ass prosecutor. As far as he's concerned, the guilty guy is already on death row."

"Duncan knows me, Justin, and deep down he's gonna believe me when I tell him my own client did it."

"Won't he be able to figure out which of your clients is the guilty person? You have some pretty notorious clients."

"That's the beauty of my plan. This guy is not one of my notorious clients. He's a one-shot client. Walked in off the street on the day of the Williams shooting, before they fingered Odell. He thought they might go after him. No one even knows that I represent him. I haven't seen him in months. Once they picked up your guy, he disappeared into the woodwork. Calls me once a month to check in."

"Could the cops find him if they knew who he was?"

"Probably. He's keeping a low profile, but they could probably find him if they really wanted him badly. Hasn't gone underground or anything. Without his name, nobody would think of him. He looks a bit like Odell when he smiles, but to most of the cops, all thin twenty-seven-year-old blacks look alike. You won't believe it when you hear the motive. Nothing political."

"Nancy, I really appreciate this," Justin said, placing his arm on her shoulder. "You're doing the right thing."

"I hope you're right. And I pray that it works."

"I thought you were an atheist."

"At a time like this I can use all the help I can get," Nancy said with a worried smile.

Chapter Eighteen

Nancy Rosen's plan failed miserably. The prosecutor, Kevin Duncan, not only refused to grant her client immunity, he also accused Nancy, Abe, and Justin of concocting a false story in order to save Odell's life.

"There *is no* Rosen client," Duncan told a journalist. "Ringel and Rosen are two radicals who are making this whole thing up in a misguided attempt to save Odell. Remember, this is the same Ringel who told Odell to stop taking his medicine. He'll stop at nothing."

Justin and Nancy were back to square one, and there were no good moves on the horizon.

Charlie O. had been restored to competency, all appeals were exhausted, and the execution date was now three weeks away. All that stood between Odell and the injection was Nancy Rosen and her anonymous client.

Justin called Nancy to discuss what else they could do. "Are you willing to give me the name now?"

"Not yet."

"What do you mean, 'yet'? Will you give it to me in time to save Charlie? I don't want Charlie to end up like Leo Frank— dead! It's just three weeks."

"I know that, Justin. I told you I won't let him die, and I keep my word."

"What are you going to do?"

"I can't tell you yet," Nancy said. "You'll know soon enough."

A week later Abe got an angry call from Duncan. "Mr. Ringel, Nancy Rosen has told us that a client of hers named Rodney Owens killed Monty Williams, and that she can prove it. Can you come to my office tomorrow to discuss this development? And please bring your associate, John Justin Aldrich."

"How about this afternoon?" Abe asked, flipping through his pocket flight guide. "Is four o'clock okay?"

"Four will be fine."

"Why do you want my associate?"

"Because Ms. Rosen told us that she has been dealing with Mr. Aldrich on this matter."

On the way to the airport, Justin called Nancy on his cellular phone. "How come you told the prosecutor and not me?"

"Because I needed a few days' lead time. Let me tell you what we're up against. Is it safe to talk on this phone?"

"Yeah. We bought one of those cellulars with a security system—for just this reason. Go ahead."

"I reached my client Owens," Nancy continued, "and urged him to turn himself in."

"What did he say."

"He refused, as I thought he would."

"So? What did you do then?"

"I told Owens that I was mailing the prosecutor a letter that afternoon, disclosing that he was the killer, what his motive was, and what he had told me when he came to my office on the day

149

of the Williams shooting. He told me things that only the killer would know. I made a file memo."

"What did Owens say?"

"He went crazy. Threatened to kill me. Threatened to have me disbarred."

"What did you say?"

"I told him that I had made up my mind, and that I was calling to give him a day or two lead time to do what he had to do before the prosecutor got the letter."

"Oh, my God, Nancy, you told Owens to skip town?"

"Not in so many words. But that was the message."

"So what happened?"

"Owens skipped town. The prosecutor got my letter, looked for Owens, was told that he had left in a hurry the day before. No one can find him. I think I know where he may be."

"What did the prosecutor do?"

"You won't believe this, Justin. He threatened *me*, with obstruction of justice and disbarment."

"I do believe it. You really put your bar certificate at risk for Charlie."

"What else could I do? I have to save Odell. And I had to give my client a fighting chance. They wouldn't give him immunity, so I gave him a chance to give himself immunity by disappearing. Not perfect, but the best I could think of. Hell of a lot better than what that old lawyer did in the Leo Frank case. Your client is not going to die."

"Thanks, Nancy. I really owe you. If there's any trouble over this, you can count on me." And Justin anticipated that there certainly *could* be trouble for Nancy. Big trouble.

Abe and Justin arrived at the prosecutor's office on the fifth floor of the old courthouse a few minutes after four. Justin had briefed Abe about what Nancy had told him on the phone. It always bugged Abe that prosecutors were housed in the same building as the judges, while defense attorneys were relegated to offices a few blocks away. One look at the dreary gray walls and institutional furniture in the office quickly reminded Abe of why he preferred to be an outsider.

District Attorney Kevin Duncan was there with his chief assistant and a state trooper. He got right down to business.

"Let's be straight with one another, Mr. Ringel. You've got a guy on death row who you say is innocent. There is no way you can prove his innocence in court without Ms. Rosen's client, Owens. Rosen's own testimony would be hearsay and probably not admissible on lawyer-client privilege grounds. If you want to save Odell, you've got to help us find Owens."

"I have no problem with that," Abe replied. "I've got no responsibility to Owens. He's not my client. How can *I* help you find him? I don't know anything about him."

"Nancy Rosen does. She knows about his friends, his family, where he probably went. We have reason to believe that if Nancy Rosen wanted to help us find Owens, she could."

"So why don't you ask Nancy? What do you want from me?"

"We've asked Nancy, and she won't help us. Claims she knows nothing. We don't believe her."

"So what do you want me to do?"

"You can help us put pressure on her. We intend to indict Nancy Rosen for obstruction of justice, and we believe Mr. Aldrich could help us prove that Ms. Rosen advised her client to flee. We want Mr. Aldrich to testify against Nancy Rosen."

"No way I'm gonna testify against Nancy Rosen," Justin said.

"You've got no choice, Mr. Aldrich. Odell's on death row, and that's where he's staying unless you help us find Owens. The only chance we have of finding Owens is by squeezing Rosen's tit in a wringer. And, Mr. Aldrich, *you're* the wringer."

"You son of a bitch!" Abe jumped out of his chair as if he were about to attack Duncan. "You're holding Charlie Odell hostage against Nancy Rosen."

"That's your characterization, Mr. Ringel. I would put it differently. Mr. Aldrich has information that could help us prove that a local lawyer committed a felony—an ongoing felony, since Owens is still at large. *We* have an interest in finding Owens, and *your client* Odell has an interest in finding Owens. Can we work together? Or does the status quo remain?"

"By the status quo, you mean Odell dies."

"That *is* the status quo, Mr. Ringel."

"We'll think about it," Abe said, knowing that he couldn't ask Justin to help the prosecutor put his friend Nancy in prison. "You're scum, Duncan. You would actually allow a man you know is innocent to be executed if my young associate here doesn't testify against Nancy Rosen?"

A sardonic smile appeared on the prosecutor's lips. "I don't know that he is innocent. I only know that your friend Rosen claims that another man, who is conveniently missing, apparently admitted that *he* did it. We get these false confessions all the time, Mr. Ringel, especially in high-profile cases, you know that. And I don't even know for sure that Owens ever really admitted anything to Rosen."

"What about the stuff that only the real killer would know?"

"I don't know what you're talking about, Mr. Ringel. Information gets out. Rosen probably heard about it through the courthouse grapevine. Wouldn't be the first time."

"Duncan, you really are a worm."

"And one more thing, Mr. Ringel. I don't want you or Mr. Aldrich telling Nancy Rosen about my offer to you. If you do, she might decide to follow Owens into hiding, and then we would come after the two of *you* for obstruction of justice. You've got exactly three days to decide whether Odell dies or Rosen goes to jail. There is no third alternative. It's a tough choice. I hear you're both good at making tough choices. Mr. Ringel, Mr. Aldrich, have a nice day."

Chapter Nineteen

Haskel's condition was worsening every week. Now there were days of absolute silence. Abe would visit almost every morning on the way to his office and talk to his old mentor. Sometimes he would get no response at all. Other times he would see a smile, a frown, a tear, a twinkling of Haskel's deep old eyes. Abe wasn't even certain he was really seeing these responses. Maybe Haskel was reacting to his own inner dialogue rather than to Abe's soliloquy. On some days Haskel would speak, often in delphic terms, occasionally with long, rambling stories.

Today Abe sat at Haskel's side to ponder his response to the awful choice the New Jersey prosecutor had inflicted upon him and Justin. In recounting the meeting with Duncan, Abe characterized Charlie Odell as a hostage and the prosecutor as a tyrant. Suddenly Haskel began to speak, softly and indistinctly at first, but then in a singsong voice reminiscent of a young student learning the ancient Talmud. Abe listened carefully to every word.

"There was once a walled city in Roman-occupied Judea in which a thousand Jews lived peacefully. A Roman general laid siege to the city, and no food or water was allowed in. The tyrannical general sent a message to the elders of the city that they had two choices. Either they must turn over to the Romans one citizen of the city for execution or everyone in the city would die of starvation."

After telling the story, Haskel stopped and nodded off to sleep. Abe tried to arouse him, but to no avail. His visit was over. There would be another tomorrow. In the meantime, Abe had to figure out what Haskel meant by his cryptic story and whether it provided any guidance to him in the tough decision he now had only two days to make.

"Justin," Abe called out as he walked into the reception area of his office, "I need you to do an unusual bit of legal research this morning."

Justin bounded out of his office with that eager look only recent law school graduates seemed to have all of the time. "Sure, Abe. Library? Computer? What's the task today?"

"Neither," Abe responded. "Today you study one of the oldest legal documents in history."

"I love legal history, especially the old English dooms. What do you want me to look up?"

"This isn't English. It isn't even *in* English. I need you to look up something in the Talmud."

"The Talmud? They don't teach that stuff in law school, and I don't read Hebrew."

"Actually, it's in Aramaic, which was the everyday language of the Jews at the time the Talmud was compiled. It's a bit like the case reports that we read today. The Talmud records legal discussions among the leading rabbis during the third, fourth, and fifth centuries."

"Abe, don't you think we have enough on our plate without digging up ancient rabbinical decisions?"

"Haskel told me a story today. I think it comes from the Talmud. Maybe it has some answers that could help us in the Odell case."

"How can a fifteen-hundred-year-old discussion help us in the Odell decision?"

"Couldn't hurt," Abe replied, shrugging. "Got any better ideas?"

He recounted Haskel's story about the walled city and asked Justin to find out how the old rabbis had resolved the dispute over whether to sacrifice one innocent person in order to save an entire city. He told Justin to call around to various rabbinical seminaries to get a lead on the story and to find out if any English translations were available.

A few hours later Justin was back again. He had found the talmudic reference to which Haskel was referring, and it was as elusive as Haskel's story. The old rabbis had agreed that if the tyrant requested a specifically named hostage, he should be turned over and the city saved. However, if the tyrant requested just any hostage, none should be selected by the city elders for execution, even if that meant the destruction of the entire city and its inhabitants.

"There was a certain logic to their thinking," Justin explained. "If the tyrant picked the victim, it became the responsibility of the tyrant. If the elders decided, the burden would be on them."

"No wonder so many of us Jews become lawyers," Abe said. "These talmudic distinctions are even more difficult to figure out than the legal distinctions in the English common law. How does it help us with the Duncan decision?"

"Let me think about that a little more."

"Okay. But do it quickly. We have only two days to make our decision."

Chapter Twenty

When Abe arrived at his office for the morning confrontation with Joe Campbell, the athlete was already in Abe's inner office, pacing quickly back and forth in his designer sweat suit as if he were warming up for a game. He was, in fact, in the midst of the NBA playoffs. The Knicks had swept the Heat in the previous round and were awaiting the outcome of a closely contested series between the Pacers and the Bulls that would determine their next opponent.

"Well, Joe, you're here early. I thought ballplayers like to sleep late."

"Has it occurred to you that I'm anxious to get this bit behind me? I need to concentrate on earning a living."

"Yeah, except you have nothing to worry about. You're innocent, right, Joe?"

"You know that better than anybody."

"Do I?"

The question hung between them.

Abe took a file folder out of the old oak file cabinet adjoining his desk, riffled through the papers, and looked at Joe. "We've got a big problem that I've got to put to you directly."

156

"What do you mean *we*, Kemo Sabe?" Joe asked. "Only I have a problem, remember. You're not accused of anything."

At least not yet, Abe thought as he turned the conversation more confrontational. "I do have a problem, and my problem is you."

"What do you mean?"

"I don't think you've been leveling with me."

"I told you I was sorry, and that it wouldn't happen again. Can't we put that behind us and get on with my case?"

"I'm not talking about *that* lie," Abe said. "Justin and Rendi believe that your entire story of when you met Jennifer and found out about her harassment suit is a bald-faced lie."

Suddenly Joe Campbell's entire demeanor seemed to change. He was no longer the polite young man who had so impressed Abe at the Four Seasons. Now he was a trash-talking jock.

"What the fuck are you saying? How dare you? I told you that I would tell you the truth, and I expect you to believe me. I'm not paying you to sit here and insult me," Joe said angrily, starting to get up. "Every goddamned lawyer in the country would give their right testicle to be representing me. And you sit here and call me a liar. Fuck you."

Abe hated this part of the lawyer's job—looking your client straight in the eye and telling him that you question his entire story. They didn't teach you how to do it in law school, and there was no instructional manual among the volumes that lined Abe's office. A quarter century of experience had taught Abe how important this kind of confrontation could be in winning a case, especially when the client was lying but might still be innocent of the charges—a phenomenon more common than most outside observers might suspect.

Abe was prepared for Joe's reaction, and he responded in an even tone. "Please stop acting. I am actually trying to help you. I'm your doctor and I've just read your CAT scan and it shows me you have operable cancer. Do you want me to pretend you don't or do you want me to try to cure you?"

"What the hell does this have to do with CAT scans and cancer? You can't see a lie on a CAT scan."

"My staff and I look at the evidence, and the evidence shows our trained eyes—just like a CAT scan shows a doctor's trained eye—that you may not be telling us the truth. Why would you lie to us, Joe, if you're innocent?"

"Holy shit! Now you're telling me—my own goddamned, highly paid *defense* lawyer—that I'm *guilty*. Who appointed you prosecutor? Who appointed you *God?* I don't have to take this. I'll go down the block, I'll look in the Yellow Pages. Any kid out of law school could win this case, especially after what we've dug up on Jennifer."

"I'm not telling you that I think you're guilty. The truth is I still believe that you're probably innocent, though I'm not as sure as I used to be, and I don't think you've told me the truth about everything. I do have to tell you, though, that Justin and Rendi believe you're guilty. And they have found some troubling documentation that supports their view."

"What the hell are you talking about? What documentation? What about the facts concerning Jennifer?"

"Justin and Rendi think that you knew everything about Jennifer *before* you decided to go out with her. That's why you picked her. They believe it was a setup from the get-go, that you always pick women who have something in their past—a false accusation of rape or sexual harassment, something that will make it impossible for them to bring a successful rape charge. Are they right, Joe?"

Joe looked stunned. Then he muttered, "Well, Counselor, do *you* believe them?"

"I don't know. Justin has found some interesting stuff on the computer. Like the fact that you got the printout on Jennifer a few days before you went out with her. Also the computer request you made was for cases of false sexual allegations."

There was a look of total shock on Joe's face. It was clear that Joe Campbell had never before been confronted with this accusation. Abe could not tell whether the look was one of shocked guilt or shocked innocence. For the first time, Joe Campbell was speechless. Abe waited a beat and then continued. "You're not making it any easier. I need to find out who you really are."

This time Joe was not silent. "Who the hell do you think you are, Sherlock fucking Holmes? Cut the shit and get back to earth. You're a goddamned criminal lawyer. You work for me. Your job—your *only* job—is to get me off. Not to tell me I'm lying, and not to tell me your associate—whose hourly fee I'm paying—thinks I'm guilty because of some computer games he's playing with himself. It's all bullshit."

"Explain to me why it's bullshit, Joe. I'd love to be persuaded. Here, take a look." Abe handed Joe the folder with the computer printouts and explained Justin's theory of how they showed that the search had predated Joe's "chance" encounter with Jennifer. Joe studied the printouts carefully, his demeanor pensive.

"It's all rather complicated, Abe," he said, pointing to the Jennifer Dowling printout. "Actually, I did several searches. The first was for Jennifer Dowling. I did that search after I met her— like I told you. I don't know why there's no time notation. Maybe CompuLaw did that only for law firms. Maybe the last part of the printout was irrelevant so I threw it away. Maybe CompuLaw just screwed up. That kind of thing happens, you know."

"What about the more general search for all false sex complaints?"

"I did do that—right after I did the Dowling search and found out about her false complaint. I wanted to know more about why women make false complaints."

"Why did you want to know?"

"Intellectual curiosity, I guess—and I wanted to understand

Jennifer Dowling. I wanted to be sure she wasn't the kind of woman who might try to set me up."

"That's just what Justin thought—originally," Abe said. He was impressed by Joe's ability to come up so quickly with a plausible explanation.

"Justin was right—originally. Why did he change his mind?"

"Because there's more, Joe—even if you're telling the truth about the computer stuff."

"What?"

"Our investigator, Rendi Renaad, has come up with disturbing information about your sexual predilections from some of your groupie friends."

"You got *our* investigator to dig up dirt on me?" Joe asked, his demeanor once again belligerent. "Who the fuck do you think you are, the *National Enquirer?*"

"No, I'm your lawyer, and hard as this may be for you to believe, I'm trying to help you. She's found some pretty nasty stuff."

Joe paused, got up, and hovered above Abe, looking at him menacingly. Abe put his finger on the silent alarm he had installed several years earlier, after a woman client accused of murdering her abusive husband had attacked Abe during an emotional confrontation. He was about to press when Joe walked away, turned back, and said softly:

"Mr. Ringel, I have no choice but to insist that you fire Rendi and Justin. I want them off my case. They don't believe in me, and I don't want to pay for people to dig up dirt on me."

"I'm sorry, Joe. That's my call, not yours. If I'm in charge of your defense, I decide who works with me. I need them. And I need them to dig up everything on you. Better them than the prosecutor. Everything Justin and Rendi learn is confidential."

"I don't care. They're off my case."

"The only way they're off your case is if I'm off your case."

"Okay, if you insist. You're fired, too—effective immediately, along with your entire team. I will not be needing your services any longer. Send me your final bill."

Abe was prepared for that response. "I wish it were that easy, Joe, only it's not."

"What do you mean, it's not? I have an absolute right to fire you and your team, don't I?"

"Of course you have that right, but you may not want to exercise it."

"Why the hell not? You think I'm afraid of you?"

"That's not it," Abe answered him. "I promised you I would never disclose anything I learned about you as your lawyer, and I'm bound by that commitment. You have to understand how the system works. If you and I part company at this point—no matter how we put it for public consumption—it will send a clear message."

"Yeah, that you're a shyster and that I want to replace you with a real lawyer. No skin off my back, only some off yours. No big deal. You'll survive."

"That's not the message."

"Then what is it?"

Abe stood up and grabbed a law book from the shelf, quickly finding the page he wanted Joe to look at. "Since the Supreme Court's decision a couple of years back in a case called *Nix* versus *Whiteside*, there has been an epidemic of lawyers dropping out of cases on the eve of trial. And no matter how they try to explain it, everybody in the system knows what it means. Here, read this paragraph."

"Well, I'm not in the system, and I don't want to read any damn law books. You tell me what it says."

"It covers the situation where the lawyer believes his client is planning to lie on the witness stand. If a lawyer knows that, he either has to drop out of the case or blow the whistle on his client, and no lawyer can survive with a reputation as a whistleblower, so they take the easy way out."

"What's the easy way out?"

"They quit, or more likely they arrange to be fired. Every judge, every prosecutor, every journalist, every court watcher, knows what it means. Firing me at this juncture would be like taking out a full-page ad in the Sunday *New York Times* confessing your guilt. Do you want to do that?"

"Goddamn it. You win."

"This isn't about winning. At least, not against you," Abe said. "Part of me wishes you would fire us without shooting yourself in the foot. You can't, and I can't quit, because I would be screwing you if I did. So now *I* have a problem, Kemo Sabe. My problem is that I know too much for both our good. I still suspect, despite your explanation, that you may have used your computer to find out about Jennifer *before* you met her. I don't know why. And I don't know whether you raped her. My gut still tells me you didn't, but not because of anything *you've* told me. It's because Jennifer Dowling's story is so weak. I have difficulty believing anything you tell me. And I also know that whether you're innocent, guilty, or somewhere in between, it will still be difficult for the state to convict you because you're a great con artist."

"Well, at least I'm glad to hear that you think it will be difficult to convict me," Campbell said, looking out the window. "If you're gonna stay being my lawyer, I want you to do everything in your power to make sure it stays difficult—no matter what you may think of me or what your damn assistants believe."

"I'll do everything the law allows me to do, but I'm not doing anything improper for you or anyone else," Abe responded.

"What does that mean? What exactly *won't* you do for me?"

"I can't allow you to lie on the witness stand."

"Hold your horses, Counselor. I'm gonna make your life easy. I'm a reasonable guy. I understand your problem, and I'm

162

going to solve it." Campbell looked Abe solemnly in the eye. "I swear to you that I won't lie on the witness stand."

The athlete had gained control over himself. Suddenly he looked sincere. This guy is a trip, Abe thought as he imagined Campbell using this same show of sincerity in his countless seduction routines. Was there anything that threw him out of control? Maybe that was the key. Campbell never lost control. That could be hell on anyone's sex life.

Joe was now talking quietly, though there was velocity behind his words. "One thing is not negotiable."

"What's that?"

"If I decide that I want to testify, I'm damn well going to testify. I'm not going to lose this case—and my freedom and career—because my own lawyer doesn't believe me. I'm telling you right now, I'm innocent and I'll testify truthfully."

Abe started to get angry. "Who do you think I am? Some dumb groupie who will fall for that show of sincerity? I have a friend in Hollywood who always tells me that 'sincerity is the essence of good acting; if you can fake that, you can fake anything.' Who do you think you're conning here? You want me to feel good because you've looked me straight in the eye and lied to me?"

"No, I really mean it," Campbell said. "This whole situation has been hell for me, and I'm beginning to realize that I do have a problem. There is something sick about looking up the secret backgrounds of women I'm dating. I'm going to go to some shrink."

"You're right again." Abe shrugged. "At least legally. If you tell me that you're going to testify truthfully, I am legally bound to accept that, since I can't know *for sure* that you're lying. I don't have a crystal ball. After all, some defendants whose lawyers think they're lying tell the truth. *Personally,* I'm not sure whether I believe you. *Legally,* I have to believe you, because I have no hard proof to the contrary. I don't know how I'm going to deal with the conflict."

"Is that supposed to be some kind of a threat?"

"No, it's just a human being talking to himself as a human being. As a lawyer, I'm satisfied with what you've told me. I have to be, despite my doubts. As your lawyer, I am required to err on the side of believing you."

"That sounds very schizoid."

"Maybe, but some of us are human beings as well as professionals. And every so often there's a conflict between those personas. It's not your problem. It's mine. *You're* my problem."

"Where does that leave me?" Campbell asked.

"With a lawyer who believes you may be lying, and who isn't sure whether you're innocent or guilty, but who has to try to prevent the prosecution from proving that you're lying and guilty. I hate being in that position. But that's *my* problem."

"As long as it doesn't become *my* problem," Campbell replied. "I mean what I say about my right to testify."

There was a menacing look on his face as Abe showed him to the door. Abe couldn't worry about that now. He had to worry about how to defend his client without losing his bar certificate—or his soul.

PART II

A Jury of
His Peers

Chapter Twenty-one

Although one part of Abe wished that Campbell could have fired him, another part wanted desperately to continue on as Campbell's trial lawyer. Like every lawyer, Abe dreamed about that one great legal victory that would propel him into the casebooks that law students read and the popular TV talk shows that everyone watched. Few lawyers achieved that dream, but those who did—Abe thought to himself—had it made for life. They would always be known as "the lawyer who won the 'X' case." F. Lee Bailey would always be known as the lawyer who won the Sheppard case; Howard Weitzman as the lawyer who won the De Lorean case; William Kunstler as the lawyer who won the Chicago 7 case; Roy Black as the lawyer who won the William Kennedy Smith case. And a part of Abe Ringel wanted to be known as the lawyer who won the Campbell case.

Abe Ringel was already well-known around Boston and among his professional colleagues. He hoped a victory in the Campbell case would propel him into that small circle of lawyers whose names were immediately recognized around the country. Abe smelled that victory, and he resented the complications Justin and Rendi had uncovered.

This was also the part of him that Abe Ringel was most

167

ashamed of. He never discussed his ambitious side with Haskel. Haskel wouldn't have understood, and he certainly wouldn't have approved. To Haskel, the law was not a business or an entertainment. It was a high calling, a learned occupation, an honorable profession. Haskel hated self-promotion, lawyer advertising, public relations, and everything else that went along with the new trend toward lawyers as moneymakers and headline grabbers. "A lawyer's only advertisement should be the quality of his legal work," Haskel had always taught his skeptical students.

Abe wanted to believe in Haskel's approach to the practice of law, yet he couldn't always live by those principles. Abe rationalized his frequent appearances on radio and television by telling himself that Haskel's way was right for Haskel's era, but that the increasing competitiveness of law practice and the increasing use of the media by ambitious prosecutors had made Haskel's way anachronistic for today's lawyers.

In Haskel's times a lawyer was respected for his integrity, for his ability to be counsel to the situation, for resolving conflicts. Sure, winning was important, even back then, only it wasn't everything. Today, with lawyers advertising their wares like cereal or dog food, winning had become paramount. Lawyers, like athletes, were judged by their won-and-lost record, by the amount of media coverage they received, by their latest high-profile victory.

Rudy Giuliani was the perfect example. He had catapulted media coverage of his prosecuting years into the job of New York City mayor. If Rudy had followed Haskel's advice, where would he be now?

Yet a part of Abe yearned for the bygone era in which Haskel was able to emerge as the greatest and most respected lawyer in Boston without ever seeing the inside of a television or radio studio. "I never comment about a legal matter outside the courtroom," Haskel would always say in response to media requests. And he always abided by his beliefs.

There was, of course, another side—a better side—to Abe. He had done more than his share of pro bono work for obscure defendants who had no real shot at winning. And why? Not for glory or fame or money—but just because he believed in the adversarial system of justice, under which every defendant was entitled to the best defense. He knew that using the media to level the playing field was part of that system. Yet he also knew that it fed his personal ambitions as well. "The adversarial system," Haskel had taught his students, "is the worst possible system of justice—except for all the others." Haskel understood how easily the system could be abused by unscrupulous and ambitious lawyers, yet how essential it was to the survival of liberty. He never had any difficulty striking the appropriate balance. For Abe it was always a struggle.

Even though Abe was embarrassed about his ambitious side, he needed to discuss his present dilemma with Haskel. As usual, Jerome let him in, and as usual, Haskel was seated at his desk. Rather, he was dozing at his desk. How sorry he looked and how sad. Abe decided to let the old man snooze while he soaked up the atmosphere of Haskel's quiet study. His eyes focused on a black-and-white photo from Haskel's wedding to Estelle. The bride was slightly taller than the groom, so that she seemed to dominate her husband. The young Haskel had his hand on her shoulder. He was dressed in a black morning coat, his tallis peeking out from beneath his jacket.

"I'll tell you a secret."

Abe jumped. Haskel had startled him.

"I had to stand on a box for that. I was a head shorter than Estelle, at least. Did you ever notice?"

Abe smiled, shook his head. "How do you feel today?"

"Well enough. Have you come to babble at me or will you let me take part in the dialogue for a change?"

"I don't babble, Haskel. Sometimes I just don't want to disturb you."

"So you talk to yourself and pretend it's me?"

"Something like that."

"So talk."

"Wait a minute. Do you mean all this time you heard me talking to you and just pretended to be, well, you know, out of it?"

"No, when I'm out of it, I'm gone. I don't know where I go. Sometimes I let you blabber so I can sleep." Haskel's impish grin made him appear for one instant to be the young groom of the faded old photograph.

Abe ran down the entire scenario for Haskel, who up till now had only heard bits and pieces of the Campbell situation. He did not tell Haskel that he had already decided to remain on the case, because he wanted Haskel to believe he was really seeking advice on what to do.

Haskel seemed to sense that Abe had reached a decision, but he mistakenly assumed that Abe had decided to abandon Campbell to protect his own career. He pointed a finger at Abe, almost pedantically, as if he were back in the classroom, admonishing a student who was about to make a mistake. "Can one abandon a client upon learning unpleasant facts?" Haskel asked. "Is that not when the client needs you most?" Then, diverging from his usual approach, Haskel gave Abe direct advice. "You cannot leave the case now, because if you do, the world will perceive a message from your leaving. And it is a message you have a sacred obligation not to send.

"Moreover," Haskel continued, "it is always possible that Justin and Rendi may be wrong. The client may yet be innocent in spite of the unpleasant facts. The great talmudic commentator Rashi wrote that a magistrate who had changed his mind about a defendant's innocence must 'search out every possibility, on the minuscule chance that perhaps his original judgment was correct and the accused really is innocent.' "

That part was easy for Abe. What bedeviled him was his realization that he was remaining on the case as much for his own self-aggrandizement as for his ethical obligation to Campbell. He wondered whether he would stay on if the case involved some poor schnook named Jones who was certain to be convicted rather than a rich superstar named Campbell. Might he not have found an ethical loophole through which to crawl out? Might he not be more easily convinced by Justin's and Rendi's evidence? He thought he knew the answer. Yet he wasn't absolutely sure. What he was sure about was that now he had to believe in Campbell's innocence, and he wanted to win, badly. Maybe so badly that it was clouding his judgment.

"Leave now, Abraham. I'm tired, and soon I'll probably be raving. How bad do I look when I slip out of this dimension, can you tell me?"

"You look like you," Abe lied.

"When I die, Abraham, will you make sure they bury me with my glasses? Jerome is too flighty, and I'm afraid that by the time the undertaker gets here, with all the commotion, I'll be separated from my glasses."

"Of course I will, Haskel." Abe turned to go.

"Thank you, Abraham."

"For what?"

"For not asking me why on earth I would want to be buried in glasses."

"I think I know."

"Do you know me so well?"

"I know myself. I would be afraid I'd get bored and not be able to read."

Abe could hear the music of Haskel's laughter all the way down the front stoop and into the street.

Chapter Twenty-two

It was now only ten days before Charlie Odell's scheduled execution, and this was the day Abe had to tell Duncan, the New Jersey prosecutor, whether Justin would testify against Nancy Rosen. Abe had tried everything—from the Supreme Court, to the governor, to *Nightline*. Nothing had worked. The prosecutor had persisted in his claim that Odell was the killer and that Abe, Justin, and Nancy had contrived a phony story about a fugitive who would never be caught.

"If Nancy Rosen is telling the truth," Duncan had responded on *Nightline*, "then let her tell us where the real murderer is so we can catch him and hear a confession from his own mouth."

Nancy remained unwilling to tell the prosecution anything about her client's whereabouts. The prosecution was prepared, however, to stop the execution if Justin would testify against Nancy. "At least that would show that you're not in a conspiracy together," Duncan said to Abe. "And if she goes to jail, she'll tell us where Owens is—eventually."

It boiled down to Justin and Abe having to choose between sacrificing Nancy's career or saving Charlie's life. There were no other options, and time had run out. If Justin were to testify

172

against Nancy, it would still take a couple of days to work out the mechanics of halting Odell's execution. It was now or never. Abe and Justin had to make the tough decision.

"Abe, this is one decision you've got to make for me," Justin said. "I'm just too emotionally involved. I'm too close to Nancy. I know what I want to do. I just don't know what I should do."

"You've really got no choice but to testify against Nancy. I know you're Nancy's friend. You're also Charlie Odell's lawyer. And Charlie's innocent life is on the line." Abe thought of Haskel's talmudic story about the Roman general who demanded that one person be handed over for execution or the entire city would perish. "Duncan wants Nancy in particular, and for good reason. After all, she *is* guilty of alerting her client and encouraging him to escape. Odell, on the other hand, is innocent."

"I know you're right, Abe, only that doesn't make me feel any better about it."

Abe phoned Duncan. "You will have your pound of flesh," he said.

"Have Mr. Aldrich in Newark tomorrow, nine A.M., in front of the grand jury," Duncan ordered. "And if Ms. Rosen finds out, the deal is off. He testifies at nine. We have an indictment by ten. Ms. Rosen is arrested by eleven. With any luck we'll have Owens in custody by the close of business."

"The deal is as soon as Justin testifies, Odell walks— whether you find Owens or not."

"That's right. As long as you don't tip Rosen so that she can join Owens."

"Don't worry," Abe said. "You've got me over a barrel."

"That's exactly where I want you. Tomorrow, nine A.M."

The morning went as planned. Justin testified that Nancy Rosen had told him she'd given Owens advance warning so that he could skip town. Nancy was arrested, and Odell's case was dismissed on the motion of district attorney Kevin Duncan, who announced that a nationwide manhunt was under way for the real killer.

Late that afternoon Charlie Odell was transferred from death row to the state mental hospital, where he would stay for several weeks before being released. Abe and Justin were there to meet him. After tearful thank-yous from Odell, Justin was off to the Newark jail to visit Nancy.

It was ironic, Justin thought, that he had helped save the life of a career criminal—even one who was innocent of *this* crime—by destroying the life of a career do-gooder—even one who may have violated the law *this* once. In the Newark Women's House of Detention he went through the familiar routine. Nancy was brought to the visitors room, wearing her blue prison garb. If anyone could look dignified in a convict's outfit, it was Nancy. Once seated, they picked up their prison telephones and spoke through the Plexiglas.

"I'm so sorry, Nancy. I had no choice."

"I know. I knew it would probably end this way when I sent my letter."

"You're going to be convicted and probably disbarred—and I'm the government's star witness. I feel awful."

"If it makes you feel any better, Justin, I would have testified against you if our situations had been reversed. You did the right thing."

"But *you're* paying the price."

"Look, Justin, I never thought I'd last this long in the profession. I'm a radical, a revolutionary. I knew that someday I'd have to choose between my bar certificate and my conscience.

And this is a hell of an exit. How many lawyers can have their professional tombstone read 'She saved an innocent life'?"

"You realize that you're going to be sentenced to prison."

"That's where a radical belongs. I'm going to be one hell of a jailhouse lawyer."

"Nancy, I'm not going to rest until we get you out of here and your bar certificate returned."

"First you've got to help Duncan put me in and take it away."

"Don't I know it. That's the last position I ever expected to find myself in: helping an SOB prosecutor put my friend in prison for doing the right thing. I feel like an absolute shit. You're a real heroine. I wish we could change places, like Darnay and Carton in *A Tale of Two Cities*."

"This is not a tale," Nancy replied as her eyes filled with tears.

Chapter Twenty-three

This was a busy time for Justin. In addition to his unwelcome role in the Odell case, the young man had been put in charge of researching the ethical limits of exactly what a lawyer could do in defense of a client who had lied to him. It was a murky area with only a few clear signposts.

Today, a Sunday, was being devoted to this issue. Abe and Justin were anticipating a full day of work. Emma had been ticked off, Abe knew, because she had wanted to lasso him into going to the artsy cinema house she loved so much, and he hated putting her off. He felt guilty. Did all fathers feel this way, he wondered, or just the ones who were bringing up their kids alone? Oh, well, he'd make it up to her later—somehow.

"If Moses came down from Mount Sinai with a list of commandments for lawyers defending clients they thought were guilty," Justin joked, "he wouldn't have needed two tablets."

"How so?" Abe asked him.

"There aren't more than a handful of rules. The problem is every one of them is riddled with exceptions, loopholes, and uncertainty."

"Give me a for-instance," Abe said, using a phrase his fa-

176

ther had loved. (And to which his mother would always respond, "A for-instance is not an argument.")

Justin thought a moment. "A lawyer can't knowingly mislead the judge. As an officer of the court, he owes the judge an obligation of candor."

"Okay. That's the first commandment. It seems all too clear."

"It's not," Justin replied. "You can certainly plead your client '*not* guilty,' even if you know he *is* guilty."

"Yeah, but that's just a formal plea. Nobody is misled by that. A plea of 'not guilty' means that you are demanding a trial, not that you *believe* your client didn't do it."

"In other words, it's a legal fiction, like so much else in the law," Justin said. "Okay. I'll give you that one. How about cross-examining a witness you *know* is telling the truth and trying to make her out to be a liar? Can you do that to Jennifer Dowling in this case?"

"You bet I can, and I will, because she *is* a liar. She lied to the police about a whole bunch of stuff."

"That's a cop-out, Abe," Justin insisted, "because *we know*—but the judge and jury don't know—that Jennifer is telling the truth about the ultimate issue: that Campbell raped her."

"I don't *know* any such thing, and neither do you. In any event, that's for the jury to decide."

"Sure it is, but you're deliberately trying to mislead them into deciding it falsely."

"Look, I don't make the rules. Nobody says I can't cross-examine a witness who I may suspect is telling the truth. In fact, I'm *obligated* to, under the rules."

"In other words, you just follow orders—like the psychiatrist in New Jersey."

"Cheap shot, Justin. These are good rules."

"Well, maybe, and yet there's no question that they often lead to bad results. They create confusion and uncertainty because they're so unclear."

"Why the hell do you think they're so unclear?" Abe felt like banging his fist on the desk, but he settled for shouting. "It's because most of the bar association honchos who wrote them don't know the first thing about real life. And because those who do, don't want to confront the tough issues."

"Calm down, Abe. You asked me for the rules, and I'm telling you there's not much there, except for the one pretty clear one."

"Which one is that?"

"You can't call Campbell as a witness if you *know* he's going to lie about *anything*—that's clear."

"Really? Is the word *know* all that clear? Do *we* really 'know' what you suspect about Campbell?"

"No," Justin admitted. "We don't know for sure. You *choose* not to know for sure. Listen, you're absolutely correct that the word *know* is the lawyer's out—the fudge word. Even some of the Supreme Court justices recognize that. I guess it's up to each lawyer's conscience as to whether he 'knows.' What does your conscience say, Abe?"

"Hey, wiseguy, I haven't checked lately. I only do that as a last resort, and I haven't reached that point yet."

"You will soon."

"I'm not so sure. What if I call him and limit his direct examination so that he doesn't get close to any possible lies?"

"How can you possibly do that?"

"I didn't say I could. But what if? What if I just ask him about the events leading directly up to the rape? I don't ask him how he first met her, and I stop before I get to the ultimate act."

"How could you do that without the jury knowing that you're trying to pull the wool over their eyes?"

"I don't know, but let's think it through before we abandon that possibility."

Abe loved this part of his work: the one-on-one exchange with his bright young protégé. The effort to outthink and outmaneuver his opponent. The attempt to fit a winning tactic into an acceptable ethic—to use his brain to avoid his conscience.

"Okay, let's run through it," he told Justin. "You be Campbell and I'll put you through my direct examination. Let's see if it works. You've gotta testify truthfully, without volunteering anything, okay?"

"Okay, shoot."

Abe stood up and gave his best imitation of himself examining his client. He walked Justin through the New York meeting, careful not to ask any question that would require the defendant to disclose that it wasn't a chance encounter:

"Describe how you and Ms. Dowling began to converse on March 10."

"Tell the jury, please, how you came to agree to meet in Boston the following week."

"How did you end up in her hotel room?"

The questions were all carefully crafted to elicit only the truth—yet as both Abe and Justin knew, it might only be a partial truth. However, it was enough to satisfy the ethical responsibility of the lawyers.

Abe continued to elicit "the truth" as he led Justin through the early evening of March 15 and into the hotel room. Here he had to be very careful.

"Did there come a time when Ms. Dowling excused herself and went into the bathroom?"

"Did she tell you why she was going?"

At this point Justin stepped out of his role. "Abe, you're getting me to tell *some* truth, not the whole truth."

"Hey, that's my job. One of the most important functions an advocate performs is to separate the part of the truth that helps the client from the part that hurts."

"And to withhold the part that hurts," Justin asked rhetorically, "even if without it you get a half-truth?"

"Exactly. Any criminal lawyer who disclosed the 'whole truth,' if it hurt his client, wouldn't be practicing long."

"Sounds better in theory than it feels in practice," Justin groaned as Abe resumed his role.

"Did she say or do anything to you that led you to believe she wanted to become sexually intimate with you?"

"Please tell the jury what she said and did."

"Did you understand that to constitute consent?"

"No further questions!"

It was a masterful job of taking the witness to the edge—the legal equivalent of sexual foreplay. Let the jury *infer* what happened next, and let it also infer that Abe did not ask any more questions in order to spare everyone in the courtroom the indelicacy of a clinical description of intimate sexual acts.

"Great job, Abe," Justin acknowledged. "You got me to tell the truth—or at least not to lie—and still convey the impression that it was consensual. However, you've only *postponed* the inevitable ethical crisis."

"How so?"

"I'll show you. Now *you* be Campbell and I'll be Puccio."

"Go ahead."

Justin gave his version of the prosecutor's stare at the mock defendant: "Mr. Campbell. Your very fine attorney has taken you up to the point of intercourse. Now I'd like to ask you some questions about the act itself. It is a fact, is it not, Mr. Campbell, that just before the act of intercourse, Ms. Dowling withdrew her prior consent and told you to stop?"

Abe tried his best Oliver North face: "No, sir, that is not a fact. She was more anxious than ever for me to enter her. In fact, she pleaded with me to enter her as quickly as possible."

"Wait a minute, time out!" Justin shouted, making a "T" with his hands. "You're breaking our rule. You just had Campbell lie through his teeth. If he did that in real life, you would be obliged to stand up and tell the judge that he was lying."

"No, I wouldn't. You think he's lying. *I* don't—at least not with any certainty."

"Okay then, I'll ask another question: 'Is it not a fact that

180

you picked Jennifer Dowling to go out with because you knew that she had lost a sexual harassment case?' "

"No, I wasn't aware of that until after we made love."

"Stop, Abe. You know that's a lie."

"Yes, I do, now show me a rule that says I have to correct a lie that is elicited *by the prosecution* on cross-examination."

"Right here," Justin said, opening a thick volume to the Supreme Court decision to the *Nix* v. *Whiteside* case. "It says in black and white that a lawyer may not assist his client in committing perjury or elicit an answer he knows to be false."

"Now, Justin, think for a minute. Did *I*—the defense attorney—*elicit* that false answer from Campbell? Or was it *you,* the prosecutor, who elicited the false answer on cross-examination?"

"So, what's the difference?"

"Everything," Abe said emphatically. "It makes all the difference in the world that it is the prosecutor who is eliciting an answer which *he* doesn't know is false. I'm not responsible."

"That's just plain sophistry," Justin replied.

"Those sophists were great lawyers," Abe said. "All of law is sophistry. On these kinds of distinctions are civilized societies built."

"It's a bullshit distinction, Abe, and you know it."

"I know it. You know it. Yet the law doesn't explicitly forbid it. And what the law doesn't forbid, it permits. And what the law doesn't forbid a defense attorney to do to help his client, it *requires* him to do."

"So you think that the law permits or even requires you to put Campbell on the stand so long as *you* don't knowingly elicit false answers on direct examination, even though you believe that the *prosecutor* will elicit false answers from him on cross-examination?"

"Yes, if it would help Campbell win. That's what I think unless and until you can show me otherwise."

"It's a cop-out, Abe. Even if you don't believe Joe's guilty.

You know—I mean really know—that he lied to you about how he used his computer, and that he has a history of kinky sex."

"I'm not going to ask him about that, and the prosecutor doesn't know about the computer stuff, and even if she were to find out about his history, she can't use it."

"So you're taking advantage of the prosecutor's limitations?"

"Of course I am, and there's nothing wrong with that."

"Depends on how you define wrong."

"Now, Justin, please write a memo to the file summarizing our little discussion."

"One cover-your-ass memo coming up."

"Enough. Let's get Campbell in here to prepare him in case he has to testify. This is going to be a tiptoe through the bird droppings."

"No sweats today, Joe," Abe said over the telephone. "When you come to my office, you should wear a conservative suit or a blue blazer. Like you will wear in court. I want to approve each of your court outfits."

"So this is the dress rehearsal, costumes and all."

Normally Abe laughed when a client tried to ease the tension with humor, but he was beginning to distance himself emotionally from his client. He realized, of course, that while in the courtroom or the courthouse corridors, he would have to be chummy. That was a big part of a criminal defense lawyer's job—pretending to like the client.

And some lawyers pretended better than others. When Mike Tyson's trial lawyer, Vince Fuller, distanced himself physically from the former champ, the media and the jurors picked up on it. At the other extreme, John Gotti's lawyer, Bruce Cutler, always went out of his way to embrace his client. Abe Ringel generally took a middle position with his clients, whether he really liked them or not—patting them on the back affectionately, but not intimately.

There was no need for Abe to pretend in the privacy of his own office on that Sunday afternoon. No one except Justin and Rendi would be there. Only when Emma came by to join them for dinner did he have to put on something of a show. Emma was totally unaware of any of the negative information Rendi and Justin had turned up about Campbell. As far as she was concerned, Joe was still Mr. Nice Guy, and Abe could not tell her otherwise. The constraints of confidentiality did not permit disclosure to a seventeen-year-old with a boyfriend who lived and died for the Knicks star.

Campbell flew up from New York on the noon shuttle. He only had a few hours, since the Knicks were leaving for the next round of the playoffs that night, and he had to be back at La Guardia by eight P.M.

At one-thirty Campbell sauntered into the office, where Abe awaited him along with Justin and Rendi. Abe figured having the whole legal team there might lend an air of formality to the meeting. It was time Campbell started to take his situation seriously.

Unfortunately, his mode of dress made it plain that he had not gotten the message. He was sporting a casual light brown cashmere jacket, a dark brown shirt, a bright pink tie knotted loosely, rust pants, and brown Mephisto shoes. His expensive cologne seemed to match his outfit.

Abe took one look and shook his head. "You're not trying to *seduce* the jurors. You're trying to *convince* them. None of those glamour boy clothes. I want something conservative. You're dressed for sex, Campbell, not for court."

"I'm sorry, Abe, this is about as conservative as I've got. I wore this to Reggie Lewis's funeral."

Abe noted that Campbell's demeanor had toned down a bit since their confrontation, as though the athlete wanted to smooth things over between them. "Then go out and buy something more conservative," he said, "unless you want the trial to be *your* funeral. Go to Brooks Brothers or Saks. I want a white button-down shirt, dark suit, blue tie, muted colors. You're not a Benetton ad. I want you to look like a choir boy, understand?"

"Yeah, I understand. I'm getting clothing advice from the man who was voted the worst-dressed lawyer in Boston for three years running."

Abe had to force a smile. He paid scant attention to his wardrobe, which consisted primarily of old-fashioned, loose-fitting, rumpled suits and a few birthday sweaters he had received from Emma and Rendi. "When I win a case," he said, "everyone knows it wasn't the clothes. In any event, I'm not the one on trial. You are."

"I thought you were so big on the truth. Yet you're telling me to wear a lie, aren't you?"

"You don't dress under oath," Abe replied, thinking back to one of his first draft card–burning cases in which he'd represented a long-haired hippie. Abe had insisted that the hippie shave before the sentencing, but the client had refused. Abe had warned him that his defiant attitude could cost him several extra months in jail. When the sentencing judge had seen the defendant's long hair, he'd smiled and said: "Finally, an honest defendant who didn't get a haircut just to impress the judge. How refreshing! I'm going to take six months off your sentence for your honesty." Since that case, Abe had often been hesitant to second-guess judges and juries on matters of dress and appearance. This time, however, he was sure.

Rendi wasn't. "Wait a minute, Abe. Let's think this through. Would it be so bad if some of the women jurors saw exactly how sexy Campbell really looked in his seduction outfit? After all, he's not on trial for seducing Jennifer Dowling. He's on trial for raping her."

"You're thinking like a woman, not like a lawyer," Justin said.

"Maybe that's exactly what we need," Abe responded. "Rendi, do you really think that women jurors want to be seduced by a defendant?"

"No, what they want is to be able to determine for themselves whether the alleged victim could have been seduced."

"Rendi may have a point," Abe said. "A friend of mine who specializes in rape cases tells me that it's a lot easier to win when the defendant is good-looking than when he's ugly. Jurors have a hard time believing any woman actually consented to have sex with a really ugly guy."

"I still think Campbell should dress for the courtroom and not the barroom," Justin said. "It sends a message of arrogance when a defendant dresses too casually. Court is a serious place."

Campbell had been watching the verbal volleys like a spectator at a tennis match. Now he spoke. "Okay, I'm convinced. No rust pants, all right? I get your drift. I'll dress conservative, but with an attitude. I'll be seductive, but not obvious. Does that satisfy everyone?"

Abe, Rendi, and Justin nodded in agreement.

"Okay, now that we've got that settled," Abe said, "the next subject is your size."

"I'm a forty-four extra-large. Why? Are you gonna buy me a jacket?"

"I'm not talking about your jacket size," Abe said, looking directly at Campbell. "I'm talking about your penis size."

"What the hell are you talking about? Have you gone crazy? You want to talk about the size of my dick?"

"Look, if you feel more comfortable talking about this with Rendi out of the room, I'm sure she would understand."

"I'd feel *more* comfortable," Campbell said, glancing at Rendi, who was having difficulty keeping a professional poker face, "discussing my dick size with *Rendi* rather than with *you*. It's none of your goddamned business. And it would only make you jealous, anyhow." He shot a triumphant look at Rendi, who smiled politely.

"Am I to take that remark as confirmation that your penis *is* unusually large?" Abe asked. Without waiting for an answer, he continued, "Your penis *is* my business, because your penis caused a vaginal abrasion in Ms. Dowling that can be explained in only two ways: rape or consensual sex with a man who has an unusually large penis. Which is it?"

"All right, if you insist. I've got a big dick. I'm a big guy. Big guys have big dicks."

"Not all of them," Rendi chimed in. "I've done research in the medical journals on this issue."

"*I've* got a big dick," Campbell insisted. "And so do most of my teammates."

"All right, enough of this," Abe said. "I only raised the issue to decide whether to have you examined by a doctor, who could take actual measurements. I didn't want you going to any doctor if you had a small penis, because the prosecution would have access to the medical reports. Now I can set up an appointment with Dr. Costello at Mass. General."

"No doctor is gonna measure my dick."

"Why not?" Rendi asked playfully. "Afraid you won't measure up?"

"Cut it out, Rendi," Abe said, though he understood her reason for joking. As the only woman in the room, she was setting the comfort level. "This is serious stuff. Look, Joe, you have no choice. If we don't produce specific medical evidence of your penis size, the prosecution will make medical hay out of the abrasion. We need equally solid medical evidence from you."

"Speaking of solid," Campbell said, "does the doctor have to give me an erection before he measures me? After all, I did have an erection when I bruised her. How the hell is he gonna give me an erection? Are they gonna use a pretty nurse?"

"I have no idea," Abe responded. "They know how to do those things. Please spare me the details. Just agree to see Dr. Costello."

"No way. I won't do it. I don't have to do it."

"Yes, you do—if you want to win."

"No, I don't. Can't you just argue to the jury that since I'm such a big guy I *must* have a large penis and then let them surmise the rest?"

"I guess I could, except it wouldn't be nearly as effective as medical testimony about your specific size."

"It would depend—wouldn't it—on whether the actual size was bigger or smaller than what the jury would surmise from your brilliant advocacy?" Campbell smirked as he realized he was beating Abe at his own game.

"Are you trying to tell us something?"

"Why don't we just leave it at that. I'm gonna refuse to submit to an exam. You're gonna point to my height and suggest to the jury that my dick is proportional to the rest of my body. And the jury is gonna believe what it wants to believe. Now can we *please* turn to a more comfortable subject?"

"Okay, if you insist." Despite his misgivings, Abe had to concede that he was impressed with Campbell's ability to grasp the subtleties of legal maneuverings. "Let's move on to your testimony."

"I'm testifying. It's that simple."

"I wish it were that simple, only it's not, because you lied to us, and if you lie to the jury, we have to tell the judge, and I just can't take that chance."

"No problem. I won't lie to the jury."

"That's correct. If you do testify, you're going to do it our way."

Abe then explained his contingency plan—he, Abe, would not ask how Joe came to meet Jennifer or about the sex itself. He would stop at the point where Jennifer consented.

"You're selling me down the fucking river to protect your own ass," Campbell responded angrily. "The jury will see right through you. They'll scratch their heads and wonder why you didn't ask me the sixty-four-thousand-dollar questions."

"Well, I can't ask you the sixty-four-thousand-dollar questions, because I'm afraid you may give perjured answers."

"I don't give a flying fuck what you're afraid of. I'm afraid of going to prison. Your ass is no more valuable than mine, and I'm *paying* you to protect mine. I told you I'm going to tell the truth, and *that's* the truth."

"I'm sorry, Joe, I just don't feel comfortable asking you questions that I suspect you're going to answer falsely."

"The prosecutor is sure as hell gonna ask me. And I'm gonna give her the same answer I would give you."

"She doesn't *know* that the answer is false. She just *thinks* it's false. In any event, that's *her* problem, not mine. And you're not her client. You're her adversary. The rules are different."

"God, what a bullshit profession law is. These rules don't make sense to anyone but a lawyer."

"They're no sillier than the 'illegal defense' rules in the NBA. Every profession has its own silly rules. I've gotta live by mine, just like you've gotta live by yours. If you violate the illegal defense rules, you get a technical foul. If I ask you a question that I know you'll answer falsely, I get a technical."

"So take the technical. That's part of the game. Coach Riley tells us that drawing a technical at the right time can be a great move."

"The difference is if you get a technical, your opponent gets one point. A technical in law means I'm out of the game—for good. No way I'm putting my license on the line for you."

"Well, there's no way I'm putting my ass on the line for your license."

"In life you have to make compromises. I think this compromise would work—if we ever have to use it."

"I don't compromise when my life's on the line. How about if I just blurt it out in answer to another question? Say you ask me, 'Did she say she wanted to have sex with you?' And instead of me just saying, 'Yes, she did,' I add, 'And then we had sex, and it was entirely consensual.' "

"Not good enough. I might still have to stand up and tell the judge what I know, since it was in response to *my* question."

Campbell shook his head. "It's just such bullshit, such bullshit."

"You can call it bullshit if you like. For me it's the law, and I've got no choice but to follow it."

"We'll see," Campbell said mysteriously. "We'll see."

They might have gone on longer except that Emma entered Abe's office. She looked especially pretty, as if she had dressed up to meet Daddy's star client. Surprised at how quickly the afternoon had gone, Abe rose, signaling the meeting was over.

"Hello, there, little miss—or I should say 'ms.'?"

Campbell had stood to greet Emma, and at his full height Abe had to admit he was a handsome man, especially dressed the way he was.

"You look cool, Mr. Campbell," Emma blurted out, surprising everyone, herself most of all.

"Thank you—and so do you."

Abe followed this exchange with his legal ear as he thought about what an impact Joe would have on a jury, on or off the stand.

Joe prepared to leave. "I have to get to the airport. I have a driver downstairs. Can I offer anyone a lift anywhere?"

What a sweetheart he could be—or at least appear to be—when he wasn't feeling cornered, Abe thought. He'd have to remember to make his client feel safe in the courtroom.

"Well, I do want to extend an invitation to all of you to a Celtics game—next season."

"Sounds like a plan!" Emma said, looking at Abe with the expression she always used when she wanted him to agree.

"We'll let you know, Joe," Abe demurred. "Emma's leaving for college soon, and she won't be around much next year."

"Hey, that's great—where are you going?"

"Barnard," Emma said.

"Good. You can become a Knicks fan and root for a winning team."

Chapter Twenty-four

"Older women. Lots of them," barked Henry Pullman. "With grandchildren. Stable families. No screwing around. No divorces. Kids who got married young. Miami Beach–in-the-winter types. Snowbirds. Italians, Irish, Jews, Greeks, maybe even some WASPs. No black women. No young women, regardless of race. And absolutely no well-educated or well-read people. Not dunces. Just not geniuses. And boring lives. No excitement. Their most adventurous trip should be a Princess cruise. No bungee jumpers, or hang gliders. They drive Chevys or Buicks. No BMWs. Boring. Boring. That's our jury. That's who we want." Satisfied with his statement, Henry Pullman toyed with his bearded chin.

They were sitting in Abe's office, poring over a pile of survey results, demographic data, and investigative reports. Pullman, a slim, gray-haired, gray-bearded man in his early seventies, was the expert Abe had hired to help pick the jurors who were most likely to acquit Campbell. Pullman was a veteran of many high-profile trials. A former union organizer from the Bronx, he had pioneered the science—or was it an art?—of helping lawyers select jurors who would be most sympathetic to their case. When he'd begun his work back in the late 1960s representing radicals who were charged with anti-Vietnam draft protests, he had been widely criticized by the established bar for trying to skew juries in favor of one side rather than helping to secure an unbiased venire. Now, even the most established law firms were using him and the clones who had followed him into what had become one of the great growth industries of the 1980s— scientific jury selection. Despite the competition, Henry Pullman was still the expert's expert.

"What about sports fans?" Abe asked.

"Don't worry. Puccio will get rid of them, especially Knicks fans. That won't hurt us. Sports fans can be dangerous. They idolize their heroes, and they can be the most vicious if they're disappointed. Stay away from fans, especially fanatics."

"What about young men? Yuppies, jocks?"

"Bad news. They're jealous. They're also trying to score with feminists. Bad news."

"Why are older women so good?"

"Because they disapprove of young women going to hotel rooms with men. They were taught that only sluts go to a man's room. Also, they want to justify their own conservative lives. Limits—they understand limits," Pullman said. "They will believe that Jennifer Dowling asked for it. They're good for us. Believe me. Older women are the ones who got William Kennedy Smith acquitted."

Rendi would be responsible for doing the investigative field work on the jury panel once it was available. She was sitting next to Abe, seething at the sexist and other stereotypes that Pullman was invoking.

"You're assuming that all older women think the same," she said.

"*Au contraire,* my dear," Pullman replied as if he had heard this criticism a million times—which he had. "Every person is an individual. We don't have the luxury of learning enough about every person to make an individualized judgment. Indeed, that's where *you* come in. The more you can learn about every prospective juror as an individual, the less we will have to stereo-type. So it's all up to you. If you get me the personalized data, I'll base my recommendations on that. Where you can't, then it's back to basics. And the basics tell me that, as a rule, older women are the best in date rape cases."

"It seems so manipulative."

"Look," Pullman replied, "the prosecutor has vast re-sources at its disposal—police, investigators, data banks. Defen-dants need me to help level the playing field."

"Only rich defendants get to use your talents," Rendi shot back. "Legal aid can't afford you. Even middle-class defendants can't afford you."

"I'm a luxury," Pullman acknowledged, showing off his expensive brown tweed jacket with the leather elbow patches. "Just like Abe Ringel is a luxury. Poor defendants can't afford him, either. It's not a fair world."

"You know, people always complain when rich defendants get expensive lawyers," Abe said. "No one ever complains when rich people get expensive doctors."

"Rich people have earned the right to have the best," Pull-man replied.

"You've certainly come a long way from your radical labor days, Henry," Abe chided him.

"So have you, Abe. We've both become full-fledged capital-ists, and we both feel a bit guilty. Just not enough to keep us from making a good living."

"What else can you tell us? What do your polls show? Do people believe Campbell or Dowling?"

"It depends on who you ask. It's all in the demographics. Young women believe Dowling. Old women don't. The most important poll result we've got is that almost everyone—even those who believe Dowling—seem to *like* Campbell. People like him, even if they think he may be guilty."

"That means we should put him on the witness stand," Jus-tin said to Abe.

Before Abe had a chance to respond, Pullman interjected. "Not so fast, young man. Maybe it means exactly the opposite."

"How so?"

"People seem to like Campbell from *afar*. Without having heard him testify. Maybe my poll results mean that he *doesn't* have to testify—that his favorability rating will be *better* if they don't hear him try to wiggle out of this."

"Interesting point," Abe said. "We'll have to wait and see. That's going to be *my* call."

"What about a shadow? Do you want a shadow? And if so, how many? Four? Six? Twelve?"

"What the heck is a shadow?" Justin asked.

"A shadow jury," Pullman explained. "After the real jurors are picked, I try to find a group of people—twelve is best—who are just like the real jurors. Same age, sex, background, race, politics, attitudes. I hire them to sit in the courtroom and listen to everything the jury hears. When the jury leaves, they leave. I call them the shadow jury."

"What good do they do?"

"Every day after court is over, I interview each of them—separately. I try to find out what impact the testimony and arguments had on them: who they believed, what arguments were persuasive, who they liked, who they hated, what they don't understand. Then I tell Abe what he has to do to improve his case. It's all based on the assumption that the shadow jurors are similar to the real ones and are evaluating the evidence and arguments the same way."

"Quite an assumption," Rendi said. "It could be all wrong."

"It could be, but it's the best we can do. Much better than *lawyers* making these judgments alone. My research shows that lawyers, even the best ones, are often out of touch with ordinary jurors."

"Isn't the shadow idea similar to what the prosecutors did in the O. J. Simpson case?" Justin asked.

"What do you mean?"

"They put together some kind of a mock jury in Phoenix to try out their case."

"What happened?"

"They acquitted him."

"I bet the prosecutors changed a few things after that," Rendi said.

Pullman is certainly right about lawyers needing help," Abe added. "When I first began to practice, I couldn't afford a shadow, so I had my mother, Sylvia, come to court."

"How did she do?" Justin asked.

"Great—when the jury consisted of older women. Not so great when we drew young men."

"It's the same principle," Pullman said.

Abe continued, "Even Haskel, who was certainly never a man of the people, used to tell his students that on the weekend before a jury trial, a lawyer should go to the movies, watch television, and ride on the subway, instead of working in the library. 'Do what the jurors will be doing,' he advised. 'Read what the jurors will be reading. Watch what they will be watching. Get inside their heads.' "

"It's all so damn manipulative," Rendi said. "I bet Haskel never used a jury expert."

"Wrong again, my dear," Pullman said with a smile. "Haskel hates what I do. Still, he did use me—most reluctantly. How do you think I got to meet Abe?"

"He did hate to use you," Abe confirmed. "He wouldn't allow his personal feelings to hurt a client."

"And he even listened to me," Pullman said proudly. "I'll never forget when he was appointed to be one of the defense lawyers in the antiwar conspiracy prosecution against Dr. Spock, the baby doctor. It was one of my first cases. I was a rookie. There was a juror named Charles White. Gentile name. Haskel had learned from a local rabbi that he was Jewish. He wanted him on the jury because he felt that a Jew would be more sympathetic to draft evasion, since so many Jews had come to this country to avoid serving in the Czar's army. I disagreed. 'A Jew who changed his name to Charles White wants to prove he's more American than Uncle Sam,' I told him. He will be utterly unsympathetic. He listened to me, and he struck him from the jury. Later Charles White wrote to Haskel, criticizing him for defending draft dodgers. I was right."

"Are you always right?" Justin asked.

"I wish. The frustrating part of my job is that I rarely find out if I was right. Even when my side wins, that doesn't prove I was right about a particular juror. I know I've been wrong a few times, and I try to learn from my mistakes."

"Try not to make too many in this case, please," Abe implored him. "I've really got to win this one."

"That's a funny way to put it. You didn't say I shouldn't make mistakes because *Campbell* is innocent, but because *you* have to win. That's not like you, Abe. Are you trying to tell me something?"

"No, Henry, I'm not trying to tell you anything. Just get me the best damn jurors you can. The twelve real ones, and the twelve shadows."

"It's only the real ones who count," Rendi noted with her usual cynicism.

Chapter Twenty-five

The opening day of a high-visibility criminal trial was generally a media circus, with TV cameramen pushing and shoving each other to get into position to capture the video images that would make it onto the evening news. Lawyers likewise competed for the perfect sound bite. Walking confidently yet humbly through the camera gauntlet, and expressing the appropriate sentiments could be a daunting experience even for the most seasoned advocate. This day was no different as Abe and his legal team made their way into the nineteenth-century courthouse in which the case of *Commonwealth* v. *Campbell* would be conducted.

"Ask yourself one simple question," Abe said as a dozen microphones were shoved in his face. "Why would a handsome basketball star who had women running after him *need* to rape?" The question hung in the air as the lawyers and spectators entered the large baroque courtroom over which the Honorable Marie Gambi presided.

The trial had been set to begin as soon as the playoffs concluded. The Knicks' surprising loss in the Eastern Conference finals had given Campbell a few days' respite between courtside and courtroom. He had used the days to rebound from media speculation about the impact the rape accusation had had on his playoff performance—which had been good, but not great. Now he was determined to do whatever he had to do. This was not a game. If he lost, there would be no next season.

"Let's get on with jury selection," Judge Gambi said, banging her gavel.

Marie Gambi—"everybody's favorite aunt," as she had been described in a recent newspaper article—was universally regarded as the epitome of fairness. A former nun, she had married a wealthy computer executive after leaving the convent and then entered law school at the age of forty. After graduation she had become a well-respected prosecutor and then a judge. She was the only Massachusetts judge who refused to wear a robe in court. "Makes me look and feel too much like a nun," she'd explained.

Today, like most days, Judge Gambi was wearing a blue jacket, white blouse, and gray skirt. Even now, in her late fifties and twenty years after forsaking the veil, Abe thought she still looked like a nun. She had also retained some old-fashioned attitudes, such as not allowing her courtroom trials to be televised—a policy that had not endeared her to the media. Yet she didn't seem to care. "Trials are serious events. Nobody is going to sell dog food during recesses in my trials," she had said.

Abe quickly used up his six peremptory challenges— challenges for which a lawyer did not have to give a reason— after picking only eight of the jurors. So he was pretty much stuck with the remaining four. Abe could smell cigarette smoke on the wool of Pullman's jacket. It wasn't often that he felt claustrophobic in a courtroom, but this jury selection was beginning to drag on: because of all the pretrial publicity, Judge Gambi had taken the unusual step of allowing the lawyers to question the jurors. Campbell was quiet and had given Abe no trouble, thank God, because right now the luck of the draw was working against them, and Abe had all the trouble he could handle— especially when the clerk called the woman who quickly became known as "Pullman's nightmare" and then later "Ms. Scuba Diver."

Ms. Julianne Barrow was twenty-nine, a Wellesley graduate who worked as an investment banker in downtown Boston. She was tall, well dressed, and beautiful, with long blond hair cascading over her dark blue designer jacket. She exuded an air of comfortable confidence, just the kind of woman to stay away from. "That's your foreperson," Pullman warned. "Do everything you can to get rid of her."

While he proceeded to ask questions of Julianne Barrow, it became clear to Abe that he could uncover no disqualifying features in her background or opinions. No one close to her had ever been raped or accused of rape. She believed in date rape, but also believed that not all women always tell the truth. So how could he get rid of her?

There was one possible chink in her armor. "Have you ever been married?" Abe knew the answer since Rendi's hasty investigation had discovered she was divorced.

"I think you must know the answer to that, Mr. Ringel. You've investigated me, I'm sure."

She was smart, and not one to take anything lying down. Was that good or bad for them? Abe wondered.

"You're right, Ms. Barrow," he said. "I know you are divorced. How recently?" He knew exactly how recently, but he had to say something.

"Six months."

"That's recent. I'm sure you're still smarting, am I right?"

"You mean am I still a man hater?" She smiled.

Abe couldn't help smiling back. She was a charmer, this one, pretty smooth. He wanted desperately to get rid of her. This woman might just be the one juror who saw through his client.

"I mean, are you distracted at all by those recent personal events?" he asked her. "You must have lost a lot of personal time and might feel pressured if the trial goes on for a while."

"Don't worry about my personal life, Mr. Ringel. I have

the right and privilege to serve on a jury, without regard to my marital status, isn't that so?"

That was an odd answer, Abe thought. Most busy people tried to stay away from jury duty. It certainly couldn't have been the way she wanted to spend a few weeks, unless she was filling up time. Abe had seen jurors like this before—lonely, even desperate people with little personal adventure. That could be trouble. Jurors like that tended to draw things out and drag the process on. Yet this did not seem to capture her essence. After all, she had a good job. Maybe she wanted to serve on the jury because she believed in the system? Or because she had an ax to grind?

Ostensibly Abe changed the subject. "Do you have hobbies, Ms. Barrow?"

"I scuba dive, I rock climb."

"A regular daredevil, aren't you?"

"I stay busy."

Abe tried to get the judge to strike Julianne Barrow "for cause." However, he couldn't come up with a reason that persuaded Judge Gambi. "You should have saved more of your peremptories," she said.

For a moment Abe thought he heard a scolding in the judge's voice. When he walked away from the bench toward the defense table, he took a deep breath and realized it was just the critical voice in his head scolding him.

He *should* have saved more of his peremptories. It was always a gamble. In his last case he had saved two of his peremptories till the very end and then never used them, because the last few jurors had been okay. Then he'd wished he had used them on some of the earlier jurors. He had lost and decided not to waste his valuable peremptories in future cases by saving them. Now he was sorry.

Abe apologized to Campbell for his blunder. Campbell seemed unconcerned.

"Let me handle Ms. Scuba Diver," Campbell sent a flirta-
tious smile in her direction.

The jury selection dragged on. Three other jurors he would
have liked to challenge got on the jury. They weren't night-
mares; they were just not that good. One was a Hispanic man in
his thirties who was a construction worker on the new tunnel
being built to the airport. He was married with two daughters.
Two others were white, male civil servants in their fifties of non-
descript background. The last regular juror was a black woman
in her thirties who was a single mother of two boys and a part-
time nurse.

Pullman wanted Abe to try to strike the black woman for
cause. He whispered to Abe: "My research shows that black
women are murder on men charged with rape, regardless of the
race of the defendant or the complaining witness."

"I've got no cause to strike her," Abe said in a low voice.
"And in any event, I have a good feeling about her."

"Your feelings are diddley compared with my research,"
Pullman insisted.

"Maybe so. But we're stuck with her, so we just have to
make the best of it."

Abe was basically satisfied with nine of the twelve jurors,
plus the two alternates. Four of the regular jurors had come
right out of Pullman's central casting: gray-haired grandmas who
could have come straight from a mah-jongg or canasta game at
the Fontainebleau Hotel in Miami Beach. One was Irish from
Somerville; one was Italian from North Cambridge; one was
Jewish from Lexington; and one was Armenian from Watertown.

Then there was a black man, a plumber in his early forties
from Winchester. He was married with no children. The other
four "good" jurors were working-class white men—two Italians,
one WASP, and one Greek.

Finally, after three days of contentious selection, Judge
Gambi was able to say, "We have a jury."

Abe turned to Pullman with a look of resignation. "Now

get me twelve good shadows so we can find out how bad it really is."

As Pullman and Rendi left the courtroom in search of shadows, Abe and Justin hunkered down for the trial. It could be as short as two or three days—if Campbell didn't have to take the stand. Or it could go as long as two weeks if he did testify and the state put on a rebuttal case. Nothing was ever predictable about a criminal trial, especially when a man like Joe Campbell was the defendant.

Chapter Twenty-six

Judge Gambi directed Prosecutor Cheryl Puccio to call her first witness. Joe Campbell, dressed in a blue blazer with gray pants and a red tie, seemed to be in a different world. He didn't even lift his head as Jennifer Dowling walked past him contemptuously. He was deep in thought.

Abe looked at Campbell and wondered what could be going through his client's mind. Campbell was still unfathomable to him, as were most of his clients—innocent or guilty. No matter how many different types of defendants Abe had dealt with, he never could think the way they did. Thank God. Abe recalled an accused stock swindler he'd once defended who spent the entire trial immersed in red herrings and stock tables. He was acquitted *and* he made a killing in the market at the same time. For all Abe knew, Joe Campbell might be thinking about his next game—or planning his next predatory adventure. In any event, Abe needed him to focus on events in the courtroom.

"Pay attention, please," Abe insisted. "I need you to tell me when Jennifer is lying, even about the most minute details, so that I can zero in on cross-examination."

"Sure, sure," Campbell said, quickly returning from whatever universe his head was in.

"I also need you to make eye contact with the jurors,"

Abe added. "Jurors sometimes look for a defendant's reaction to the evidence." He could see that he was getting nowhere with Campbell, so he decided to tell him an anecdote that Haskel used to relate to his students. "Joe, please listen to this little story."

"If you insist."

"I insist." At this point he'd do headstands if it meant Joe would pay attention to the proceedings. What next—a marching band? Anyway, Abe tried on his best raconteur skills.

"A defendant was once on trial for murdering his wife. No corpse had been found, but the circumstantial evidence was convincing. During his closing argument the defense lawyer told the jurors that they were in for a great surprise: when he counted to ten, the allegedly dead wife would walk through the courtroom door. 'One, two,' the lawyer began. By 'seven' every juror had his eyes riveted on the door. 'Eight, nine, ten,' the lawyer counted. The jurors waited expectantly, but the door remained closed. The defense attorney smiled and explained to the jurors, 'See, each of you turned your eyes to the door. You each must have had a reasonable doubt about whether the wife was really dead. My little experiment,' the lawyer declared victoriously, 'proved that you had a reasonable doubt and you must, therefore, acquit the defendant.' Despite this logic the jury convicted the defendant. Afterward the disappointed defense lawyer asked one of the jurors how she could have voted for conviction after the jurors had all looked at the door. 'Yes, *we* all looked at the door,' the juror explained, 'but we noticed that the *defendant* didn't. *He* knew nobody was walking through that door.' "

Abe placed an arm on Campbell's shoulder. "Take that story to heart, Joe. You damn well better be looking at the door."

This time, it seemed, Campbell had listened to Abe. He stared intently at the jurors as Jennifer Dowling began her testimony.

Cheryl Puccio was a first-rate courtroom performer. She was a handsome woman in her late thirties, not too glamorous

203

or sexy, and very credible to jurors. She wore gray tailored suits that made her look a bit masculine, without being threatening. Her voice was soothing, if a bit monotonic. She spoke quickly, never smiling. Cheryl Puccio was all business, no nonsense. She exuded sincerity. No one would choose her for a partner at a long formal dinner party, yet Abe knew that she was perfect for the role in which she was cast—the champion for a young woman victimized by a predatory man.

"Please tell the jury your name."

"My name is Jennifer Dowling," the witness said firmly as she fiddled with the bottom of her dark business suit. Abe was pleased to notice how similarly Campbell and Dowling had dressed for their courtroom confrontation.

"What do you do for a living?"

"I work in advertising for a Manhattan firm."

Out of the corner of his eye, Abe studied Joe's reaction to Jennifer. Did he project pity? Anger? Contempt? The amazing thing to Abe was that Joe's emotion was zero. It was hard to imagine that there had ever been anything between them. Jennifer, he noticed, seemed to be expending a lot of energy avoiding the defense side of the courtroom. If the jury picked up on this, how would they interpret it?

"When did you first meet the defendant, Joseph Campbell?"

"I met him on March 10, near the office building where I work."

"Was it a chance meeting?"

"Yes."

Abe heaved an inaudible sigh of relief at Jennifer's answer. He had been fairly certain that neither Cheryl Puccio nor Jennifer Dowling was aware of Justin's theory about how Campbell had come to meet Jennifer.

Cheryl Puccio took Jennifer uneventfully through the first meeting and then the subsequent dinner at Stellina's in Watertown. At the mention of Stellina's, the juror from Watertown whispered something to the woman on the adjoining seat.

"No talking to other jurors until all the testimony is complete," Judge Gambi admonished.

Everyone in the law business knew that jurors disregarded this ritualistic warning. But rituals were essential to the survival of all institutions—even trials.

Now Puccio was taking Jennifer to the Charles Hotel. This would be the next crucial test. Would Jennifer tell the truth about her original desire to have sex with Campbell? Or would she fudge? Abe hoped she would fudge. Most date rape victims did, he knew, because they feared that if they told the whole truth— including the fact that they had originally consented to sexual foreplay or more—the jury would conclude that they'd been asking for it.

In one of their strategy planning sessions, Abe had shown a videotape of the cross-examination of Patricia Bowman, the complaining witness in the William Kennedy Smith case. At one point Bowman denied that she had even had any sexual interest in Smith. When she said she couldn't remember how her panty hose ended up in her car, Abe had stopped the videotape.

"That's when the case ended," he'd said. "After that the jury stopped listening to Patricia Bowman, because they stopped believing her." Turning to the Campbell case, Abe had continued, "We've got to look for a point like that in Jennifer Dowling's story. If we can catch her in a lie—even an insignificant lie—the jury will stop listening to the rest of her story, even if it's true."

"Why would a woman who has really been raped ever lie about what went on before?" Justin had asked.

"Because they believe that if they were to tell the truth about welcoming the man's advances up to a certain point and then saying no, some of the jurors would refuse to convict, even if they believed her testimony."

Rendi had been angry over this. "Some people just can't

seem to get it through their thick skulls that rape isn't a crime of morality. It's a crime against a woman's right to choose whom she will or won't have sex with."

"*We* know that, Rendi," Abe had replied. "Not all jurors believe it."

To Abe's surprise and chagrin, Jennifer Dowling told the truth about who had initiated the sex. Possibly, Abe calculated, Puccio had shown her the same Patricia Bowman videotape.

Jennifer told the jury the details: that she had wanted to have sex with Campbell, that she went into the bathroom to put in her diaphragm, that she returned wearing only her unbuttoned shirt, that she had initiated the discussion about sex with Campbell, and that she had reached for his genitals.

While Jennifer went through her catalog of consent, Joe gently nodded his head in agreement. Abe noted that Campbell had positioned himself so that he seemed to be directing all his silent commentary toward the jury—specifically the assertive Ms. Scuba Diver.

Now Puccio was up to the critical point in the testimony.

"So you were willing to have sex with Joseph Campbell as you both lay in bed. Did something then happen that caused you to change your mind?"

"Yes."

"What happened?"

"Mr. Campbell whispered something in my ear."

"What was it that he whispered?"

"At first I wasn't certain. Then he whispered it again, this time a bit more loudly and more clearly."

"Are you now sure you know what he said?"

"Yes, I am positive. He made it crystal clear."

"Please tell the jury exactly what he said."

As Jennifer began to answer, Abe turned to watch Campbell's reaction to what Jennifer would say. This would be the first time he would hear the words Joe had allegedly spoken. He wondered what words could have so quickly changed

Jennifer from a willing sex partner into an unconsenting rape victim.

"He said these words." Jennifer was speaking softly but clearly. " 'Give me as good a blow job as you gave Nick Armstrong at your office. I hear you give world-class head in order to get ahead.' "

Jennifer began to weep softly. Several of the jurors were looking at her as she sobbed. Ms. Scuba Diver's eyes were fixed firmly on Campbell's head, which was shaking gently back and forth. He must have been aware that the forewoman was observing him as he squinted slightly and formed a silent *tsk, tsk* sound. The effect of these subtle movements by Campbell was to send a pained message of disappointment in Jennifer for finally crossing the line from truth to falsehood.

At first Abe didn't understand what Campbell was trying to do. Then it hit him: Campbell was *testifying* without taking the witness stand. He was having a running, silent, private conversation with Ms. Scuba Diver, the most important and dangerous member of the jury. Campbell was trying to seduce her, but not physically. He was going for her mind. And from the look on Ms. Scuba Diver's face, Joe Campbell seemed to be scoring, as usual.

Puccio, who was busy comforting Jennifer, missed the entire scene, as did Judge Gambi. Jennifer stopped weeping, wiped her eyes with a tissue, and continued with her testimony.

Puccio asked her to explain the significance of Campbell's words.

Jennifer spoke haltingly as she disclosed the secret that had nearly destroyed her life. "Last year I performed oral sex on the vice president of my company in an effort to obtain a promotion."

As soon as she uttered these words, a collective gasp could be heard through the courtroom. It was as if the prim and proper Jennifer Dowling had suddenly stripped naked in front of the jury. Courtroom observers and jurors turned to each other in astonishment and began to converse.

"This is not a spectator sport," Judge Gambi shouted, banging her gavel. "There will be no sounds from the audience, or the press, and especially the jury. Continue, Ms. Puccio."

Cheryl Puccio had known, of course, the answer Jennifer Dowling would give to her question. Still, she had no choice but to ask it. If she didn't, Abe would, and it was always better to blunt the impact of cross-examination by bringing out the worst material first on direct examination. In any event, her answer was a crucial, if risky, building block to the state's case.

After the audience quieted down, Puccio continued her direct examination.

"Are you proud of what you did?"

"No, I am mortified. It was stupid, immoral, and desperate. I really believed that it was the only way I could avoid losing my job."

"And did you lose your job anyway?"

"Yes, I did."

"How come?"

"Because the man on whom I performed oral sex told his boss, the president, that I give 'world-class head.' The president then asked me to perform oral sex on him, and I refused. So he fired me."

Abe could have objected on hearsay grounds to Jennifer's testimony about what the vice president allegedly told the president, but he wanted the story to come out so that he could prove she had lied during the deposition in her harassment suit.

Puccio then asked Jennifer a question that made Abe's heart skip a beat. "Do you know how Mr. Campbell learned about what had happened between you and your bosses?" Abe waited for Jennifer to answer. He wondered whether they had somehow found out about the computer printouts.

Fortunately Jennifer said, "I have no idea."

At this point Campbell shrugged and raised his hands slightly, as if to signal both pity and triumph. Then he shook his head again to make it clear that Jennifer Dowling was simply not telling the truth. This time Abe could see Ms. Scuba Diver respond with her own modest gesture of disbelief. Abe hoped that Ms. Barrow was directing her disbelief at Jennifer Dowling rather than at Joe Campbell.

Abe had been surprised by Puccio's last question. She must have known that Jennifer's answer would now give him a basis for challenging her entire story. He began to compose his argument in his mind: "Of course Jennifer Dowling has 'no idea' how Joe Campbell could have learned of her deep, dark, and shameful secret, because there is no corroboratory evidence that Joe Campbell *did* know of it." He'd been spared the ethical quandary of whether he could ask Jennifer the question on cross-examination because Puccio had asked it on direct. Abe surmised that Puccio simply did not want to leave a loose thread hanging. Lawyers often made the mistake, he mused, of believing that it was their job to tie up all loose ends—to create a neat, symmetrical little bundle. However, life was full of loose ends, and lawyers often hurt their cases by being too fastidious and neat when it didn't serve their clients' interests. Cheryl Puccio had asked one too many questions.

"It's like the wrestler," Abe explained to Justin and Rendi over a quick lunch at recess. Campbell had declined his offer to join them, preferring to work out in a nearby gym.

Rendi groaned, and Abe knew he must have bored her with the wrestler story ten thousand times. But it was new to Justin.

"Okay," Justin said, knowing he would regret it, "tell me about the wrestler."

"It seems this wrestler was accused of biting off the ear of another wrestler during a match. The defendant wrestler's lawyer was cross-examining the only eyewitness—the referee. Reaching the apex of his examination, he asked, 'You didn't actually see my client bite off his opponent's ear, did you?' The witness responded, 'No, I didn't actually see him bite it off.' Instead of stopping, the lawyer asked one more question: 'So how do you *know* that he actually bit it off?' Without hesitation, the witness replied, 'Because I saw him spit it out!' "

Chapter Twenty-seven

Puccio continued her examination of Dowling after the lunch break.

"After Campbell asked you for 'as good a blow job as you gave Nick Armstrong,' what did you say?"

"I told him to stop. I yelled 'Stop!' The more I yelled, the more persistent Campbell became, until he forced me to submit. He raped me. He hurt me. He knew I wanted him to stop, but he deliberately raped me, and he enjoyed it."

"Are you absolutely certain," Puccio asked, "that you communicated your lack of consent to him?"

Jennifer Dowling looked directly at Campbell as she answered: "I have never been more certain of anything. He knew I wanted him to stop. Yet that seemed to turn him on even more. He wanted to rape me, and he did."

Campbell locked eyes with Jennifer Dowling. He shook his head almost imperceptibly. Then he turned ever so slightly to make fleeting contact with Ms. Scuba Diver. Now her look of disbelief seemed to be directed at Jennifer Dowling.

"Your witness, Mr. Ringel," Cheryl Puccio said.

This was the ethical lawyer's nightmare: cross-examining a rape victim who he suspected was telling the truth. It was not as bad as in the old days, when defense lawyers could ask about the complaining witness's entire sexual history and when some juries

211

wouldn't convict unless the victim had been a virgin. In those days defense lawyers had no choice but to do the "sleaze thing," as Emma called it. Thank God for the rape shield laws, Abe thought. At least we don't have to do *that* anymore. Nonetheless, the defense lawyer still had to try to prove the complaining witness was a liar—regardless of what he personally believed.

As Abe approached Jennifer Dowling and introduced himself to her, he tried to forget about his ethical qualms. She is the enemy, he repeated to himself. It is my job to discredit her. She is all that stands between Campbell's conviction and acquittal. I've got to get the jury to disbelieve her.

Abe always began his cross-examination by going for the jugular. None of this "work your way up to the killer question" stuff for him. There may be a role for foreplay in sex, but not in cross-examinations, he thought. If there's a weakness, exploit it during the first minute. Get the jury on your side right away, and then they'll be rooting for you during all the rest of the cross-examination.

"Ms. Dowling, you admitted on direct examination that you have no idea how my client, Joe Campbell, could have found out about your little problem at work. Is that correct?"

"Yes, it is."

"You certainly never told him, did you?"

"No, I didn't."

"You have no friends or work associates in common, do you?"

"Not to my knowledge."

"What do you mean, 'not to my knowledge'? You would *know*, wouldn't you, if you had friends or work associates in common?"

"I guess so."

"So, the fact is that you don't know anyone in common, right?"

"That's right."

"And you know of no way, do you, for Mr. Campbell to have learned about your problem?"

"No, I don't. That's why I was so surprised."

"Your Honor," Abe said pointedly to the judge, "I move to strike Ms. Dowling's statement about being surprised as not responsive to my question."

"Sustained," Judge Gambi agreed. "Please limit your answers to Mr. Ringel's questions."

"Okay, Ms. Dowling. So it seems right to you that my client could not have known about your problem at work, is that correct?"

"Yes, that is correct."

"Now, Ms. Dowling, that seems to leave only two choices, doesn't it: one, that my client knew something that it seems impossible for him to know; or two, that you weren't telling the truth when you swore to the jury that he whispered to you about that problem. Which is it, Ms. Dowling?"

"Objection, Your Honor." Puccio shot up. "He's arguing with the witness, not questioning her."

"Overruled, Ms. Puccio. There's a fine line between an argumentative question and a questioning argument. This one is close, but it falls on the right side of the line. You may answer, Ms. Dowling."

"I am telling the truth, Mr. Ringel."

"So it's your position that my client is capable of doing the impossible, is that right?"

"Objection."

"Sustained. This time you've crossed the line into argument, Mr. Ringel. That question will be struck. You need not answer it, Ms. Dowling."

"Thank you, Your Honor," Abe said. "Now, Ms. Dowling, you say you are telling the truth, right?"

"Right."

"Well, let me ask you this. Were you telling the truth when

213

you initially told the police that it was my client who first made sexual advances toward you?"

"I don't remember telling that to the police."

"May I please show the witness the police report that describes her account of what happened?"

"Do you want it in evidence?" the judge asked.

"Yes."

"No objection from us," said Puccio.

Abe gave Jennifer a copy of the police report and asked her to read it silently. "Is that a generally accurate summary of what you told the police on the night you claimed you were raped?"

Jennifer nodded her head in the affirmative.

"Now, would you read the first sentence to the jury."

Jennifer read out loud: "Complaining witness acknowledges that she initially consented to perpetrator's advances, including cunnilingus."

"Now, a fair reading of that sentence suggests, does it not, that it was my client who made the initial advances?"

"Objection." Puccio rose. "The document speaks for itself."

"Sustained."

"Okay," Abe acknowledged, "the document does speak for itself, and the jury can decide for itself what it means. So, let me ask you about what *you* told the police. Did you tell them during your initial interview that it was *you*, and not my client, who *first* suggested having sex, and that it was *you*, and not my client, who made the first physical sexual advance?"

"I didn't feel comfortable telling the officer—"

"Please answer *my* question first," Abe interrupted. "Did you or did you not tell the police you were the aggressor during the first interview?"

"No, I did not. I can explain."

"I'm sure you can. But the *fact* is, is it not, that you withheld information from the police when you were first interviewed?"

"That's correct, but the reason—"

"Ms. Puccio will, I'm sure, give you an opportunity to explain why you didn't tell the whole truth. Right now, I'm just interested in the *fact* that you didn't tell the whole truth."

"Objection."

"Sustained. Mr. Ringel's speech will be struck. You are to ignore it. Please ask the next question."

"Ms. Dowling, is there anything else you didn't tell the police at your first interview?"

"Probably. I can't remember."

"Well, let me try to help you remember. Did you tell them that you had removed your bra when you went to the bathroom?"

"No, I didn't."

"Did you tell them that you returned from the bathroom with your shirt unbuttoned and the rest of your clothing removed?"

"No."

"Did the police instruct you to tell them everything that happened?"

"Yes, they did."

"And yet you withheld these facts."

"I didn't think they were that important."

"Yet *today* you thought they were important enough to tell the jury."

"Yes, I did."

"Is that because Ms. Puccio advised you that you should testify about these facts?"

"Objection."

"On what grounds?"

"Lawyer-client advice," Ms. Puccio said halfheartedly.

"You're not *her* lawyer, Ms. Puccio," the judge ruled. "You know that. You're the *state's* lawyer. Objection overruled. You may answer."

Jennifer looked to Puccio, who nodded as if to give her

permission to answer. "Yes, Ms. Puccio told me to tell every-thing—to hold nothing back."

"And are you holding absolutely nothing back now?"

Jennifer hesitated. "I don't think so, but it's possible I may have forgotten a few things."

Abe knew he had succeeded in planting in her mind the possibility that he might know certain facts that she had forgotten. Her confidence was shaken. Now was the time to question her about the incomplete information she had given the police.

"It is a fact, is it not, that you did not tell the police that it was you, rather than my client, who initiated the sex because you thought they wouldn't believe you if you told them the whole truth. Is that not the fact?"

"I thought they wouldn't take me seriously."

"And they wouldn't believe you, is that right?"

"Yes, that's right."

"So you were willing to tell less than the whole truth in order to be believed, is that correct?"

"Everything I said was true."

"But not the whole truth, right?"

"Not every detail."

"You deliberately left out the fact that you initiated the sex because you wanted to be believed, right?"

"I guess that's right."

"And several months before that, you deliberately lied under oath in a deposition about whether you had oral sex with your boss, because you were afraid that if you told the truth, no one would believe you were sexually harassed. Right?"

"Yes, but then I told the truth."

"Only after your friend testified about what you had admit-ted to her. Right?"

"That's right. But I did tell the truth."

"And it is the fact, is it not, that you would be willing to tell *this* jury less than the whole truth in order to get them to believe you. Is that right?"

216

"No, I'm telling the whole truth now."

"You weren't telling it when you spoke to the police, right?"

"I left out a few things."

"Deliberately, right?"

"I guess so."

"And is it fair, in your view, to characterize a statement that omits important facts as a 'half-truth'?"

"I guess so."

"And what, then, is the half that is *not* the truth, Ms. Dowling?"

"Objection. The term *half-truth* is self-explanatory."

"Sustained."

"Fine," Abe said. "Let the jury decide what the half that isn't the truth should be called."

"Objection."

"Sustained. The jury will ignore Mr. Ringel's speeches, and Mr. Ringel will stop making them. Do you understand, Mr. Ringel?"

"Yes, Your Honor. May I resume my questioning?"

"Go on."

Abe continued to pound away. Jennifer became more confused and distraught until he sensed he might be risking a backlash. He had been caught up in the heat of battle. Now he knew he had reached that critical point when he began to feel a personal tinge of disgust overtaking the pleasure of professional success. The time had come to pull back and show his warmer self. Was he doing this out of genuine concern—or as a tactic?

"Would you like to take a break, Ms. Dowling?"

The judge waited silently while Jennifer remained mute, breathing heavily. Perspiration formed on her forehead and tears welled up in her eyes. If Abe hadn't psyched himself up to objectify her as the enemy, he would have felt a more extreme set of emotions: guilt, pity, sadness, sorrow. He couldn't afford that now. He had to win.

"Ms. Dowling?"

"Let's get this over with, if you don't mind, Mr. Ringel." Her voice gained strength as she uttered these words. Behind him, he could sense Campbell concentrating on their exchange.

"Actually, a short recess is a good idea," Judge Gambi said. "Let's all take a five-minute break. Ms. Dowling, you may step down."

Jennifer exited the courtroom with the prosecutor by her side. Abe could imagine what that little tête-à-tête would be like. He'd been involved in a few of those himself—like with Charlie, for example. It was a merry-go-round of emotions being a trial lawyer, yet it was a whole lot worse being on the witness stand. Women lawyers, Abe thought, seemed better at handling the client's emotions, even if that seemed a sexist attitude. Or maybe it was just Abe Ringel who had trouble handling the shifting emotions of a trial.

Abe took a seat beside Campbell, who was rubbing his forehead with eyes closed. The jury had been instructed to remain in the courtroom during the brief recess. Ms. Scuba Diver, Abe noted, was looking intently at the defendant, as were several of the older women, all of whom seemed too galvanized to move. Many of the court spectators also kept their seats, probably afraid to lose them.

The courtroom began to fill up, and then the bailiff announced that recess was over. Whenever Abe heard that phrase, he thought back to the monitor in elementary school signaling the end of the punchball game he and Alex O'Donnell always played during recess.

Just then Joe glanced over at the jury box and smiled openly at Julianne Barrow, Ms. Scuba Diver. To his horror, Abe found himself urging on his client silently. He couldn't help it; Joe's rapport with the prospective foreperson was important. She is the enemy, he told himself, repeating it like a mantra several times as he watched Jennifer reenter the courtroom. It was clear she had been crying. He could sense her fear.

"You are still under oath," Judge Gambi reminded Jennifer as she retook the stand.

Jennifer nodded silently. Abe approached the stand. Joe smiled once more at Ms. Scuba Diver. The trial went on.

"Now, Ms. Dowling, is it not a fact that after you were fired from your job, you went to see a psychologist—"

"Objection, objection. Sidebar," Puccio yelled.

"In my chambers, now," Judge Gambi ordered them.

"What is this all about?" the judge asked Abe when they reached her tiny, run-down suite. "You know that we have a psychotherapist-patient privilege in this state."

"We also have the Sixth Amendment, Your Honor," Abe insisted. "And that gives Mr. Campbell the right to confront his accuser with all relevant evidence that could help him defend himself."

"Your Honor," Puccio countered, "Ms. Dowling confided in the psychotherapist on the basis of an explicit promise that what she said would be confidential. She bared her soul at a time of real emotional need, and it would be unconscionable to have that all spread out on the public record."

"Your Honor," Abe rebutted, "what if she admitted to the psychologist that she had made up the entire story of the alleged sexual harassment episode in order to cover up her own inadequacies at work?"

"Do you have any evidence of that, Mr. Ringel?" Judge Gambi shot back.

"No. That's why I want to *question* her about it—to develop evidence."

"It's a goddamned fishing expedition," Puccio objected. "He's just fishing for dirt. He's got no basis."

"Do you have any basis, Mr. Ringel?"

"Yes, I do. My client tells me that Ms. Dowling told him that she had gone to a psychologist after an unpleasant episode several months earlier. It is fair to infer that she was referring to the events that led up to her firing."

"Do you have any basis for believing that she told the psychologist anything that would be relevant to your defense?" the judge pressed.

"We can only find that out by asking either the witness or the psychologist—or by looking at the psychologist's notes," Abe said.

"I'm sure there is nothing relevant there, Your Honor," Puccio insisted. "It was a series of psychotherapeutic sessions, not a confessional. Jennifer didn't confess to her psychologist that she lied, because she didn't lie."

"With all due respect, Your Honor, how does Ms. Puccio know? Has she seen the notes? Has she spoken to the psychologist?"

"No, I haven't, but neither have you."

"That's my point," Abe said triumphantly. "Nobody knows. For all we know, Ms. Dowling may have sought treatment because she is a pathological liar, and the psychologist will tell us she isn't cured even now!"

"You're reaching, Mr. Ringel," Judge Gambi said.

"Of course I am," Abe acknowledged. "Because I can't get the evidence and I have to assume the worst. What if—just what if—I'm right?"

"How can we find out without breaching the confidentiality of the privilege?" Judge Gambi asked.

"I have a suggestion," Abe said.

"I'm not surprised. What is it?" the judge asked.

"Why don't *you*, Your Honor, review the notes *yourself*—if there are any notes. If not, question the psychologist. If you conclude that there is nothing of relevance to my defense, I will not persist down this line. On the other hand, if you do find that there is relevant material—material that I could use to impeach Ms. Dowling's credibility—then it will be turned over to me and I can use it to question her."

"Well, Ms. Puccio, what do you think?"

"I object strenuously. It's not that we don't trust you, Your

Honor. What Ms. Dowling confided to her psychologist was not intended for *anyone* else's eyes or ears, even a judge's. They were matters of the utmost privacy."

"Mr. Ringel?"

"Your Honor, there is no right to that kind of privacy in the text of the Constitution—no psychotherapist-patient privilege. There is a right to confront witnesses and to subpoena evidence. And I have a right to ask Ms. Dowling about what she told her psychologist. I also have a right to ask her—and I fully intend to—whether she went to a rape counselor *after* she had sex with my client."

"Why is that relevant?" the judge asked.

"Because she *claims* that she was raped, and my client denies it. If she didn't go to a rape counselor, that would corroborate my client's denial. And if she did, then I would have a right to know what she told the rape counselor. Again, she may have admitted to the rape counselor that she made the whole thing up."

"This is outrageous, Your Honor," Puccio complained. "If defense attorneys are allowed to get the records of rape counselors, then no rape victims would ever confide in them. It's like the lawyer-client privilege. I can't subpoena Mr. Ringel's notes of what Mr. Campbell told him, even if they were to show he admitted raping Ms. Dowling."

"They would show no such thing."

"I'm just making an analogy."

"It's not analogous," Abe said, "because the lawyer-client privilege is protected by the Bill of Rights, whereas these other privileges aren't."

"The psychotherapist-patient privilege is protected by a statute in this state," Judge Gambi said.

"The Bill of Rights trumps a statute, Your Honor."

"Yes, Mr. Ringel, it does. However, the statute is also important. It protects an important relationship that the state wants to encourage—between a patient and her psychologist or rape counselor. I will not allow a fishing expedition into these thera-peutic records—certainly not without more than the unsupported inferences you've come up with thus far."

"Well, can *you*, at least, look at the records?"

"No, I won't. They are confidential—even from me. As a lawyer, Mr. Ringel—and a very good one—you must surely appreciate the sacrosanct nature of privileged and confidential information. You would raise the roof if anyone suggested that *I* read the notes of your lawyer-client meetings. I understand your desire to fish for some poisonous eels, Mr. Ringel. I'm not going to let you ask any questions about Ms. Dowling's psychologist or rape counselor—if she had one. These issues are out of bounds."

"With respect, I preserve my objection for appeal—if we have to appeal—and having preserved it, I have no further questions for Ms. Dowling."

After the lawyers and the judge returned to the courtroom, Puccio rose for redirect examination. She asked Dowling to explain why she had not told the police everything. Now a bit calmer, Dowling did a credible job explaining her fear that the police—who were all men—might scoff at her if she acknowledged that she had initiated the sexual advances.

Abe's point had been made, and he did not need to re-cross-examine her. He concluded that Jennifer Dowling's testimony, standing alone, would probably not be enough to convict Campbell. He had created—manufactured?—a reasonable doubt about her credibility, even though he suspected that she might have been telling the truth. He had done his job well.

Yet the case was far from over. Although Jennifer's testimony *by itself* would probably not convict Campbell, if it were to be corroborated by hard scientific evidence, the jury might still find him guilty beyond a reasonable doubt. That was why the state's next witness, Dr. Mary Stiller, a gynecologist at Massachusetts General Hospital, was so crucial. Dr. Stiller had examined Dowling on the night of the alleged rape and had observed and photographed the intravaginal abrasion. She testified that the abrasion was consistent with forcible sex.

Abe asked only three questions on cross-examination.

"Is it not the fact, Dr. Stiller, that Jennifer Dowling's abrasion is equally consistent with consensual sex between a man with a large penis and a woman who has never given birth to a child?"

"Yes, it is."

"Is it not the fact that your physical examination cannot distinguish between these two possible causes?"

"That is true."

"Is it not true, therefore, that the abrasion alone cannot prove, to a reasonable medical certainty, that Jennifer Dowling was raped?"

"That is true."

"No further questions."

Cheryl Puccio rose for redirect.

"The abrasion would be consistent *only* with rape, would it not, if the man who caused the abrasion had a *smaller*-than-average-sized penis?"

Abe jumped to his feet. "Objection, objection. I move for a mistrial. How dare Ms. Puccio try to put those words in Dr. Stiller's mouth! She knows that there is no evidentiary foundation for her factual premise about the size of the penis at issue here."

"Into chambers, both of you," Judge Gambi barked. "Now. I don't want any of this discussed in front of the jury."

Abe was steaming as he entered the judge's chambers. "I've never seen such a cheap shot," he growled at Puccio. "I thought you were above that."

Judge Gambi called for order and directed her anger at Puccio. "That *was* a cheap shot, Ms. Puccio. You know there's no evidence in the record of Mr. Campbell's size."

Cheryl Puccio responded calmly, "Your Honor, I have a

223

good faith basis in fact for my question. My next witness will testify as to the size of Mr. Campbell's penis."

"That's ridiculous," Abe said. "The prosecution has not even asked to examine the item at issue. How could she possibly know?"

"There's more than one road to Rome," Puccio said with a smile.

"Okay, Ms. Puccio," Judge Gambi directed. "If you've got any evidence, I want to know about it now. No more games."

"I do have the evidence. My next witness is Charlene Green, a young woman who has had sex with Mr. Campbell on several occasions. She will testify as to the size of his penis."

"Your Honor, that is entirely inadmissible and prejudicial. I don't know who this Green woman is. Unless she takes a tape measure to bed with her, she can't possibly give evidence as to Campbell's size."

"No, she doesn't use a tape measure, but she has had quite a bit of experience. She is what they call a 'groupie,' Your Honor. She has slept with many basketball players, and she can qualify as something of an expert on penis size. She can't give you inches, Your Honor, but she is prepared to swear under oath that in her experience, the defendant in this case is smaller than average."

"Your Honor," Abe interjected, "even if she were an expert—which we dispute—she would only be an expert on basketball players. And even if my client were smaller than the average basketball player—which we do not concede—that would not necessarily mean that he was smaller than average for the entire population. This woman has a skewed view of size from sleeping with too many large basketball players."

"Okay," Judge Gambi said. "I've heard enough. We're not going to turn this rape trial into a debate about what is an average-sized penis. I will not allow my courtroom to be demeaned in that manner. No, Ms. Puccio. No discussions of penis sizes. I will strike your last question, Ms. Puccio, and tell the jury to disregard it and forget it."

"That's not enough, Your Honor," Abe demanded. "Telling the jury to forget that Ms. Puccio implied that my client has a smaller than average penis is like telling a group of people not to think about an elephant—or in this case a mouse. The jurors are going to assume she was telling the truth. I've got to be able to combat that impression."

"What do you propose as a remedy, Mr. Ringel?"

"Let me at least argue to the jury that there is no evidence in the record to support any conclusion other than that the size of my client's penis is proportional to the rest of him."

"It *isn't*," Puccio insisted.

"So says some groupie."

"So say several groupies we interviewed. Unfortunately, none of the others would testify."

"Enough, enough," Judge Gambi ruled. "You can both argue anything you please, as long as it is based on evidence that is before the jury. This Green woman will not be allowed to testify. Now let's wrap up the trial, please."

Puccio had no further witnesses. Her case would stand or fall on the testimony of Jennifer Dowling and the corroborative medical evidence described by Dr. Stiller. Now the big question was whether Campbell would testify. If he did, the entire dynamic of the trial would change. Everything else would fade into the background as the jurors focused on only one question: Was Campbell telling the truth or was he lying? If Campbell did not testify, that same question would focus on Jennifer Dowling. Abe had to make the decision before morning.

"I have this friend in New York who gets a million dollars to try a case," Abe mused over dinner with Justin and Rendi. "He tells me that fifty thousand of it is for the time and expenses. The remaining nine hundred and fifty thousand is for his judgment on whether the defendant should testify or not. That's how important this decision is."

"Edward Bennett Williams used to say, 'Always put the defendant on, unless he has a record as long as Long Island,' " Justin said. "I read it in his autobiography."

"Gerry Spense says, 'Never put a defendant you think may be guilty on the stand,' because the jury will always see through him," Rendi added.

"They're both wrong," Abe said. "A lawyer should never say 'never' or 'always.' Every case is different. There are no universal rules. That's why I'm less certain about your theories of Campbell's guilt. I'm still not sure whether he did it. And I'm still operating on the assumption that he didn't. You've got to sit and listen to the government's case and then evaluate your client's individual strengths and weaknesses."

"Look at those Menendez kids," Rendi interjected. "Guilty as could be, and great actors. They put it over on enough of the jurors to get a deadlock in the first trial."

"So what's the right approach here?" Justin asked.

"I don't know yet. I'm still thinking."

"What does Campbell want to do?" Rendi asked.

"He *says* he wants to testify. I'm not sure that's what he really wants. He wants me to *think* that's what he wants."

"Why do you say that?" Rendi asked.

"Because he hasn't pressed me in the last day or two. He didn't even want to come to dinner tonight, even though he knows we're talking about this. He's out with some friends."

"Will he go along with your recommendation?" Justin asked.

"I don't know. All I can do is give him my best judgment."

"What is your best judgment?"

"My best judgment at this point is that we probably have it won without Campbell taking the stand, yet it's far from certain that we've won."

"Can Campbell help us or hurt us?" Justin asked.

"Yes."

"What do you mean, 'yes'?" Justin asked.

"He can help us *and* he can hurt us, and I just don't know how he'll do."

"You've been over his story ten times with him."

"Right. And every time it comes out a bit different. Not the words, but the music. His affect changes all the time, and jurors look at that kind of thing."

"What about the ethical problem?" Justin asked.

"The ethical problem has become more of a tactical problem at this point. The ploy we practiced of bringing him right to the edge and then not asking him the crucial questions would backfire in light of how explicit and direct Jennifer Dowling was."

"So what's it going to be, Abe?"

"I'm going to leave it to Campbell. I'll lay out the options, give him my best assessment of the costs and benefits, and let him decide."

"That's not like you. This is your call. You're the guy with all the experience."

"Yeah, except this is not an experience call. Campbell is unique, and this case is unlike any I've ever had before. This guy has a rapport with the jury like I've never seen. It's his life. It's his call. Try to reach him, Justin. He's eating at Chef Chang in Brookline. I told him he might have to cut his dinner short. Tell him to meet us at the office in half an hour."

The trio rushed through dessert and hurried over to the office. Campbell arrived a few minutes later with Emma in tow. "My friends got tied up in New York. I called your house. Your daughter answered and was kind enough to join me for dinner. She told me all your secrets."

"I don't tell her any secrets. Not mine and not yours."

"Your daughter knows a lot about basketball—for a girl." Campbell smiled teasingly.

"I know a lot even for a boy," Emma shot back.

"All right, Emma, you got your treat—dinner with an NBA star. Now it's time for you to skedaddle. We've got decisions to

227

make and you can't participate in them." If Abe had any thoughts about Emma having dinner with Campbell, he kept them to himself.

"I hope Joe takes the stand. He'll be a great witness," Emma asserted.

"Thank you, F. Lee Ringel, and good night."

"Good night, Daddy. Good night, Joe. Justin, Rendi, see you around."

As Emma was leaving, Abe gestured to Joe to sit next to Justin. "Okay, let's get down to business. It's decision time. Joe, it's your call. To testify or not to testify—that is the question."

"To testify," Campbell said matter-of-factly. "Now wasn't that easy?"

"Wait a minute. It's not that easy. Even putting aside the ethics issue, Puccio will grill you like you've never been grilled before."

"No, she won't."

"Why not? Have you seduced her, too?"

"She wishes. No, I haven't seduced her. And you're right, she would grill me if she could."

"Well, she can—if you testify."

"No, she can't," Campbell said with a smile, "because I've testified already, and I don't have to take the witness stand."

"How many Chinese beers did you have for dinner?" Rendi inquired. "Don't you understand that if you testify, you get cross-examined. And you haven't testified yet."

"Yes, I have," Campbell replied smugly. "Just before the trial began, Abe told me this story about a guy on trial for murdering his wife—"

"You mean the corpse-walking-through-the-door story," Justin broke in. "We've all heard that one."

"Well, I hadn't. And it gave me a great idea. I'm surprised none of you noticed it."

"I noticed it," Abe said.

"What the hell are you talking about?" Justin asked.

"I've been testifying throughout the prosecution's case. I've made eye contact with several jurors, especially the scuba-diving one you were all worried about. She knows what my position is. She knows what I admit and what I deny. And she believes me—without my ever having said a word."

"He may be right," Abe said. "I did see what he was doing. He may already have given his best testimony, without even having sworn an oath to tell the truth. At least as far as Ms. Scuba Diver is concerned."

"My God," Justin said. "You learn something new every day in this game. I've never heard of this one before, testifying without saying a word."

"Actually, I've seen it before," Abe said. "An entirely different context, but the same principle."

"What happened there?" Justin asked.

"It was a Mafia case. A former associate of a major crime figure had made a deal with the feds and was testifying against his former boss. The boss never said a word. He looked the witness right in the eye as if to say 'You rat on me and your entire family is dead.' "

"What did the witness do?"

"He freaked. Changed his entire testimony. The mobster got off."

"That's what I call confronting the witness," Justin said.

"That wasn't the same principle at all," Rendi said. "The mobster used fear. Joe used lust."

"Getting back to Campbell," Abe said, "Henry Pullman tells us we're in trouble. Most of his shadow jurors, especially the young feminist and the black woman, believe Jennifer Dowling. Another shadow was very impressed with the doctor, and several of the other women keep talking about the vaginal abrasion and the size of Campbell's penis. Right now there's six for conviction, only three for acquittal, and three up in the air. The majority seems likely to swing the others to their side. Henry says we've got to put Campbell on."

"That's because I haven't made eye contact with the shadow jurors," Campbell said. "The shadows haven't heard—or seen—me testify, only the real jurors have."

"What about the abrasion?" Justin asked. "Several of the shadows seem impressed with that and were clearly influenced by Puccio's question about your being smaller than average."

"I've taken care of that." Campbell smiled.

With that comment, every eye in the room turned to Campbell's gray cashmere trousers, which were unusually tight around the inner thigh. The outline of his penis was plainly discernible.

"I dress left, and my tailor knows how to bring out the best in me."

The boast seemed justified as six eyes looked down on what appeared to be a cylindrical bulge in his pants.

"You're wearing falsies!" Rendi exclaimed with a mixture of admiration for Campbell's ingenuity and disgust for his duplicity.

"If that's not his," Justin said, "we may be participating in a fraud on the court. Don't we have an obligation, Abe, to check the evidence?"

"Don't be silly," Abe replied. "We don't know whether it's true or false, and in the absence of evidence to the contrary, we have an obligation to believe our client." He turned to Campbell. "That's the last time you're wearing those pants. You've made your point, so to speak. Now, please, back to baggy pants. I don't want Puccio or the judge seeing what you're doing."

"No chance," Campbell said. "That's the last place either of them would ever look. Ms. Scuba Diver has had her eyes on me since the time Puccio asked the question, and when I wore these pants the next day, she gave me a knowing glance as if to say you've proved your case to me."

As much as Abe hated to admit it, he knew he could trust Campbell's reading of people—the man had made his reputation on his ability to read the opposition.

"Well, I guess the decision is easy," Abe said. "Campbell

has certainly convinced me that in light of everything we now know, the defense should probably rest."

"And it certainly avoids the ethical issues we were worried about," Justin added.

"Well, at least it *changes* the ethical issue," Abe said. "I'm still going to have to tiptoe through a lot of ethical tulips in my closing argument."

"So it's decided," Rendi declared with a sigh of relief. "No defense. We rest."

"It's gonna shock the hell out of Puccio," Justin said with satisfaction. "She's been preparing for weeks to cross-examine Campbell and to put on a strong rebuttal case. I heard through the grapevine that she even got the son of one of her friends—a college basketball player—to act the part of Campbell in a mock cross-examination. What do you think she'll do?"

"She has no choice. The prosecution has rested. The defense will rest first thing in the morning tomorrow. She had better be ready with her closing argument. I'm sure as hell not ready for mine yet, but at least she goes first."

Chapter Twenty-eight

"The defense rests, Your Honor. We're ready for closing arguments," Abe announced.

Cheryl Puccio showed her surprise. "Wait a minute, please, Your Honor. Can we meet in chambers?"

"All right, everyone in my chambers."

As they were walking toward Judge Gambi's chambers, Puccio whispered to Abe, "You son of a bitch. You really sandbagged me. I was sure you were going to put Campbell on. And I was ready for him."

"That's why I didn't put him on." Abe smiled. "My job is to sandbag you."

"This isn't a game, Mr. Ringel," Puccio said angrily. "You're representing a dangerous rapist, and you know it. That's why you're not putting him on. You would be suborning perjury if you put him on."

"I'm glad you know so much about my tactics—and my ethics."

When they entered Judge Gambi's chambers, Puccio immediately asked for a one-day delay in the trial so she could work on her closing argument.

"No way, Your Honor," Abe objected. "My client is entitled to a speedy trial and a speedy verdict. Lawyers are supposed to be prepared for anything."

"Mr. Ringel deliberately lulled me into thinking that he was planning to put on a defense."

"I *was* planning to put on a defense. I prepared Mr. Campbell to testify. Ms. Puccio's case turned out to be so weak that I don't have to put him on."

"That's entirely your call," Judge Gambi said. "And the prosecution should have been ready for it. I certainly wasn't surprised. I thought it could go either way. I'm ready with my instructions. As a courtesy, I will give the prosection the morning to do its homework, but the state's closing argument begins at one P.M. sharp and ends at two forty-five P.M. Defense goes from three P.M. to five P.M. Prosecution gets fifteen minutes for rebuttal. This case is not all that complex. My instructions begin at nine A.M. tomorrow. I'll be done by ten, and the jury will have the case by ten-fifteen. With any luck, we could have a verdict by tomorrow afternoon."

That afternoon Puccio's closing argument, like the woman herself, was direct, no-nonsense, without dramatics. After speaking for twenty minutes, she came to the heart of her case:

"There is one unusual aspect of this case that I will now touch on. Joe Campbell did not rape in order to get sex. He could have gotten sex from Jennifer Dowling without raping her. She testified that she was willing, indeed eager, to have a sexual relationship with him. Then Joe Campbell deliberately said something to her that led her to change her mind. Why he did that we can only surmise, but that is not part of our burden of proof. We do not have to prove to you *why* Joe Campbell wanted to rape Jennifer Dowling—only that he *did* rape her. Somehow he found out something that he knew would upset Jennifer, and he whispered it to her. We don't know how he found out, and that's not something we have to prove, either. All we have to prove is that Jennifer said no for whatever reason and that Joe Campbell forced her to have sex with him for whatever reason.

"And you heard her testify that she did say no. Why would

she lie about something like that, especially after she acknowledged that she originally did want to have sex with him?

"Moreover, Ms. Dowling's testimony is corroborated by
physical evidence. Mr. Campbell caused an abrasion that you
heard Dr. Stiller say is consistent with forced sex. Oh, sure, it's
also consistent with consensual sex with a man with a very large
penis. We have heard absolutely no evidence, however, about
the size of Joe Campbell's penis, and there is no reason for you
to assume that it is anything but average."

Several jurors murmured at the mention of Campbell's penis
size, but a rap from Judge Gambi's gavel quickly silenced them.

Cheryl Puccio ended her argument with a logical review of
all the prosecution's evidence and a simple request for a verdict
of guilty so that Jennifer Dowling might get on with her life.

Now it was Abe's turn. His only turn. Puccio would get to
rebut Abe's argument. She would get the last word. He had to
make his argument so convincing that even Puccio's rebuttal
would not change the juror's minds. He could feel the adrenaline.

"Men and women of the jury, you have heard a truly brilliant presentation by one of the best prosecutors in the county.
She has to be good, because the facts of her case don't make
sense. Think about how many times she admitted to you that she
couldn't explain what she claimed were facts. Review them in
your own minds. She couldn't explain *why* Joe Campbell supposedly raped Jennifer Dowling if he knew that Jennifer was ready,
willing, and eager to have sex with him voluntarily. She couldn't
explain *how* Joe Campbell supposedly learned about Jennifer's
very private secret, or *why* he would whisper it to her just before
they were beginning to have voluntary sex. She had no idea
whether this six-foot-three-inch man has a penis that would be
average for a man who is five feet nine inches or for a man who
is six inches taller than the average man.

"The prosecutor has made a heroic effort to fill these gaping
holes in her Swiss cheese by trying to persuade you that she does
not have the burden of proving these unknowns. And the judge

will tell you that she is right, as a strict matter of law. However, as a matter of simple logic, how can you convict a man of one of the most heinous crimes on the books without understanding *why* he would do it, *how* he obtained the secret information that the complaining witness claims he had, and *whether* his physiology is consistent with evidence of rape or consensual sex. There are just too many I-don't-knows, maybes, and uncertainties in this case for you to find Joe Campbell guilty beyond a reasonable doubt.

"There are only two pillars to the prosecution's house of cards, and both are shaky at best. The first is Jennifer Dowling. She makes a good witness. Smart, attractive, and with no obvious motive to lie. Yet she admitted to you that she deliberately lied about her sexual harassment claim and changed her story only after her friend testified against her. She admitted that she told a half-truth to the police in order to get them to believe her. And the other half of a half-truth is a half-lie. Would she not also be willing to present a half-lie to you in order to get you to believe her?

"Most of what Jennifer Dowling told you was the truth. Indeed, only a small portion of it was false. She did want to have sex with Joe Campbell. That is true. She did put in her diaphragm. She did take off her bra in the bathroom. She did suggest sex to my client. She did reach down and touch his genitals. All of this is true."

Throughout his summation, Abe fought to stay focused on the here and now. For one instant, as his eyes caught Jennifer's, he was distracted. A wave of self-doubt swept through him. He thought fleetingly of Nancy Rosen's valor compared with his own conflicting motivations, and—not for the first time—he silently cursed Alex O'Donnell for the "favor" of bringing him to Joe Campbell. Then he pushed his doubts back. It was too late now—now he must win.

"What is *false*—and what defies common sense—is that Joe Campbell would suddenly change from a warm, gentle person into a monster who is whispering strange things into Jennifer Dowling's ear and then pouncing on her like a teenage boy whose hormones are raging out of control. Such transformations from Dr. Jekyll into Mr. Hyde may make interesting fiction, but they are not the stuff of real life. Why would Joe Campbell take by force what he was offered willingly? Why would he deliberately destroy the mood of romance? Why would he risk his entire career, his fortune, and his liberty for something that Jennifer Dowling was all too willing to give him without any risk?

"Yes, sex is a strong and powerful force. It makes people—both *men* and *women*—do and say things that seem entirely out of character. Still, you cannot answer these difficult questions by general speculations about sex. You must look to the evidence, and there is nothing in the evidence in this case that answers those questions."

Abe looked at the jurors to try to get some sense of how he was doing. How did the women react to his suggestion that women were sometimes driven by sex to lie? How did the men react to his Dr. Jekyll and Mr. Hyde reference? He hoped to see signs of approval so that he could skip the next—and most dangerous—part of his argument. There were no overt signs, just cold stares. He had to go on.

"Now we come to what may be the hardest part of your job. If you conclude—as I urge you to under the evidence—that Joe Campbell is innocent, your job is easy. You are required to go with your conclusion and find him not guilty. If you are uncertain about his innocence or guilt, your job is also easy. You must find him not guilty.

"Now here's the hard part. If any of you think he is *probably* guilty, you must *still* find him not guilty, because 'probably' isn't enough. You must be certain beyond a reasonable doubt. It's hard to vote not guilty when you believe the defendant is *probably* guilty. In your personal decisions about important matters, you generally go with the probabilities. And why not? If something is more probable than not, you should go with the more probable, rather than with the less probable.

"A criminal trial is different. Our tradition says that it is better for ten guilty defendants to go free than for even one innocent defendant to be wrongfully convicted.

"Sometimes I wish our country had the Scottish verdict of 'not *proven*.' That's easier to say than 'not guilty,' when you think the defendant probably *is* guilty, but when you're not convinced beyond a reasonable doubt. I sincerely hope that none of you will have to reach that hard decision and that all of you will agree with me that the evidence in this case points unerringly in the direction of innocence. Since I cannot know what is in each of your minds, I must take the precaution of talking to you as if some of you may believe that Joe Campbell is probably guilty. If there are any of you on the jury who think that, I ask you to listen to the judge's instructions on reasonable doubt and to remember that a vote for a verdict of not guilty is not a vote for *innocence*. It is a vote that the prosecution has not satisfied its heavy burden of proving beyond all reasonable doubt that the defendant is guilty."

Abe was nearing the end. Now it was time for a gambit that he himself had invented and used successfully in numerous cases—none, however, quite like this one.

"One final request before I turn the lectern back to my distinguished adversary. The prosecutor always gets the last word. That is a powerful advantage. I cannot anticipate and answer every argument she will make. Indeed, some prosecutors deliberately reserve certain arguments for rebuttal because they know there will be no opportunity for the defense to respond to them."

"Objection, Your Honor. He's charging me with something that *other* prosecutors may do."

"Well, if you don't do it, Ms. Puccio, his argument will ring hollow. No harm, no foul. Overruled. Please wrap it up, Mr. Ringel."

"Thank you, Your Honor. Back to my request. As Ms. Puccio is making her final argument, I would ask each of you to think of what I would probably say if I had a chance to reply to her. When you hear her make an argument, try to listen to it from my perspective. In that way, you will help level the playing field. In that way, the trial will become a search for truth, rather than a game in which the home team gets the advantage of batting last.

"Let me give you an example. If Ms. Puccio were to argue that Ms. Dowling told the truth by admitting that she had inserted her diaphragm, you should reply—because you know I would reply if I had the opportunity—that she had no choice but to tell the truth about *that,* since the rape kit showed the presence of spermicide. That is the sort of thing I would like you to do for me—and for justice. Play the role of defense lawyer during the prosecutor's rebuttal. In that way, no arguments will remain unanswered. I thank you for your attention, and I urge you to think carefully about your verdict. If you do, I am confident that it will be not guilty."

Abe sat down, satisfied that he had put forth the best possible case for Campbell without crossing into any ethical minefields. At this moment he even believed his client was innocent. Were the jury to vote now, he was convinced it would acquit. Unfortunately, the jury didn't vote after the defendant's closing argument. It voted after the prosecutor's rebuttal and the judge's instructions. Either or both of these could change the dynamic of the deliberations.

Cheryl Puccio was known for her rebuttal summations, which were the true test of a great prosecutor. A lawyer could plan the main part of her closing arguments. The rebuttal summation—the last word—could rarely be planned. It had to pick up on the strongest points of the defense lawyer's summation and turn them against the defendant and in favor of the prosecution. Puccio was a master of this art form. Now it was her case to win.

She picked up her notepad and walked to the jury box, pausing just long enough to look each of the jurors in the eye, as if to say to them "This isn't a game. Don't be hoodwinked by Ringel's clever arguments. Get back to basics. This man Campbell is a rapist." That's what her eyes said. Her words were different, more subtle.

"Ladies and gentlemen, Mr. Ringel is right. There are some I-don't-knows and maybes in this case. This is not *L.A. Law* or *Perry Mason*. This is real life, where no announcer tells you before the last commercial break what actually happened. There are always uncertainties in real-life cases. That is why the judge will instruct you that proof beyond a reasonable doubt is not proof to an absolute certainty. Fanciful doubts, such as those which Mr. Ringel has tried to plant in your minds, are not enough for acquittal. For you to acquit this man, your doubts must be *reasonable*. They must be based on reason, not whim, not gut feelings, not sympathy, but rather on facts, evidence, reality.

"With that in mind, let's return to the evidence in this case. The central question is, Do you believe Jennifer Dowling? If you do, then you can have no reasonable doubt about the defendant's guilt. There is no wiggle room there. If *she* is telling the truth, then *he* is guilty beyond a reasonable doubt. This is not a case where reasonable people could have different views about whether Jennifer Dowling did or did not consent. If you believe her, as you should, she clearly withdrew her prior consent in unequivocal language: 'No,' 'Stop.' Mr. Campbell could not have misunderstood that withdrawal of consent. Nor is he entitled—as a matter of law—to believe that 'stop' means 'go' and 'no' means 'yes.' If you believe Jennifer Dowling, then you must convict Joe Campbell.

"Now, let me tell you why you must believe that Jennifer Dowling is telling the truth. If she were lying—if she were trying to frame an innocent man—why would she admit that it was she who asked for sex? She could easily have said it was Campbell who asked. After all, there were no other witnesses. Second, she admitted that she made the first sexual move with her hands. She could easily have lied about that—if she were a liar. Again, no other witnesses to contradict her. Finally, she admitted that she took off her undergarments."

At this point Campbell looked directly at Ms. Scuba Diver, who nodded in recognition, as if to say "Of course she admitted all that. Once the presence of spermicide was shown, Dowling had little option but to acknowledge that she had initially consented to sex."

Several of the other jurors, having been asked by Abe to act as his surrogate, also seemed to understand that Puccio was overstating her case. Several furrowed brows and questioning looks made Abe very hopeful about what was going on.

Puccio resumed her closing argument, unaware of the interplay between Campbell and Ms. Scuba Diver but a bit concerned about the furrowed brows. Quickly she improvised a response.

"To be sure, there was some physical evidence that Jennifer Dowling had consented to sex—the spermicide, for example. Remember there was no hard evidence of *who* initiated the sex. And yet she told the truth—a truth that certainly doesn't help her cause. She trusts you, ladies and gentlemen of the jury, to believe that she changed her mind, as she had every right to do. She trusts you not to hold the truth against her. And you should not.

"The medical evidence is merely corroborative of Jennifer Dowling's testimony. It helps you decide whether or not to believe her. Our case stands squarely on her credibility. If you conclude she is telling the truth, you should convict. If you conclude she is lying, you should acquit. It really is as simple as that.

"Before you retire to deliberate, I ask you to do one thing. Please. Look Jennifer Dowling straight in the eye and ask yourself: 'Is she lying?' "

When Cheryl Puccio issued this solemn challenge to the jury, Abe could not bring himself to accept it. He could not look Jennifer Dowling in the eye. He hoped the jurors were not looking at *him*. Out of the corner of his eye, he saw that the other jurors had accepted Puccio's clever challenge. They were looking directly at Jennifer Dowling. All except for Julianne Barrow. She was looking Joe Campbell in the eye. Joe was not glancing back at her. He was looking Jennifer Dowling straight in the eye and shaking his head, as if to accuse her of lying. What a piece of work this guy is, Abe thought. He really took to heart the story about the corpse walking through the door.

Again Cheryl Puccio missed this byplay. It was becoming apparent to Abe that Joe played to the jury only when Puccio was focused on examining witnesses and Judge Gambi's attention was elsewhere. Now the prosecutor finished her rebuttal summation:

"Ladies and gentlemen of the jury, I ask you not to brand Jennifer Dowling a liar. I ask you to believe her. And if you do, you have no choice but to convict Joe Campbell of rape. Thank you."

It was vintage Puccio. Unemotional, factual, and compelling. She had used Abe's arguments in her favor. She sat down, and every eye in the courtroom turned to the jurors' faces in an effort to read their minds. Had she gotten through to them? Had the dynamic shifted away from Abe and Campbell and in her favor?

A few apparent nods of agreement seemed to suggest that Puccio had gotten through to some of the jurors. That was to be expected. So were the poker faces on several other jurors. There was no way of counting noses from the few ambiguous signs. And in any event, minds could change even after all the arguments. The judge's instructions changed minds. The discussion in the jury room changed minds. A restless night of sleep sometimes changed a mind. Even with all the scientific breakthroughs in jury evaluation, the dynamics of a jury decision were still largely in the realm of speculation. Abe knew enough never to be cocky in a jury case.

At dinner that night, Henry Pullman gave his report on the

shadow jurors. "The jurors liked Puccio's argument that Dowling didn't have to tell the truth about who initiated the sex. Puccio has managed to turn that negative into a positive."

"Anything else?" Abe asked.

"Yeah. There are still a couple of shadows who tell me in private that they can't vote to convict a guy for rape if the woman was asking for it, even if she changed her mind."

"That's good for us, right?" Justin asked.

"Wrong. That's what they're willing to say in private—to an old man like me. Most likely they won't be willing to say that to their fellow jurors. They may be afraid to vote for acquittal on that basis and be thought of as sexist, or worse."

"So it's bad?"

"No, not necessarily. It's a wild card."

"Bottom line, Henry?" Abe inquired.

"Bottom line is that it doesn't look like a unanimous acquittal to my shadows. But then again, my shadows have not had the dubious benefit of being made love to by the eyes of the great White Knight. Who knows!"

"Nor can they look into the eyes of Jennifer Dowling," Rendi added.

"Is there anything I can ask the judge for in her instructions that could help us with the issues your shadows came up with?" Abe asked.

Pullman thought for a moment, consulted his notes, and replied, "Yes, there is."

"What?"

"My jurors were very impressed with Puccio's argument that this isn't a case about reasonable doubt. It's a case about whether or not you believe Jennifer. They like that because it empowers them. They're used to deciding whether someone is telling the truth or lying. They think they're good at that. It requires basic common sense. They hate this reasonable doubt stuff. They don't know how to think that way—about probabilities and stuff like that."

"So what can the judge tell them that will help us?"

"You're asking the wrong guy *that* question," Pullman said. "Abe, you're our expert on jury instructions."

"I've got to think about that one, Henry. Thanks for the info. I'll try to have an answer for that problem by morning."

Chapter Twenty-nine

"Any proposed changes in my instructions, Counsel, before I deliver them?"

"Yes, Your Honor. I have two," Abe responded. "First, I would respectfully request the court to give a specific instruction requiring the jury to find *beyond a reasonable doubt* that Dowling is telling the truth."

"No way, Your Honor," Puccio responded quickly. "Our burden is not to prove the truth of any particular witness's testimony beyond a reasonable doubt. Our case as a whole must meet that burden—not each component of it."

"How can your whole case be proved beyond a reasonable doubt, unless your *critical* witness is believed beyond a reasonable doubt? You yourself argued yesterday that your whole case turns on whether the jury believes Jennifer is telling the truth."

"Good point, Mr. Ringel," noted Judge Gambi. "How do you respond, Ms. Puccio?"

"Let me give you an example," she replied. "Assume that the jurors believe Jennifer's uncorroborated testimony, but not beyond a reasonable doubt. Then they hear this corroboration, which they also believe, but not beyond a reasonable doubt. In that case, neither the testimony *standing alone*, nor the corroboration *standing alone*, would satisfy the standard of proof beyond a reasonable doubt. Yet *both together*—they can add up to proof beyond a reasonable doubt."

"*Better* point," Judge Gambi acknowledged. "Now it's your turn, Mr. Ringel." The judge was obviously enjoying this exchange between two very able lawyers. Abe was not, because he knew he had been bested by Puccio. He tried to respond to her compelling point, without any real hope of success.

"Ms. Puccio is trying to argue that two weak pieces of evidence, neither of which alone satisfies the standard of proof beyond a reasonable doubt, can be slapped together, and somehow the heat of the collision will magically produce a result that is greater than the sum of its parts. That defies both the laws of physics and the laws of logic."

"Nice try, Mr. Ringel. Ms. Puccio wins this round. I will not require the jury to conclude beyond a reasonable doubt that Ms. Dowling's testimony, standing alone, establishes guilt, because in this case her testimony does not stand alone. It is the jury's decision whether the medical evidence provides corroboration."

"My next request, Your Honor, is that you not give the standard instruction in which proof beyond a reasonable doubt is defined as that 'level of proof on which you would act in the most important decisions of your life.' "

"What's wrong with that instruction, Mr. Ringel? I give it all the time and nobody ever objects to it."

"What's wrong, Your Honor, is that rational people always make important decisions on the basis of a mere preponderance of the evidence, as well they should. For example, if there are two medications for a particular heart condition, and one is slightly better than the other—say one has a fifty-five percent cure rate and the other a forty-five percent cure rate—and both have equivalent risks and side effects, only a fool would go with the forty-five percent when he could have the fifty-five percent."

"What does that have to do with reasonable doubt?"

"That's exactly my point. It has nothing to do with reasonable doubt."

"Now you really are confusing me, Mr. Ringel."

"Let me try to explain."

"Go ahead. It's your motion."

"Okay, Your Honor. In a criminal case, the jury is *supposed* to go with the forty-five percent, *not* the fifty-five percent. If the jury concludes that it is fifty-five percent likely that the defendant is guilty and only forty-five percent likely that he is innocent, they should go with the forty-five percent and acquit, not with the fifty-five percent. Even if it's seventy-five percent to twenty-five percent, the juror should go with the twenty-five percent for innocence. That's what it means to say 'better ten guilty go free than one innocent be convicted.' And that type of thinking is counterintuitive for most jurors, because it is *not* the way they decide other important issues in their lives. So you should explain the difference to them."

"What *would* you have me say?"

"With respect, Your Honor, I would like you to say exactly the opposite from what you usually say."

"You certainly know how to ask for the moon, Mr. Ringel. Be more specific."

"I would respectfully ask Your Honor to instruct the jury that they should *not* make their decision in this case the same way that they make decisions about important issues in their own lives. You should tell them that a decision in a criminal case is *very* different from other decisions, because we are much more afraid of an erroneous guilty verdict than of an erroneous not guilty verdict."

"Go on, Mr. Ringel."

"Therefore, even if, for purposes of deciding whether to hire him as a baby-sitter or allow him to date your daughter, you would conclude that Mr. Campbell *probably* did rape Ms. Dowling, you should not conclude that he did it for purposes of deciding this criminal case, *unless* you believe that the evidence that he did it is so strong that it leaves you with absolutely no reasonable doubt."

"Well, Ms. Puccio," Judge Gambi said, turning to the prosecutor, "Mr. Ringel makes a convincing argument that I've been giving the wrong instruction for ten years. Can you help me convince myself that I've been right all these years?"

"I'll try, Your Honor. People understand that important decisions aren't always made on a mere preponderance of the evidence. You don't have open-heart surgery unless you've resolved all your reasonable doubts. The traditional instruction reflects that common sense, and you've been right to give it all these years."

"I'm flattered by your support, Ms. Puccio, but I think that Mr. Ringel is correct. I'm not going to give my usual instruction. Nor will I give Mr. Ringel's understandably pro-defendant instruction. What I will say is that criminal trials are different and that the jury should not convict merely on the basis of the usual level of certainty it requires in other decisions, but rather on the basis of proof beyond a reasonable doubt. I'll leave the rest to their good old-fashioned common sense."

"That's agreeable to me, Your Honor," Abe said.

"I don't agree, Your Honor," Ms. Puccio said.

"Ms. Puccio, I've made up my mind."

Judge Gambi then ordered the marshal to lock all the doors, requested quiet in the courtroom, and solemnly read her instructions. It always bothered Abe how much more seriously judges took their own instructions than they did the arguments of the lawyers. Spectators were free to walk in and out during the lawyers' arguments. When the judge instructed, it was like a papal mass.

After reviewing the elements of the crime of rape and the rules of evidence, Judge Gambi gave the "reasonable doubt" instructions she had promised. The jurors seemed to pay particular attention to that part of the judge's presentation.

Then Judge Gambi issued her final words to the jury: "Your

first task is to select a foreperson who will preside. He or she has no greater or lesser influence than anyone else. You should listen to others and maintain an open mind until the final vote. In the end, you must decide whether or not you believe that the defendant has been proven guilty beyond a reasonable doubt. If you so conclude, you should vote to convict, without regard to your feelings toward the defendant, the complainant, or anyone else. If you conclude that there is a reasonable doubt, you should vote to acquit, without regard to your feelings toward the defendant, the complainant, or anyone else. Now, go and do justice."

Abe was satisfied with the instructions. It was fair, down the middle. Henry Pullman soon confirmed his assessment. "She didn't change a single vote. It's still the same. They're all over the lot."

As the jurors left the courtroom to deliberate, none gave any sign as to which way they were leaning—no smiles, no glances at the defendant, no clue at all. Even Ms. Scuba Diver averted her eyes from the direction of the defense table and walked straight out.

Now it was time to play the lawyer's favorite guessing game: When would they return? Would a short deliberation mean an acquittal or a conviction? Would a long deliberation signal a hung jury?

"I sure hope it's not a hung jury," Campbell said with a sigh. "That would be terrible for my endorsements. And we would have to go through the whole thing again."

"A hung jury would be a hell of a lot better than a conviction," Justin replied.

"There won't be a conviction," Campbell added quickly. "I'm not worried about that. Ms. Scuba Diver would never allow that."

"How can you be so sure?" Abe asked.

"Don't worry, Abe. I'm not a Mafia defendant. I didn't bribe any jurors. I just know women. That's my expertise, like yours is knowing judges."

"I don't try to seduce judges."

"We each have our way."

"There's no legitimate way you can be as certain as you sound," Justin insisted.

Abe interjected: "Let's not open up any cans of worms, Justin. Your curiosity will just have to remain unabated."

"Hey, c'mon, guys," Campbell interrupted. "I don't want you to think I'm some kind of corrupter of jurors or some kind of nut psychic. So I'll tell you my deep, dark secret. It's very simple. When I play basketball, especially on the road, I often pick out an attractive, unaccompanied woman in the stands and make eye contact with her—while I'm on the court and when I'm on the bench. I've developed this ability to make love with my eyes. And I know when it's working. If it's working, I arrange to have one of the ball boys deliver a note to her in the stands, inviting her for a drink. It almost always works. I know what I'm doing."

"That's a drink. This is a verdict. Could be different," Rendi said.

"We'll see who is right," Campbell said. "When this case is over, I'll meet Ms. Scuba Diver for a drink and ask her. That's how confident I am."

A stunned silence greeted Campbell's display of bravado.

Five o'clock arrived with no verdict. The jury was sent to the Howard Johnson's Motor Lodge for dinner and a good night's sleep. Deliberations would resume at nine A.M. the next morning.

There was no more frustrating time for a lawyer than when the jury was deliberating. There was absolutely nothing Abe could do to affect the outcome of the Campbell case. Yet he was so focused on the case that he couldn't possibly turn his attention to other matters.

Like most lawyers, Abe hated not to be in control—not even to know what was going on. Part of him wanted to get away from the entire case—to be with Emma, to talk about her schoolwork, her plans for Barnard, her boyfriend, her life. This was her last year at home. He would miss her, despite his periodic trips to the Big Apple. After she left home, their relationship would never be the same.

Abe had arranged a dinner with Campbell, Justin, Rendi, and Pullman. There was really nothing to talk about except speculation concerning the outcome of the case. Why not invite Emma, Abe thought. This wouldn't be a lawyer-client confidential meeting. It was more of an obligatory social event. He could sit next to Emma and talk to her, while the others gossiped about Judge Gambi, Cheryl Puccio, the jurors, and Jennifer Dowling. He called her.

Emma was thrilled with the invitation. "Thank you for finally treating me as a grownup, Daddy, and for finally recognizing that I *can* be trusted with secrets."

"Nice try, Emma. Rules are rules. You can't be trusted with *legal* secrets yet. No one outside the legal team can be. This is a social dinner. No secrets tonight."

"Okay, at least I get to talk about the case."

"In a general way. No specifics."

Abe told everyone that he would meet them all at the Changsho Restaurant. He had to do something first.

Haskel's house was on the way to the restaurant, and Abe decided to drop in on his old friend.

When Jerome opened the door, Abe knew it was an off day. The Haitian aide was sensitive, his feelings tended to show easily in his eyes, and no matter how many old and sick people he might have tended to, he never seemed inured to Haskel's bad spells. Abe knew the routine by now, so he went immediately to Haskel's bedroom, bypassing the study. He wondered just how long it would be before they closed up the study for good.

Once upstairs, while Haskel's mind roamed, Abe told him of the trial. "I can't be torn like this too many more times, Haskel. How did you manage to keep your ethics together?"

Silence, of course, greeted him. This time Abe joined the

long silence, which was finally broken by the ringing of the old rotary phone next to the bed. Abe was deciding whether or not to answer it when Jerome called on the intercom next to Haskel's bed. "It's for you, Mr. Ringel, it's your lady friend."

"Abe?" Rendi asked.

"Am I that predictable?"

"Yes. How is he today?"

"Not so good," Abe whispered into the phone. "Out of it. But not cantankerous. He's getting past that point, unfortunately."

"I thought you'd want to know. You just got a call from New Jersey. They've got Owens in custody. I don't know whether he turned himself in or they caught him. But he's in jail."

"So, there is a God, after all."

"What does this mean for Nancy?"

"It's too early to tell. It can't hurt."

"I'll see you at dinner?"

"Do me a favor. Make sure Campbell has a lot of beer and talks to everyone else. I want to spend some time with my daughter."

"Later, then."

"I need you in my corner. Have I told you that?"

"Rarely, but it shows anyway."

After they hung up, Abe got ready to leave. As he bent down to bid Haskel good-bye, the old man grabbed his wrist. "The verdict of a court is not the verdict of history."

Was this Haskel's usual delphic pronouncement? What was he trying to say?

"I love you, my friend," Abe told him.

Haskel smiled. Maybe he wasn't that far gone after all.

All the way back to the restaurant, Abe thought about Haskel's message.

* * *

By the time Abe arrived at Changsho, everyone else was already seated at a large round table. "I tried to order a bottle of champagne to celebrate the end of the trial," Emma said in her most grown-up voice. "They said I had to wait for you, since I'm underage."

"No champagne yet," Abe said. "There's nothing to celebrate."

"Sure there is." Campbell smiled. "I can stop wearing these gray suits. Armani, here I come. Champagne for the table, even for Emma, if her father will permit."

"All right, one glass for Emma. Don't invest heavily in your new wardrobe yet, Joe. You may still end up wearing government issue."

Abe sat on one side of Emma, Rendi on the other. He tried to talk to Emma. However, she was more interested in talking basketball with Joe, who was seated across the large table. After a few minutes of banter about the Knicks, Justin redirected the conversation to the trial.

"What did you folks think of Judge Gambi?"

"Great judge, that Gambi," Rendi said. "Really fair to everyone."

"And smart," Abe added.

"Of course you think she's smart," Justin said, "because she ruled in your favor on the reasonable doubt instruction. I remember how you carried on for weeks about Judge Schneider after she ruled in your favor in that sewer case."

"It was a brilliant decision," Abe said with a broad smile, as Rendi laughed out loud.

"What could possibly be so funny about a sewer case?" Campbell asked.

Abe explained. "I was representing a law school classmate in the leather tanning business who was being charged exorbitant rates for using water that eventually found its way into the sewers. I had cited a case involving a beer brewery that used even more water but was charged less. The judge asked me whether there isn't a big difference between a leather tanner and a brewery: 'The leather tanner's water ends up in the sewers, Counselor, whereas the brewery's water ends up in the drinker's body.' "

"So how did you respond?" Campbell inquired.

"I told the judge that if she waited about half an hour, the brewery's water would also end up in the sewers. She laughed and ruled in my favor. A great judge. She brought justice to the sewers."

"We need more women judges," Rendi chimed in.

"Oh, yeah," Justin said cynically. "Have you ever been before Judge Mary Mahony? That kind of a woman we don't need more of. She hates men."

"Well, what about Judge Bailey? He hates women."

"So what are you saying, Rendi? We need more men-hating women judges to balance the women-hating men judges? Maybe we should just get good judges without regard to sex."

Emma joined in: "I read somewhere that women judges are generally fairer than men judges because they've experienced more discrimination." God, was Abe proud of her. She knew just what to say and when to say it.

"Do you think Puccio will be made a judge?" Rendi asked.

"If she wins this one," Pullman said.

"She wouldn't be bad," Abe said. "She's fair—for a prosecutor."

Silence spread across the group like stains over the linen tablecloth.

Campbell recovered first. "We're not going to lose this case thanks to my great team here, so everyone can stop looking so hangdog."

"That's nice of you to say, Joe," Emma said.

When Abe looked at her he saw the hero worship in her eyes and wondered whether he could ever tell her what Rendi and Justin had dug up on the basketball star.

"Not so fast, Joe. There are only twelve people who can

dictate how this thing will turn out, and until we hear from them, I don't want to bait the gods."

"You mean you don't want a *kenaynahura?*" Campbell smiled.

Emma laughed. "Where the heck did you learn to speak Yiddish?"

"From your buddy Alex O'Donnell. He says he learned it in the old neighborhood. He always tells me that when I'm on a streak."

Emma picked up the conversation where it had ended. "Daddy, you know Linda Fairstein, the rape prosecutor in New York? Well, her new book, *Sexual Violence,* argued just the way you did when we first talked about this case. That false complaints of rape really hurt actual rape victims. In fact, the women in my group agreed that falsely accusing someone is almost as terrible as rape itself."

Abe knew she was playing to her audience here, so he kept silent.

"Where does your group stand on my case?" Campbell asked. "Do they think I was falsely accused?"

"Split verdict," Emma said. "Some do, some don't."

"What do you think?"

He was smooth, Abe thought.

"I think my father is going to prove you're innocent."

"Smart kid you got, Ringel. And she dresses a lot better than her father."

For the moment Abe appreciated Campbell's agility at negotiating difficult conversations. "No thanks to me, I might add."

"No, she's clearly an original." Campbell winked across the table at Emma.

Pullman said, "Emma's group actually is close to the shadow. I told you it might be a hung jury."

"There's only one jury that counts," said Rendi. "Not the shadows. Not Emma's group. Not even us. Just those twelve people who are now eating hotel food at the Howard Johnson's Lodge."

"With the food they feed them at Ho-Jo's, I'll bet there'll be a verdict first thing tomorrow. I think it will be before lunch," Justin predicted.

"If it's tomorrow, you're dead," Pullman said, shaking his head. "A long deliberation could be a hung jury. A short one in this case sounds like a conviction."

"I think it will be tomorrow, and I think I'm going to win," Campbell said, holding up a glass of champagne.

"To Campbell being right," Justin toasted.

"To justice," Emma added, clinking Abe's glass.

Upon hearing Emma's words, Abe was tempted to tell the old joke of the lawyer who cabled his client, "Justice has prevailed," to which his client responded, "Appeal immediately." Abe thought better of even joking about his cynicism, lest he tip his suspicions of Campbell to Emma and Pullman.

Abe and Emma walked home after dinner. During the fifteen-minute walk, Abe praised Emma for articulating her viewpoint so sensitively. "I really am a dinosaur when it comes to women's issues. Seeing you, listening to you, knowing you, has been more educational than a hundred books."

"Really, Daddy? Do you mean that?"

"Yes, I do. You know how much I rely on Haskel for his wisdom. And I rely on you for your directness, your truth, your commitment."

"Daddy, you're the smartest man I know."

"Clever, Emma, clever. There's a world of difference between the cleverness of my generation and the wisdom of Haskel's generation."

"What about my generation?"

"You've got something we lack, too. A kind of passionate honesty. It's great to be sandwiched between two such different generations, each of which teaches me so much about myself. We were brought up on the quick fix."

"You really do take me seriously sometimes, Daddy, even when you seem to be ignoring me."

"I really love you, and I love what you are and what you're in the process of becoming."

"Don't get sentimental on me," Emma said softly, holding Abe's hand. "I *need* a dinosaur to rebel against."

"Let's not grow apart when you move to New York. I'm not sure what the rules are. Can I call you every day? Or is that too clingy? You've got to tell me."

"There are no rules, Daddy. Just call whenever you feel like. I'll call you whenever I need money. That's the main rule."

"Good. Then I'll give you a dollar at a time. Seriously, though, I want you to have your own money, so you don't have to call me just for money. I want you to call me when you *feel* like it."

"I will. I just may have to do it from a pay phone. It isn't cool for a college freshman to call her daddy all the time."

"We'll be fine, Emma. I know it. Now let's enjoy our last few months together as housemates. How about a Red Sox game this weekend—if the verdict is in and it's good?"

"Sorry, Dad, I'm all booked for this weekend. Jon has tickets for a concert."

"Next weekend, then. The Vineyard. Charlotte Inn. The Black Dog."

"Sorry, Dad. Next Saturday night is my feminist group dinner. Even Jon doesn't get to go to that one. So I have to go out with him on Friday."

"All right. We'll just play it by ear. You'll fit me in sometime."

"I'll try my best, Daddy," Emma said with the Hannah smile that brought back so many memories.

Chapter Thirty

"We have a verdict," the clerk shouted to the lawyers and spectators milling around the hallway outside the courtroom. "It will be announced in ten minutes."

Abe looked at his watch. It was 11:15 A.M., just a little more than two hours since the jury had resumed its deliberations. "Now I guess we'll see who's right," he said to Pullman as they walked toward the front of the courtroom.

A few minutes after everyone was seated, the jurors were brought in. Abe quickly looked at Ms. Scuba Diver. Her head was down. She was not looking in the direction of the defense table. She was not smiling. Campbell looked in her direction. There was no response. Abe put his arm around Campbell's large shoulder, as if to comfort him. Campbell shrugged it away, as if to say "I don't need your pity. I can take it, whatever the verdict may be."

Henry Pullman made his way to the lawyer's table and whispered two words in Abe's ear: "Expect trouble." Abe expected trouble even without Henry's warning. He knew from experience that when a jury had acquitted, it generally smiled and looked at the defendant when it entered the courtroom to deliver its good news. When it was about to deliver bad news, it looked as though it were on the way to a funeral.

Only Campbell was still optimistic. "I know what you're

thinking. Don't worry. Of course they're not looking up. They're embarrassed about concluding that Jennifer is a liar. Some of them may even feel a bit guilty for doubting her, but they have a reasonable doubt. Believe me."

Abe shook his head in bewilderment. Was this man a crystal ball reader? Or was he always so self-deceptive?

"Be seated, please. We have a verdict," Judge Gambi announced.

"Ms. Foreperson," she said, "please rise." Ms. Scuba Diver stood up. "Has the jury reached a unanimous verdict?"

"We have."

"Please give the verdict sheet to the clerk, who will hand it up to me."

Judge Gambi received the one-page verdict sheet, looked at it, and showed no expression.

"Please announce your verdict."

At this point Ms. Scuba Diver glanced past the defense table and looked directly at Jennifer Dowling. Then she looked down at the verdict sheet and read: "We, the jury, find the defendant, Joseph Campbell"—she paused and looked directly at the defendant as she finished reading the verdict—"*not* guilty of rape."

The spectators reacted with a mixture of cheers and boos and loud buzzing. This time Judge Gambi did not try to quiet them down. The case was over, and those who had come to see justice done were entitled, Judge Gambi believed, to express their feelings—briefly. After about a minute, she rapped her gavel once.

"Mr. Campbell, you are free to go. Ms. Puccio and Mr. Ringel, I want to thank you both, and your staffs, for excellent presentations. Ladies and gentlemen of the jury, I never comment on a verdict except to say that you have performed an important function of citizenship. You should be proud of your willingness to take time out of your busy lives to do justice. Thank you. Court is adjourned."

Abe had spent enough time with Campbell to know not to

expect the customary hug from a grateful client. He was right, and relieved. Instead he got a cool handshake from Campbell.

"You did a good job," Campbell whispered, looking in the direction of the jury, which was leaving. "Especially considering what you think of me. Don't worry, you'll never have to see me again, except in commercials and at Celtics-Knicks games. I do want you to know that I am innocent. That's the truth. Thank you. I'll send you my last installment on your bill. Now you'll be the most sought after lawyer in America. Congratulations."

"Congratulations to you, too," Abe said. "And please get some help. Stay out of trouble."

Abe looked at Jennifer Dowling, who was sobbing uncontrollably in Cheryl Puccio's arms. Suddenly Jennifer looked at Abe and shouted across the room at him, "You're worse than Campbell. He's a sicko and a pervert. You're supposed to be a decent man. You got the jury to believe I'm a liar. And you know—deep in your heart—that I'm telling the truth. You bastard."

"I'm sorry you feel that way, Ms. Dowling," Abe said, walking toward her with his arm extended to shake her hand. "The jury didn't find you to be a liar. They just had a reasonable doubt."

"Bullshit," Jennifer replied, pulling her arm away. "You made them think I am a liar, and I'm not."

"I'm sorry. That's the way our system works." Abe walked away, his head reeling from a combination of confused feelings—ego gratification for winning, professional satisfaction at fulfilling his role as a defense attorney, and personal guilt over what he had done to Jennifer Dowling.

The defense team left the courtroom, with Campbell behind them, signing autographs. Suddenly the media descended upon them.

"Any comment, Joe?"

"Are you mad at Jennifer, Joe?"

"Abe, what do you think was the main reason for the acquittal?"

Abe responded for Campbell. "We are satisfied that justice was done and Mr. Campbell can get back to his life and his profession. He isn't mad at anybody. The reason we won is because Mr. Campbell is innocent. The state had no case. It never should have come to trial. Beyond that, we have no further comment. Ms. Puccio did an excellent job, and so did the judge and jury. Botton line, there was no case."

"So it wasn't your brilliant defense?" one journalist was shouting at Abe as they were getting into the car.

"No, it's easy to win when you have an innocent client."

That was Abe's standard response whenever he won a case. Some lawyers were quick to take credit for victories, and when they did, they created the risk that their statements would be interpreted as a suggestion that it was a difficult case because the client was really guilty. Abe always credited the client's innocence. Only this time the words did not come out so easily.

Henry Pullman was not in the car. He had stayed behind in the hope of cornering some of the jurors. He always did that in order to check the accuracy of his methods so that he could fine-tune them. It was all perfectly proper, at least in most states, and extremely educational for Henry.

Back at Abe's office there was the usual champagne and cookies that followed all victories. It had been a long time since the last victory party. There had been no champagne following Charlie Odell's release from prison, since Charlie's freedom had been achieved at the cost of Nancy Rosen's indictment. Today there was nothing—at least nothing public—to tarnish Campbell's victory.

Abe proposed a toast to Joe's freedom, and then he smashed the glass on the floor. Everyone was shocked at his uncharacteristic display of apparent violence. But he quickly explained: "There is a Jewish tradition of breaking a glass at even the most joyous events such as weddings. It reminds us that no joy is ever without some sorrow. Today there is joy in Joe Campbell's victory. Yet there is still sorrow, because Nancy Rosen remains in prison, even though the man she was convicted of helping to escape is now in custody."

Campbell, who had heard bits and pieces of the Rosen drama from Abe and Justin, joined in: "To Nancy's freedom."

Abe would never be able to fathom the man. So much of him seemed—at least on the surface—to be so decent, so normal. If Justin and Rendi were right, where did his demons come from?

He had to put the most positive face on Campbell's acquittal, especially since most of the people at the party—including Emma—knew nothing about Campbell's secret. One day he would tell Emma the truth about Joe's background, Abe thought to himself. But not for many years.

About an hour into the party, Henry Pullman came bursting through the door. He grabbed Abe and Rendi and pulled them into an empty conference room. "You're not going to believe this. I spoke to four jurors, including Julianne Barrow."

"What did they tell you?" Rendi asked.

"This guy Campbell is really something. In all my years in this business, I've never seen anything like him."

"How so?"

Henry took his notepad out of his jacket pocket. "The first guy I spoke to was Harrison Fowler, the truck driver from Malden. Listen to what he told me. I wrote down his exact words."

Henry started to read his notes. " 'When I first heard Jennifer's testimony, it sounded true. Then I believed Campbell's denial.' "

"He didn't deny anything," Rendi said.

"Well, Fowler sure thought he did," Henry insisted. "When I pressed him on that, this is what he said: 'Oh, I know he didn't actually take the witness stand, but I was watching him very carefully. His denials looked very sincere. I believed him.' "

"What else did Fowler say?" Abe inquired.

"He said that Puccio really blew her credibility with that small dick question. Nobody believed that."

"Why not?" Rendi asked.

"Fowler didn't want to get into that. He just said, 'We didn't believe it.' "

"What about Ms. Scuba Diver?" Abe asked.

"I couldn't get too much from her. She seemed almost embarrassed. She talked about reasonable doubt. She said that Jennifer may have been angry because Campbell didn't treat her well. She wanted to know what Campbell was going to do now. She seemed more interested in him as a person than in the case."

"Son of a bitch. He really did seduce her. And she knows it. That's why she feels guilty. That's why she wouldn't look at us when she entered the courtroom. She voted her crotch, not her brain. Joe really did get to her hormones. Son of a bitch."

"Don't worry, Abe," Rendi teased. "The press will never know that. They'll think you won the case with your brilliant legal arguments. You're going to be a superstar."

When Abe returned to the party, Campbell was already gone. "He wanted to catch the shuttle back to New York," Emma explained. "He told me to give you a kiss good-bye and say thanks. He also said anytime *we* want tickets to a Knicks game, they're on him. That'll be great when I'm in New York. We can go together when you come down to visit."

"Maybe. We'll see," Abe said, his attention wandering to the reporters who were talking to Justin on the other side of the room.

"Justin tells us—off the record, of course,—that it was your tactical decisions that won the case," said Mike Black of the *Globe*, walking over to Abe. "Is that true?"

"Let's stay off the record for a minute, okay?" Abe replied. "Tactical *mistakes* can lose a case, and I don't think we made any. However, tactics alone rarely win a case. You've got to have the right client and the right evidence. Now back on the record. This was a team victory. Everyone on the team deserves credit."

"Abe," Black persisted, "if you had such a good client, why didn't you put him on the stand? Wasn't it risky allowing the jury to conjecture about why he didn't testify?"

Abe was pleased that even Mike Black, who was among the most perceptive law reporters in the country, wasn't suspicious. "It's always a risk to put a client on. And it's always a risk not to put a client on. That's what I get paid for—to weigh those risks in a particular case."

"Abe," called Gayle, "it's Tammy Gross from *Larry King Live*. They want you live at nine P.M."

"Fine. Have them send a car here."

"There are also calls from *Good Morning America* and the *Today* show. They both want you tomorrow. They also want Campbell."

"Try to work it out so I can be on both. Tell them no Campbell."

Abe stopped drinking champagne in anticipation of his upcoming TV interview. He went back to talking to the reporters, carefully feeding them a mixture of background material and quotable sound bites for publication.

"Abe, can you come into the office for a second?" Gayle whispered discreetly. "A new client."

"Who?"

"It's Ice Puppy, the rap singer. His real name is Mohammed Kenya. Actually his *real* name is Malcolm Royce."

"How do you know so much about him?"

"There's an article about him in the current *People*. He's been indicted for raping one of his backup singers. It's all over the papers."

"I haven't looked at a paper since before the trial. Quick, bring me a few clips while I talk to him."

Abe picked up the phone.

"You the man who got that White Knight dude off?" came the abrupt question.

"Yes, I am," Abe replied.

"Then you the man I want to be my mouthpiece. I don't care what you charge. My record company's pickin' up the tab."

"Can you come to Boston to see me, Mr. . . . . What do I call you?"

"*You* can call me Mo or Mal. My old friends call me Mal. My new friends call me Mo. I can be in Boston anytime. I got wings."

"Can it wait till the day after tomorrow?"

"Fine. First thing in the A.M., I'm there."

After Abe had finished his call, Gayle came in with another message. "Call Senator Bergson. The guy who's been accused of harassing his staff members. He wants you. Everyone wants you."

"Until I lose the next one."

"Well, you're not going to lose the next one," Gayle gushed. "You're on a roll. You're on top of the world. You're a winner."

A few minutes later, as Abe was savoring the victory, Gayle pointed to the phone again.

"Another new client?"

"No, it's a woman named Darlene Walters. Says it's about Joe Campbell. Should I tell her to call back?"

"I'll take it," Abe said, motioning for Justin and Rendi to join him in his private office. He put the call on the speaker-phone.

"Hello, Ms. Walters, I'm here with two of my associates, if that's all right. If this is about the Campbell case, you should know it's over. He was acquitted."

"I heard. That's why I decided to call. I know you were asking about me before the trial—a woman named Rendi something talked to a couple of my friends. I didn't want my name to come up at the trial, so I didn't get in touch with you."

As she spoke, Rendi whispered in Abe's ear, "She's the account executive Margie told me about. Remember, the rough sex."

"So why are you calling now?"

"I was hoping he would be convicted and put away."

"The jury has spoken, Ms. Walters."

"They didn't know what he did to me. It was just like what he did to that poor Jennifer woman."

"Look, Ms. Walters, I can hear that you're upset. But there's really nothing I can do. He was acquitted."

"He's done it before, and he's going to do it again. Somebody has got to stop him."

"I'm sorry, Ms. Walters. There's nothing I can do."

Abe started to hang up the phone when Justin stopped him. "Ms. Walters, I'm Justin Aldrich, Mr. Ringel's associate. Mr. Ringel is right. There is probably nothing we can do, but I would like to hear what you meant when you said that what he did to you was like what they say he did to Jennifer."

Abe was upset at Justin's intrusion. He didn't want to hear what he knew was probably coming. Unfortunately it was too late. He couldn't hang up the phone now, as Darlene Walters began to tell her story.

"I met Joe at a party and really had the hots for him. It was after my divorce, and I was going through a wild phase. When he asked me out, I was thrilled. After dinner, I invited him back to my apartment and we started to make out. I *wanted* to get it on with him. Then he started to accuse me of having done something terrible during my divorce. He made me cry, and I told him to leave. He wouldn't. He really got turned on when I fought off his advances, and he beat me up. And then raped me." Darlene Walters was now sobbing into the phone.

"Did you call the police?"

"No."

"Why not?"

"I just couldn't. I don't want to get into it."

"How did Campbell find out about your divorce?" Justin asked.

"I don't know. I certainly didn't tell him. I didn't want him to know I had children. Turns off some men."

"We really appreciate your call," Justin said. "I just don't think there's anything we can do. Did you call the prosecutor?"

"No. I don't want to bring a case. I just thought you should know. Maybe you can have some influence over him. He's a real sicko. Unless he gets help, he's going to hurt someone real bad. And I didn't think you'd want that on your conscience."

"Thanks, Ms. Walters," Abe said, and hung up the phone.

Even before the line was disconnected, Rendi spoke up. "Oh, my God. Now it makes sense. Why didn't I think of it before?"

"What, what makes sense?" Abe asked.

"What Chrissy Kachinski—remember, the 'groupie' who got married to the meat guy from the south shore?—told me as I was leaving."

"What?"

"Chrissy said something about Campbell having picked the right victim, because Darlene would never complain. I figured she just meant that groupies protect the players, but it could have meant . . ."

"What, what?" Abe pressed.

"Don't you see? It all fits together. Maybe Campbell found Darlene the same way he found Jennifer, stalked her, pretended to meet her, dated her—all the while planning to rape her—knowing that she, too, was a perfect victim—a victim who would never complain."

For a moment there was silence, as they contemplated the enormity of this suspicion.

Then Justin bolted out of Abe's office in the direction of the computer room. Abe and Rendi followed, carefully skirting the office party so as not to invite questions. "What are you looking up?" Abe demanded.

"Not *what*," Justin replied as he pressed keys. "*Who*. I'm looking up Darlene Walters."

Within minutes a case appeared on the screen, a Boston appellate case. Two years old, it involved a divorce, in which the wife had accused her husband of sexually abusing their son. The judge had made a finding that the wife had made up the entire story, and custody had been awarded to the husband. The wife had appealed, and the appellate court had affirmed the lower court's ruling. Three pairs of eyes looked intently at the name of the wife on the computer screen. It was Darlene Walters.

Here was the last piece of the puzzle, the final bit of evidence that would make it impossible for Abe to deny to himself that Joe Campbell was guilty. Justin had been right: Abe had been sorely afflicted with defense lawyer's blind spot. He now realized that the truth had been there for him to see much earlier—if he had only wanted to see it. And the most disturbing part was that he couldn't be sure what he would have done if the Walters call had come before the trial or during the trial. And now—after the trial—his hands were tied.

Abe turned slowly to Justin and Rendi as his face grew pale. "You were right all along. He was guilty. And Jennifer Dowling may not have been Campbell's first."

Rendi completed Abe's thought for him: "And Jennifer Dowling may not be Campbell's last."

As Abe contemplated the horrors of this prospect, Gayle handed him yet another list of new clients and media requests. He tried to shake off the effects of Darlene Walters's call. After all, there was nothing he could do, especially now—after the acquittal.

He looked down at the list Gayle had given him. Most lawyers would sell their souls to have these kinds of calls. Yet his thoughts kept returning to Joe Campbell. What would Campbell be doing tonight while he, Abe, answered Larry King's questions? A disturbing image jumped into Abe's mind. It was of Campbell sitting at his computer, punching in another request for vulnerable women like Jennifer Dowling and Darlene Walters. Maybe this time it would be Ms. Scuba Diver, Abe fantasized as he recalled Joe's promise to have a drink with her. No, he said to himself, there's nothing in *her* background to suggest vulnerability.

The image of Joe at the computer left as quickly as it had come. It was time for Abe to leave his office for the first of his many interviews. Abe Ringel would now be known forever as "the lawyer who won the Joe Campbell case."

For better or for worse.

PART III

Better Ten Guilty
Go Free . . . ?

Prologue

The blond woman and the tall man walked quickly past the hotels on Central Park South—Park Lane, Hampshire House, all of them elegant, as was the woman herself.

Finally they reached the circle before the grande dame of Central Park hotels, the Plaza—Trump's pride and joy. What a wonderful place to have a brief encounter with the tall handsome stranger seated beside her. She was pleased that her magazine had decided to put her up in such high style.

The woman walked confidently past the doorman up the stairs, through the lobby, and to the bank of elevators to the left of the hotel's dining room. The Oak Bar would be nice this time of night, but one look at the man's nervous facial expression— even under his large hat—and she knew that he wouldn't want to be hanging around in public places.

"Would you like to come up for a while?" She pretended innocence, standing beside the elevator bank.

The suite was blue with white furniture, and a basket of fruit had been delivered, compliments of the hotel. "My company does a lot of work with the hotel."

"Advertising, right?"

"No, that must have been some other girl. I'm in magazines." She smiled to soften her gibe. "Can I get you something from the bar?"

"No, actually, I don't think I'll stay. I just wanted to walk you upstairs. I have an appointment in the morning, and you, my sweet, deserve more time than I could give you tonight."

"And more concentration." She smiled.

The man felt a quick stab of paranoia. Why was she talking about that? What had she heard about him? "What makes you say that?"

Midge was surprised to hear a note of harshness in his tone. "I was kidding, silly."

As she walked past him, she stroked his cheek, so lightly he barely felt it. "Come on, one drink, then you're on your way. You won't regret it."

The man felt the numb feeling inside him grow a little denser as the woman walked toward him with passion in her eyes.

This woman was bolder than the others, and the action soon heated up, so he quickly hauled out the secret he had dug up from her past and slammed against her as she lay exposed and vulnerable.

Instead of just pulling back, she took him on at his own game—threatening him about what might happen to a man who had already been accused of date rape. He hadn't realized that his trial—even with the acquittal—would so fundamentally change his control over the game.

The evening suddenly spun out of control; the game got away from him. He closed his hands around her neck to block out her harangue, and the familiar surge of power masquerading as desire forced him to hurt her.

"I'm sorry," he whispered as he left the hotel room.

Chapter Thirty-one

The last two months—since the Campbell victory—had been the most productive of Abe Ringel's life. He had experienced more professional successes and kudos in that period than in the prior twenty years. He had gotten the Ice Puppy indictment dismissed when the complaining witness withdrew her charges.

Even Senator Bergson had received merely a slap on the wrist from the Senate Ethics Committee after Abe threatened to put the entire Senate on trial for tolerating sexual harassment over the years. A terrific new case, with high visibility written all over it, had just come into the office. It involved a wealthy young man named Brian Bulger, who had killed his elderly mother to spare her the agony of learning he was HIV positive and gay. Other well-paying clients were so plentiful that many had to be turned away. A TV movie was being produced of the Campbell case, and Sam Waterston, an Emmy winner, had been signed to play Abe.

"It's just the beginning," said Arthur Berg, the public relations consultant Abe had hired following the Campbell victory. Life was good at work.

Even the Nancy Rosen case seemed to be moving in the right direction. The police had learned that Monty Williams had

273

seduced Rodney Owens's sixteen-year-old niece and made her pregnant. Owens, they believed, had killed Williams in revenge. Without Nancy's testimony, however, they had only a circumstantial case. So Duncan had offered Nancy a deal: her freedom in exchange for testifying against Owens. They did not ask her to testify as to what Owens had told her concerning the murder itself, since that would constitute a lawyer-client-privileged communication, which would be inadmissible at a trial. Instead they wanted her to testify about the allegedly criminal conversation that had led to his fugitivity. That conversation would be admissible since it dealt with a future crime—becoming a fugitive. The prosecutor believed that this incriminating discussion, which showed consciousness of guilt, coupled with the circumstantial evidence of his involvement in the Williams killing would assure a conviction.

Not unexpectedly, Nancy had turned down the deal. So the prosecutor turned to Justin, offering him the same deal: if he testified as to what Nancy had told him about the conversation, Nancy would be freed. Nancy, of course, urged Justin not to testify.

Despite her plea, Justin decided to help her. He owed nothing to Owens, and Nancy had not told him about the Owens conversation in confidence. So he was free to do the right thing. Although Justin's testimony would be double hearsay—he would testify as to what Nancy told him Owens had told her— Abe and Justin believed that a judge would probably allow it to be introduced into evidence. Hearsay was generally not allowed as evidence, but there was an exception for certain kinds of hearsay—if they had special qualities of truthfulness. What Nancy had told Justin was an admission of wrongdoing on her part— encouraging her client to become a fugitive—and the law presumed that people didn't go around admitting crimes unless they were really guilty. Therefore the law allowed this kind of hearsay to be used. The same was true of what Owens had said to

Nancy before he flew the coop. It was an admission of intended wrongdoing.

In any event, it didn't look as if the case would actually come to a trial.

When Owens's lawyer heard about the proposed deal, he decided to strike one of his own, whereby Owens would plead to manslaughter and get ten years. It was not quite a done deal, but unless there were complications, Nancy could be out in a couple of days. She would be angry at Justin and Abe, but that was okay. Better an angry and free Nancy than a friendly imprisoned Nancy. For Abe, as well as for Justin, this was a liberating prospect.

Life was good, except for the bittersweet reality that Emma was leaving in a week for New York. "Can't you stay until your birthday?" Abe asked her. "We always spend September 1 together."

"Not this year, Dad. I've got to be in New York on September 1. My roommate and I are going out to celebrate the beginning of college."

"Can I come?"

"Oh, Daddy. You've got to get used to the fact that I'm moving on. There'll be plenty of time for us together. This is an important time for me. New friends. Even new boyfriends. Jon's not invited. I want to meet new people. We've agreed that we should see other people. I don't want to be a holiday dater who waits for her man to come east from Stanford on Thanksgiving and Christmas."

"I think that's a good idea, Emma. I like Jon, but you seem to be outgrowing him. I don't think you should go steady with anyone. Play the field."

"God, you are a dinosaur. 'Go steady,' 'play the field.' I didn't think anyone talked like that since *The Brady Bunch.*"

"You know what I mean."

"I love you, Daddy. Let's go to a Red Sox game this week before I go to New York."

ALAN M. DERSHOWITZ

"Sox are out of town. *You* know that. Stop patronizing me."
Abe hugged Emma and kissed her good-bye.

Abe took a cab downtown to see his investment adviser.
He had hired the company that currently handled the Clintons'
finances. Since the Campbell case his income had skyrocketed.
Last year he had earned $250,000, which was pretty good by
Boston small law firm standards. This year, over the past three
months alone he had earned $400,000, and it looked as though
he would soon break into seven figures for the first time in his
career.

In the cab he began to leaf through the second section of
The New York Times. Abe had always been fascinated by New
York. After law school he had given some serious thought to
moving there. But Boston had a firm grip on his allegiance. Now
that his daughter was moving to New York, he tortured himself
by reading the crime stories, especially those that took place on
the Upper West Side, where Barnard was located.

Suddenly Abe's eyes focused on a small headline: MAGAZINE
EDITOR KILLED IN MIDTOWN HOTEL. He began to read the all-
too-typical story: "The body of Midge Lester was found in the
Plaza Hotel room in which she had registered the previous day.
Ms. Lester, who was an editor at *Chicago* magazine, had died of
asphyxiation. Detectives confirmed that she had been sexually
abused. There was no sign of forced entry, and hotel personnel
said that the killer was probably an acquaintance of the dead
woman. No one saw anyone with Ms. Lester after she arrived at
the hotel, and telephone records showed no phone calls. The
police acknowledged that they had no suspects or leads."

Abe gasped out loud as he read the story. "What's wrong?"
asked the startled driver.

"Turn around and take me back to Harvard Square!"

"Are you okay?"

"I'm fine. I just need to get to my office."

He took his cellular phone out of his briefcase and called
the office. "I need Justin now!"

276

Justin was on the phone in an instant. "What's up, Abe?"

"Do you have a copy of *The New York Times*?"

"Yeah."

"Turn to page B-four, bottom right hand column."

There was silence on the phone as Justin found and read the story. Then, suddenly, Abe heard him scream, "Oh, my God! It's Campbell. It's his MO!"

"Let's not jump to any conclusions. It sounds like dozens of run-of-the-mill rape-murders in New York. There's nothing that ties it directly to Campbell."

"Then why did you call me so upset?"

"Because there's only one way to find out whether it is Campbell."

"I'm off to the computer room."

"I'll meet you there in ten minutes."

Chapter Thirty-two

Abe raced up the three flights of steps to his office, bolted past Gayle and into the computer room, locking the door behind him to make certain no one else wandered in. Then, without saying a word, he walked over to the computer and looked directly at the screen, hoping against hope it would show that he and Justin had reacted too hastily to the news story.

Justin was staring at the words that had just materialized on the screen as if they were the text of a death sentence—which is exactly what they may have been, if and when Campbell had punched them up at some point in the not-too-distant past.

Abe's eyes quickly found the name he was hoping he wouldn't see. The news story was several years old, from the *Los Angeles Times*. It told a sordid tale of a beautiful young married woman in Beverly Hills who had become a high-priced prostitute in order to be financially independent of her husband. The details of the news account weren't important, but the conclusion was as clear as the name *Midge Lester* on the screen: somehow Campbell had managed to find this account of yet another perfect date rape victim. No woman who had been a prostitute and who had obviously moved to another city and started a new life would be eager to bring charges.

Joe's violence had apparently gotten out of hand during this rape, and Midge Lester had ended up dead. Maybe this death was accidental, but it was certainly predictable. Campbell's appetite for sexual violence was obviously getting harder to satisfy.

Abe and Justin both peered at the screen as if hoping the awful telltale letters glowing there would somehow disappear. Neither could speak. It was the criminal defense lawyer's worst nightmare: *they* had caused the death of an innocent woman by successfully defending a violent rapist they suspected was guilty. Every decent criminal lawyer obsessed about this possibility. Few ever experienced it.

The silence was broken by Justin bursting out in tears. Abe put his arm around the younger man's shoulder and tried to console him, yet he could find no words of comfort either for Justin or for himself. Finally Abe spoke.

"There's nothing anyone can say, Justin. And there's nothing anyone could have done to prevent this. We live under a system of rules, and we had no choice but to play by those rules."

"I can't live with rules that produce *this*. We're not talking about only rape anymore. Jennifer Dowling will eventually recover. Midge Lester won't. It's over for her. And the worst part of it is that we had it within our power to save her life."

"No, we didn't," Abe said, "not without breaking the rules."

"I don't give a damn about the rules! Who knows which poor woman will be next? Abe, we've got to do something—"

"Take it easy. We can't just call the cops on our client. We believe he killed Midge Lester only because we have confidential information we obtained from him as his lawyers. I *promised* him that I would never reveal his computer secret. Just because he's not our client anymore doesn't mean we can blow the whistle on him."

"Well, what *can* we do?"

"First thing we *can* do is call Campbell and confront him with our knowledge."

"Okay, you call him. I'll listen on the extension."

Abe dialed Campbell's home number, hoping to find he was away at preseason training camp and hence could not have been in New York when the killing took place. No such luck.

"Hello?"

"This is Abe Ringel. You know why I'm calling, Joe."

"Hey, Abe, it's nice to hear your voice. To what do I owe the pleasure?"

"Cut the bullshit. We've read today's newspaper, so there's no use beating around the bush. We know you did it."

"I don't know what you're talking about. What part of the newspaper are you referring to?" Campbell asked.

"Don't bullshit us, Joe," Justin interjected angrily. "A woman named Midge Lester was killed Saturday night at the Plaza Hotel, and you killed her."

"I still don't know what you're talking about. I was home Saturday night watching TV. Do you want me to tell you what was on?"

"I'm sure you could tell us. You probably taped it. But we're not buying it," Abe said. "You were at the Plaza Saturday night, having sex with Midge Lester. Things got out of hand after you got her to say no. You grabbed her around the neck. She choked to death. And you did it."

"I'm not the only guy who has sex with women in hotels," Campbell said nonchalantly. "You guys have really been watching too many Perry Mason reruns. Why don't you leave it to New York's Finest to solve this one?"

"Because they don't know what we know," Justin replied. "They don't know about your little computer-assisted rape game. But we do—and we're going to tell them."

"No, you're not, damn it," Campbell said, showing anger for the first time. "If you tell them *anything* I told you while you were my lawyers, I'll have you disbarred and I'll sue you for everything you're worth."

"Some things," Justin said, "are more important than

money. Don't try to threaten us. We're going to do the right thing, no matter what it costs us."

"Well, the right thing is to preserve your obligation to me—to shut up. In any event, you're barking up the wrong tree. I didn't kill that woman in the hotel. If you try to blow the whistle on me, you'll both end up looking like idiots when they find the real killer."

"We've got you dead to rights on this one, Joe," Abe said. "Justin searched for the name of the dead woman in our various databases, and he came up with the same kind of background that has characterized your previous victims. We now have three women—all of whom fit the same modus operandi. If Cheryl Puccio ever got her hands on that piece of information, you'd be on trial for murder before you could say 'guilty as charged.'"

"It's just a fucking coincidence, Abe. Lots of women have backgrounds, especially those who go to hotel rooms with guys they've just met."

"Somehow you manage to find them all," Justin said. "It's a pattern, not a coincidence. And we know how you find them. It's there in the public record—if Puccio just knew where to look."

"So now *you're* threatening *me*, right? What are you planning to do? Write an anonymous letter to Puccio telling her to do a Nexis search on the dead woman and Jennifer Dowling?"

"And maybe a few other women we've learned about," Justin added.

"Abe won't let you do that. It would ruin his career. He'd no longer be known as the lawyer who *won* the Joe Campbell case, but rather as the lawyer who falsely accused his own client of murder."

"And maybe also," Abe added pensively, "as the lawyer who caused the death of Midge Lester."

"See, Justin," Campbell said. "I'm right about Abe. Your boss is too much of a realist to blow his hard-earned reputation on your little game of show-and-tell. In any event, you're both wrong about this killing. It wasn't me."

"Right," Justin replied. "And you didn't rape Jennifer Dowling, either."

"That's right. And that's what I like to hear. *My* lawyers—who were very well paid to defend me—taking *my* side for a change, not trying to become amateur prosecutors. By the way, you'll be relieved to know that I'm going to begin seeing a shrink once a week—she's a psychologist who specializes in athletes with anxiety. If talking to her will relieve *your* anxiety, you have my permission to call her. Otherwise why don't *you guys* find a shrink who specializes in *lawyers* with anxiety." Campbell slammed down the phone, leaving them hanging.

Justin cursed. "What did you expect from that manipulative son of a bitch—a full confession? Permission to turn him in?"

"No, but I hoped he might be a bit more frightened. He saw right through your bluff."

"I'm not sure it is a bluff," Justin said. "I really am thinking of turning him in."

"Justin, you know you can't do that. It would be the end of your career."

"And *yours*. That's why I'm not gonna do anything alone. We're in this together. And we've got to come up with something that stops this guy. There has got to be a way."

"I'm all for it—if we can find some way to stop him without breaking too many rules. Maybe stretch them a bit, but not break them."

"Okay," Justin said with a small smile, his first since getting the call from Abe. "I'll look at the existing law, and you start thinking about how to make *new* law."

Chapter Thirty-three

"Haskel, I really need your judgment."

"Do I have any judgment left?" Haskel asked, lifting his head slightly from where it had been resting on his chest.

"How have you been? Have you been taking your medicine?"

"Not very much. I will have eternity to be free of pain and to be asleep. I cherish the few remaining hours of lucidity I have left, even if they come with the price tag of pain and anxiety."

"I have something for you to read," Abe said, opening up *The New York Times* to the story about the Plaza Hotel killing.

"Please, Abraham, read it to me. My eyes hurt when I read."

Abe read aloud the brief news account.

"A terrible tragedy. I know how worried you must be with Emma going to New York."

"It's not about Emma, although I am worried about her. It's about Joe Campbell."

"I'm so proud of you, Abraham. You won that difficult case without violating any ethical rules. I was worried about you during that case, especially after you confided in me what you had found."

Abe felt fortunate that today seemed to be one of Haskel's good days. "I must confide in you again, Haskel. Both Justin and

I think that Joe Campbell was responsible for this killing in New York."

"Did he tell you?"

"No, no," Abe responded. "Quite the opposite. He denies it vehemently. Says he was at home."

"So how can you be so sure? There are hundreds of such killings in New York every year."

"We are sure, Haskel. As sure as anyone can be. Remember how I told you that Campbell would use his computer to look for women who would be unlikely to report a rape? Well, this woman fit that description, and her story could be found through his computer database. We checked it."

"Abraham, you know I don't understand computers. Is there any other possibility? Could it be coincidence?"

"There is always another possibility, but the circumstantial evidence points to the conclusion that Campbell found out about her secret, just like he found out about Jennifer Dowling's secret, and deliberately stalked her and raped her."

"And killed her?"

"Probably not *deliberately,* but I can't even be sure of that."

"And you know all this because of what you learned when you were representing Mr. Campbell?"

"Yes. He confided in me about his use of computer searches only after I explicitly promised him confidentiality. Without his confidential admission to me, we could never have figured out the pattern."

"So now, my dear Abraham, you have information that would help to stop this awful man from doing further terrible injuries, yet you cannot disclose this information because you obtained it in confidence?"

"That's exactly right, and I need *your* help in figuring out a way to disclose this information and stop this guy."

"Are you sure you are asking the correct question, my dear Abraham?"

"What do you mean?"

"Do you really want to figure out a way to disclose what you learned in confidence?"

"I don't know, Haskel. What I do know is that I must do something. I can't wait for him to kill again. I feel responsible for this woman's death."

As Abe uttered these words, a vision of Hannah crossed his mind. She was driving her car, distracted by her concerns about Abe and Rendi.

"Do you feel that responsibility as a lawyer?"

"What do you mean, Haskel?"

"As a lawyer, did you have any other option than silence?"

"Well, maybe not as a lawyer, but certainly as a human being I had the option of blowing the whistle on him. I could have done what Shakespeare said: 'Tell truth and shame the devil.'"

"Aha," Haskel said. "Did you really have that option, Abraham? Were you really freer as a human being than as a lawyer?"

"Haskel, now I'm really getting confused," Abe said, wondering to himself whether it was Haskel who was confused.

"Abraham, think about Abraham," Haskel said.

Abe did not know whether Haskel was asking him to think about *himself* or about the biblical patriarch after whom he was named. Haskel made it clear in his next sentence:

"And then think about Socrates."

Haskel fell asleep as Abe wondered what Abraham and Socrates had in common. While waiting for Haskel to awaken, he recalled one similarity between the two historical figures. Both were prepared to sacrifice that which was most dear to them—in Abraham's case, his beloved child, Isaac; in Socrates' case, his own life—in order to demonstrate their faith. Abraham demonstrated his faith in God, who vindicated that faith by saving Isaac. And Socrates had demonstrated his faith in the Athenian system of justice, which failed to vindicate him by ordering his death. How this all related to Joe Campbell and his deadly computer eluded Abe. But at least he had an opening for when Haskel awoke.

A full hour passed before Haskel stirred. And when he did awaken, it was not the same Haskel as the one who had fully understood Abe's dilemma. He seemed more confused, less focused, and even more elliptical than usual in his questions.

"Haskel, I hope you had a good nap."

"I don't dream anymore."

"I think I understand your reference to Abraham and Socrates."

"Menschen. They were both menschen," Haskel mused, employing the Yiddish-German word for "man" or "human being."

"So?"

"So, you're a mensch, too, Abraham. Act like a mensch."

"I think I understand what you are telling me," Abe said now. "I must search for a *single* answer to the question of what is the right thing to do. There is no correct *human* way, unless it is also the right *legal* way. That is why Socrates willingly swallowed the hemlock and why Abraham willingly set out to sacrifice his son."

"You are one person, Abraham. You must find one answer."

"Where do I find that one answer?" Abe implored.

"Where others before you have looked," Haskel said, his eyes beginning to cloud over.

Abe watched the old man struggling to convey some last thoughts before he drifted off once again. He placed his ear close to Haskel's mouth to make out the words.

"The old books give guidance, not answers. Sometimes there are no answers. Always make sure you are asking the right question."

As Abe thought about the question, he watched his dear friend drift off into a troubled sleep.

This time he could not wait around for Haskel to awaken. He had exhausted the old man, and he was no nearer a solution, except that he realized Haskel was right in rejecting the dichotomy between the human solution and the legal solution. That was one characteristic Haskel had in common with Emma. Both had integrated their ethics into their personalities. Maybe that's what wisdom really is, Abe thought. He needed to search for a wise approach rather than a clever gimmick.

Was there such an elegant solution?

Chapter Thirty-four

As he was walking from Haskel's house back to his home, Abe found himself thinking about Nancy Rosen, that she was really in prison for a conspiracy to *achieve* justice. She had sacrificed her freedom to resolve a conflict between saving the innocent life of a stranger and hurting her own client. She had opted for an *inelegant* solution that had saved Charlie Odell's life and preserved her own client's freedom—at least for a time—but at the high cost of her own imprisonment and disbarment.

In Nancy's heroic act of self-sacrifice, Abe thought, there must be a lesson—a clue as to what he should do. As he entered his home, still thinking about Nancy, his phone rang.

"Abe, it's Nancy. Guess where I'm calling from? I'm home! I've just been released, and I want to thank you—and I also want to argue with you and Justin."

"I'll accept the thanks, Nancy. I'm so happy you're finally out."

"The Lord giveth and the Lord taketh away. Justin put me in and Justin got me out. It's almost biblical."

"I guess it's true what they say about everyone getting a little religion in prison."

"Not really, but if you tell them you're Jewish, they give you kosher food, which is a hell of a lot better than the regular prison fare. So I got some religion—temporarily. It's called playing the system."

"Owens did the deal?"

"Yeah, and he's not that unhappy. He's looking to serve no more than about eight. He'll be younger than I am when he gets out. It all worked out okay, I guess. Though I disagree with Justin's willingness to testify."

"Look, you know he plays by the rules. The rules said he could testify, and we both wanted to help you."

"I know, but I wouldn't have done it, even to help Justin. He knows that."

"We both know that, Nancy. You are a very different lawyer—and person—than we are. Now let me ask you a question."

"Okay, shoot."

"What if you knew that Owens was going to kill someone else? Would you still not have ratted him out?"

"Depends on who he was going to kill. Remember, I'm a revolutionary."

"Cut the rhetoric, Nancy. I know that you could never sit back and allow your client to kill an innocent person."

"No way. If life has taught me anything, it's that standing by when you should be doing something always comes back to haunt you. I would definitely do something."

"What?"

"I don't know. I wouldn't just play by your rules. Remember, those are the rules that put me behind bars. Got to go now. I haven't even called my mother yet. Ask Justin to call me when he gets a chance."

"Bye."

As Abe hung up the phone, the doorbell rang. It was Justin. Without even walking in, he began to speak loudly.

"Abe, I think I've figured out what to do!"

"Calm down, Justin. And come in. Everyone on Brattle

Street can hear you. By the way, Nancy's out. Call her. She's pissed at you."

Justin caught his breath and sat down in the living room. "That's great about Nancy, and typical. We'll patch it up. Don't worry about her. Now here's my plan for Campbell. We should start doing exactly what Campbell has been doing—searching through our computer databases for vulnerable women. As soon as we find anyone who fits the profile of Campbell's victims, we warn them—anonymously, of course—to stay away from Campbell."

"Nice try, Justin, only it won't work," Abe replied. "Campbell is right. There are too many vulnerable women out there. We have no idea how he picks and chooses among them. We'd be calling hundreds of women. And some of them might call the cops. We would still be blowing the whistle on our client on the basis of lawyer-client confidences."

"Well, something *has* to work, Abe. Unless you can come up with something better, we're just going to have to go with an imperfect plan," Justin said. "I couldn't take reading another news story like the one about Midge Lester. It would drive me into a mental hospital."

"Haskel told me to look for an answer where others before me have looked. You've searched out the legal ethics materials, have you found anything?" Abe asked.

"Same old clichés about a lawyer's duty to his client and to the court. No way out of this one. There is no exception to the obligation of confidentiality in a case like this. The rules provide that if Campbell were to *tell* us that he was planning a future crime, we could blow the whistle on him. That's the only out."

"The 'future crimes exception,' " Abe agreed. "But he has to tell us. It's not good enough that we figure it out from what he told us about the past."

"And Campbell hasn't *told* us that he's planning to commit any future crimes," Justin said. "Maybe we can trick him into telling us about his future plans—and then we can blow the whistle."

"No way he's going to tell us anything. That's wishful thinking. He vehemently denies everything. And whatever we know, we learned in the course of representing him for a *past* crime. He told us about his computer MO only after I promised him confidentiality."

"Damn it, he really conned you into making that promise. Remember his bullshit speech about how his reputation as a gentleman would be ruined if you ever disclosed that he checks out women on his computer? I think it was all a ploy."

"It wouldn't be the first time."

"How so?"

"Remember Paula Hawkins?"

"No. It was before my time."

"Awful case. It almost destroyed me. Paula was accused of poisoning her much older husband. She shocked me by actually confiding that she did it. I'll never forget her words: 'I killed the old man in self-defense. He was boring me to death.' "

"Did she want to testify?"

"No. She knew I couldn't let her."

"So what happened?"

"I defended the case on forensic grounds, and the jury came back with manslaughter."

"Not bad."

"Not good enough for her. She hired a new lawyer who accused me of 'ineffective assistance of counsel' for not letting her testify."

"So what happened?"

"The prosecutor asked me for an affidavit explaining why I had decided not to put her on the stand. He had a hunch she might have confessed to me."

"I hope you gave it to him. After all, she was accusing you of screwing up the case. You're allowed to defend yourself."

"No way," Abe replied. "I don't help prosecutors keep my former clients in prison—even if I have to fall on the sword."

"So what happened?"

"The judge ruled that I had been ineffective and freed Paula."

"Do you think she set you up?"

"Probably."

"What about Campbell?"

"I don't know. Maybe. If I could prove that it was a ploy—that it was a fraud from the get-go—I probably could blow the whistle, but there's no way I can prove it. We're just guessing."

"Sounds like a pretty good guess to me."

"It's not enough. I made the promise. And I'm just not allowed to blow the whistle," Abe insisted. "No way. If I do, I'm in clear violation of the Code of Professional Responsibility. No wiggle room. None."

"I guess you're like a priest who learned something terrible during confession."

"Father Ringel." Abe smiled. "Somehow I can't conjure up the image, but it does give me an idea."

Chapter Thirty-five

In all of Abe's years in the Boston area, he had never been to this place. It frightened him a little, putting him in mind of the stories his grandfather Zechariah had told him about growing up in Poland amid religiously inspired anti-Semitism. Now he was entering the rectory of the Boston Catholic Archdiocese for an appointment with Father Stanislaw Maklowski, Boston's leading authority on the Catholic confessional. Somehow Abe had expected dark corridors, with eerie shadows. Instead he saw bright rooms, with colorful portraits of past cardinals bedecked in red.

Father Maklowski was as bright and accessible as his surroundings. He was sitting on a large comfortable ottoman, smoking a cigar. "I picked up the habit when I worked in Cuba before the revolution," he explained. "I wish I could offer you a Montecristo, but domestic is the best I can do. Want one?"

"No thanks, Father," Abe said.

"Please, call me Stan. You're not here for confession, Abe. So we can dispense with titles. What can I tell a famous lawyer like you about our arcane rules regarding the seal of the confessional?"

"As I told you when I called for the appointment, this is

going to have to remain fairly abstract, because it involves a real case that I can't tell you about. Okay?"

"So you don't even trust a priest?" Father Maklowski joked.

"It's not that I don't trust you, Stan. I'm just not allowed to tell you. I hope you understand."

"Sure I do. I guess you don't know I'm a lawyer, too. I don't practice. I graduated Notre Dame Law School, passed the Illinois bar. I'm also a canon lawyer, but I've done the priest thing all my adult life. I keep up with legal ethics and occasionally do a guest lecture at Boston College. So go ahead, throw me your best hypothetical."

"Okay, Stan. Here it is. What if a priest learned information during a confession that led him to believe that the penitent was going to kill someone? Could he reveal it to prevent a murder?"

"Hey, Abe, that's *my* favorite hypothetical. I always use it when I'm teaching new priests about the seal."

"So what do you tell them?"

"Under our rules, it's not even a close question. No way can a priest disclose it."

"What can he do?"

"Plead, cajole, threaten eternal damnation. Anything short of disclosure."

"Do priests really stick to that rule?"

"You bet they do. Look, Abe, in real life almost no one ever gets information about a future crime. Of course, it has happened, and we just don't tell."

"Has any priest, to your knowledge, violated the rule and disclosed?"

"Yes, just recently. In Italy, of all places. Practically in the shadow of the Vatican."

"What happened?"

"A well-intentioned local priest—I'm told he's a real good guy, I don't know him personally—took confession from a penitent who told the priest that he had committed several murders on behalf of the Mafia."

"They were *past* murders, right?"

"Hold your horses, Abe. I'm getting to that."

"Go on."

"The priest believed that if he disclosed that the murders— which had been unsolved to that point—were done by the Mafia, this disclosure would prevent future Mafia murders."

"So he thought he would be saving lives by blowing the whistle on his penitent."

"No, he never blew the whistle on the penitent. That would have gotten him in real trouble."

"What did he do?"

"He just delivered a sermon in his local church in which he disclosed that an *unnamed* person had confessed to having committed the murders on behalf of the Mafia."

"Didn't people want to know the killer's name?"

"Sure, but the priest refused to disclose *that*."

"So what happened?"

"It's still under consideration. Everybody agrees he did the wrong thing."

"I bet the prosecutors are happy."

"It's interesting. They're not so happy, because it's caused something of a backlash. Even the press has condemned the poor priest. Everyone is on his case."

"Even you?"

"Even me, though I'm praying that he won't get into any more trouble. He did what he believed was right."

"Do you think he was wrong?"

"As a matter of Catholic law, there can be no doubt about that. He was wrong."

"What would you have done, Stan, if you had a choice between saving lives and disclosing a confession?"

"I know what would be the right thing to do."

"What?"

"Preserve the seal."

"Even at the cost of human lives?"

"Abe, I know this is hard for laypeople to understand. Our job is to save souls, not lives. We have to leave it to others to save lives. If we were ever to breach the seal of the confessional, it would make it impossible for us to save souls, because no one would confess."

"Sounds like the kinds of arguments that lawyers make."

"Lawyers are not in the business of saving souls. They are in the business of saving lives."

"No, we're not—unfortunately. We're in the business of defending people charged with crime. And if we break our 'seal,' no one will trust us. It's a very similar argument."

"Abe, you obviously came to me for information, not advice. Luckily I'm in the advice business, too. Do you mind if I offer you some?"

"Sure, go ahead."

"It's your decision, but I think that if you could save an innocent human life by disclosing a legal confidence, you should do it."

"Father . . . Stan, isn't that inconsistent with what you said you would do?"

"Yes, it is inconsistent, just as our roles are inconsistent. My role is to save souls. Yours is more earthly, and there is no higher calling here on earth than to save lives. I wish I were free to do that, but I'm not."

"Our situations aren't really that different, Stan. By *not* disclosing the information, I might in the long run be saving *more* lives, because more clients would confide in me and I could talk them out of doing terrible things."

"Look, Abe, it isn't the role of a lawyer to play God and take a life in the short run in the hope of saving more in the long run."

"I made a *promise* of confidentiality to my client. Are you telling me to break a solemn promise?"

"Saving a life is more sacred than keeping a promise—for a lawyer."

"Remember, you're a lawyer, too."

"Yes, I am. However, I don't take confession *as a lawyer*. I take it *as a priest*. If someone told me something *as a lawyer*, not as a priest, which could save a life, I would disclose it."

"Has that ever happened to you?"

"No. Nor have I ever been told anything, *as a priest*, that could save a human life."

"I wonder what you would really do if that ever happened? If you really *could* save a life by disclosing what you learned as a priest in confession? You seem like too good a person to sit idly by watching an innocent human being, whom you could save, die."

"I wonder, too. I hope my faith will never be tested," Father Maklowski said.

"Mine sure *is* being tested, and I feel like I'm failing the test."

Abe left the archdiocese more uncomfortable than ever. He was still convinced that he could not do to a client what a priest would not do to a penitent: violate the rules.

He went back to the office, where Justin was waiting, hoping that the meeting with Father Maklowski had changed Abe's mind. Abe related his conversation and got right to the bottom line.

"Nothing Father Maklowski said persuades me to blow the whistle on Campbell."

"Nothing you or anybody else has said persuades *me*," Justin answered, "that we have to stand idly by while our former client rapes and maybe kills yet another innocent woman."

"Justin, the reality is that lawyers, priests, even doctors, often have to stand idly by, because of the importance of confidentiality. It's the price society pays for encouraging confidential communications," Abe replied.

297

"Doctors have to disclose child abuse when they observe symptoms, even when it means blowing the whistle on a patient."

"And look at what that's caused."

"What?"

"A lot of abusing parents have stopped taking their kids to doctors, because they're afraid of being turned in," Abe said. "That's why lawyers have rejected the whistle-blower approach taken by doctors and psychologists."

"I guess there's no easy answer," Justin acknowledged.

Abe noticed a box on the desk next to the computer. It was marked "Davka CD-ROM Aggadic Midrashim, Second Edition."

"What is that?"

"It's that computerized Talmud program I told you about. It came from the Hebrew College. I've been playing with it."

"Have you found anything helpful?"

"Not really. Just a story about an old judge who used to be the vice president of the Sanhedrin—the old talmudic supreme court."

"What's the story?"

"You're not going to like it. I certainly don't."

"Why not?"

"Believe it or not, this old judge—his name was Shimon, the son of Shetah—actually confronted a situation a bit like ours."

"How so?"

"Well, he had presided over a case in which a guilty murderer was let off because there was only one witness. The Bible expressly requires at least two witnesses—in capital cases. The acquitted murderer then goes out and kills again, and the judge sees him with 'the sword in his hand, the blood dripping, and the dead man still twitching.' "

"Quite graphic."

"Yeah, these guys knew how to write some gut-wrenching stuff."

"So what does the judge do?" Abe asked.

"Nothing. That's the point. He asks the murderer the same question we've been asking ourselves."

"What?"

"Here, let me read it to you, straight from the Talmud: 'Wicked one, who killed this man? You or I?' "

"So what does the judge answer?"

"He answers that *he*, the judge, is surely *not* responsible, because he followed the biblical rule, requiring two witnesses."

"Well, that seems right, doesn't it?"

"Maybe for a judge, certainly not for a lawyer," Justin said.

"To the contrary. It seems to me more justified for a lawyer than for a judge."

"Why so?"

"Well," Abe explained, "both have to obey the law. A lawyer's primary responsibility is to his client, while a judge's is to society in general. If a judge does the right thing by occasionally letting a guilty person go free—perhaps even to murder again—it would seem to follow that an advocate can't be blamed for doing the same thing."

"Maybe that's the source Haskel was referring to when he told you to look where others have looked."

"Maybe he was referring to *all* the sources we've found. So far it's three to zip. Legal, Catholic, Jewish—they all point in the same direction. We must keep quiet. Hard as it is, that is the *right* thing to do—both as lawyers and as human beings."

"Even if Campbell rapes and kills again?"

"We can't know that for sure, Justin."

"Yes, we can. I've also done some research on serial rapists."

"What did you find?"

"It's a fairly frequent phenomenon. There have been an average of ten each year in New York alone."

"What do they have in common?"

"First, they stalk particularly vulnerable women who are afraid to complain—such as prostitutes, drug addicts, unregistered aliens. Second, they don't stop until they get caught. Third, they leave few clues. Finally, they become increasingly violent with time."

"That sounds a lot like Campbell, except that he's turned to high tech."

"The worst part of it is that it's virtually certain he won't stop on his own."

"How can you be so sure?"

"Let me quote Lisa M. Fried, a sex crime expert in the New York DA's Office," Justin said, shuffling through his notes. " 'This is the most repetitive type of crime in the world. It's not just a fear, it's a knowledge. A serial rapist will rape again.' "

"Those are statistical generalizations, Justin. We can't know for sure that Campbell will rape or kill again."

"Yes, we can. You know it and I know it. There's no reason to believe he's any different from the others except that he's smarter."

" 'The prince of darkness is a gentleman,' " Abe said, quoting his favorite playwright.

"That means it's going to take even more time until he's caught, leaving an even longer trail of victims."

"Under the rules, *we* are not responsible, even if Campbell were to rape or kill again—any more than the priest or the judge would be. We, too, have an obligation to a higher authority. We are bound by our oath. We must remain silent. We have no choice."

"We always have a choice, Abe. There's always the option of civil disobedience. That's what Nancy Rosen did. She went to jail because she chose to break a bad law for a good purpose."

"That's not *our* decision to make, Justin. Diderot was right when he warned that anyone who takes it upon himself to break a bad law thereby authorizes everyone else to break the good ones."

"*I* urged her to break the law."

"That was *your* job. *Her* job was to resist your urging."

"I was *right*, Abe. It was for a higher good."

"Maybe. This particular situation wouldn't be for a higher good. Remember that our whole system, especially the role of defense counsel, is based on the theory that it's 'better for ten guilty to go free than for one innocent to be wrongly convicted.' "

"It's a nice theory, Abe. Does it make sense when one of those ten guilty is bound to kill yet another innocent?"

"I don't know, Justin. I don't know. What I do know is that I won't break the rule. I just can't do it. I *believe* in these rules, damn it. And I just won't break them."

"Let me ask you this, Abe," Justin persisted, assuming the role of Socratic teacher. "What if you not only knew for sure *that* Campbell was going to kill, but you also knew for sure *whom* he was going to kill?"

Abe tried to squirm out of the question. "How could I know who unless Campbell told me?"

"No fair, Abe. Stick to my hypothetical. Say we figured it out by the computer, or some other way. Say it turned out to be Ms. Scuba Diver, the jury foreperson. Remember, he said he would meet her for a drink. Could you live with yourself if you knew that a *particular* woman, Ms. Scuba Diver, was about to be killed—not some *statistical* woman, but an *actual* woman whom you knew. Could you really play by the rules and stand idly by while the blood of this woman was spilled?"

"I don't know, Justin, I really don't know."

"If you're uncertain about *that* situation, how can you be so damn certain about *our* situation?"

"Because in our case, we don't know *who* the woman will be."

"Why does that make a difference?"

"I don't know, it just does. At least to me."

"Yeah, me too. And yet it's a psychological difference, not a moral one, damn it. It's harder to let someone die if you know who she is than if she's just some abstract statistic. But it *shouldn't* make a difference."

"You're very convincing, Justin. You'd make a great law professor."

"Maybe that's what I ought to become. At least they don't kill people the way we did."

"We didn't kill anyone, damn it. Don't ever say that, Justin. It's not fair."

"Tell that to the mother of Campbell's next victim—the one whose life we're *not* going to save because you have to follow some damn rules."

Chapter Thirty-six

"Abe, I've known you for more than ten years," Rendi said, pouring him a glass of 1982 Château Margaux, "and I've never seen you so upset about a work-related matter."

"This isn't only about work," Abe said, guzzling the fine wine as if it were root beer. "It's about what it means to me to be a lawyer and a human being. This is the worst position I've ever been placed in during my career. I feel absolutely impotent."

Rendi and Abe both smiled—sadly—at the sexual reference, since Abe had in fact lost all interest in sex of late.

Rendi had invited him over to her Beacon Hill apartment for a warm, friendly, perhaps even romantic dinner, without sexual overtones—except perhaps to restoke the flames for the future. Rendi's small one-bedroom home always seemed entirely out of character for its occupant. It was warm, gracious, and beautifully decorated with antiques from the archaeological digs in which she'd participated over the years. Abe could never imagine Rendi—the most impatient person he knew—digging slowly, cautiously, and reverently through layers of dirt in search of small treasures from the ancient past. Even the gentle Elizabethan lute music seemed to reflect her aspiration toward serenity, rather than the chaotic reality of her life.

Rendi remembered, painfully, how Abe's guilt over having slept with her just weeks before Hannah's death in that tragic accident had made it impossible for him to become sexual with her for more than a year afterward.

"This isn't like Hannah's death," Rendi insisted—getting right to the point, as usual. "*This is* about your professional life. It's a horrible dilemma you're in, but it's not about people you love. It's not about Emma. It's not about your health, though it's having an effect on your health. It's not about us," she added tentatively, not quite certain how their relationship could be classified.

"I know that," Abe said without quite convincing himself, "and I'm thankful that this isn't *that* kind of a personal crisis. Still, it *is* a personal crisis. It's tearing me apart, both as a lawyer and as a person. It's making me realize how much of my personal self is tied up in my professional role as a defense lawyer. It's making me challenge everything I've believed in and advocated for a quarter of a century. It's driving me nuts, Rendi. I've made up my mind not to blow the whistle on Campbell, and my decision is eating at my guts."

Like most professional advocates, Abe had developed a talent for making hard decisions quickly and then immediately distancing himself from the emotions of the decision. "A litigator does not have the luxury of *mutcher*ing over past decisions," Haskel used to say, employing the Yiddish word for "obsess" or "torment." Yet that was precisely what Abe was doing: *mutcher*ing himself to distraction over his decision not to blow the whistle on Campbell.

"And that bastard Campbell really knows that he's bedeviling you. I wonder if that turns him on, too?"

"It's not really his fault, Rendi. He is what he is—a sick, miserable person. There are plenty of others out there like him.

If it weren't Campbell, it could be someone else. Every advocate has his or her devil. Mine happens to be Joe Campbell."

"That's because this is not a problem that is capable of being answered by some snap of the fingers. This is the kind of problem that plagues philosophers. It's the eternal conundrum. There is no perfect solution. You have to choose the least imperfect one."

"When I was younger I could do that, and then put it behind me. I can't seem to do that with this one."

"Good. Because recognizing complexity, ambiguity, and uncertainty is a sign of maturity. You're finally growing up."

"And I don't like it one bit," Abe said, allowing himself his first small smile of the evening.

Rendi got up, walked over to him, and gently sat down on his lap. She sat there for a full minute, just looking at his troubled face. Then she spoke, almost in a whisper. "Look, Abe, there's a time to think. God knows you've done enough of that. And you're not comfortable with your decision."

"How do you know?"

"It's obvious. Sigmund Freud was once asked how he made up his mind on difficult choices."

"What did he answer?"

"He said he flipped a coin."

"Not very original."

"Yes, it was. He said he would then see how he reacted to the coin flip—was he comfortable with the way it came out."

"Clever."

"Well, you fail the Freud test—you're *mutcher*ing over it."

"It's a decision that warrants *mutcher*ing."

"You've done enough of that. Now's the time to act."

"So what do you think I should do?"

"I think you should break the rules and turn him in. Do it because it's the only right thing to do. I'll be proud of you. Emma will be proud of you. Hannah would have been proud of you."

"It *isn't* the right thing to do. Don't you think Judge Gambi was right when she denied my motion to find out what Jennifer told her psychologist?"

"Yes, I do, but that was different."

"Why was that different?"

"Because Jennifer wasn't going to kill anyone."

"Maybe she was falsely accusing someone."

"You know she wasn't."

"The *judge* didn't know that, and yet she wouldn't let me find out what Jennifer told her shrink, because she understood the importance of keeping a promise of confidentiality."

"It's still different, Abe, and I think you should call the cops on Campbell."

"I know that a lot of people would praise me for blowing the whistle on a guilty rapist and murderer. I can't. It would be breaking a fundamental rule of my profession."

"Abe," Rendi said without thinking, "it wouldn't be the first rule you broke." As soon as the words passed her lips, she regretted having spoken them.

Abe responded by sending a clear message to her that he would like her to get off his lap. When she stood up, he extended a comforting hand to her. "I know I broke a rule and a promise in the past, and we both wish I hadn't. That night with you just before Hannah's accident was the worst thing I ever did. If I could take back any hour of my life and live it differently, that would be the hour."

"For me too. Even before the accident, I regretted what we had done. A few weeks ago I went back to my computerized diary and reread the entry for the day after that night. Do you know what it said?"

Abe paused. "You've kept a diary?"

"Yes, on my computer."

"You know, Rendi, that makes me a little nervous. How secure are those things? Any sophisticated hacker could break into it."

"Don't get paranoid on me, Abe. Nobody would want to read my journal—except maybe *you*. And I've got a password that nobody could figure out."

"What is it?"

"You think I'm telling *you*? I've got stuff in there that you'll never know about."

"Rendi, you've got to be concerned about the security of your computer."

"Stop it—listen to me. We're not talking about hackers now. I'm telling you what I wrote in my diary," Rendi said, placing an arm around Abe's shoulder.

"Tell me."

"It said that the sex was great, but it wasn't worth it, because you would always feel guilty about betraying Hannah's trust."

"You were right, especially in light of what happened."

"We couldn't have known what was going to happen. And what happened wasn't our fault."

"I can never know that for certain. What is even worse is that I will always have a secret from Emma."

"Believe me, Emma will have plenty of secrets from you."

"Not like this one."

"Look, Abe, the flesh is weak. We weren't the first, and we won't be the last decent people who succumbed to temptation. And we enjoyed it."

"Yes, we did. And look what it did to us. If we hadn't, we would probably be married today."

"Boring. It's more fun this way."

"I can't play fast and loose with rules anymore, Rendi. I paid too high a price that time. I'm not going to let this son of a bitch destroy my commitment to the rule of law." Abe sat and stared straight at the small fragment of the statue of Justinian that sat atop Rendi's mantelpiece.

Chapter Thirty-seven

Abe felt like a juggler with four balls in the air. He spent every minute of every hour obsessing about Campbell. Even though he knew he was doing the right thing, he couldn't stop himself from running for his *New York Times* every morning to look through the metro section in search of a new crime that might fit Campbell's MO. He watched the New York news every night on the cable TV superstation. He was worried sick—his blood pressure had skyrocketed—that Campbell would strike once again.

It was as if a sword of Damocles was hanging not only over the head of Campbell's next victim, but over Abe's head as well. Part of him actually wished that Campbell would commit his next crime already and get caught. The real horror of the sword of Damocles, Abe realized, was not in its dropping, but in its hanging.

At the same time, he worried about Emma's upcoming move to the high-crime neighborhood around Barnard. He bought her a portable siren at Sharper Image. He gave her a book about how not to be a victim in New York. He paid for the self-defense course—it was called "model mugging"—she was taking at the Cambridge Y and was relieved to hear from her that she was now capable of disabling a mugger with a quick knee to the groin. Abe was confident that he had satisfied his religious obligation to teach his daughter to swim. He had much less confidence in the city whose cross-currents she would be trying to navigate.

Abe's third worry ball was Haskel. His health was deteriorating even more rapidly. Now when Abe came to visit, Haskel would sometimes just sit staring straight ahead, his eyes glazed, his mouth hanging open, and his hands twitching uncontrollably. On his last visit Haskel had seemed particularly anxious to advise Abe about some impending crisis, but had been unable to articulate his warning. He'd kept repeating the biblical names *Amalek* and *Hamen* and mumbling something about "future generations." It had been even less to go on than usual, so Abe had told Justin to check out the names and come up with any relevant sources.

During every visit with Haskel, Abe wondered whether this would be the last time he would see his dear friend alive. He thought constantly about all the things he wanted to say to Haskel before the old man died, but he couldn't bring himself to deliver his farewell speech lest it be perceived by Haskel as though his friend were giving him permission to die.

Then there was Nancy Rosen, still disbarred for doing the gutsy thing, although she was at least out of prison and working as a paralegal back in Newark. Abe couldn't get Nancy out of his mind, for two reasons. The first, he knew, was irrational: he continued to blame himself and Justin for Nancy's disbarment, even though he knew it was not their fault. Neither was it her fault. The blame lay directly at the doorstep of that prick of a prosecutor, Duncan. The second reason Abe thought so much about Nancy was that he believed somewhere in her noble actions lay a clue as to what *he* should do about Campbell. Yet he couldn't figure out what the lesson really was.

Nancy had sacrificed her liberty and career to save the life of an innocent stranger—Charlie O. To Abe, that pointed toward blowing the whistle on Campbell to save the lives of Campbell's future rape victims. Ironically, Nancy was disbarred for her *refusal* to blow the whistle on her own guilty client, Rodney Owens. It was a mixed message, much like Haskel's arcane talmudic stories, and unlike the legal ethics course Abe had taken back in law school, where simple answers solved simple problems. One thing was crystal clear to Abe: If Nancy Rosen were in his position now, she would do *something* to stop Campbell. I guess that's what makes her a radical and me a cautious lawyer, Abe thought grimly.

These images—each so different from the other—cascaded through Abe's mind, causing him anguish, confusion, and sleepless nights.

Now there was a new worry. The morning after Abe's visit to Rendi's apartment, she had called him in a panic. She had logged onto her computer diary from her modem at the office and had noticed something strange.

"If not for your little bit of paranoia last night, I probably wouldn't have even spotted it," Rendi said.

"What?" Abe asked nervously.

"Somebody logged into my computer yesterday for almost an hour, and it wasn't me."

"How can you be sure?"

"Don't you remember, Abe? I was away all day yesterday, except for the evening. I never was near my computer."

"Could it be a mistake?"

"Could be, but I doubt it. I think you were right. Somebody was reading my diary."

"Well, it wasn't *me*, Rendi—if you're thinking that."

"No, I'm not thinking that. You wouldn't have a clue how to break in."

"Could it be Campbell?"

"Could be, but why?"

"Maybe he's looking for some dirt that he can use as insurance in case I decide to blow the whistle."

"Sounds plausible. Maybe he's looking for something on *me*," Rendi speculated.

"Why?"

"I don't know."

"It just gives us something else to worry about."

With all these concerns, Abe preferred to focus his attention on Emma. At least with her he could do something positive—enjoy her last few days at home, lecture her about safety, give her advice about courses, teachers, restaurants, and boyfriends. He could joke with her about her new, more sophisticated wardrobe. He could be with her at home, sharing a Chinese take-out dinner from the Lucky Garden, with the final movement from Mahler's Fifth playing in the background.

"I'm really worried about you, all alone in New York."

"I'm a grown woman, Daddy."

"Yes. I know that, and that's exactly why I'm worried about you. You think you're invincible."

"I am woman. Hear me roar," Emma sang in a mocking voice, momentarily drowning out the Mahler.

"I am mugger. See me mug," Abe sang back in an equally mocking tone.

"You really don't have to worry. I've gotten my certificate—with honors—from the model mugging course at the Y."

"That worries me even more, because now you really believe you can take on a professional career mugger."

"Daddy, the first thing they teach you in mugging school is to *avoid* muggers. The second thing is how to escape from them. They teach us how to fight back only as a last resort."

"That sounds sensible. Will you follow their advice?"

"You bet I will. Do you think I want to spend my college years in a wheelchair? Forget it. I know how to run, and I'm damn fast," Emma said, pointing to a trophy she had won in a prep school track meet.

"You do understand why I'm so worried?"

"Yes. Because that's your job, and because that's your nature. I worry, too, Daddy. The apple doesn't fall far from the tree. I also worry about you. You seem so preoccupied, and I heard you on the phone yesterday, talking to Dr. Gurewitz about your blood pressure. Why has it shot up? I hope it's not because of *me?*"

"No, it's not because of you. It's a work thing that I can't talk about."

"Daddy, you always told me that it was wrong to get depressed about work. Depression, you said, should be reserved for personal or family crises, not for work. You can get upset, angry, or worried about work—you always say—but never depressed. And you seem depressed."

"I am a bit depressed, and my pressure is up a bit. And it is because of something at work. Even my rules don't always make sense. This is something at work that affects me very personally."

"Is it about Rendi?" Emma asked. "Are you two finally making some decisions now that I'm out of the way?"

"No, it's not about Rendi, though I suspect that your absence may either bring us closer together or drive us farther apart."

"Can't you share it with me, Daddy? My friends all tell me I give good advice."

"No, I can't, Emma. It's about a client. And it's confidential. I can't discuss it with anyone outside the office."

"That rule sucks, Daddy. Fathers should be allowed to discuss confidential stuff with their adult children."

"And children should be willing to discuss confidential stuff with their parents," Abe said pointedly. "Yet you keep secrets from me, don't you?"

"That's part of growing up, making our own mistakes. I wish you could share with me what's bugging you, Daddy."

"I wish I could also. I know I would benefit from your advice. Unfortunately, it's against the rules."

"And Abe Ringel is a stickler for rules," Emma added, knowing that she had lost the argument. "By the way," she added almost as an afterthought, "I'm leaving for New York day after tomorrow, on Thursday, one day early. I'm doing something special for my birthday on Friday, and my new roommate, Zoe, is taking me shopping the day before at her uncle's boutique in SoHo."

"What are you doing that's so special?"

"Can't tell you. Don't worry, it's perfectly safe. I'll tell you afterward. I'm sworn to secrecy for the moment."

"Even from your daddy?"

"Especially from my daddy," Emma said with the Hannah smile that always melted him.

Abe was tempted to play the adolescent game of "I'll tell you my secret if you tell me yours." Yet he knew he couldn't reveal Joe Campbell's terrible secret under any circumstances.

"I guess I have to trust you," he said, squeezing Emma's hand in his own.

"You sure do, especially since I don't even have to tell you what I'm doing anymore, except if I want to."

"I hope you'll always want to," Abe said with a touch of sadness in his voice.

"Well, probably not *always*," Emma said. "Maybe sometimes."

"I love you, Emma. And I do trust you."

"I love you, too, Daddy. And I know you'll always be there for me."

Chapter Thirty-eight

It was September first—Emma's eighteenth birthday. Abe so wished he could spend it with her, as he had spent all of her previous birthdays. Since September 1 always fell between the end of summer camp and the beginning of school, it was not a time for parties or group celebrations. When Emma was a child, she had bemoaned her fate, since she was deprived of the school or camp birthdays her friends celebrated. Abe and Hannah had developed the tradition of getting all dressed up and taking her to a grown-up restaurant and a show.

This year she was starting her new life in New York. Abe knew that she was getting dressed up for dinner and maybe a show—that part of the tradition would never change—only this time it was with someone else. Maybe her new roommate. Maybe a new boy she had met in New York. Maybe Jon was coming down for a last fling. Abe hoped she would have a great time, only not quite as great as the times she had experienced with her parents. Memories have their place, he thought, even in the life of a quickly maturing young adult.

Abe was spending Emma's birthday in the office, trying to catch up on correspondence. Typically, his mind was on Campbell. He imagined his devil at the computer, searching for yet a new victim. Abe shut his eyes tight as if to focus his imagination more sharply, perhaps even to be able to see the new name on Campbell's computer. Would it be another ad executive, an editor, an investment banker, maybe a lawyer? Abe tried not to visualize the victim in his mind's eye.

While he drifted off into his day-mare, Rendi burst into the office. She had a worried look on her face.

"What's wrong?" Abe asked.

"I don't know for sure. I was at home working at my computer—actually erasing some of my journal entries that I didn't want to fall into anyone's hands . . ."

"Closing some barn doors after the cows have gotten out?"

"In any event, that's not what I came down here to talk about. Emma called me this morning—just a little while ago. She was in a giddy mood, and she wanted to talk. Girl talk. She told me not to tell you. And I probably shouldn't."

"Why not?"

"Because it's going to upset you. It would upset any father."

"What do you mean?"

"Promise me you won't tell her I told you."

"I promise. Now, please, what did she tell you?"

"It's not what she *told* me. It's what she asked me."

"How so?"

"She asked me about woman stuff. The kinds of things she could never discuss with you."

"She's talked about that kind of stuff with you before, hasn't she?"

"Yes, in the abstract. Today there was an immediacy, as if she needed to know now—today."

"She told me she had something special planned for tonight, and she wouldn't tell me what it was until afterward," Abe said.

"Abe, it sounds to me like your little girl is planning to lose her virginity as a birthday present to herself."

"That is upsetting to me, Rendi. You're right. It's inevitable. I guess I'm glad she waited until college. And I'm certainly glad she's talking to you about it. I wish I'd learned about it *after* it happened. Now I'm going to be sick to my stomach all night trying not to think about it."

"I know. That's why I didn't want to tell you."

"So why *did* you tell me? It's so out of character for you to break a promise of confidentiality to Emma, especially since there's nothing I can do about it except drive myself crazy."

"Abe, if that were all there is to it, I wouldn't have told you. And maybe that's all there *is* to it, and I shouldn't have told you. Except she said something that I *had* to tell you. Maybe it doesn't mean anything. I'll leave the decision to you."

"Now you're really getting me worried—and confused. What did she tell you?"

"Not tell me. *Ask* me!"

"What?"

"She asked me about the difference between sex with someone her own age and with someone a lot older."

"Oh, my God. She's having sex with a professor—already? Those goddamned exploitative bastards. I just read about that schmuck from the University of Massachusetts who believes that it is his academic mission to 'cure' his students of their virginity. I'll sue the bastard who's taking advantage of Emma. Do you know who it is? Can we stop him?"

"No, I don't know who it is—for sure. It's not a professor. She implied to me that it's someone she has known for a while and went out with in Boston."

"Who the hell could it be?"

"I don't know. There's just one guy who fits the description."

"Who? Damn it, stop playing games. One of her high school teachers?"

"Abe. *Think.* Stop blinding yourself. It's not like you."

"I can't think. I'm too scared and too confused. Who, Rendi? Who?"

316

"It could be Joe Campbell."

Abe stopped breathing. His heart literally skipped a beat. He felt nauseated and dizzy simultaneously. Why had he not thought of that? Why had his two major obsessions—Campbell and Emma—remained on two separate tracks? Why had he not put them together? Had his DLBS blinded him even when it came to his daughter's welfare? He retraced the clues that should have led him to suspect this awful possibility.

Emma had been open about her "crush" on Campbell. She had come to the trial. She believed he was innocent—and Abe never tried to disabuse her of that fantasy. She had gone to dinner with him, maybe even flirted a little. It seemed so innocent at the time. It simply never occurred to Abe that there could be anything sexual or romantic between them. Campbell was almost fourteen years her senior—a man of the world. Now it all came together. Well, not quite all, Abe realized.

"Emma doesn't fit Campbell's MO," he said excitedly. "She's not at all like the others. If he ever dared to do anything against her will, she would be the first one to press charges. Campbell has to know that. And there's nothing in any computer about Emma, is there, Rendi?"

"Well, there were a few references to her in *my* computer, but nothing like the stuff about the other women."

Justin walked into Abe's office, where he had heard her and Abe in animated conversation.

"What's going on? Are you okay?" he asked Abe.

"I don't know, Justin. Rendi just told me something that makes us suspect Emma may be going out with Campbell tonight."

"Oh, my God, are you sure?"

"No, because Emma doesn't fit Campbell's MO."

"You're probably right," Rendi interrupted, "though you wouldn't be the first father not to know everything about his daughter's secret life."

317

"Not something Campbell would be interested in," Abe insisted. "She'd never keep anything like that from me."

"That raises the second scary possibility," Rendi went on.

"What second possibility?" Abe asked in panic.

"Okay. I don't think this is likely, but it is *possible*. Maybe the death of Midge Lester was no accident. Maybe Campbell's perverse need for sexual violence has escalated to the point where he *needs* to *kill* in order to achieve gratification. Remember what his former wife told me about how his need for violence had escalated even back then. Maybe now he *needs* to kill."

"Emma doesn't fit Campbell's MO," Abe repeated, finally sitting down. "I don't care what you say, she's not like those other women."

"Abe, stop," Rendi said. "You're not thinking. If Campbell has now decided to *kill* the women he rapes, he doesn't any longer *need* women who fit his old MO. They don't have to be women with sordid pasts, because they're not going to be alive to testify against him. Abe, Campbell may be planning to *kill* Emma."

Upon hearing those words, Abe stood up and dialed Emma's number in New York. The phone rang three times, and then a voice answered: "Hi, Emma and Zoe are out exploring this great city. Please leave a message at the beep."

Abe dialed Campbell's number: no answer. He called Zoe's parents in New Rochelle. They were home, but they had no idea where Zoe was. She would be home for dinner after 6 P.M., they told him, and he could call her then. Abe asked for the name and number of the uncle's boutique in SoHo, and they gave him the number.

Next, Abe called and reached Zoe's uncle, who confirmed that Zoe and Emma had been in yesterday and that Emma had bought a red dress. Emma had a special date with a very important person, Zoe had confided to her uncle. She wouldn't reveal his name.

While Abe was making the calls, Justin remembered what

he had found out about the biblical names that Haskel had babbled during his last visit with Abe. "Now it makes sense," Justin said. "I couldn't make heads or tails of the story when I found it."

"What is it?" Abe demanded.

"It's a story about the evil king of Amalek, whom God had condemned to immediate death. King Saul delayed the king's execution, despite God's order not to be 'too merciful.' The delay allowed the evil king to sire a child. A descendant of that evil king's child then endangered the life of the descendants of the man who had been merciful to him. It led the rabbis to conclude that 'showing mercy to an undeserving person is as sinful as not showing compassion to a deserving person.' "

"Oh, my God. Haskel was trying to warn me that Campbell might go after Emma, and I wasn't smart enough to figure it out." Abe realized that it wasn't the absence of any smarts—no one could be faulted for that. It was once again his defense lawyer's blind spot—and that was entirely his own fault. He was to blame for the reality that Emma's life was now in danger.

Abe decided to call the New York City police. He had an old friend from Dorchester who was president of the Shomrim Society, the Jewish policemen's benevolent group in Manhattan. He reached David Rothman at headquarters, where he currently served as head of the hostage rescue unit. Suddenly all of Abe's ethical qualms had gone up in a puff of smoke.

Abe had stopped being a lawyer. Now he was a father determined to save his little girl's life. Maybe it was better for ten guilty men to go free than for one innocent to be wrongly convicted—but not if one of those guilty men was going after your own daughter! Abe was now willing to disobey any rule, violate any law, break any commandment, to stop his diabolical former client from hurting his daughter.

But was there anything he could do?

Chapter Thirty-nine

Abe quickly told Rothman the whole story. Rothman was aware of the Midge Lester murder, and he couldn't believe Campbell was the murderer. "Hey, I'm a Knicks fan. No way. Joe Campbell's not a rapist. You showed that at his trial. And he's certainly not a killer. No way."

"I can prove it," Abe insisted, and he explained Campbell's computer MO.

"Holy shit," Rothman said. "Holy, holy shit. Any leads? Where are they going?"

"To a fancy restaurant. Maybe a show. And then probably to a big hotel. He wouldn't take her back to his place or to hers. He probably has a hotel room already under someone else's name, and he's concocted some cover story as to why he wants to take her there. More romantic or something."

"Not much of a lead. There are a thousand fancy restaurants, hundreds of shows, and dozens of big hotels. I could never convince the brass to watch them all—especially on the basis of what you've got. It's all circumstantial. You don't know for sure she's even out with Campbell."

"It's him, Dave. I know it. It's my daughter. I can feel it."

"How quickly can you be in New York?"

Abe looked at his watch: it was 1:45 P.M. "I can get the two-thirty shuttle and be at police headquarters by four, four-fifteen at the latest."

"That gives us maybe five or six hours to stop this mother-fucker," Rothman said. "I'll do what I can to get the troops out while you're in transit. I can't promise much. Nelson Mandela's in town, and a lot of cops are tied up in that. Bring whatever documents you have. We may need to try for a warrant. And fax a recent photo of Emma."

Abe grabbed his files, instructing Justin to stay behind and man the phones in case Emma called. He also told Justin to try to break into Joe Campbell's computer files. "Maybe there's a clue in there somewhere to where he's taking Emma."

"Let's give him a little bit of his own medicine—and hope it works," Justin said as he flipped on his modem.

Rendi had already called a cab. Now she and Abe ran down the stairs and ordered the driver to speed to the Delta shuttle.

During the flight to La Guardia, Abe was on the phone, calling the Barnard security people and begging them to search Emma's room for any clues as to where she might be planning to spend the night of her eighteenth birthday. He thought back to her birth, remembering it as though it were yesterday. Hannah had been calm and in control. Abe had been a nervous wreck. He had wanted a boy, Hannah a girl. They hadn't known what it was going to be until Emma had emerged into Abe's waiting arms. When he'd announced it was a girl, he'd been thrilled. He'd never even remembered that he had wanted a boy, until Hannah had reminded him several years later.

Abe looked at his watch as the plane touched down: it was 3:45. How much time until Campbell got her alone in the hotel room?

It was nearly five o'clock when Abe finally worked his way through the Midtown Tunnel traffic, onto the FDR Drive, and over to the downtown brick building that was headquarters to the New York City Police Department. In the cab, Rendi had a brainstorm. Why not notify all the local TV and radio stations and have them show both Campbell's and Emma's faces? That way they would surely be identified by restaurant patrons, hotel desk clerks, and others. Campbell was one of the most recognizable figures in New York. Rendi's plan made sense.

When they arrived, Abe pleaded with Rothman to implement Rendi's plan. Burt Riley, the police department's lawyer, wouldn't hear of it.

"We don't even have probable cause here. We've got a guy who was *acquitted* by a jury. A lawyer who now says he *believes* his own client is guilty, even though he made his name telling everyone in the world he believed the man was innocent. A nervous father who is understandably concerned about his daughter's taste in men, though he doesn't even know for sure who she's out with tonight. And so far no crime."

"I don't give a shit about the technicalities," Abe shot back. "We're talking about my daughter's life here."

"I've always said that a conservative is a liberal whose kid just got mugged," Riley said, shaking his head.

"Yeah, and a civil libertarian is a cop who's been asked to take a urine test for drugs," Abe replied. "That's got nothing to do with whether you call the TV stations."

"No way I'm gonna call with what you've got," Riley said.

"Then *I'll* call the TV stations myself," Abe insisted.

"Don't waste your time, Mr. Ringel," Riley said. "No TV station is going to risk a libel suit by accusing one of our leading citizens—and one who was acquitted, to boot—of planning another rape or murder. It just won't happen. Not without an arrest warrant, which we can't get, at least not in time for the six o'clock news."

"We've got to try, damn it!"

"Okay, if you want to waste another precious hour," Rothman said with a sigh. "Look, I believe you. I think you're on to something. And I'm willing to put my ass on the line for you by getting a dozen or so cops working this case—but discreetly. If we go public, we'll get our ass kicked in. No judge is going to give a warrant on the basis of this crap."

Abe knew that Riley and Rothman were right. He also knew that if he could get the story out, it would stop Campbell. Campbell would, of course, deny he had any evil intentions toward Emma, and Abe would be in the position of having blown the whistle on his former client for *past* crimes. But Abe couldn't care less. All that consumed him was the need to help his daughter—at any price.

He called his friend Howey Green at the local CBS station and told him the story.

"Wow, what a great TV show that would make," Howey said. "But we can't go with it as news, Abe. Certainly not without checking with our lawyers first, and that always takes time. If it turns out to be true, we would be interested, of course, but not on the basis of what you've got."

Panic was beginning to set in as Abe again checked his watch: it was 5:50, time to try Zoe's parents again. Maybe she was home early.

No luck. Nor had the Barnard security cops had any more luck. They had searched Emma's room and had come up empty. Nothing on her desk calendar except a heart, drawn by red felt pen next to September 1. Several people had seen Emma leave her room, dressed in a short red dress. She was going out for the day and wouldn't be back till morning, she had told a friend in an adjoining room. She'd been whistling as she left, carrying a small pocketbook.

Rothman had secured ten cops—eight men and two women—to make the rounds of several of the city's most popular large hotels. They had given up on the restaurants, because there were so many. If no one was spotted by ten P.M., a few of the police would drive around the theater district, looking at the crowds as they exited the shows. They were carrying the photograph of Emma and a newspaper picture of Campbell.

Abe decided that he would remain at police headquarters

and continue to work the phone. Rendi ran down to a local bookstore and bought a restaurant guide, then started to call every fancy restaurant in the city. Pretending she was one of the paparazzi, she offered each maître d' $1,000 for the tip if Campbell showed up.

At 6:45 Abe again called Zoe's parents. She was still not home.

Finally, at 7:25 P.M., Abe reached Zoe. He asked her whether Emma was out with Joe Campbell.

"I'm sorry, Mr. Ringel. I can't tell you that. You should ask Emma."

"This is an emergency, Zoe. Emma doesn't know that Campbell is a rapist. You must tell me."

"Oh, my God!" Zoe shrieked. "Emma told me that Joe was innocent, that he was a real sweet guy."

"I have evidence that he's not so sweet. I couldn't tell Emma. It never occurred to me that she would go out with him."

"She's gone out with him a few times already—in Boston. I guess you didn't know that. She was afraid that if you found out, you'd object because he was your client and he's so much older."

"She's right. There's no time for that now. I take it you're telling me that they're out together."

"Yeah, only you don't have to worry about him raping her, Mr. Ringel."

"Why not?"

"I don't know how to tell you this, Mr. Ringel. I guess I have to. Emma *wants* to spend the night with Joe. She's all prepared. Birth control and all."

"Zoe, you don't understand. Joe Campbell is a real sicko. Emma's life is in danger. Did she tell you which hotel they were going to?"

"Emma didn't know. Joe told her it would be a surprise. A very romantic hotel. He had a room all reserved under a friend's name—to avoid a lot of gawking."

"Do you know whether they're having dinner?"

"Yeah, at some small Italian restaurant in midtown. She told me the name, but I can't remember."

"Are they going to a show?"

"Yeah, a matinee."

"Thanks, Zoe. Let me give you my number in case you think of anything else, or in case Emma happens to call. If she does, please tell her to get away from Campbell and not to go to his room."

"She's not going to call me until she's alone."

"Just in case. My associate Rendi is going to call you and read the names of all the Italian restaurants in midtown. See if that jogs your memory."

Abe immediately dialed his old friend Alex O'Donnell, Campbell's agent. He remembered that Alex had mentioned the pseudonym Campbell sometimes used when he checked into hotels.

No answer. Alex's secretary told him that her boss was on a plane going to Europe.

"Does he have a sky page?" Abe asked her.

"Yes, but I don't know whether it will work halfway across the Atlantic."

"Try, please."

Abe racked his brain and finally remembered that Campbell had used a name that was somehow related to his nickname, the White Knight. But he still couldn't remember the precise name Campbell had used to register in the Boston hotel.

However, he *did* remember the name of the Boston hotel: the Four Seasons. He called Justin and told him to call over to the hotel and find out the name Campbell had used to register there. In the meantime, Rendi had gotten Zoe to narrow down the list of restaurants to half a dozen. She called each of them. No Campbell. It was now 8:45.

The phone rang.

"Bad news and good news, Abe," said Justin. "Bad is that

325

I can't break into Campbell's files. I've tried everything. He's probably randomized his password. Good news is I found out what name he uses to register in hotels: 'Mitch White.' "

Abe and Rendi quickly started to call all the large hotels on the list provided by the police. New York Palace: no luck. Park Lane: no luck. Regency, Waldorf-Astoria: no luck. Emma's life was quickly ticking away, and she didn't even suspect it.

In desperation, Abe turned to Rendi. "Please, do whatever you have to do. Whatever they taught you in the Mossad. No limits. We've got to stop him."

Even before he'd completed the last sentence, Rendi was out the door, a look on her face that Abe had never seen before.

Chapter Forty

Peter Luger's Steak House is tucked under a bridge in Brooklyn, right over the East River from Manhattan. It is one of Brooklyn's major attractions for sophisticated Manhattan residents and a steak lover's paradise. Joe Campbell loved beef. Although he had made reservations at Gianini's in Midtown, after the show was over he'd decided that he was in the mood for a steak. So off they went in a taxi over the Brooklyn Bridge.

The restaurant seemed like an oasis in the middle of an asphalt desert, steaming with poverty, drugs, and homelessness. Normally Emma would be consumed by the disparity of wealth inside and outside the restaurant. However, this was her day, a time to think only of the pleasures that awaited her. It was her first real date with Joe Campbell, not an afterthought of one of her father's meetings. Joe had called her and asked her if he could be her "first date" in New York. Somehow he also knew that it was her birthday. Her father must have mentioned it once, Emma thought.

"I can't believe how good you look," her new roommate, Zoe, had said as Emma was dressing for her date. While shopping at Zoe's uncle's boutique in SoHo, they had picked out a frothy short red chiffon dress, cut below the bust. High-heeled pumps completed the outfit. Emma was used to wearing Dr. Martens and Birkenstock sandals, so she had to practice walking on the heels for a while before getting dressed. She couldn't believe that her study dates with Jon had been enough to satisfy her all this time.

Emma's secret was too terrific not to share with someone. So Zoe knew of her plans, but she was sworn to secrecy. No one would learn from Zoe's lips where Emma was spending the evening. Emma had made one promise before she'd left: "I'll call you as soon as I'm alone, no matter what time. Wish me good luck."

Now she was alone with Joe Campbell—well, alone among hundreds of diners. Soon she would really be all alone with him.

"You really look sexy, Emma. I knew you would when you started dressing like a woman."

"It's fun to get dressed up every so often, though I feel a lot more comfortable in my usual clothes."

"Does anyone know you're out with me?" Campbell asked, reaching over to touch Emma's hand.

"No, I would never tell my father. He'd freak." Emma giggled, not volunteering that she had shared the secret with Zoe.

"Good. We can tell him about us if and when we become an 'us.'"

During dinner Joe was a perfect gentleman, thoughtful, funny, complimentary, and commanding. Emma asked him to order for her. He selected porterhouse steak, roasted potatoes, sautéed okra, and a 1989 Pomerol, of which they each had only one glass. Both were anticipating a long, sensual night.

After cheesecake for dessert, Emma excused herself to use the ladies' room. In it she saw a pay phone and decided to call Zoe and report on the progress of the evening.

Zoe's line was busy, so she decided to redo her makeup and then try again. Checking her watch, Emma saw that it was eight-thirty, just a little more than three hours left on her birthday. A few minutes later she dialed again. This time she got Zoe's answering machine and left a message: "Wow, Zoe. Am I having a great time! We went to a film festival at the Museum of Modern Art. Then we decided to go to Peter Luger's for dinner over in Brooklyn. Joe felt like steak, not Italian. Now I'm in the ladies' room and we're about to leave for his hotel. He still won't tell me where. But he said it would be romantic. Near Central Park. I can't wait. I promise I'll tell you everything. Everything. See you soon."

Emma hastened back to the table.

While Emma was crossing the Brooklyn Bridge on her way back into Manhattan, Abe was sitting in police headquarters, almost in view of the bridge, waiting for the phone to ring with some news of Emma. Finally it rang.

It was Zoe. Her voice was shaking. Emma *had* called her while she'd been in the shower. She played back Emma's message. Abe listened to Emma's giggly voice, wondering if he would ever hear his daughter happy again.

"Mr. Ringel, God, I'm so sorry. I don't know how I could have missed her call."

"That's okay, Zoe, it's not your fault." It seemed to Abe he'd been saying that a lot lately. "I've got to go."

"Please have Emma call me as soon as you get her away from that creep. Please, I won't sleep a wink."

"Sure." *If* he got her away.

He called Peter Luger's. Yes, Joe Campbell had been there. Yes, he had been with a woman. They had called a cab—to take him and the young lady he was with to Manhattan. No, they didn't know where, but they knew the name and number of the cab company.

A call to the cab company turned out to be a dead end. They had sent half a dozen cabs to Peter Luger's. However, they agreed to send out a message on the car radio.

Abe continued to call the hotels, limiting himself to the dozen or so that bordered Central Park. Still no luck.

Finally, as 10 P.M. approached, Abe decided to go up Central Park South and make the rounds of the hotels. Maybe Joe had used a third name. Maybe the cabbie hadn't recognized Joe Campbell.

Rothman drove Abe uptown in a squad car while another cop manned the phones. It was 10:15 P.M.

Chapter Forty-one

MANHATTAN—FRIDAY, SEPTEMBER 1

The St. Moritz had seen better days, yet it was still an old favorite for romantic interludes. Its views of the park were spectacular, and its high-ceilinged rooms still reflected the detail and charm of a bygone age.

Campbell had a cap pulled down over his head and was holding an umbrella that was wet from the light summer shower outside. Despite his height, no one seemed to recognize him as he and Emma walked the short distance between the revolving door and the elevator that would take them to the room he had rented in the name of Jason Crane. No "Mitch White" tonight, Campbell thought. Using his familiar pseudonym wouldn't be a good idea this time.

He had created a perfect alibi in the event anything went wrong. First, he had reserved the hotel room several days earlier by computer, sending a postal money order to cover the cost of the room. Then, on the way from Peter Luger's to the St. Moritz, he'd stopped at his apartment for a few minutes, telling Emma he had to get some toiletries. He'd asked her to stay in the cab, which was parked around the corner from the entrance. He had gone past the doorman, making sure to tell him he was turning in for the night. Then he'd gone down to the basement, exited through a side door, which he left ajar, and returned to the cab.

As they rode up in the empty elevator, Joe hoped desperately that tonight would be different. He had been attracted to Emma because she was so unlike the others. Perhaps her innocence—indeed, her virginity—would be enough of a challenge and a turn-on to feed the monster. Maybe tonight would be like his first night with his ex-wife, Annie. That had been wonderful, mutual, gentle, and explosive. Could Emma bring that all back to him?

Maybe.

He put these thoughts out of his mind as he turned the key and opened the door to room 1017. Emma was thrilled as she slipped inside and saw flowers and champagne on the table adjoining the large double bed. The stereo was soon playing Brahms's Fourth symphony, which Emma had confided was her favorite. This was going to be a night to remember.

Emma's body swayed sinuously as she walked across the room in the unfamiliar high heels. Touching the flowers, she said, "These are so beautiful."

Drawn to the sight of her thigh outlined against the delicate fabric of her dress, Joe came up behind her and gently put his arm around her. Then he kissed her passionately.

Emma emitted a low sigh as Joe began to move his hands down her sides. Cupping one soft breast, he recalled the feel of young skin.

He felt the surge of desire emanate from his mind to his groin. It was the first time in years he had felt any arousal in a normal fashion. "Come here," he murmured.

He drew her to the bed and slipped her expertly out of her dress. "You've been shopping at Victoria's Secret, I see." He smiled at the sight of the young innocent in a see-through black bra and lace bikini panties. He saw her blush. "Don't be embarrassed. You're a lovely woman, and I am delighted that of all the men in the world you chose me to celebrate your birthday with."

Carefully he removed her bra. Again he felt the thrill of sexual arousal.

"Now you." Emma began to unbutton Joe's shirt.

"Not yet. I want to just enjoy you some more." The truth was he wanted to see how long he could keep his erection. And just as he thought it, he felt himself recede.

Emma saw the look cross his face and knew he was experiencing what Rendi had warned her about with older guys. She tried to take the pressure off.

"Whew, let's take a breather."

"Would you like some champagne?"

"Sure, a little."

Campbell opened a bottle of French champagne and poured them each a glass. As he was handing Emma hers, some of the champagne dripped on her body. He leaned down and surprised her by licking the wine from her skin. Again he felt a brief rise.

"Why don't you get undressed?" Emma said, pulling off her underpants.

Joe removed his remaining clothes quickly, but then he went limp again. This time was more humiliating because he was naked.

It wasn't working. Emma didn't seem to mind, but Joe was becoming angry and frustrated. The monster was growing ugly. This would not be a reprise of the first night with Annie Higgins. It was beginning to feel like a reprise of more recent nights with other women.

Suddenly Joe moved his body so that his mouth was close to Emma's ear. Gently he whispered something into her ear. At first Emma did not even hear the words. All she felt was the lovely sensation of his mouth blowing softly into her ear. Then she heard him distinctly—and couldn't believe what he was saying. But there was absolutely no room for ambiguity.

"Your father had sex with Rendi just before your mother died, and your mother found out about it."

"That's a lie!" Emma screamed.

"No, it's not. I broke into Rendi's computer diary, and it's there in black and white."

"Oh, my God. Oh, my God, why are you doing this?" Emma cried, tears filling her eyes. "Why are you ruining the most important night of my life?"

She got up from the bed, reached for her dress, and headed for the bathroom. Joe followed her and grabbed her around the waist, pulling her toward him.

"Let go of me. I don't want you to touch me. If you don't let go, I'll yell rape."

"No, you won't," Joe said, placing his giant hands around her mouth and nose. As he did so, he felt an enormous surge of sexual energy through his body. . . .

Chapter Forty-two

It was 11 P.M. by the time Abe and Rothman made it uptown to the row of hotels that dotted Central Park South. They started at the Plaza and worked their way west. As they were entering the Park Lane, Abe looked down at his watch: it was 11:15.

As Abe and the detective left the lobby of the Park Lane, a uniformed policeman ran up to them. "Call for Mr. Ringel. It's being patched through."

Abe grabbed the police phone and heard Rendi's voice, breathless, on the other end.

"I'm calling from inside Campbell's apartment. Damnedest luck—the basement door of his building was ajar."

"What did you find?"

"A computer printout of parts of my diary—you were right—and a reservation receipt for the St. Moritz in the name of Jason Crane."

"We're on our way to the St. Moritz. Meet me there."

"I'm on my way."

Abe ran up Central Park South toward the St. Moritz, while Rothman called the hotel and asked for Jason Crane's room. No answer. Suddenly the quiet night air of Central Park was disturbed by the blast of sirens. Abe, panic-stricken, ran toward the sound. An ambulance, a paramedic truck, and three police cars had formed a circle in front of the main entrance to the St. Moritz, blocking traffic. While Abe focused his eyes on this terrible scene, Rothman came running behind him, screaming, "There's been a call for an ambulance! Something happened on the tenth floor—I don't know anything else."

Abe ran through the phalanx of cops that had quickly encircled the ambulance. Rothman was screaming, "Let him through, let him through!" The two of them approached within a few feet of the waiting ambulance and saw a handful of paramedics pushing a gurney through the hotel lobby. Abe couldn't tell whether there was any sign of life in the patient. He raced to catch up with the paramedics, still imagining the worst. The awful image of Emma, not breathing, ashen faced and stone dead, focused in his mind's eye as his daughter's brief life flashed before him. How unlucky she had been to lose a parent so young. To lose her own life so violently and so early. To have a father who was such an idiot for sticking to the rules.

At that instant Abe felt a tug on his arm. "Not now, Rendi," he said automatically, trying desperately to get a look at the face on the passing gurney while trying just as hard to avert his eyes from a sight he did not want to see.

Again there was a tug on his arm, this time even more firmly. "Daddy, Daddy," he heard. The voice was tearful and frightened. Abe was certain he was hallucinating. It sounded like Emma's voice. Where was it coming from?

Suddenly he saw the face on the gurney out of the corner of his eye. It was a man's face—Joe Campbell's face. He heard one of the paramedics say, "He's in shock." Then Emma, frightened and tearful, came into full view.

"Daddy, Daddy," she said. "He tried to rape me. He tried to kill me."

Abe embraced her. Emma continued to cry, "He was really trying to kill me."

"I know. I know," Abe said, hugging his shaking daughter.

"He told me something terrible about you and Rendi, Daddy. He knew it would upset me."

"That's the way he does it, Emma. That's his MO."

"Why didn't you tell me?"

Abe wasn't sure whether she was referring to what Campbell had told her or to what he had known about Campbell. He didn't try to answer. There would be time for that later. For now he asked, "Are you okay? Did he hurt you?" Before she could even answer, Abe saw an enormous welt and a deep scratch on her mouth and cheek. Her nose was bleeding slightly, and her eye was blackening.

"I'm fine, Daddy. I think I might have hurt Joe. I kicked him very hard in his groin—the way they taught me in model mugging. Then, when he bent over, I kneed him in the face. Then I hit him with a champagne bottle and called downstairs. I thought he was dead. I ran out of the room."

"You did the right thing, Emma. You saved your life. You had to. You had no choice."

"Thank God for the model mugging class," Emma said with the first hint of a smile. "We trained with some really big guys."

Abe gently embraced Emma.

"All I could think about is how much I wanted to see you safe."

"All I could think about," Emma responded, "was how I wanted to spend every birthday for the rest of my life with you, Daddy."

"Well, we still have about ten minutes until this birthday ends."

Epilogue

Joe Campbell was arrested in his hospital room at Lenox Hill. He was charged with attempted rape and attempted murder.

He suffered permanent injury to his left testicle and severe contusions to his right testicle. The injury to his reputation was, if anything, even more enduring, especially after the mortifying New York Post *headline, which became a classic:* JOCK STRAPPED. *The subhead read "Campbell Arrested, Suspended from Knicks."*

Four months later Campbell was tried for the attempted rape and attempted murder of Emma. His new lawyer, Raul Kramer, raised an insanity defense and subpoenaed Abe to testify about his conversations with Campbell concerning psychiatric treatment. Abe was reluctant to testify about a former client, but since Campbell had waived any lawyer-client privilege by subpoenaing him, he did testify truthfully as to what he had recommended to Campbell. He also testified fully about the computer scheme. Kramer believed that by disclosing these bizarre facts, he would increase Campbell's chances of being found insane.

The testimony backfired. Jurors later told the press that no one who was capable of calculating so carefully in advance could really be insane. Campbell was sentenced to fifteen years' imprisonment, eligible for parole in ten years with good behavior.

However, he was not tried for the murder of Midge Lester; the prosecutor concluded that the evidence was too circumstantial. Currently Joe Campbell is studying computer programming in Dannemora prison.

Nancy Rosen was finally readmitted to the bar after Abe got several dozen prominent lawyers to sign a petition urging a one-year suspension rather than a permanent disbarment. She is still practicing in Newark, working out in the local gym, and walking a thin line between being a lawyer and a radical.

Late on the eve of Yom Kippur, Haskel Levine died in his sleep. Abe had visited him just hours before his death, on the way home from Kol Nidre services. Haskel was almost completely uncommunicative during this last visit. But he did seem to ask—at least Abe thought he did—how Emma was doing.

Emma was doing very well at Barnard. The assault by Campbell had traumatized her more than she had first realized. What upset her even more was learning that Campbell had told the truth about her father and Rendi. Even after many tearful talks with her father and several months of intense therapy, she was still a long way from getting back to normal, but her classwork was improving and she was even beginning to date. Her current love was a young Russian immigrant, a rabbinical student at the Jewish Theological Seminary and a philosophy major at Columbia. "He reminds me of what a young Haskel Levine might have been like," she told Abe.

One aftermath of the Campbell case was Emma's immutable decision not to become a lawyer. This came during one dinner, after Abe had tried for several hours to explain why he had not been able to warn her about Joe Campbell. "There are serious consequences when a lawyer breaks a promise and a rule," Abe had explained.

Emma's face showed that she was thinking about the promise and rule that he had broken with respect to Hannah. She didn't say a word, except to place some of the blame on herself. "If I had broken my promise to Joe Campbell and told you that

I was going out with him that night, I'll bet you would have told me the truth about him."

Abe acknowledged that she was right. He did not try to dissuade Emma from pursuing a career in which she did not have to make such tragic choices.

"In the end, the law didn't save me. I had to save myself," she told Abe. "Daddy, I want a career in which doing the right thing always helps people—not one where you always have to make tragic choices between people." Emma is studying child psychology.

Abe's romance with Rendi underwent a change following the emptying of his nest. They spent alternate nights in passionate pledges of undying love and then cursing each other and swearing to stick to a strictly professional relationship. Yet once purged of the curse of their secret, Abe and Rendi drew inexorably closer. It looked as if they might finally stabilize their rollercoaster relationship.

The American Bar Association is considering a change in its rules of lawyer confidentiality following the publicity surrounding the Campbell case. Under the proposed new rule, a lawyer will be allowed to disclose a confidence from a client if such disclosure is necessary to save an innocent life, even if the client did not say he was planning a future crime. The lawyer must, however, tell the client of this new exception at the beginning of the initial lawyer-client interview.

Critics of the proposed change—which has come to be called the "Ringel rule"—argue that if the new rule is enacted, clients will simply not trust their lawyers with information that the lawyers might eventually have to disclose. One prominent critic, Professor Monte Fireman of Hofstra Law School, has argued that if the Ringel rule had been in effect when Joe Campbell had come to Abe Ringel, Abe would never have learned the information from Campbell that enabled him to try to save his daughter's life.

Abe Ringel has taken no position on the proposed new rule.

ALAN M. DERSHOWITZ

In a letter to the American Bar Association, he stated, "Some existential moral issues are so complex that they are not amenable to simple solution by the adoption of a blanket rule. Every lawyer will have to continue to struggle with the dilemma of whether or when to blow the whistle on a client."

Prior to sending this letter, Abe read it aloud in front of Haskel's tombstone.